P9-DHN-524

RICHARD HERMAN
POWER CURVE

Other Books by Richard Herman

IRON GATE
DARK WING
CALL TO DUTY
FIREBREAK
FORCE OF EAGLES
THE WARBIRDS

And in Hardcover

AGAINST ALL ENEMIES

RICHARD HERMAN

POWER CURVE

AVON BOOKS ◆ NEW YORK

This is a work of fiction. Names, characters, places, and incidents either are the product of the author's imagination or are used fictitiously. Any resemblance to actual events, locales, organizations, or persons, living or dead, is entirely coincidental and beyond the intent of either the author or the publisher.

AVON BOOKS, INC.
1350 Avenue of the Americas
New York, New York 10019

Copyright © 1997 by Richard Herman, Jr., Inc.
Excerpt from *Against All Enemies* copyright © 1998 by Richard Herman Jr., Inc.
Excerpt from *The Warbirds* copyright © 1989 by Richard Herman Jr., Inc.
Excerpt from *Force of Eagles* copyright © 1990 by Richard Herman Jr., Inc.
Excerpt from *Firebreak* copyright © 1991 by Richard Herman Jr., Inc.
Excerpt from *Call of Duty* copyright © 1993 by Richard Herman Jr., Inc.
Inside cover author photo © Melanie Mages
Visit our website at http://www.AvonBooks.com
Library of Congress Catalog Card Number: 96-45324
ISBN: 0-380-78786-5

First Avon Books Paperback Printing: August 1998
First Avon Books Hardcover Printing: May 1997

AVON TRADEMARK REG. U.S. PAT. OFF. AND IN OTHER COUNTRIES, MARCA REGIS-
TRADA, HECHO EN U.S.A.

Printed in the U.S.A.

WCD 10 9 8 7 6 5 4 3 2 1

For my children,
Eric, Susan, Marianne,
and Neil

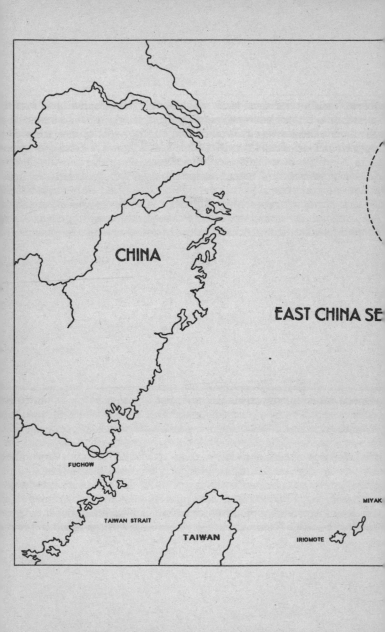

CHINA

EAST CHINA SE

FUCHOW

TAIWAN STRAIT

TAIWAN

IRIOMOTE

MIYAK

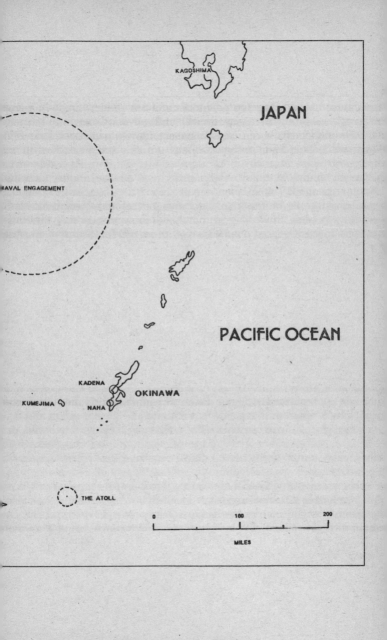

Prologue ⟵

St. Louis, Missouri

"General, please stand back."

Robert Bender gave the Secret Service agent a cold look. After seven months, the institutional paranoia of the Secret Service was wearing thin, and he was tired of being moved around like a piece of unwanted furniture. But all very necessary, he rationalized. He stepped farther back into the wings where he could still see the vice president standing at the podium. He split his attention, watching the agents and listening to the speech.

". . . this administration is one hundred percent dedicated to the advancement of equal rights." A loud round of sustained applause echoed over the stage. *Turner's telling the delegates what they want to hear*, Bender thought, *like any good politician.* Most of the audience had bought into the vice president's carefully constructed image as "the most intelligent and engaging personality in American politics." The "engaging" he agreed with.

Another agent hurried by, speaking into the whisper mike hidden under his sleeve cuff. He shot a worried glance at Bender and skidded to a stop. "Sir, it might be better if you left the stage."

"The vice president gets upset when I'm not around," Bender replied. *Hanging around like a trained lap dog*, he thought.

The agent jerked his head in agreement. The agents

1

standing post for Turner felt sorry for the three-star general—when they weren't laughing about his predicament. The vice president liked having an Air Force lieutenant general dance attendance as a personal aide, and the agents chalked it up as another ego stroke for Turner. "Please display your badge, sir."

Bender fished out his White House area badge and let it dangle from his neck on the outside of his class A blues. *Why am I here?* he wondered for perhaps the thousandth time. Bender's wife claimed it was because the vice president liked the way he looked: tall and lanky with gray hair and steel-blue eyes. Nancy Bender was determined to get her husband through this assignment with his sanity intact and teased him. "It keeps you humble. Besides, you make a cute little go-for, although you are a bit overpaid."

Chuck Sanford, the agent-in-charge of the vice presidential detail, came up the steps from the lower dressing rooms where the Secret Service had set up a temporary command post. "General, have you seen Mr. Shaw?" he asked. A trace of agitation gave his voice a rushed sound.

Bender frowned at the mention of Turner's chief of staff. "Not recently," he answered, his words clipped and abrupt. *Why is Sanford upset?* he thought. *He's the cool one and never flaps, not even when that crazy preacher had taken two potshots at the president's limousine.*

"We need to get a message to Magic"—Magic was the code name a Defense Department computer had generated for Turner the day after the inauguration—"and can't find Mr. Shaw."

The general relented. Now it was his turn to feel sorry for the Secret Service. It angered him the way Patrick Shaw controlled access to the vice president. It wasn't worth an agent's career to bypass Shaw, and even Bender was very correct in dealing with the prickly chief of staff. Shaw had a well-earned reputation for destroying anyone he saw as a threat to his authority. "I saw Shaw about thirty minutes ago, leaving with the brunette in the short black dress."

"Damn," Sanford groaned. "We'll find him, but he's going to be pissed if we catch him with his pants down—again." He hurried away, speaking into his whisper mike.

Bender's frown deepened. He had never before heard Sanford use profanity, and the agent had to be under enormous pressure to be so talkative. Normally, the Secret Service was good for only the time of day, if that. He focused on the activity around him and decided something unusual had to be going down.

The general allowed himself a rare excursion into profanity. *That bastard,* he thought. *Why can't Shaw keep his pecker in his pants? How many guests in the hotel would be rousted, bullied, or disturbed just because Shaw's gonads did his thinking whenever a pretty and eager girl on the make came around?*

Sanford hurried up the steps with two more agents and moved them into place to scan the audience. *Some fool has probably threatened the vice president,* Bender reasoned. An Air Force master sergeant, one of the communication specialists assigned to *Air Force Two,* the vice president's airplane, rushed up the steps carrying a secure cellular telephone and gestured at Sanford, trying to catch his attention. But before Sanford saw him, two agents grabbed the sergeant and frog-walked him back down the steps.

Fitzgerald is a good man and doesn't deserve to be manhandled for doing his job, Bender told himself. Besides, those agents should know him from *Air Force Two.* Bender moved down the stairs in time to see the agents slam the sergeant against a wall and frisk him down. The general clamped an iron control over his anger. "What's the problem?" he demanded. The agents ignored him and spun the sergeant around, still searching him.

"Agent Adams," Bender said, his voice heavy with command, "I asked you a question."

Wayne Adams looked at Bender. The general's voice carried a punch that demanded his undivided attention. "Ah, sorry, sir." He paused, breathing rapidly and deciding how much he should say. "You haven't heard—the president is dead."

Bender blinked once, the news pounding at him with an intensity he couldn't understand. Then he was back in control, rigid and unbending. "Sergeant Fitzgerald, is that why you were bringing the phone?"

"Yes, sir," Fitzgerald answered. "The National Military Command Center needs to authenticate the change of command."

Bender took charge, overriding the Secret Service. "Do it."

"We can't allow that," Adams said.

"Why not?"

"Because the vice president hasn't been told yet," Adams answered.

"Why not?" Bender repeated.

"Mr. Shaw," came the answer.

Bender shook his head. "Are you that afraid of him?" No answer.

"Tell her now," Bender ordered. "Don't wait until you find Shaw."

Adams shook his head.

Bender looked at Fitzgerald. "Tell me the details," he demanded. The sergeant repeated what he knew. Bender jerked his head once. "Give me your message pad," he said to Fitzgerald. He quickly wrote a note and ripped off the page before returning the pad. He trotted up the stairs and past Sanford and the other agents posted in the wings.

"General!" Sanford barked.

"You know me," Bender shot back, flashing his White House badge and not slowing as he walked on stage.

Madeline Turner heard the commotion and turned to look. Bender handed her the note and walked back into the wings.

"Goddamn you," Sanford rasped.

"Without a doubt," Bender replied, his voice sharp and unyielding. He looked back toward the podium. Turner was unfolding the note, still looking at him. He watched as she read. *So this is how history is made,* he thought, recalling the exact words he had jotted down moments before:

Madam President, President Roberts died of a massive cerebral hemorrhage at 2:18 this afternoon in the White House. Your presence is needed immediately on board Air Force One.

Madeline O'Keith Turner looked up at him, her mouth slightly open. Tears filled her eyes and streaked down her face.

"For God's sake, woman," Sanford groaned. "Not here. Not now." He never took his eyes off Turner. "You should have waited until we found Shaw."

PART ONE
APPEASEMENT

Who is Madeline O'Keith Turner? She has been
described as "the most intelligent and engaging
persona" in American politics. She is certainly
that. But she is also a political lightweight with
a thin record centered on domestic issues. But
as Harry S. Truman warned, although domestic
policy can hurt you, foreign policy can kill you.
So what foreign policy will emerge when President Turner is confronted with the reality of
the new world order? Will it be isolationism or
engagement? Only time will tell.

ELIZABETH GORDON
CNC-TV News

Washington, D.C.

Robert Bender stood up when the reporter was ushered into his basement office under the West Wing of the White House. The press aide made the introductions. "General Bender, may I introduce Elizabeth Gordon of CNC News?"

"You're a hard man to find," Gordon said, extending her hand. Her cameraman halted in the doorway, wondering how he could set up the interview in the small, windowless office while the press aide escaped, eager to join the real action upstairs.

Bender allowed a tight smile as they shook hands. "I'm not very newsworthy, Miss Gordon." He wasn't good with reporters or TV interviews. But like all the president's staff, he had been told to make himself available for media interviews on what Patrick Shaw was calling Media Blitz Day.

The media had been in a feeding frenzy since Turner had been sworn in as president on board *Air Force One*. But Shaw, her new chief of staff, had held them at bay for ten days, throwing them tidbits and claiming the funeral and period of mourning for the dead president was paramount. Shaw had used the time to sort out the confusion in the White House, moving his people into place and restructuring the staff. Now it was time to throw the press a bone with meat.

9

"Please call me Liz," the reporter said. "What do you think, Ben?" she said to her cameraman, turning to business.

"Too small," the cameraman answered. "Maybe we could do it outside, in the park."

"Fine by me," Bender answered as he grabbed his flight cap and motioned at the door. A frown crossed Gordon's face, and Bender suspected she was worried what the late afternoon August heat and humidity would do to her makeup. "I know a cool spot," he told her. He led the two upstairs and through the corridors crowded with the journalists, TV reporters, and camera crews who had finally been released from their confinement in the press room.

A Secret Service agent held a door open for them that led out of the West Wing and onto the veranda of the colonnade that connected the West Wing to the mansion. "Thank you," Bender said. A thought clicked into sharp focus: He hadn't seen the two Secret Service agents Chuck Sanford and Wayne Adams since returning from St. Louis ten days ago. He added it to his action list.

A hot blast of humid air rocked Liz Gordon back as she stepped outside. "It's not far," Bender said, jamming his flight cap on his head, automatically denting the top seam in the back. It was a violation of Air Force dress regulations but a holdover from the days when he flew solo pilot for the Air Force aerial demonstration team, the Thunderbirds.

They walked down the veranda, and suddenly the air became cooler as they neared the White House. "A venturi effect," he explained.

"Perfect," the cameraman said. He went to work and rapidly set the interview up, positioning Gordon for the best exposure.

"This is actually quite pleasant," Gordon said. "How did you find it?"

"I try to get outside whenever I can," Bender answered. Nancy, his wife, claimed the way he roamed the President's Park was a subconscious attempt to break free of his cage inside the White House. He agreed with her.

The cameraman gave Gordon her cue, and she looked

into the Betacam. A gentle breeze ruffled her blond hair, creating an attractive effect. "Lieutenant General Robert Bender has been President Turner's military aide since she was vice president. As we have heard many times, he was the individual who told her the president was dead." She turned to Bender and tilted the microphone in his direction.

"As Mr. Shaw has repeatedly explained," Bender said, "I was only the messenger, nothing else."

"But you wrote the message," Gordon said, not willing to drop the subject.

"I can't add anything to what Mr. Shaw has already said," Bender replied. "I just happened to be there."

Gordon realized she would not get anything new out of the general on that subject, regardless of the rumors flying out of the White House about what had really happened back stage at the conference.

"General, you were on board *Air Force Two* on that fateful flight back from St. Louis. I don't recall seeing you when President Turner took the oath of office."

Bender paused and stared at her, not liking the way Gordon implied she was there when, in fact, she was referring to the much played videotape of Turner being sworn in by Justice Lorraine Worthing. *Do that again, Miss Gordon,* he thought, *and we're in trouble.* "To be technically correct," he replied, his voice flat and boring, "the aircraft becomes *Air Force One* when the president is on board. It was very crowded, and I was on the flight deck with the crew." He didn't tell her that the flight deck was the only sane refuge on that flight.

"What was your reaction to the first woman president being sworn in by Chief Justice Lorraine Worthing?"

"The symbolism is obvious," Bender said, trying not to sound like a pompous ass. "But it was fortuitous circumstance. Justice Worthing had flown to the Bar Association conference with President Turner, and it made sense for her to administer the oath on the flight back to Andrews Air Force Base."

"On the videotape," Gordon said, "I saw very few men at the swearing in."

Nice recovery, Bender thought. "Men were there," he replied. "It was just the camera angle." He didn't mention that Patrick Shaw had deliberately surrounded Turner with women.

"You seem to enjoy a special relationship with President Turner," Gordon continued. She caught the look on Bender's face and paused.

You keep pushing it to the limits, Bender thought. *This had better not lead into some sleazy question about her being a widow.* Turner's husband had died of a heart attack while playing tennis during an early primary election campaign, and Shaw had played it to the max, milking images of a grieving widow with a thirteen-year-old son and nine-year-old daughter soldiering gamely on. It had been a major factor in capturing the women's vote for the Roberts–Turner ticket.

Gordon was momentarily rattled, caught off guard by the general's silence and cold look of disapproval. Normally, she would have taken it as an opening or a weakness to be exploited. But an inner alarm warned her not to push this man. "Ah, ah," she flustered, "I meant, considering her well-known distrust of the military, some would even say contempt."

Bender relented. "I was a liaison officer. But more than anything else, I acted as an interpreter explaining military jargon and how the Department of Defense works."

"So what are you doing now?" Gordon asked.

"Not much. The president is a fast learner and the chairman of the Joint Chiefs of Staff is her military advisor now. I'm hoping for a quick reassignment, which will happen as soon as the dust settles and they realize I'm an unneeded body taking up space."

"I imagine anything after the White House would be very boring. What type of assignment do you want?"

A warm smile spread across Bender's face and his eyes came alive. He wanted to end his career by commanding ACC, Air Combat Command, the fighting arm of the Air Force. "Anything to do with operations, flying."

Gordon realized the interview wasn't worth much, and Bender was living up to his reputation as being a tight-lipped, noncommunicative bastard. She brought the interview to a close as quickly as possible, and the Betacam was turned off. "Thanks, General," she said, not meaning it.

"Miss Gordon, Ben, my pleasure," he replied. He glanced at his watch: 1710, twenty minutes before the presidential press conference that would cap the day's blitz. Because he wasn't needed inside, he headed for the southwest gate and the parking spaces on West Executive Avenue, where his car was parked. It was the one perk that he appreciated.

Gordon watched him as he walked away. "The general is not a happy man," she said.

"He wants out of here," the cameraman added. "Not that I can blame him." *And he remembered my name*, he thought.

Maura O'Keith sat patiently in the sitting room on the second floor of the White House. She liked the room for its southwestern exposure and was content to wait for her daughter. She shifted her body, feeling for a comfortable depression on the couch. "There," she murmured, finally finding a friendly soft spot that accommodated her aching back.

Pouring herself another cup of tea, she ignored the little puffs of pastry a White House chef had baked specifically to entice her. "That wicked devil," she murmured, giving into temptation and helping herself to one of the delicate creations. Maura O'Keith was a plump sixty-eight-year-old woman who had few illusions about herself, her daughter, and, more importantly, her grandchildren.

No, she decided, reaching a conclusion about her four-teen-year-old grandson, *much better to keep Brian in boarding school. This place will spoil him rotten. Sarah, on the other hand, will do fine here. And I can make sure she isn't spoiled by the arrogant fools who think they're important just because they work in a place that is.* She smiled at the thought of her ten-year-old granddaughter. The little girl had a practical streak that rivaled her grandmother's, and although she wasn't as smart as Brian, she could read people like a book.

The door leading into the bedroom opened, and Madeline O'Keith Turner, the forty-fourth president of the United States, came through. Maura O'Keith gave her daughter an appraising look. "You look nice, Maddy," she said.

"Then you think this is OK for my first press conference?" Turner asked.

Maura cast a critical eye over her daughter. Turner's makeup was perfect, highlighting her high cheekbones and brown eyes. Her severe, light gray summer business suit draped in a straight line, giving little hint of her figure. The long hemline ended six inches above the floor, and a modest slit up the right side ended below her knee. The light silk scarf around her neck contrasted nicely with her suit and did not conceal the single strand of small pearls looped outside her white blouse. "Oh, yes," Maura conceded. "Sit down, your hair isn't quite right." She rummaged in her ever-present handbag and pulled out a comb.

"Mother, it's the stylist's job," Turner said as she sat down in a corner armchair, giving in to the inevitable.

"I got you all the way through college and law school as a hairdresser—"

"A stylist," Turner corrected.

"A hairdresser," Maura replied. She gave Turner's dark brown hair a few deft strokes, smoothing and simplifying the arrangement, accentuating the red highlights. "The pearl earrings are lovely but always hide your ears. They stick out too far."

Turner laughed. It was musical, low pitched, and captivating. "Thank you, Mother. I didn't know that."

Maura gave her daughter's shoulder a little snap with the comb. "Don't get sassy now."

Again the laugh. "I don't know what I would do without you."

Maura became serious. "Oh, I don't know—I'm worried. I've seen what reporters can do to presidents. What they did to poor Mr. Reagan—"

"I'm not President Reagan," Turner interrupted. "We've been working on this for two days." A knock at the door caught their attention. "Come," she said.

The door opened, and Patrick Shaw stuck his big head in. "Y'all ready, Mizz President?" he asked. As usual, his southern drawl and lopsided face reminded Maura of a court jester. But the chief of staff was not a comedian.

The rest of Shaw emerged through the door. He was a shaggy bear of a man, hunch shouldered, wearing a rumpled brown suit and in need of a haircut.

"All set," Turner answered.

"Is there anything you want to go over one last time?" Shaw asked. "Any dots or t's you want to give one last twist?" Turner shook her head, and a big grin spread across Shaw's face, lighting his hazel eyes. "Good," he said. "Personally, I'm as nervous as a young filly being eyed by a big stud who's about to—"

"Please, Patrick." Turner laughed. "No barnyard humor today. This is the White House, and you've never been close to a farm."

"True," Shaw conceded. "But it fools the opposition." His southern accent was less marked. "You look great and will do fine. We'll be ready in fifteen minutes."

"I'll be there."

"Make an entrance," he said.

"I know the script," she reassured him. Shaw nodded and ambled out the door.

Silence. "I don't trust him," Maura finally said.

"It would be chaos without him," Turner replied. By mutual consent, they dropped the subject of Patrick Flannery Shaw.

The old refrain was back, haunting the old woman. *Oh, Maddy,* she thought, *why can't you see Shaw for what he is?*

Maura O'Keith hated Shaw.

Patrick Shaw studied the reporters seated in the East Room for Turner's first press conference. The elegant ballroom was packed with reporters, sound technicians, still photographers, but only three TV cameras. The cameras and sound technicians were controlled by Shaw, and the networks received their audio and video feeds through a White House control room in the basement.

He joked with the two assistants hovering at his back. "It's like the folks say in showbiz: Give 'em what they want and they'll come out every time." The assistants dutifully laughed while one scribbled Shaw's latest homily in a notebook. Shaw liked the analogy to show business for this was an opening night and he had left nothing to chance. He scanned the room again, determined to bring off a perfect show. His heavy eyebrows knitted in mock consternation when he saw Elizabeth Gordon sitting in the first row by the center aisle. It was not her assigned seat and a violation of White House protocol. "What's Liz doing in CBS?" he asked.

One of the assistants moved forward, not happy to be the center of Shaw's undivided attention. "She sat there at the last minute."

Shaw focused on the errant reporter. "That's Whiteside's seat. Where did he go?"

"He moved to the back on his own," the assistant said, amazement in every word as he pointed out Peter Whiteside. "He didn't make a big deal out of it and took Gordon's seat."

"That means I owe the bastard," Shaw grumbled. He made a show of calculating the payback. "He'll want more than a young bedmate on the next presidential trip." He paused, thinking. "Whiteside gets the last question. No, let him ask two questions. Make it happen." The assistant scurried off, glad to have survived. Shaw spoke into the small microphone attached to his lapel that linked him with the control room in the basement. "Add Liz Gordon to the list," he growled, loud enough for the other assistant to hear.

That ensured the rest of the White House staff would hear about Liz Gordon's banishment and two or three would leak it to the press—another way to keep the reporters in line like obedient ducks. The controller on duty added Elizabeth Gordon's name to the Do Not Admit list that barred individuals from entering the White House. Once the reporter left, she would never get back in and her career would take a serious, perhaps fatal, hit.

A late arrival hurried past, anxious to find his seat among the reporters. "You've really got us packed in here, Mr. Shaw."

Shaw laughed. "The White House is like a tight pair of pants," he quipped loud enough for a few other reporters to hear, his southern accent much heavier now. "Not enough ballroom." That homily had been recorded before,

and the assistant laughed with the reporters as Shaw
slipped through the door leading into the Green Room.
Clear of the crowd, he headed for the White House television unit, also in the basement. "Keep laughing," he muttered to himself.

He moved quickly, with surprising agility for a big man,
and reached the TV control room in minutes. He slipped
on a headset and stood behind the row of technicians con-
trolling the video and audio feeds. He spoke into his mike.
"OK, folks. Here we go."

The carefully staged press conference opened with the
press secretary leading Turner's fourteen cabinet secretaries and the chairman of the Joint Chiefs of Staff out of
the Green Room. They split into two groups and stood
against the wall to the left and right of the entrance to the
main hall that connected the East Room to the State Dining Room. The press secretary approached the podium
near the hall entrance and stood looking at the crowd.
When Shaw judged the honor guard formed by the cabinet
was in place, he snapped one word. "Now."

The press secretary said nothing as the center camera
did a slow zoom up the main hall. Madeline Turner was
walking down the red carpet alone, carrying a thin leather
folder, her briefing book, in the crook of her left arm. Her
head was held high, and there was no hesitation in her
step as she approached the East Room. The nine reporters
Shaw had placed in the audience in a rough diamond pattern sprang to their feet, paying the price for a seat at the
conference. They were the catalyst that brought the rest
of the audience to its feet well in advance of her arrival.

"Ladies and gentlemen," the press secretary intoned,
his deep voice carefully modulated, "the President of the
United States."

The reporters waited quietly as Turner approached the
podium. She laid the leather folder on the podium and
folded her hands on top. For a moment, she gazed over
the standing crowd. The room was eerily quiet. "I would
give all that I have," she began, "not to be here today."

The reporters that formed the diamond exploded in applause and carried the others with them. Tears caught at

the corner of her eyes while she waited for the ovation to subside. "But we must continue. We know the way."

Again applause, this time without being instigated by the diamond formation, rocked the room. "Perfect," Shaw said into his mike. He smiled when a camera zoomed in on Turner. The tears were gone as she opened the briefing folder and made her opening remarks. The press conference was off to a good start. "The hard part is behind us," Shaw said.

The reporter from ABC started the questioning. "Madam President, you inherited the China problem and what has been called the Taiwan Crisis from the late President Roberts. Critics in Congress claim your administration has rolled over by letting the People's Republic of China occupy Taiwan. Is this an invitation to further territorial aggression by China, and are you going to oppose their takeover of this strategic island?"

Shaw allowed a tight smile as Turner answered. He had expected that question and planned for it. "As you know," Turner said, "the Chinese established sovereignty over Taiwan the day President Roberts died. But I don't think you can call the arrival of the new Chinese governor and his staff from Beijing on an unarmed civilian transport an occupation or a takeover. Certainly, no military force was used by the People's Republic of China.

"President Roberts had been dead less than eight hours when the Chinese ambassador was called to the State Department. He assured the secretary of state that his government was not trying to exploit the situation and was deeply apologetic about the timing of Taiwan's reversion to Chinese control. In view of the historical claim that China has on Taiwan, the acceptance of the Taiwanese, and the lack of protest from China's neighbors, the United States is not in a position to intervene."

"Perfect answer," Shaw announced. The press conference continued to play out as planned.

Then the sound technician with a boom microphone walked past Elizabeth Gordon. "Madam President," Gordon called.

"Yes, Liz," Turner said.

"Why did she recognize the bitch?" Shaw grumbled

for the benefit of the technicians in the control room. "That's not in the script."

"Madam President," Gordon said, "you have been described as a political lightweight only nominated to run on your party's ticket to bring in the women's vote. Your record in the California state senate supports that allegation and can at best be described as thin since you have focused primarily on one issue: women's rights. Madam President, what *are* the issues that define your administration?"

"I think," Turner answered, "that if you carefully examine my record, you'll find that—"

Shaw came to his feet, shouting, not waiting to hear the rest of her answer. "Gawd damn!" he roared, filling the control booth with his anger. "Everyone of those meatheads knows what your record is." He could hear the reporters shouting for attention as the dam burst.

Behind Shaw, a voice blurted, "It's out of control."

Rather than listen to what was being said in the East Room, Shaw barked new marching orders into his microphone. "Get to Whiteside, tell him to change the subject. Turner will recognize him when he stands up." He pushed a technician out of his seat and overrode the script reader in the president's podium. He typed furiously:

RECOGNIZE PETER WHITESIDE IN THE BACK—NOW

He looked up at the TV monitors. A press aide was talking to Whiteside who immediately stood up and raised his right hand. On cue, Turner's voice rang out. "In the back—Peter."

A sound technician was already in place and thrust a boom mike in front of him. "Thank you, Madam President," Whiteside called.

"Peter," Turner said, her voice amazingly calm, "what are you doing way back there?" A few titters ran through the audience. Whiteside was renowned for the way he lorded it over the lesser lights in the press corps and took offense at the slightest infringement of his preeminence or prerogatives.

"Madam President, I have no idea. But it's a lot safer

here than up front." The titters turned to laughter, and
Shaw relaxed. "For one, Madam President, I am not concerned with your past record but with the future. Right
now, our economy is in a slump. Unemployment is spreading, and we're seeing more and more homeless people on
the streets everyday. What are your immediate plans to
get this turned around?"

The reporters quieted as Turner answered. "Back on
track," Shaw said, wiping his face with a huge handkerchief. He was quiet until the press conference ended and
Madeline Turner left the East Room, retreating up the
main hall, still walking alone. Again per Shaw's script.

Shaw's staff crowded into his large corner office for the
postmortem on the press conference. They were surprised
to find him so expansive and relaxed after the near disaster
caused by Elizabeth Gordon. "Folks," Shaw said, "it got
tense out there today. We gotta learn from our mistakes
'cause there's no more second chances."

The intercom on his desk buzzed, and he jabbed at a
button with a stubby finger, missing on the first attempt.
"Damn machines," he muttered, punching again. This
time he made contact.

"Mr. Shaw," his secretary's voice said, "the president
wants to see you in ten minutes. She's in her private study.
And you might want to watch CBS. Peter Whiteside is
on."

A young assistant was poised by the TV, ready to do
Shaw's bidding. Shaw punched off the intercom and nod-
ded. Peter Whiteside's face immediately filled the screen.
"President Turner weathered her first press conference
today," Whiteside was saying, "with grace and dignity.
Her elegant, but understated business suit—"

Shaw flicked a remote control at the TV, turning it off.
"They're still looking where we want 'em to look," he
said. "So we survived after all. We won't be so lucky
next time. So remember, no fuckups next time around or
someone loses their balls." He looked around the room.
Only the male members of his staff were nodding in unison. "Or their titties as the case may be." Now everyone
was nodding. He laughed. "It's equal opportunity, folks,

equal opportunity." His staff filed out, taking his threat very seriously. He hit the intercom button to his secretary, this time swift and sure. "Tell Mizz President I'm on my way."

He hummed as he left his office. "Oh, my Gawd, how the money rolls in," he half sang, half mumbled.

Madeline Turner was working in the small office off her bedroom in the residence, the second and third floors of the White House. It was a comfortable nook, not rigidly formal like the better-known rooms, and suited her personality. Books and magazines were strewn around the floor in casual disarray, and she was sitting in the corner of a couch wearing a short-sleeved dark blue sweatshirt, matching warm-up pants, and fuzzy socks.

"Patrick," she called when he came in, "sit here." She patted the couch beside her and took off her reading glasses. She laid the thick blue briefing book she had been reading on the floor.

Shaw noticed that the TV in the corner was on and tuned to CNC, Elizabeth Gordon's network. He glanced at the briefing book but couldn't read its title. *What is she boning up on now?* he wondered. Turner was a voracious, very fast reader and could read and watch TV at the same time—a trait that bothered him.

"I thought it went well today, didn't you?" she began.

Shaw settled his bulk into the designated spot and tugged at his tie, loosening it even more. "It could have been worse."

"The Liz Gordon thing?"

Shaw dumped his chin onto his chest, not looking at her. "You shouldn't have recognized her. She was out for blood and opened a floodgate." He stood up and paced the floor, a sure sign that he was worried. "I ran the videotape. We've got problems with the press and—"

"Patrick," she interrupted, "we don't have problems with the press. Not yet—the honeymoon, remember." The tone in her voice warned him to drop the subject. She watched as he paced the carpet.

He finally stopped and stood by the fireplace, looking at the small brass bell sitting on the mantle. "That's the bell, isn't it?'' Turner nodded an answer. "I haven't seen it in years,'' Shaw mumbled, remembering.

Maddy Turner had been a young, idealistic, and dazzled first-term California state senator when they first met. She was two years out of law school and had run for the senate in the East Bay district of San Francisco more as a lark than with any expectation of winning. Much to her surprise and that of both parties, she had won. Once in the California senate, the egos stalking the halls of the state capitol relegated her to the sidelines. As the old men running the California legislature in those days liked to say, she was "marginalized" and there was nothing she could do about it. It was simply a matter of waiting for her defeat in the next election.

Out of frustration, she had turned to Patrick Shaw, her party's state chairman. From the very first, it was a political marriage made in heaven. Turner was eminently electable, and Shaw couldn't be elected as an animal control officer. She could charm, Shaw could raise money. But no one was listening to her in the senate. Then Shaw gave her the bell.

For four sessions, the bell sat on her desk on the senate floor, and whenever she felt her colleagues were ignoring or trying to intimidate her, she rang it loudly until they listened. While she made a name for herself, Shaw funneled campaign money her way. And as he was fond of saying, "Money is the mother's milk of politics." He often regretted that he hadn't said it originally.

When Turner swamped her opposition in the next election and carried two other candidates with her, all thanks to Shaw, the bell disappeared. Turner was on the road to power, and Shaw was the force behind her.

Shaw stroked the bell's ebony handle. Then he picked it up and rang it. Turner looked at him, and all the warmth and nostalgia of that time was back. "That was a long time ago,'' she murmured.

Shaw knew she was listening now. "Mizz President, we've got problems with the press. It was the women reporters leading the attack, not the men." Turner was silent, and Shaw knew he could continue. "You're not one of the sisters anymore. For them, you've gone over, become part of the establishment. They're sending you a message."

"What's the message, Patrick?"

"Stay a sister, advocate the issues that are important to us or we will nail you. Mizz President, I know how you feel about the feminist movement, but you're the president of everyone now. You've got to move beyond it."

Turner tilted her head and looked at him. "OK, Pat. What's the real angle?"

Shaw sprawled on the couch opposite her and dropped his chin on his chest. "There's a stridency in any militant movement that turns the voters off. You've got to disassociate yourself from any group not near the center."

"Especially one that can be called bitchy," she added.

Shaw grinned. "Your word, Mizz President, not mine. But you saw one at work today."

"Or maybe she was being a good reporter," Turner replied. "Don't worry about it—not yet." She looked at him. "Where was General Bender? I didn't see him at the press conference."

So that's why she wanted to see me, Shaw thought. *Why is she worried about him? What's the connection there?* "Ah, he did an interview or two and took off. Itchy feet." He paused, wondering if this was the time to get rid of the stiff, reserved officer. "Mizz President, he doesn't have anything to do, so put him out of his misery. Send him back to the Pentagon. There's really no place for him on your staff."

"So he's bored?"

"Stiffly."

"Then give him something to do." No answer from Shaw. "No suggestions? Well then, tell him I want a detailed briefing on what's going on in the Far East. I haven't got the slightest idea what the Chinese are up to."

So she was reading the briefing book on China, he thought. He would have to spend some time reading it. "Rawlings or Murchison can do that for you." William Rawlings was the national security advisor and Clement Murchison, the secretary of state she had inherited from the former president.

"I also want to know what my military options are."

"That's Overmeyer's job." General Overmeyer was the chairman of the Joint Chiefs of Staff. "He's very territorial and—"

"It will give Bender something to do," Turner interrupted.

Shaw smiled. He knew when to capitulate. "Can do. Mr. General Robert Bender is going to be one busy man. Anything else, Mizz President?"

She shook her head, dismissing him. He headed for the door. Her voice stopped him. "Patrick, did you put Liz Gordon on the Do Not Admit list?" He nodded. "Take her off."

"Yes, ma'am," he said, closing the door behind him. He whistled a tuneless melody as he ambled back to his office. He filed away a few more pieces of information in his mental computer about Madeline O'Keith Turner. For some reason, she wanted to keep Bender around and was concerned about China. The Senate Foreign Relations Committee chairman would be interested in that.

He was vaguely aware that it was dark outside when he entered his office in the West Wing. His long-suffering secretary was still there, waiting for him with the president's schedule for the next day along with a guest list. He initialed off the schedule and handed it back to her for distribution.

"Elizabeth Gordon has called twice on your private line," she told him. "She wants to know why she is on the Do Not Admit list."

"Go home, Alice Fay," he said. He waited until she had left before picking up his private phone and punching in a number. He managed a "Liz" before the reporter hit him with a stream of invective.

"You bastard!" she screamed, piercing his ear. "You put me on the Do Not Admit."

The grapevine is a little too fast and way too accurate, he thought. He would have to do some fine tuning. He smiled and let her wind down. "You got it wrong, darlin'. I took you off the list." He smiled. This was the stuff of disinformation and kept the reporters off balance. By implication, the president had put Liz on the list and he was spending his *obligata* getting her off. "You did good out there today."

After hanging up, he scanned the names on the guest list. His eyebrows came together, and he frowned as he deleted a senator's name. *No way,* he thought. *You're so crooked that if you ate a nail, you'd shit a screw.* He smiled. *Remember that line,* he told himself. He buzzed for the duty officer to pick up the revised guest list and made one more phone call. "I hope you're thinking what I'm thinking," he said, his voice low and husky. He smiled at the answer and walked into the deserted corridor.

Not a bad day, he decided, shuffling past the lone Secret Service agent still on duty outside the Oval Office.

Okinawa, Japan

It was still dark when the F-15E Strike Eagle taxied into the flow-through at Kadena Air Force Base on Okinawa, Japan. The crew chief marshaled the jet into the last bay of the long, carportlike structure with its sawtooth roof. The canopy came up as the engines spun down and the crew unstrapped. The backseater was the first out, throwing two small canvas bags of flight publications, checklists, and charts to a waiting crew chief. She scampered down the crew boarding ladder and waited for her pilot, Captain Chet Woods, to descend.

"What's the hurry, Laurie?" Chet asked. "Got a hot date?"

"At this hour?" she shot back. "Sure."

Chet could tell she was anxious to get going, not that he could blame her after the long training mission. Unfortunately, a maintenance problem had delayed their launch, and what should have been a relatively short flight had turned into a grueling twelve-hour crew-duty day.

Then the tanker that was scheduled for a night airborne refueling had canceled, another maintenance problem, and they had to divert to Osan Air Force Base in South Korea for gas. The flight profile back to Okinawa had been a stresser because Laurie had simulated a failure of the Eagle's navigation computer, her idea of having fun.

26

The production supervisor's panel truck pulled up, and a grizzled master sergeant got out. "Anything for Maintenance, Cap'n?" he asked.

"She's good to go, Sergeant Contreraz," Laurie answered. "Out kickin' butt this early?"

Master Sergeant Ralph Contreraz frowned. As the production supervisor, he was responsible for the care and feeding of the Forty-fourth Fighter Squadron's twenty F-15Es and eighty crew chiefs. He had heard about the problems Laurie and her pilot had launching and was going to solve the problem. "My people screwed up, Cap'n. It won't happen again."

Laurie called to the pilot. "Chet, you got any write-ups?"

"Just what's already in the forms," he answered.

"We'll take care of it," Contreraz told them.

Chet thought for a moment. By rights, he and Laurie should review the videotapes from the mission and debrief the flight. But it had been a long night. "Laurie, you're cleared off hot. We'll debrief the mission after the change of command ceremony this afternoon."

"*Sigh-oh-nar-ah*," Laurie said, drawing out the Japanese word for good-by.

The pilot and Contreraz watched her walk away. "She's a real squatty-body," the sergeant said.

"A bundle of energy moving at warp 8," Chet said.

"I hear she's a pretty good wizzo."

"Oh, yeah," the pilot allowed. It was the truth. She was an excellent wizzo, Air Force slang for WSO, weapon system officer.

Laurie drove to the BOQ, trotted up the stairs, and took off her flight boots before letting herself into the room. Without turning on the light, she unzipped her flight suit and pushed it past hips that no amount of exercise could make smaller. But Laurie was happy with her body, all five foot four inches and 140 pounds of it. She peeled off the athletic bra she preferred for flying, not that her small breasts needed much support to fight the g's that came with flying the F-15 Strike Eagle. Because of her compact and sturdy frame, she could sustain over 12 gs without passing out, an impressive number. She slipped out of her panties and ran her fingers through her short dark hair, fluffing it out. Now she had another use for her body.

She slipped into the bed and cuddled against the back of its occupant. When the back didn't stir, she whispered, "Come on, Robert Junior, wake up." No response. "There's always plan B," she coaxed. Still no response. She reached into his shorts and had his attention.

"What time is it?" he mumbled.

"After five."

"Must've been a hell of a mission."

"A real ballbuster," she said, kissing his neck. Now he was responding.

"Do you always come home horny?"

"Always," she answered.

"It's the flying that does it," he said.

"You're the shrink, you know about these things."

"I don't want to be around if you ever fly in combat."

"Why?" she murmured.

He sucked in his breath. "According to everything I've read"—a long pause as he tried to breathe normally—"the sex drive goes into supercharged overdrive in combat."

"I hope you're up to it."

The long line of officers and their wives or husbands snaked out the door of the Officers' Club ballroom and into the hall. Laurie moved with the line, hoping that Robert would arrive in time to go through the reception line with her to meet the new wing commander. Probably some problem at the clinic, she reasoned. She was wearing trousers and high heels with her class A blue uniform, but her heels weren't high enough to let her see over the crowd.

He found her just before she reached the reception line. She looked up, suppressing an urge to kiss the tall and lanky captain. Lately, she had been wondering if their kids would have blond hair and blue eyes like him. "Lucky dog," she kidded. "You missed the change of command ceremony. Boring."

"I've seen enough of them," he said.

"Seen one, seen them all," she quipped.

They reached the reception line, and he went first because he was more senior in rank than Laurie. The wing commander's executive officer made the introductions. "General Martini, may I introduce Captain Robert Ryan, Jr., one of our flight surgeons. Captain Ryan is also doing psychiatric research while at Kadena."

Brigadier General David Martini extended his hand. He was a heavy-set man, almost six feet tall, barrel-chested, and with a head of jet black, barely controlled, curly hair. His narrow-set brown eyes darted around, never resting, and his handshake was firm but abrupt. "Captain Ryan," he said, "I understand you're an expert on stress."

"Not an expert, General," Ryan answered. "But I am researching the physical and mental ramifications of stress and how it affects flying and judgment."

Martini gave a short nod, little more than a jerk. Based on that short introduction, Robert Ryan knew he was dealing with a classic type A personality, a hard-driving, tightly wound, aggressive overachiever. Martini turned to the officer standing behind Ryan. "General Martini," the executive officer said, "may I introduce Captain Laurie Bender, one of our weapon system officers from the Forty-fourth."

They shook hands. "Any relation to Lieutenant General Robert Bender?" Martini asked.

"He's my father, sir."

The Pentagon

The staff car dropped Lieutenant General Robert Bender at the River Entrance to the Pentagon. He trotted up the steps, through the entrance, and past the Bradley Corridor and the office of the chairman of the Joint Chiefs of Staff. He took the escalator to the fourth floor and walked directly into the Air Force corridor. He turned left into the Air Force chief of staff's outer office and was ushered directly into the office of General "Wild Wayne" Charles, the Air Force chief of staff.

No one had called General Charles "Wild Wayne" in years, at least not to his face. But the ferocious drive that earned him the nickname, four stars, and his current position was still very much a part of his personality. "Bob," Charles called, waving Bender to a seat, "I understand you've got a problem."

Bender told him about the briefing the president wanted on the Far East and her military options. Charles spun around in his chair and looked out a window. The Potomac sparkled in the summer sun, and a power boat cruised slowly upstream. "Not good. Briefing the president is the chairman's job. You've *really* got a problem."

"What a surprise," Bender allowed, irony caught in every word.

Charles turned around and laughed. "I'll be damned, Bob. Are you lightening up at last?"

"Somebody has got to tell the chairman."

Charles nodded. "I'll do it right away. Expect the shit to hit the fan."

Bender nodded, understanding only too well the reaction of General Tennyson Overmeyer, United States Army, the current chairman of the Joint Chiefs of Staff. Overmeyer would read the situation exactly as Bender would have: A three-star general was playing politics in the White House and had gained access to the president, bypassing him, who, along with the secretary of defense, advised the president on all matters relating to the military. Bender fully expected Overmeyer to crunch him hard and force him into retirement. He would never see his fourth star and reach his ultimate goal, the capstone of his career: the command of Air Combat Command. It was all he had ever wanted.

"Chief," Bender said, "this was not my idea. All I want is out of that place."

"Which is exactly what we want," Charles assured him.

"So what do I do?"

Charles said nothing and was silent, turning the problem over in his head. Finally, "Brief her."

"Thanks, chief."

"I may be able to salvage this," Charles told him. "There's things you don't know, and as long as you're talking the party line, the chairman may think you're just his mouthpiece. I'll try to convince him."

"I hope so," Bender said, not feeling hopeful at all.

"Bob, the only guy I know with a backbone as rigid as yours is Overmeyer. But he knows the truth when he hears it. Now chase your body down to Plans and OPs"—Plans and OPs was the deputy chief of staff for Plans and Operations—"and get your act together. I'll do what I can with Overmeyer."

Bender stood up. "Thanks, chief. I appreciate it."

Charles watched him leave. *You are about to get your eyes watered,* he thought.

Bender left Charles's office, turned left, and took the few steps down to the office of the DCS for Plans and Operations. In short order, he found himself inside and talking to the three-star general who headed the directorate. What Bender heard was worrisome, and there was no doubt that China was well on the road to becoming a major military power. The DCS for Plans and OPs calculated that if China sustained its current rate of military buildup, the United States would be facing a very credible threat within three to five years.

"How many people know this?" Bender asked.

"The chairman has briefed everyone in the current administration. But our take on China's trending is not a popular position right now and no one is listening. But we're doing exactly what we've always done, looking at military capability, not political intentions.

"As we speak, China has the capability to project its military power well into the Pacific and envelop Japan. Think of China as being Germany and Japan being England at the turn of the twentieth century. But there are two major differences when you compare them. First, Japan is an economic superpower that is militarily irrelevant. Second, China is the preeminent military power in Asia but an economic midget."

The pieces started to come together for Bender. "Then the Chinese takeover of Taiwan is nothing but a grab by the biggest bully on the block for the goodies and we can expect to see more of the same."

"That's guessing at China's political intentions," the three-star said. "But we think so. Unfortunately, the State Department and the national security advisor have a different take on the situation." A knock at the door cut off any conversation. A lieutenant colonel entered and handed the three-star a note. "General Charles wants to see you ASAP."

A worried Bender made his way back to the Air Force Chief of Staff's Office. His condition did not improve when he was immediately escorted into Charles's office and found General Tennyson Overmeyer, the chairman of the Joint Chiefs of Staff sitting there. "General," Charles began, "I think you know Bob Bender."

"We've met," Overmeyer grunted. He waved Bender to a seat. "I don't like the idea of you briefing the president."

"I assure you, sir," Bender replied, "it is not my idea. All I want is out of the place."

"So I've heard," Overmeyer told him. "But it will be feet first if you're not careful." He pulled out a cigar and chomped off the end. But he did not light it and chewed on the tip. He studied Bender for a few moments. "Of all the damn situations," he finally said, "this has got to be the one most screwed up." The general shot out of his chair and paced back and forth, still rolling the unlit cigar in his mouth. "Wayne assures me you will tell the president exactly what we want."

"You can rely on it," Bender said.

"We're dealing with too many unknowns here," Charles said. "We better bring him on board. He can be trusted."

"So help me God," Overmeyer growled, "I'll build a gallows and hang the bastard in the parking lot if he can't."

Bender assumed he was the "bastard" Overmeyer was talking about. "Sir, you sign off on the briefing, and I'll give it word for word. For all practical purposes, it will be you up there speaking."

The two four-stars exchanged glances. Overmeyer sat down. "A few days before Roberts died"—Bender caught the derogatory sound in Overmeyer's voice when he referred to the dead president—"a satellite monitored the positioning of the Chinese fleet opposite Taiwan. The National Reconnaissance Office repositioned a Keyhole satellite—cut its useful life in half—to get the detail we needed. It wasn't just the fleet on maneuvers but a massive repositioning of the People's Liberation Army—army, air force, and navy. Much more than the saber rattling that had been going on in the nineties. I called Roberts, told him I was worried and wanted to upgrade the DEFCON. He told me, and I quote, 'Don't worry about it. Return to normal readiness and stop all internal posturing. Do it immediately.'

"The bastard knew enough to know I had already started internal measures and was moving up the readiness ladder. He shut us down, and all we could do was watch. Naturally, I talked to the DIA and the boys in the basement." The boys in the basement were the supersecret intelligence organizations that fell under the Pentagon's control. "The boys put it together." The general was chewing his cigar at a rapid rate, his jaws working like a pit bull gnawing a bone.

"Roberts had cut a deal with the Chinese under the table. Based on what happened, we probably gave them Taiwan. But for what? What do we get out of the deal? Peace in our time?" The general's face had turned beet red as his blood pressure skyrocketed. "Our president appeased the Chinese exactly like Chamberlain did when he sold Czechoslovakia out to Hitler at Munich."

That was 1938, Bender thought. *Haven't we learned anything in sixty-three years?*

Overmeyer was back in tight control, binding his emotions with an iron-hard clamp. "When Roberts died of a cerebral hemorrhage, he really left Turner with a headache."

"Sir," Bender said, "I honestly don't think President Turner knows a thing about this."

"We agree on that," Charles told him.

"That makes anything I tell her about the Far East misleading," Bender replied.

Overmeyer threw the remnants of his cigar into a waste can. "Correct. And that's the problem." He stood and walked to the door. "I want you to tell her." He stared at Bender. "And then I want you out of the White House. Dead or alive."

Washington, D.C.

The door to Robert Bender's small office was open. His coat was off as he sat at his desk trying to create a meaningful briefing on China for Madeline Turner. But he was drowning in the shear mass of information the Pentagon had thrown at him. It was too much, and he changed direction, outlining a new briefing book for the president. *The first step is to hitch the horse to the cart,* he thought. He personally doubted if Turner would ever see the briefing book or, for that matter, him once the briefing was over. That outcome didn't bother him, and as he had told Nancy the night before, "I was looking for a job when I found this one."

A "Hi" caught his attention, and he looked up to see Sarah Turner standing in the doorway. "May I come in?" the ten-year-old girl asked.

He waved to the only chair. "Sure. But it's not very comfortable." Sarah stepped inside and crawled onto the straight-back chair. She was wearing light blue warm-ups with white running shoes. But instead of the presidential logo on the embroidered name tag, it only said Brat. *She's a prototype of her mother with blond hair,* he thought, *and is going to be a beautiful teenager.* "What brings you down here?"

She slumped back in the chair and kicked her feet back and forth, the unhappy gesture of a little girl. "Just looking around."

A Secret Service agent walked by, a rarity in that part of the basement, and smiled when he saw Sarah. "Please leave the door open," he told Bender before he retreated down the hall. Bender saw him raise his left wrist and speak into his whisper mike. Sarah looked even more unhappy.

A warm smile spread across his face, and he remembered when Laurie was young. "Looking for the place?"

Sarah nodded. Like many ten-year-olds, she needed a hiding place where she could find refuge from the cares and traumas of being a little girl growing up. A niche that was hers only and safe from the prying eyes of adults.

"It's going to be hard in the White House," he told her. "But I bet your grandmother could help."

"Grams," Sarah said, fuming. "She doesn't let me get away with anything. The ushers talk to her and tell her everything. They're afraid of my mom but not Grams. Everybody talks to her."

"That's life," Bender said. "But you've got the inside track. Your grandmother loves you."

That cheered her up, and she stopped kicking. "Mom's going on a big trip over Labor Day, but I'm not going. Maybe me and Grams can find a place then."

"Lots of places to hide down here," Bender said.

The little girl gave him a serious look. "Why don't you like my mom?"

Are my feelings that obvious? Bender thought. He did not like the president, but then, he did not totally dislike her. So what was the problem? He was brutally honest with himself. His was a male-dominated, elitist world, and now women, like Madeline Turner, were shaking that world to its foundations. He did not object to change, but he was extremely reluctant to tinker with a system that had been tested in combat and worked. However, social equality was not in the equation, and his standards of success hinged on mission accomplishment, combat effectiveness, and low casualties in that order. But how could he explain that to an outsider, much less a little girl?

"Do you like your teacher?" he asked. She nodded. *You probably like all your teachers,* he thought, *because you're a perfect kid and the teachers love you.* "But what about your principal?"

"I don't know her."

"Who enforces the rules at school, I mean, really swings the big bat?"

Sarah smiled, liking the image of her principal with a baseball bat. "The principal, I guess."

"So how do you act around your principal?"

"Everyone is very polite, and we never talk when she's around."

"Does that mean you don't like her?" he asked. She shook her head. "Your mother," Bender continued, "is like my principal."

That satisfied the little girl, and she changed the subject. "Why do you like airplanes?"

"Oh, boy—"

"Shouldn't you say 'Oh, girl'?" she interrupted.

For the first time since he had been in the White House, Bender laughed heartily. "You are absolutely right. Oh, girl, that's a hard one to answer." How could he explain to a child his love of flying? The attraction of the machines? The challenge? The unparalleled sense of freedom and being in control? The sheer beauty of breaking out on top of clouds to meet a crystal blue sky? The sense of peace?

"Airplanes, especially jet fighters, are beautiful things and fun to fly," he said.

"Mom says jet fighters and bombers are killing machines."

"They can he used for that, but no one I know wants to."

"Could you shoot another plane down?"

"If I had to, yes." He wasn't about to tell her that he had shot down an Iraqi MiG in the 1991 Gulf War and watched the pilot fall to his death when he ejected too low to the ground. "But I don't want to."

"My brother, Brian, wants to go to the Air Force Academy and be a fighter pilot. But Mom says she's not going to let the military kill her son." Bender didn't know how to answer that one. "Do you have a son?" Sarah asked.

He held up a single finger. "We have a daughter."

"Oh. Girls don't have to fly, do they?"

He smiled. "No, they don't." *But kids have a way of growing up different from what parents want,* he thought.

"See you," Sarah said, flouncing out of the office.

The Secret Service agent walked by, following her. He stopped and nodded at Bender. "The kid's all over the place," he said.

"Say," Bender replied, "I haven't seen Chuck Sanford or Wayne Adams around lately. What happened to them?"

The agent looked around to be sure they were alone. "You didn't hear this from me. They've been relieved and are looking at an administrative firing."

Bender's eyes narrowed. "Shaw?" he asked. The agent

only looked at him. "Because of what happened at St. Louis when I told Turner the president was dead?" The agent grunted an answer and disappeared down the hall.

Bender leaned back in his chair, thinking. He'd have to do something about that. Another thought came to him. He knew why Madeline O'Keith Turner hated the military.

3

Washington, D.C.

The butler hovered behind the two women and little girl, ready to be of instant service. He liked the easy and warm family atmosphere that enveloped him when they ate breakfast, and of all the families he had waited on in over thirty years of service in the White House, he liked this one the best. He even liked the children, Brian and Sarah. But without a doubt, the little girl was his favorite. *If you're going to be a princess,* he thought, *you've got to start young.* And this one was going to be a princess.

"Mr. William," Sarah said, concerned about his welfare, "when do you eat breakfast?"

A warm smile spread across his dark face. "I eat in the kitchen mess early in the morning, Miss Sarah. Right after I come to work."

"Why can't you eat with us?"

"Well, thank you," he said, "but my job is to see that you get a hot breakfast. We all gotta do what's expected of us."

Madeline Turner smiled at the man. "Thank you, William." He keyed on that and withdrew, leaving them alone.

"I don't like having servants," Sarah announced. "It doesn't seem fair."

"They're helpers, not servants," Maura O'Keith told her. "They help your mother by doing little things so she

38

is free to do the big, important things. You and me get helped because we're here with your mother."

"Your Grams is right, Sarah," Turner said. "I couldn't be president without people like William. He knows that and is proud of what he does. Now hurry up, or you'll be late for school."

"I'll go with her," Maura said, standing up.

"Thanks, Mother." Turner stood up and glanced at her watch: 7:20. She had forty minutes to herself, a precious forty minutes of quiet before the day exploded around her. But she was honest with herself and admitted she loved the hustle and constant activity, the stream of people who surrounded her and never left her alone.

William was waiting outside in the corridor, familiar with her morning routine. He followed her into the study pushing a tea cart with a carafe of fresh coffee. Turner settled into her corner on the couch while he poured a cup. "William, what did you do over Labor Day?"

"We had a family reunion at my brother's place in Bethesda," he answered. "Quite a gathering, everyone was there."

"What did you talk about?"

"Mostly you, ma'am. Of course, I didn't say much. I never do." It was the truth. It was easier to get information out of the CIA than the White House's household staff. William fussed over the tea cart for a moment. "I did tell them about Sarah and the way she prowls around the mansion, trying to hide from the Secret Service and driving them crazy. I hope I didn't overstep my bounds."

Turner smiled. "You know the bounds better than I do, William." Again, that was the truth, and he would never say anything bad about the first family. Further, Turner was certain the reserved and proper African-American would never talk to the press, and if members of his family did pass on charming little tidbits about the first family, so much the better. "I appreciate your honesty. Did they talk about any major political issues?"

William understood exactly what Turner was doing. The White House was an institution that could swallow up and isolate a president. He had seen it many times and knew that Madeline Turner needed a window to the world. And she had chosen him to be one. But Patrick Shaw had warned the entire staff about talking to her alone. And he had also seen that before. Access to the president of the United States was power.

But he was eligible for retirement, and it hurt to get out of bed on cold, early mornings. "Mostly they talked about jobs, Madam President. There's a lot of unemployed or underemployed people out there. They don't want welfare, they want good jobs. Ones that allow them to raise a family."

She nodded. William had confirmed what she had sensed during her Labor Day trip. "Thank you. Please don't tell anyone what we talked about. If Mr. Shaw questions you, tell him I asked what you did over the holiday."

"Yes, ma'am," William replied. *Indeed, I will,* he thought as he left and closed the door behind him.

Shaw bumped into William thirty minutes later outside the family kitchen on the second floor. "What did you talk about this morning?" Shaw asked. The tone of his voice was warm and friendly.

"The president asked what I did over the holiday," William answered, his voice stiff and formal. "I told her we had a family reunion at my brother's."

"Was that all?"

"She did thank me for the coffee," William answered.

Shaw's tone never changed. "That had damn well better be all you talked about or your ass will be on the streets."

"She does expect an answer to her questions, Mr. Shaw."

"And I want to know what the questions are," he said. He took the few steps down to Turner's private study and checked his watch. Jackie Winters, Turner's superefficient personal assistant, was already there with the black leather organizer that was the center of her life. For the rest of the day, Jackie would shadow Turner wherever she went, waiting outside in corridors or at her own desk, never more than a few steps away. Jackie Winters was a mouse by appearance and trade, but she was fiercely protective of Turner and would willingly take a bullet for her.

At exactly eight o'clock, Shaw knocked twice and entered. Jackie was right behind him. The day had started.

Shaw sat down opposite Turner and handed her the day's schedule while Jackie retreated to a chair in a far corner. Shaw counted to three—she had read the schedule—and handed her the President's Daily Brief, the slickly printed summary of the best intelligence the CIA could produce. She read the twelve-page document in less than three minutes. He handed her a list of people she would be meeting, complete with a short one-paragraph biography on those she didn't know. He counted to twenty on this one. Then he handed her an action list, items that needed a decision in the near future. At the top of the list was the selection of a new vice president. She glanced at it and looked up.

"Patrick, I want to take a new direction."

"Yes, ma'am." He didn't like the tone in her voice.

"Over Labor Day, I got the sense that economic conditions are worse than we thought."

"Our statistics are pretty accurate, Mizz President."

She took off her reading glasses. "Once, during a senate committee hearing in California, I had to listen to a group of Ph.D.s from the university. They were trying to sell a high-powered study on welfare reform based on statistics and economic projections. Then I discovered that not one of them had ever met a welfare recipient."

Shaw smiled. "I can put our statisticians in the streets."

"Not the streets, Patrick. I want them and their bosses in the employment offices talking to the people who are looking for work." She paused for effect. "We're going to create an employment program."

"Hard to do, Mizz President, without expanding government handouts."

"Not handouts. And I'm not talking about creating a generation of hamburger flippers either. I want meaningful, well-paid jobs."

"How do you propose we do that, Mizz President?"

"We're going to overhaul the tax system from the top down with the bottom line being productivity and jobs."

Shaw was seldom at a loss for words, but he was now. "Ah, ah, that's been tried before. Didn't work, upset too many personal manure wagons." He glanced at his watch, anxious to get out of this conversation. "Your staff meeting is in—"

"Ten minutes," Turner said. "Tax reform is not going to happen overnight, but start working on it. Today. I want background on my desk by this afternoon. We've got three years to make a difference." Jackie made a note in her organizer. The material would be delivered as ordered. Turner stood and walked to the door. "And Patrick, I asked for a briefing on the Far East. What happened to it?"

"I'll check on it, ma'am." He followed her out as Jackie made another note. *What's this three years crap?* he thought. *What happened to the next election? This is what I get for working with amateurs. They always want to do the right thing.*

Shaw's blunt fingers beat a relentless tattoo on his desk as assistants darted in and out of his office, minimizing their exposure time to his anger, as they hurried to build a background file on tax reform. The West Wing was buzzing with rumors, but no one knew what or who had sent Patrick Flannery Shaw into a towering rage. At one point, he chased Alice Fay, his secretary, out of his office with, "I'd rather be a hooker than own a politician. The hooker gets to spit it out afterward."

That outburst provided the clue Alice Fay needed about the who behind his anger. But it wasn't worth her job to talk about it.

"Get me Bender," he shouted to the vacant doorway.

Almost immediately Alice Fay answered, "General Bender is on line 1."

"In person," Shaw shouted back. He wanted real meat to chew. Within moments, Bender was in his office. "What happened to the briefing you were preparing for the president?" he asked, his voice not betraying what he felt.

"The slides and briefing book are being prepared and will be ready this afternoon," Bender replied.

Shaw heard the answer, but he wasn't really listening. His mind was still working the problem Madeline Turner had laid on him that morning. The more he thought about it, the worse it got. Meaningful tax reform would kill her politically. There were too many powerful interests behind the current system, and they would take her down along with anyone standing too close—like Patrick Shaw. For Shaw, there was only one constant in his life: power. He savored it like a junkie on a heroin rush or an alcoholic when the first shot hits bottom. Of all the addictions, his was the least curable—he was a power freak—and he wasn't about to sacrifice all that he had attained over a hare-brained scheme that was political suicide.

"You sure it will be ready—when?" Shaw asked.

"This afternoon," Bender repeated. "Anytime after 1400 hours." He would have to call General Charles, the Air Force chief of staff, and have the chairman, General Overmeyer, approve the briefing soonest. But it could be done.

"Good. Be ready when I call. We'll do it in the Situation Room. The president has never used it before."

"Do you want to review the script or the briefing book first?" Bender asked.

Again, what Bender was saying didn't register. "Gawddammit! Just be ready."

"I'd suggest the national security advisor and the secretary of state be there," Bender said.

Shaw's grunt was unintelligible. Bender spun around and retreated out the door. "Leave the door open, sir?" he asked.

Shaw ignored him and went back to work on the hard problem. The implications of what she was proposing were staggering. *What a load of shit!* he thought. *Basing a tax system on productivity and jobs! Maybe I can divert her attention away from this tax reform business. I've saved her from herself before. But if I can't, it's time to get out of Dodge.*

Jesus H. Christ, he moaned to himself. *How the hell do I get out of Dodge and still stay alive in this town?*

The Marine sentry unlocked the door to the Situation Room in the basement of the West Wing. He flicked on the lights and stood back for Bender to enter. It was not a large room, perhaps twenty by fifteen feet in size, and contained a conference table and comfortable chairs. Sliding doors on the paneled walls could roll back to reveal maps, video displays, or the big screen at the far end. But other than that, it was totally devoid of the electronic gadgets and telecommunications as portrayed by the movies and TV. What was impressive, however, was the communications array in the comm center a few steps down the hall.

"I'll need to use the thirty-five-millimeter slide projector," Bender said.

"I'll set it up for you," the Marine said.

"You better let me do it," Bender said. "Believe me, your clearance doesn't go high enough."

The Marine unlocked the projection room behind the big screen and waited outside while Bender loaded the slides into the projector. He cycled through the slides to make sure they were properly reversed so the audience could read them from the backside of the screen. The Marine relocked the room when Bender came out. "I'll restrict access," he assured the general.

Bender returned to the Situation Room, plugged in the projector's remote control, and ran the slides—a double check of the slides and the projector. He was a very methodical man, willing to rely on others to do the small, critical jobs that ultimately made the system work. But if he had to, he could do it himself. And sometimes, he wanted to. Finally, he sat the blue briefing book on the table in front of the president's chair and retreated to his spot beside the screen where he would give the briefing. He sat down and stared at the briefing book as he mentally rehearsed the words he would say. This wasn't what he had in mind when he joined the Air Force.

He closed his eyes and for a few moments, he was back in the cockpit of an F-16 high above the earth, free and alone. Now he was back with the Thunderbirds, lined up on the runway, quickly going through the cockpit checks. Then Thunderbird's lead voice over the UHF radio. "Cockpit check."

The quick response from each pilot that he was ready to go. "One."—"Two."—"Three."—"Four."—"Five."—"Six."

Always a short laugh from the lead. "Thunderbirds, let's run 'em up." And the show was on.

"Smoke on." He was blasting through the show box and spiraling high into the sky, reaching, always reaching, pushing the limits, striving for the perfect show, trusting his teammates, sure that they would be there for him.

Turner's voice brought him back to the present. "Disturbing your nap, Robert?"

He looked up and felt his face blush. "Only daydreaming, Madam President." She was smiling at him from the doorway. Bender came to his feet in a rush as she walked in. He was back in control and standing quietly, his hands folded in front of him, holding the remote control and laser pointer.

"We haven't had a chance to talk in quite a while," Turner said as she sat down. Bender didn't answer.

Shaw stood aside and let the secretary of state, Clement Murchison, and the national security advisor, William Rawlings, enter. One of Shaw's strengths was his ability to read the emotional clues people transmit in their actions or words, and he caught every single one coming from Turner. *She likes this guy,* he thought. *That's why she keeps him around. The most uptight, rigid asshole in the whole fuckin' U.S. Air Farce, she likes.* Why had he missed the signs before?

Instinctively, Shaw focused on Bender, his delicate antennae tuned to every nuance. *My Gawd,* he thought, *he does look like a general, lean and mean, unbending, hungry for command.* Was he a lever to control Maddy Turner? Just as rapidly, he discarded the thought. Not because of Turner, but because of the signs coming from Bender. Bender did not like the president. But why? Shaw filed it all away and found a seat next to Rawlings, the national security advisor. He hoped the briefing would not take too long.

"Well, Robert," Turner said, "what do you have for us today?"

Shaw heard the warmth in her voice. *Damn,* he thought, *a woman talks like that to me and I'm all over her like a bear on honey.* Another thought came to him. *Has she deliberately let her guard down to show me something?*

"Madam President," Bender began, "this is the briefing you requested on the current situation in the Far East. It is essentially a summary of the briefing book in front of you."

What briefing book? Shaw thought. *Damn, I haven't seen a new briefing book.* Then he remembered the earlier conversation he had had with the general. He had been distracted and let it slip through the cracks. Bender had been straight with him.

Shaw listened while Bender ran through the basics. *Nothing new so far,* he thought. It was the standard Pentagon line: an expansionist China was rapidly increasing its military strength and was now a threat to its neighbors and world peace. Next came the scare tactics. Something about the delivery of six Xia-class missile submarines ahead of schedule; a naval task force centered on China's first aircraft carrier being operational; and finally, a long discussion on China's nuclear, biological, and chemical warfare capability. According to the Pentagon's current analysis, the biological agents developed by the Chinese were far more deadly and sophisticated than any nerve gas toxin. *Where did all that come from?* Shaw wondered.

Turner liked the way Bender ran through the briefing: fast, articulate, and well organized. Out of habit, she flipped the pages of the briefing book, reading as he talked. But she could read much faster than he could summarize the main points and was well ahead of him.

Her head came up. "General Bender, skip ahead to, ah, the topic on page 67." She looked at Shaw. "Patrick, check outside and send Jackie back to her office. Make sure the guard is down at the far end of the hall by the stairs and no one enters the corridor. Then lock the door."

"We're secure in here, Mizz President," he said. The look on her face drove him out of his chair to do as she ordered. *What the hell?* he wondered. Bender said nothing until he had returned to his seat. Bender cycled the slides forward. The words "The Beijing Pact" flashed on the screen. "What the hell is the Beijing Pact?" Shaw muttered.

"We're about to find out," Turner said. Shaw's head jerked at the sound of her voice. There was something new in her tone, and National Security Advisor Rawlings looked like he needed to make an urgent trip to the restroom.

"In this business," Shaw whispered, sotto voce, "never pass up a men's room to take a precautionary piss. You never know when you'll get another chance."

"Madam President," Clement Murchison, the secretary of state, said, "this is not the time nor place to discuss this issue. I must protest."

"Yes," Turner replied, "I imagine you would. General Bender, please continue."

"On Thursday, August 2," Bender said, "sixteen days before President Roberts died"—the camera clicked, a remote sound from behind the screen that echoed over them, and a slide of a gray Boeing 707 landing flashed on the screen—"an unmarked Air Force KC-135 landed in China at Shahe, a Chinese air base approximately an hour's drive north of Beijing."

Click. A grainy slide of Rawlings and Murchison getting off the same airplane flashed on the screen. "This photo was taken from over a mile away and had to be computer enhanced."

Click. Murchison following Rawlings into a black sedan. "They were then driven to Beijing."

Click. Rawlings and Murchison entering a house. "Where they met with the premier of the People's Republic of China, Lu Zoulin." The screen went blank. Bender's voice carried over the room, his words clipped and sharp. "This meeting was held in the utmost secrecy and a mutual accord was reached, which, for lack of a better term, we are calling the Beijing Pact. We do not know the content of the document, but we do know its effect."

Murchison stood up as if to leave. "Sit down," Turner said. He did.

"Saint Peter shit-a-brick," Shaw whispered. This was one of those times that cemented the special bond he felt existed between himself and the celestial gatekeeper. It was all in the job description. "The devil done got inside."

"General Bender, why are you the one telling me this?" Turner asked.

"Because, Madam President, the CIA does not know about it and the Pentagon only became aware of it since President Roberts's death. To the best of our knowledge, the only two people in your administration who do know about it are sitting in this room."

"Again, Madam President," Murchison said, his voice breaking at the edges, "I must protest. This issue is beyond the purview of the military."

"Is it?" Bender replied. The screen came alive. "This is a transcript of a telephone conversation between President Roberts and General Overmeyer on Thursday evening, August 16, two days before the president died."

GENERAL OVERMEYER: Sir, the Chinese are massing opposite Taiwan. We need to brief you on the situation ASAP and I want to increase the DEFCON.
PRESIDENT ROBERTS: Don't worry about it. Return to normal readiness and stop all internal posturing. Do it immediately.

Shaw had to read the words twice to fully believe them. "Does this mean—" His voice trailed off and he couldn't finish the sentence. He was having the political equivalent of a religious experience.

Bender could have been a college professor explaining a simple problem in calculus to a very thick student. "It means, Mr. Shaw, that the president of the United States, with the collaboration of the secretary of state and his national security advisor, cut a secret deal with the Chinese, giving them Taiwan."

The politician in Shaw kicked in. "The quid pro quo?"

"We don't know what the quid pro quo was," Bender answered. "We can only guess, and the military is not in the business of guessing. You'll have to ask these two gentlemen."

Rawlings and Murchison started to speak, but Turner flicked her hand up, a short gesture silencing the room. She finished reading the briefing book as the men waited. "Please run the rest of the slides," she said to Bender. He clicked through the slides. "Yes, I see," she said, standing up. "Patrick, work the problem. Don't come out of this room until it's solved.'' She picked up the briefing book. ''General Bender, please come with me.''

''I need to get the slides, Madam President.'' She nodded and waited while the Marine guard unlocked the door to the projection room and Bender retrieved the slides. She never took her eyes off him. Then she was a step in front of him, still carrying the briefing book as they climbed the stairs and walked to the Oval Office.

Jackie was waiting by the door. Turner handed her the briefing book and Bender's slide tray. ''Please destroy these immediately. Do it personally—this is important.'' Jackie nodded and disappeared down the hall. ''Please sit down,'' She told Bender, motioning to one of the couches. She picked up a phone, not sitting down. ''Trish, tea and coffee please.'' She dropped the phone into its cradle, turned to face Bender, and leaned back against the front edge of her desk, her arms folded.

They waited in silence. Bender pulled into himself, thinking. He had expected a more emotional reaction, perhaps even tears, and was surprised that she was so calm and collected. *Maybe she doesn't fully understand what it all means,* he reasoned. He looked at his president. There was no doubt she was a very attractive woman. *Nancy would love that suit she's wearing,* he thought. *But I doubt if she would look that good. That's it. Turner is mostly appearance. Put up a good front for the troops.* Another thought came to him: *She likes giving orders.* Bender was convinced he had her measure.

''Robert, we need to talk.''

Shaw was enjoying himself. It wasn't often he had a chance to disprove the old political adage that you could kill someone in politics, but you couldn't kill them dead. ''Gentlemen, have you ever attended an autopsy?'' His voice was friendly and quiet with only a soft trace of his southern accent. ''It is not a pretty sight.''

''Shaw,'' Murchison said, trying to regain control. ''Who in the hell do you think you are?''

''The man conducting the autopsy.''

Murchison stood to leave. ''Don't be ridiculous.''

"It's our autopsy," National Security Advisor Rawlings said. Murchison sat down.

Shaw stood up and plodded around the room like a friendly bear. He stopped behind Rawlings and placed a big hand on his shoulder. He knew who would break first. "First, let's examine the proximate cause of death. Disloyalty."

William wheeled a tea cart into the Oval Office. "Would you prefer coffee or tea?" Turner offered.

"Coffee," Bender answered.

She buzzed her secretary as William left. "Please show Mr. Shaw in the moment he arrives." She glanced at Bender while she poured his coffee. "Robert, I have two problems: one political, the other with foreign policy. Patrick is solving the first one, but I've got to solve the second. Needless to say, whatever I do involves the military. That's where you come in."

"Madam President, you should be talking to General Overmeyer, not me."

"But I want to talk to you about it."

"Why me? By law, the chairman of the Joint Chiefs of Staff is your military advisor."

"I will talk to him"—a long pause—"when he's ready to listen to his president who happens to be a woman."

"He'll listen, Madam President, because—"

"Because he's an officer and a gentleman? Don't be silly."

"Because you are his commander in chief." *He won't like it,* Bender thought, *but he will listen.*

"Cream or sugar?" she asked, the gracious hostess.

This is bizarre, Bender thought. *We're caught in a major crisis and playing tea party.* "Black," he said. She handed him the cup, almost touching his hand.

"Why didn't General Overmeyer tell me?" Turner asked.

"Because we—"

"We?"

"The Department of Defense." He changed his approach. "Because our intelligence operatives didn't—"

"Your operatives? Spooks like the CIA?"

Stay focused! he raged to himself. "We call them the boys in the basement." The puzzled look on her face demanded further explanation. "Certain intelligence agencies fall under the Department of Defense to avoid congressional oversight. It started under President Reagan."

"Why wasn't I told about them?"

He wanted to say, because you're not talking to the right people. Instead, "You'd have to speak to the DCI"—the DCI was her director of Central Intelligence—"and General Overmeyer about that. But to answer your original question: because our spooks didn't put all the pieces together until a few days ago. General Overmeyer thought this briefing was a good opportunity to—"

"Overmeyer thinks I'm up to my neck in this."

"I can speak for the general and—"

"Can you speak for yourself, Robert?"

"Loyalty," Shaw explained, being very friendly, "is a form of currency in politics. You exchange it for power. No loyalty, no power. If someone takes your power away, then you are free to renegotiate your loyalty. So who took your power away? What were you two shit-for-brains thinking of?"

"The agreement was President Roberts's idea," Murchison said.

"Always blame the last bastard who left," Shaw muttered.

"We were acting for him," Rawlings said.

"Nothing wrong with that," Shaw conceded. "But you should have been banging on the door of the Oval Office the moment China moved on Taiwan, a full confession on your lips, resignation in one hand, and the gawddamn Beijing Pact in the other."

"It's called the Technical Agreement for the Reversion of Taiwan," Rawlings said.

"Technical Agreement?" Shaw asked, now the confused good old boy. "What did you do? Negotiate it over the Internet?" No answer. "I want a copy. Now."

A tight smile spread across Murchison's face. "One of the protocols of the agreement dictates that if either party is removed from power, for whatever reason, the agreement is null and void and both parties will immediately destroy their copies. Which, with the death of President Roberts, has happened.''

"You are truly beyond redemption," Shaw said, back to being friendly and enjoying himself, "and suffering from a massive case of brain farts. Why do you think Lu Zoulin moved on Taiwan when he did? Do you think he burned his copy? I can see the press conference and hear the question now. 'Madam President, what about this supersecret sellout of Taiwan like Chamberlain sold out Czechoslovakia to Hitler?' No way she could've answered, 'I'm glad you asked that question.' You hung your president out to dry. What kind of loyalty is that?''

"Any question by the press would be pure speculation," Murchison said. "She doesn't have credible denial."

"What was the quid pro quo?" Shaw asked. "What did the Chinese give up so we'd roll over on Taiwan?"

Murchison was smiling. "There is no agreement in force, therefore no quid—"

Rawlings interrupted. "I've got a copy."

Speak for myself? Bender wondered. *Where are we going with this?* "The chairman is certain you didn't know about it. He took this opportunity to tell you."

The president sipped her tea. "Who knows about this in the Pentagon?"

"Very few people. It's extremely close hold."

"The secretary of defense?"

"I don't know," Bender answered. "But knowing General Charles—"

"General Charles?"

Bender bit his lip. Hard. She didn't even know who he was. Where had she been the last seven months? "General Wayne Charles is your Air Force chief of staff," he replied. "He would only be in this if the secretary of defense was in the loop." *Don't politicians understand loyalty?* he thought.

"I'm not very good with names," she explained. "I've got to put a face to the name." Another sip of tea. "Do you speak for General Charles, too, Robert?" Her voice was soft and gentle.

"In this case, yes."

"What do you think the quid pro quo was?"

Shaw sat down and drummed the table with his fingers. It was decision time, and whatever he decided to do now would drive events in the future. "Boys, we have a problem. I can turn you over to the DOJ''—the Department of Justice—"and let them work you over. Or—"

Murchison laughed, interrupting him. "Investigate us for what? We were not in violation of the Logan Act. In fact, I am empowered by the Constitution to negotiate for the president. Try reading it, Mr. Shaw."

Shaw feigned surprise. "Who said anything about violating your constitutionals?" He gave an audible sigh. "That's the problem with you lawyer types—too damn legalistic. The DOJ will tear your life apart, looking into every little dark nook and cranny where you stuck your pecker or cut a deal. I'm willing to bet that you're both like an overripe melon: Thump a little bit and you'll crack wide open. If you want to play it my way and be smart about this, you can submit an undated letter of resignation along with all the details of this sordid little mess."

"In short," Rawlings said, "you want a full confession and a letter of resignation so you can sacrifice us if this blows up."

"You are a rocket scientist," Shaw allowed.

Murchison understood exactly what Shaw was doing. "That would put us in your pocket."

"Just your balls," Shaw said. "But you still got a job. Except you don't belch around Mizz Turner without my permission. You don't see her without going through me, and you tell her exactly what I tell you to tell her. When you are alone with her, I want a blow-by-blow rehash, and you had better've said the right words. Then, when the time is right, I'll date your resignation and you can slip away into any obscurity that makes you feel good. If you've been good little dog turds, your trip reports disappear. But they won't be burnt."

"Shaw," Murchison said, "I cannot allow that. You are so crooked—"

"If I ate a nail, I'd shit a screw?" *Damn,* Shaw thought.

Why did I waste that line here? He was tired of being nice and rolled out the heavy artillery. "Let me explain the situation in terms even a lawyer can understand." Shaw's voice went cold and hard. "You have three options. You can either do as I ask *or* you will be found in bed with a dead girl *or* a live boy. Your choice."

"You'll have my resignation and the details on your desk in an hour," Rawlings said.

Murchison stood up, trying to retain a semblance of dignity. "And mine as well."

A broad smile spread across Shaw's face. He was all teddy bear now. "Boys, I want your copies of the Technical Agreement in my hot little hands in, say, five minutes?"

"But I destroyed mine," Murchison protested.

More drumming of Shaw's fingers. "Did you?"

"It will take a few hours," Murchison replied, his voice full of bitterness. For the first time in his life, he understood rape.

Madeline Turner sat on the couch opposite Bender and crossed her legs. For the first time, he noticed that she had big feet for a woman. "Madam President, I can only speculate about any quid pro quo between President Roberts and the Chinese."

"Then speculate."

Bender looked at his hands, wishing he was on some quiet Air Force base where sanity ruled. "I think we gave up Taiwan in exchange for a few promises."

"And the promises were?"

Bender responded to her voice. "No more territorial expansion on their part and they'll honor the existing status quo." Silence. Turner's face was calm.

Finally, she broke the silence. "Considering this is a done deal, I can live with that."

"If you trust the Chinese."

"I take it," she said, "that you don't trust them."

"No, ma'am, I don't."

She stood and walked to her desk. "Robert, please wait until Patrick joins us. It won't be long." She buzzed her secretary, who brought in two folders and one of the ever-present blue briefing books. Jackie Winters briefly appeared to see if she was needed.

Bender glanced at the briefing book and gave an inner sigh. *Those puppies do cause trouble,* he thought, recalling the one that had just been burned. He chastised himself for thinking of the books as puppies. He glanced at the book on her desk and read the title: "Tax Reform."

As promised, he didn't have to wait long for Shaw to join them. Shaw smiled broadly and dropped a thin, leather-bound document on her desk. "The Technical Agreement for the Reversion of Taiwan," he announced. Turner picked it up and read while Shaw poured himself a cup of coffee and sat down. "Mizz President is a speed-reader," he told Bender. "About 1,500 words a minute. Doesn't miss a thing."

Turner closed the agreement and laid it down. "As I expected," she said. "Robert, you speculate well. We gave up Taiwan for a freeze in the status quo."

"May I?" Bender asked. She nodded, and he picked it up and started to read. It was amazingly straightforward and detailed the relationship between China, Taiwan, and the United States. He had a hard time splitting his attention as he read in order to follow their conversation.

". . . a done deal, Mizz President. We can live with it . . . just don't want to talk about it in public."

Bender reread the paragraph on "respective spheres of influence." *This is like a time warp,* he thought, *and is pure balance of power politics right out of the nineteenth century.*

". . . the Chinese ambassador must have thought I was a fool when I called him in." This from Turner.

". . . doubtful that he knew a thing about it," Shaw replied.

Bender read the attached protocols that invalidated the agreement. *Why do we still have this copy?* he wondered.

". . . not to worry about Rawlings and Murchison, Mizz President . . . undated letters of resignation along with detailed trip reports, those boys did learn somethin' useful in high school . . . better to keep them on board until we can give them a proper funeral. They're finished in this town."

Bender studied the last protocol, a map at the back of the agreement. Dashed lines outlined the so-called spheres of influence. He froze. "Son of a—" he muttered, catching himself before he finished the expletive. He looked up. Turner was smiling at him.

"Did I sense a little emotion, Robert?"

Bender felt his face turn red. "We've got serious problems." He handed the open agreement back to Turner.

Shaw laughed. "How do you know that, son?" Bender's skin prickled at Shaw's patronizing use of the word *son*.

"The map." The two men gathered around Turner. "See how our sphere of influence does not include Japan?" Bender's left forefinger traced the dashed line that ended just beyond the island of Guam in mid-Pacific.

"Neither does theirs," Shaw said.

Bender's finger traced the dash line that outlined China's sphere. "But the Chinese sphere of influence *does* include Okinawa and the Korean peninsula."

"A glitch in the map," Shaw said. "Hell, North Korea has always been under Chinese influence and everybody knows Okinawa is a part of Japan."

"So what does this mean?" Turner asked.

"It doesn't mean a thing," Shaw said. "By protocol, this agreement is invalid. They got Taiwan before this poker game was called and are going to take their winnings and go home."

"This is the way it all started over the Spratly Islands," Bender said. The Spratly Islands were an oil-rich chain of 200 uninhabited reefs and shoals in the South China Sea. "The Chinese issued a map in the early 1990s that had a dotted line around the Spratlies."

"Yeah, yeah," Shaw grumbled. "And it's been China-creep in the South China Sea ever since, which is nowhere close to Okinawa."

"Korea and Okinawa are next," Bender said.

Turner shook her head slowly. "Is this the Pentagon's latest version of the Red Scare to justify a big budget? I've heard it before. You're obsessing, Robert."

Shaw walked back and forth, making a big show of being worried. He glanced at the folders and briefing book on her desk, willing them to disappear. "The general here might have a good point, Mizz President."

"Then we'll wait and see," Turner said. "I am not going to bankrupt this country with an unwarranted military buildup. Now I've got a cabinet meeting to get ready for. Thank you, gentlemen."

Shaw ushered Bender out of the Oval Office. "Most helpful, General, most helpful." He shambled down the corridor toward his office, making a popping sound with his mouth, much like a champagne cork. He closed his office door behind him and dialed a number on his private phone. "Hello, darlin'," he said. "It's me." A long pause. "I know it's been a while, but I've been thinking about you. I'd love getting our libidos together tonight." Another pause. "Break it. You won't regret it."

4

Washington, D.C.

Robert Bender was fighting the last of the evening's rush hour traffic and had almost reached his quarters on Bolling Air Force Base when his cellular phone buzzed. It was a summons from his bosses in the Pentagon. Automatically, he reversed course and called his wife. Nancy Bender answered on the first ring. "It's one of those days," he said. "I just got called to the Pentagon and have no idea when I'll be home. Don't wait dinner."

"Just come home horny," she answered.

He smiled at the old response. Nothing had changed on the home front. Nancy was one of the constants in his life, always there, always busy, down to earth, and always ready to start a second honeymoon. Or would it be the thirty-fifth? More like the 135th, he calculated. How many times had he uprooted her on a moment's notice to rush to a new assignment? But he couldn't have done it without her.

Traffic over the George Mason Memorial Bridge was still heavy but moving quickly, and within minutes, he was walking in the River Entrance of the Pentagon where an Air Force lieutenant colonel was waiting for him. "General Bender, you're wanted in the Tank." He escorted Bender to the second floor and through the double doors into the JCS section. Judging by the number of aides

58

floating in the corridor, the meeting was going to be an oil burner.

Six pair of eyes, the entire Joint Chiefs of Staff, turned on him when he entered the conference room, greeting him with silence. Not the best of beginnings, Bender decided.

"Gentlemen," General Charles, the Air Force chief, said, "I think you all know General Bob Bender." The cold stares were not reassuring. "Bob, we're waiting for the secretary of defense. He's in his office with the service secretaries and will be here in a few moments." Charles paused, considering his next words. "We just got word from the OMB"—the Office of Management and Budget—"that the president is going to slash the defense budget thirty percent over the next two years. Apparently, Shaw has lined up congressional backing—quite a bit."

"So what the hell is going on across the river?" General Overmeyer growled.

"This is the first I've heard about it," Bender said. "I've been a persona non grata since I blew the whistle"—he paused, not sure how much the other chiefs knew.

Overmeyer waived an unlit cigar at the room. "They know. You stirred the pot, no doubt about that, and this is the fallout." He snapped the cigar in two and threw it into a corner. "She dropped the budget cut on Secretary Elkins without any warning. Thirty fuckin' percent! This is turning into fuckin' Bloody Wednesday! But it doesn't stop there, she's going through us with a meat ax. All special forces, with the exception of Delta Force, gone. The boys in the basement, gone." He jammed a fresh cigar into his mouth. "It turns out the DCI had never told her about the boys, and she's really in a snit."

"I told her," Bender admitted.

More silence. Then, from the chief of Naval Operations, "I thought you enjoyed a special relationship with the president."

"I don't know what's special about it," Bender replied. "I'm a hangover from her staff when she was vice president." The look on Overmeyer's face and the condition of the cigar warned him that he was on dangerous turf. "I haven't talked to her since briefing her last Thursday, and the letter requesting my immediate transfer is on Shaw's desk.''

"Has the letter gotten past Shaw?" Overmeyer asked.

"I don't know."

"Fact," Overmeyer growled, "she's not talking to us. Fact, she does listen to you."

"She may be listening," Bender said, "but I seriously doubt if it's doing any good." *Come on,* he thought. *Get me out of there.*

"Pull the letter," Overmeyer said.

Bender looked around the room in shock. They were all staring at him and not even Charles looked friendly. An image of a lamb being led into a slaughterhouse flashed in front of him. "There is no reason for me to stay there," he protested.

"You're the only voice of reason we got over there," Overmeyer growled. He gestured at the door, and Bender didn't need any other encouragement to leave.

Overmeyer was right, Bender thought. *This is turning into Bloody Wednesday.*

The same lieutenant colonel was waiting for him. "Sir, the chief asked that you hang around in case the chairman wants to talk to you again." He looked at his watch. It was past 7 P.M. "The Secretaries' Dining Room is open for dinner. Would you care to join me?"

Bender nodded. "When did you come to work?" he asked, leading the way to the fourth floor.

"Five this morning," came the answer.

"Been a busy day?"

"It's been a madhouse—Pearl Harbor and Hiroshima rolled into one."

"I can believe that," Bender replied. His day had been a total waste, and he envied the lieutenant colonel for being in the thick of it.

The lights in the bedroom were still on when Bender finally arrived at his quarters on Bolling Air Force Base. He stopped in the kitchen and opened the refrigerator. A bottle of the German beer he loved was standing front and center, capped with an upside-down glass. He smiled.

Nancy was sending him a signal. He opened the beer and headed upstairs.

Nancy Bender was curled up in bed reading a case book. As usual, a bare leg was sticking out from under the blanket, and her reading glasses were perched on the end of her nose. She was a small, dark-haired woman, possessing enormous brown eyes and unlimited energy. A bemused look lit her eyes as he shed his uniform coat and tie, flopped out in an easy chair, and poured the beer into the glass. It was a ritual that never changed. "A bad day?" she asked.

"A nothing day," Bender answered. He took a drink and savored the taste. "I spent the day typing up the letter and answering a few inane questions from Shaw's staff, at least what I thought were inane questions. Then the call from the Pentagon. I spent all of five minutes with the Joint Chiefs and then had to hang around for three hours in case they wanted a follow-up." He took a sip of beer. "What's the book?"

"Case studies on counseling in emergency trauma centers," she answered. She looked at him, her dark eyes filled with concern. "I'm only a volunteer and have to handle cases a professional counselor could spend a year on. I get maybe thirty minutes with a shattered mother or wife and send them on their way. It's not right." Somehow, in the midst of their constant moves, Nancy had earned a B.A. and then completed a master's degree in psychology. But she hadn't stopped there and had become a licensed clinical social worker when they were stationed in California. Now she was doing volunteer work in an emergency room in the heart of Washington's inner city.

"The budget ax is falling everywhere," he said.

Nancy rightly suspected that the crisis that had called him to the Pentagon was a budget cut. "The things we do to each other," she murmured. Then, more brightly, "Did you submit your letter?"

"It's on Shaw's desk. But the chairman wants me to pull it."

A concerned look spread across Nancy's face. She knew her husband too well and was afraid the enforced period of inactivity in the White House would drive him crazy.

"Why the change? I thought they wanted you out of there?"

"So did I," Bender said. "It looks like I won't be getting a new assignment after all. I don't know what the chairman expects me to do. There are no ground rules over there, only Shaw. I'm not a politician and spinning my wheels, not accomplishing a thing. If I can't get out of there fairly soon and do something productive, we might as well retire." His eyes drew into a humorous squint. "*Then* you can get a job and support *me* in the manner you've been accustomed to for the last twenty-eight years."

"Don't count on it. You were the one who married a child bride." She rolled over and laid the book on the nightstand. The covers pulled up and he could see her bare back. She picked up a letter and tossed it to him. "From Laurie," she said.

He leaned back in the chair and read the letter, slowly sipping his beer. Occasionally, a smile would flit across his face as he relaxed. He was back with Nancy, and the cares of the White House were in a pigeonhole for a few hours. He slowly folded the letter and replaced it in its envelope before dropping it on the table beside his chair. "Do you think she'll marry him?"

"In her own good time," Nancy answered. She eyed the letter. "Must you always be so neat?" No answer. "I'm convinced there's a bit of the anal compulsive in you."

"I wouldn't know about that. You're the shrink."

"Well, if you're going to retire and become a kept man, you had better audition for the job." She threw the covers back and waited for him before turning out the light.

"Have you taken a vow of stupidity?" Shaw asked. He propped the telephone on his shoulder and listened to the reply while he rifled through the paperwork on his desk, organizing the 8 A.M. meeting that started Turner's workday.

"This isn't La-La Land over here," the director of Central Intelligence protested. "We don't make up intelligence, we only report it. And as long as I'm the DCI—"

"Which may be about one more day," Shaw said, "unless you start taking a hard look at China."

"As I was saying," the DCI continued, "as long as I'm the director, the President's Daily Brief will contain only the best and most current intelligence we can produce. Nothing is happening in China that warrants the president's attention."

Shaw looked at his watch. "In exactly seventy-two minutes, I'm going to hand the PDB to the president. Given her concern about the Far East, I'd suggest that it include a statement to that effect." He smiled. "Considering your sterling performance on the Beijing Pact, she'll find warmth and comfort in your reassurances." He waited for the DCI's wheels to grind. Sooner or later, he would realize that if China went hot, he'd be out of a job and heaped with scorn and ridicule for missing it.

"This discussion is beyond the security classification of this phone," the DCI huffed.

He needs some enlightenment, Shaw decided. "The president can take bad news," he said, "but hates surprises. I mean, she really hates them. You saw what happened to defense—" He deliberately let his voice trail off. The DCI would fill in the rest.

"An amended PDB will be on your desk in an hour," the DCI said. "With relevant intelligence on China."

"I do like dealing with you rocket scientists," Shaw said, breaking the connection. He finished arranging the stack of papers he would carry to the meeting before he picked up the letter. "Now what do I do about this?" he muttered. He jabbed at his intercom. "Get Bender in here." He glanced at his watch. Three minutes, he calculated.

Bender was standing in the doorway with eighteen seconds to spare. Shaw held up the offending letter with his thumb and forefinger. "I need to speak to you about that," Bender began.

"There's nothing to say," Shaw replied, cutting him off. "Your president needs your help." He let the letter fall to his desk. "Where's your loyalty, General?"

Who would believe? Bender thought. *He wants me to retract the letter.* Maybe it was time to do a little politicking of his own. "One of the reasons I requested reassignment is because of Chuck Sanford and Wayne Adams.''

"Who the hell are they?'' Shaw grumbled.

"The two Secret Service agents you had relieved from the president's detail after St. Louis. I hear they're undergoing an administrative discharge.''

Shaw's right fingers drummed on the desk. *Damn right I had them sacked,* he thought. *So you want to wheel and deal. I can do that. Anything to keep Maddy happy—and distracted from tax reform.* "I don't interfere with Secret Service internal matters,'' he countered, feeling Bender out. The general's look was an eloquent statement of disbelief. "But I can check into it. We don't want anyone abusing our people.'' It was a done deal.

"I'd appreciate that,'' Bender said. He picked up the letter and turned to leave. "Shall I leave the door open, Mr. Shaw?''

"Close it,'' Shaw said. He cocked his big head to one side and watched Bender leave. *So you want to play hardball,* he thought. *Never do that when I've got another turn at bat.*

Sarah Turner shot out of the family dining room and almost bowled into the serving cart William was pushing down the corridor. "Sor-ry,'' she called. Then she thought better of it and came back. "I apologize, Mr. William. I know I shouldn't run.''

"Well, thank you, Miss Sarah. I do appreciate that. You do seem happy today.''

"Brian, my brother, is coming back from school. He's going to live here and go to the Academy in Georgetown.'' She spun away and danced down the hall, not quite running. William smiled and shook his head. The staff was buzzing with rumors about the president's son returning from boarding school. The most popular gossip held that he was being kicked out because of discipline problems. But cooler heads maintained the Secret Service was worried about threats and thought he would be safer in the White House.

Madeline Turner came out of the dining room with her mother. The two women spoke quietly for a moment, out of his hearing, before they parted. Turner took the few steps to her private study, and William followed, the day's routine underway. She settled into her spot on the couch. "Well, William, I imagine the rumors are flying."

"Indeed they are, Madam President."

A pensive look spread across her face. "What's the betting?"

William poured her a fresh cup of coffee. "Two to one that it's a discipline problem."

"And your bet?"

"I don't engage in that type of thing," William answered.

"A safe bet would be that it's a security problem," Turner said.

William smiled. "Thank you, ma'am." He withdrew in time to hold the door for Shaw and Jackie Winters.

"Good morning, Mrs. President," Jackie said, preempting Shaw.

"Mizz President," he said, flopping into the couch opposite her. He handed her the day's schedule as Jackie settled into her usual niche. The PDB followed in short order.

She scanned the thin document. "China seems very quiet."

"I agree with the analysis that it's a lull while Beijing feels out your administration. But we do want to stay on top of it. Harry S. was one of the best men to sit in the Oval Office. He warned that domestic policy can hurt you but foreign policy will kill you." They continued with the routine, and he handed her the day's action list. "Mizz President, you can't put off selecting your V.P. much longer. If you want, I'll get a list together and have the FBI and Treasury check 'em out."

"Jackie, please wait for me downstairs." Her personal assistant quickly left, leaving them alone. "I've already made my decision," Turner said. "Gwen Anderson."

"Mrs. Integrity?" The look on Shaw's face resembled that of a maiden aunt who has just discovered a sexually transmitted disease has been named after her favorite niece. Gwen Anderson, the current secretary of health and human services, was considered the most ardent feminist in the administration and reported to be incorruptible. For Shaw, the first was an inconvenience, the second, a fatal liability. "Ma'am, you really need to think about this. You need balance to your administration."

"I'm concerned with ability, not balance," Turner continued. "I've spoken with her, and she'll be here this afternoon for further discussions. She has been very forthcoming and assures me there are no skeletons in her closet."

"Mizz President," Shaw protested, "surely you're not going to take her word on that?"

"You're right. Have the FBI check her out. Do it quick. But there are no dents in her armor."

"All we have to do is find the key to her chastity belt," Shaw muttered.

"Do I sense a hesitation, Patrick?"

"Yes, ma'am. You certainly do. You should be thinking ahead to the next election and choosing your running mate now. To be viable, you need a veep from an anchor state who can breeze through the confirmation hearings. Don't go revving your engine when you haven't got gas in the tank."

"Is this your lecture on spending political capital?" Turner asked.

"Yes, ma'am, it is, and we're running on about a quarter tank. It was touch and go getting the Senate to confirm Anderson for Health and we're going to run the tank dry getting her confirmed as vice president. That's gas we can't afford to burn at this point."

"I trust her," Turner replied, "and need her to head a new program." Shaw braced himself for the words *tax reform.* He didn't hear them. "We're going to give this government a face." She came alive. "For example, when someone calls a government office, they won't hear a recorded menu with a list of options. They will be talking to a real person—a person who cares about their problems."

Shaw paced the floor while she talked. When he sensed the timing was right, he stood by the mantle and touched the bell that Turner had rung while in the California senate. She smiled when he picked it up. "Patrick, I really want to make this happen." He tilted the bell, and it gave off a single ring, little more than a tinkle. She stopped talking, and he knew she was listening.

"This will be a good job for your new vice president," he told her, "whoever she or he is. But, Mizz President, choose someone near the middle. And about Government with a Face, it's window dressing, so don't micromanage. They tell the story about President Carter who insisted on even approving the schedule for the tennis courts. Use your time wisely. It's my job to handle the details."

Turner smiled at him. "You're my daily dose of reality," she said. "Work General Bender into the schedule. I want him to meet Gwen and discuss another problem."

"The subject?" Shaw asked.

"The glass ceiling in the military. We need more women in command."

He's going to love that one, Shaw thought. "Anything else?"

"No. Let's get started." She walked to the door. "Oh. I want to see action on tax reform. Today."

"What did you have in mind, Mizz President?"

"Your job is to handle the details," she reminded him.

I got to get out of Dodge, Shaw moaned to himself.

"Go right in," the secretary said. "Mr. Shaw is waiting for you."

"Thanks, Mrs. Raskin," Bender replied. The woman smiled at him. Everyone else called her Alice Fay, and she suspected that Bender was one of the few people who knew her last name. Like every staff member in the White House, there was no name plate on her desk. You were supposed to know who she was or you had no business being in her office.

Shaw was tilted back in his chair with a telephone stuck to his left ear. He waved Bender to a seat. "Senator, we'll do what we can, but we're going to need some help." He listened for a moment. "Don't think of it that way. Right, I'll be back in touch." He dropped the receiver into its cradle. "Senators are like dogs," he said. "Some learn quicker than others." He stood up and deliberately loosened his tie and rumpled his shirt. "We're going into the

Oval Office in a few moments, and you are going to meet one Gwen Anderson. Be careful.''

"I've heard about Mrs. Anderson," Bender replied.

"She'll try to bait you. Just the way she is."

"Thanks for the heads up," Bender said.

He followed Shaw into the Oval Office. The two women were sitting on the couches opposite each other, and Turner patted a spot next to her for Shaw. Bender took the remaining seat on the couch next to Anderson. She was a handsome, heavy-set woman in her midfifties with attractively streaked salt and pepper hair. A strong scent of musk perfume assaulted him. Turner made the introductions before turning to business. "Robert, we're concerned about the small number of women in the military."

Bender wished he had been warned about the topic and stifled his standard protest that she was talking to the wrong man. They were all looking at him expectantly. "The percentages have been constantly improving," he began. "Overall, we are up to approximately sixteen percent—"

Anderson interrupted. "Approximately?"

"The current figure is 16.2 percent. As you know—"

Again, she interrupted him. "What percentage are officers?"

"Overall, the percentage is a little higher."

"Be specific, General."

Why the attack dog tactics? Bender wondered. "It varies from service to service," he answered. "Seventeen percent of all officers in the Air Force are women. I'll get the exact numbers to you, by service and by rank, right after this meeting."

"Please do that." Anderson looked away from Bender. "Maddy, the real problem is the glass ceiling. Although these figures are somewhat encouraging, they mask the fact that the number of women serving as colonels is abysmally low and almost nonexistent at flag rank. We need more women generals."

Only politicians hire generals off the streets, Bender thought. "Increasing numbers of women are moving up the rank structure," he told them.

Anderson ignored him. "The key to promotion in the

military," she said, "is command of combat units, which are effectively closed to women. Maddy, you can't penetrate the military mind-set on issues like this. We learned that over gay rights. You can't discuss it with a bunch of homophobic—"

"I never did understand that word," Bender said, interrupting her.

"Pardon me for speaking while you were interrupting," Anderson snapped. "But for your information, it means fear of homosexuals."

What's good for the gander is definitely not *good for the goose,* he thought. *Shaw did warn me about taking the bait.* Bender dismissed any chance of Anderson listening to a rational explanation of the dynamics of combat and what it took to lead men and, for that matter, women into the crucible of battle. Nothing in her experience would allow her to accept the brutal reality of what happens to human beings when they are near real bullets, real danger, and real death.

"Maddy," Anderson concluded, "don't even bother to discuss this with them. You are their commander in chief, so tell them." On this last point, Bender agreed with her. The president should indeed tell the generals what she wanted. But there would be discussion.

Madeline Turner looked at Bender. "Why are you against women in combat?"

He hedged his answer. "For the most part, it's not a question of women being able to do the job—"

"But you are against women in combat," Turner interrupted.

He didn't want to answer because it was the truth. But she was his president and he would not lie to her. "Pregnancy."

"I expected that," Anderson scoffed. "What would a man know about that?"

"I know what it does to combat effectiveness," Bender said.

"Thank you, Robert," Turner said, dismissing him.

Shaw settled behind his desk and reevaluated Robert Bender. He had deliberately hung the general out to dry by not telling him the subject of the meeting. Yet, he had handled it well and had not strangled Anderson, for which no jury of his peers would ever convict him if he had. "What's your take on Mizz Anderson?"

"I didn't like the way she kept calling President Turner Maddy," Bender answered.

"Get used to it," Shaw said. "You're looking at the next vice president." Shaw guffawed at the look on Bender's face. "Do words escape you?"

"Well," Bender stammered, "they say she can't be bought."

Shaw shook his head. "Everyone can be bought in this town. It would, ah, be premature to tell your generals about Mizz Anderson."

"They are in my chain of command."

"You seem to forget who's at the top," Shaw said. He waited until Bender left before calling one of his assistants. "It's slash and burn time—Gwen Anderson. Get the children digging. Oh, and get the FBI started on a formal investigation."

It was late the following Saturday when Shaw shuffled down the corridor outside the press secretary's office, hoping for the right chance encounter with one of the seventy-three reporters currently assigned to the White House pressroom. Unlike most politicians, Shaw not only understood reporters, he liked many of them. Although he had little respect for their profession, he tantalized them with gossip, tidbits, and insights to keep the doors open. Now he was searching for the right door so he could use one of them in a very shameless manner. For their part, the reporters willingly joined in the game and let him use them. It was a marriage that could only have been made in Washington, D.C.

A woman's voice called, "This is hostile territory, Patrick. Aren't you afraid of being mugged this late at night?"

Unbidden, Shaw's lopsided grin spread across his face when he recognized the speaker, Elizabeth Gordon. "Liz, it has been a while," he said. He watched her walk toward him. She was in her early forties, tall, trim, and confident.

He admired her legs, which she displayed to the limits of journalistic propriety. "How's Jeff? I haven't seen him in some time." Jeff Bissell was her longtime, live-in lover.

Liz cocked her head and gave him an odd look. "You haven't heard? He moved out."

"A shame," Shaw replied. "I liked him."

"So did I," she said. "But he's just like you and can't make a commitment."

He looked contrite. "Liz, in those days I was young and dumb."

She laughed. "Well, you're not young now."

"A pity," he said. The door was open.

He watched her as she sat on the side of the bed and slipped on her high-heeled slippers. She stood and walked across the room, her body shimmering in the soft light. She knelt and opened a drawer, finding what she was looking for. Then she walked back to the bed, waving a long feather.

"No way, Liz," Shaw protested. "My heart can't take that."

"You used to love it," she said, rolling back into bed and laying a breast against him. He took a deep breath as she drew the feather over his stomach. "Try to ignore me," she whispered. He closed his eyes and concentrated. He felt a warm tongue in his ear as the feather moved between his legs. His erection that had been building withered away. He was winning the game. "You're not paying attention," she murmured.

"If I remember right," he replied, a slight catch in his voice, "that is the idea. By the way, what are the stakes?"

"I want an inside. What do you want?" He described the penalty she would have to pay if he won. "Oh, I can do that!" Her enthusiasm ruined what was left of his self-control, and he felt her hand massaging him into a full erection. "But I won't have to, will I? Pay up."

"Maddy wants Gwen Anderson for her veep—a bad choice. Anderson will self-destruct during the confirmation hearings."

She mounted him. "Why?" Her thighs clamped him. Hard.

"She takes lithium to control manic-depressive mood swings. She's buried it so deep that no one suspects. Gawd only knows how that will go down on the Hill when it surfaces. She's OK at Health but—" he caught his breath. "Can this wait to later?"

"Of course," Liz whispered. She had her inside.

Shaw was in his office the following Monday when Liz broke the story. He watched the TV and put on his stubborn Winston Churchill face at the unanimous response of the senators who were on the confirmation committee. Their reaction to Liz's revelation about Gwen Anderson was even better than he had expected.

His intercom buzzed. "Mr. Shaw," Alice Fay said, "the president is with her advisors and wants to see you."

"I imagine she does," Shaw replied. He picked up a folder with detailed backgrounds on potential vice presidential candidates and headed for the Oval Office.

5 ⟋

Okinawa, Japan

Brigadier General David Martini rolled into the Eighteenth Wing's Intelligence section like Typhoon Towa that had just blown over Okinawa and Kadena Air Base. He fixed the NCO with a hard look. "This had better be good," he barked. The NCO gulped and escorted him to the big walk-in vault where the lieutenant colonel who headed Intel was waiting. Martini stormed through the steel door and raised his bellow another ten decibels. "Peter, Intel comes to me, I don't go to Intel. What the hell is going on?"

Lieutenant Colonel Peter Townly motioned for the NCO to close and lock the vault door from the inside as he left. "General, I've been yelled at by pros."

Martini laughed. He liked officers who stood their ground. "Where I come from, a pro is a hooker."

"Intel has been called worse," Townly replied. "I received a message from DIA"—Defense Intelligence Agency—"that I had to decode myself. First time I ever had to do that, and there's only two people on this base with a clearance to read it: you and me." He handed Martini the message. "Under the circumstances, I thought it would be best if you came here."

Martini read the message slowly. "Son of a bitch!" he roared. "The cocksuckers sold Taiwan out to the Chinese!" He immediately regretted the outburst. A general

73

was allowed a little profanity, but he had crossed the line. He made a mental promise to tone down his language. "This gets worse. The Chinese and South Koreans are getting in bed together. The South Koreans! What the hell is going on?"

"The South Koreans and Japan," Townly said, "have been at odds over the Tok Do Islands since the end of World War II. Economic competition has only made the dispute worse. I'd say the Koreans are getting ready to switch sides, politically and economically."

Martini reread the last sentence. " 'Take no overt actions! This is for your information only!' What the hell is this supposed to mean?"

"It means," Townly said, "that the political situation is going critical, and our commanders don't want to leave you in the dark. But they are also saying they don't know what's going to happen next."

"You're an Intel officer," Martini growled. "So be intelligent."

Townly took a deep breath. "My best guess is that China is going to consolidate the western rim of the Pacific into one economic empire under their control."

Martini humphed. "Japan won't stand for that. Neither will we."

"We gave them Taiwan," Townly reminded him. "Now they're challenging Japan." Townly warmed to the subject. It wasn't often he got to play at geopolitics. "Think of this in terms of pure power politics like 100 years ago."

Martini stifled an obscenity. "Pete, this is the twenty-first century." He headed for the door. "Burn the message and the decode. Now." Townly had the match ready and set the two pieces of paper on fire. He dropped them into a wastebasket. Unfortunately, the smoke set off the alarms. Martini stared at him. "Except for that, you did good."

Martini had been blowing some smoke on his own; he knew exactly why the Defense Intelligence Agency had sent out the message. The Joint Chiefs of Staff were telling him to get ready to fight but, for some political reason, couldn't use the normal alerting system. Like the six other commanders at the Air Force bases facing China who had gotten the same message, he was going to take training to the edge. Although that would increase the risk level for accidents, he wouldn't let up until every man and woman under his command was razor sharp. He hoped his Army, Navy, and Marine counterparts were doing the same because he couldn't tell them.

The Eighteenth Wing's Operations Group commander, the colonel responsible for the three F-15 squadrons that formed Kadena's cutting edge, soon found himself the subject of Martini's undivided attention. The general was primarily concerned with the Forty-Fourth Fighter Squadron, which, until six months ago, had been an air superiority squadron. Now it was in the process of transitioning to the F-15E Strike Eagle, which could drop bombs as well as engage other aircraft. In quick order, Martini, the Ops Group commander, and the commander of the Forty-Fourth toured the maintenance side of the squadron and then examined the training folder of every pilot and weapon system officer.

"Tell me about Chris Leland," Martini said.

"Captain Christopher Leland," the Ops Group commander grumbled, "should be flying multimotors and looking for a job with the airlines."

"He also has an uncle who is a U.S. senator," Martini replied.

"That's what got him this far," the squadron commander said. "General, he's a nice kid but inconsistent as all hell. He does great one day and is a basket case the next. Overall, he's well below average. But he does meet the minimum, and given enough time, he'll be OK. Right now, he's still flying with an IP''—an instructor pilot— "and we haven't matched him up with a wizzo yet." Without a weapon system officer in the backseat, the Strike Eagle could not perform its primary mission of dropping bombs.

Martini fixed the Ops Group commander with a hard look. The colonel should have canceled Leland's fighter pilot ticket months ago and shipped him off to fly transports. Now Martini needed every pilot he had. "If he meets the minimum standard," Martini grumbled, his dis-

pleasure obvious, "he flies. Team him up with a wizzo—
one who's got a clue."

"I've got one of those," the Forty-Fourth squadron
commander said.

The civilian contractor sitting at the control console
waved Ryan into the simulator for the Strike Eagle. "Go
right on in, Cap'n. She's practicing approach and
landings."

Ryan waved back and walked into the sim room and
climbed the steps to the cockpit. Laurie was alone and
sitting in the backseat, her crew position. He climbed into
the front seat to watch the instruments and projection
screens. As a flight surgeon, he had flown over a hundred
hours in the backseat of F-15s and conducted stress studies
in the simulator. Although he wasn't a pilot, he recognized
a good approach and landing when he saw one. The audio
gave a reassuring clunk when she touched down. Then she
firewalled the throttles and turned the landing into a touch
and go. Her hands flew around the cockpit as she retracted
the gear and flaps. She reefed the sim into a sixty-degree
climb and did aileron rolls. Ryan watched the video displays and felt the onset of motion sickness. "Whoa!"
he shouted.

"Wuss," she replied. She leveled the sim and spoke
into her microphone. "Time to spin, crash, and burn,"
she told the civilian at the console. She raked the throttles
aft and slowed to stall speed. Then she pulled back on the
stick and gave it full right rudder. The sim did as she
commanded and went into a spin. She held the spin until
it was fully developed. The videos showed the sim going
straight down as the altimeter unwound at a dizzying rate.
Then she recovered, flying straight and level, the altimeter
rooted on fifty feet. "Made it this time," she said.

"You do this for fun?" Ryan asked.

"I enjoy it and it's good practice." They climbed out
of the cockpit and headed for the door.

"Practice? Are you still applying for pilot training?"

Laurie shook her head. "They just teamed me with
Chris Leland."

"The rumors say he's pretty bad," Ryan said, masking the worry he felt.

"He's not good. But like the man says, if the minimums weren't good enough, they wouldn't be the minimums." The "man" in this case was her squadron commander. "Anyone else would be looking for a job with the airlines."

"Does Martini know how weak he is?"

Laurie's lips pulled into a wry twist. "Yeah. This was his idea. For some reason, we're going balls-to-the-wall on training. I guess this is part of it."

"You're not alone," Ryan said. "He was over at the Med Center and really unloaded on us. I got tapped to set up a Personnel Reliability Program. Talk about a waste of time. There's absolutely no reason for it. None at all."

A frown crossed Laurie's face. "PRP? Isn't that the program where you have to certify the physical condition and mental stability of people working around nuclear weapons?"

"You got it," Ryan replied. "It doesn't make sense since we haven't had nukes on the island since 1972. Martini's such a raving asshole. He wants to look good to the brass and is using our bodies as stepping stones to promotion."

She nudged him with her hip. "Say, if you're not using your body, I got a use for it."

"When are you going to marry me?" he asked.

"Marriage is dull, hard work," she replied, "and not for prima donnas."

"Hey," he protested. "Who's a prima donna?"

She smiled at him. "Oh, someone I know."

Washington, D.C.

Bender stifled a mental sigh and tried to estimate how much longer he would be buried under the reams of proposed Defense Department budget cuts he was reviewing for the Office of Management and the Budget. He was angry and frustrated; angry because he was being asked his opinion where he did not have expertise and frustrated because OMB wasn't talking to the experts he kept recommending.

"Hi. Can we come in?"

He looked up at the sound of Sarah Turner's voice. She was standing in his doorway with her brother. He smiled. "Sure. But I only got one chair." Sarah flopped into the chair and started to swing her legs back and forth.

A man's voice answered from the hallway. "I'll get another one." Chuck Sanford, the Secret Service agent who had been in charge of the Secret Service detail when Turner was vice president stepped into view. "Good to see you again, General."

"Welcome back," Bender said. "And Agent Adams?" Sanford nodded and moved out of sight, searching for a chair.

"Do you remember everybody's name?" Brian Turner asked, still standing in the doorway.

"I try to," Bender answered. He studied the president's son. He was a tall and awkward fourteen-year-old discovering who he was and what he could do. Physically, he was totally different from the small and feminine Sarah. He was itchy to move and discover new places, new adventures. But there was no doubt that he was his mother's son, and some day, he would be a very handsome man. "People are important."

"That's what Grams says," Sarah said, wanting to be part of the conversation.

"Grams!" Brian snorted.

Bender laughed, understanding the boy. "I was trapped in a house full of women for a long time," he said. Brian looked at him hopefully. "Strange, but I miss it now."

Brian shot a sideways glance at his sister. "I won't."

Sanford was back with a chair. He sat it on the opposite side of the doorway from Sarah's and disappeared. Brian stepped into the small office and looked around. His mouth fell open when he saw the picture on the wall. It was a photograph of the Thunderbirds against a magnificent skyscape. Although the six F-16s were very small, the red, white, and blue of the Thunderbird motif was clearly visible against a vast sky. Yet the aircraft and sky were one, in perfect harmony with each other.

"What a great photo," Brian said. "Can I get one?"

Bender shook his head. "There were only eight prints made before the negative was ruined. That's me on the extreme left."

"You really flew with the Thunderbirds? And that was your airplane?"

"Yeah, I did. But that was a long time ago. But it wasn't *my* airplane. It belonged to the crew chiefs. They just let me borrow it from time to time to go play."

"The crew chiefs, are they sergeants?" Brian asked. Bender nodded an answer. "Oh. Just like servants."

Bender chuckled. "You've never met a sergeant. Believe me, they are not servants. They do the work and they keep the aircraft flying. Without them, a pilot never turns a wheel."

"Turns a wheel?" Brian asked.

"That's just a way of saying taxiing."

"Mom says she couldn't be president without people like sergeants doing their jobs," Sarah added. "They know that and are proud of what they do."

"Your mom knows what she's talking about," Bender said.

"Is that why you try to remember everyone's name?" Brian asked.

"Yeah. I guess that's why."

"What's it like to fly a fighter?" Brian asked.

He shot a quick smile at Sarah. "Oh, boy"—she returned his smile—"it's hard to describe. Without a doubt it is the most fun thing I have ever done in my life. But it is also the hardest thing. You have to stay in shape, study all the time, and memorize stuff."

"What do you have to memorize?" Brian asked.

"Emergency procedures."

"I won't have any emergencies when I fly."

Rather than laugh, Bender grew very serious. "The business of a fighter is combat. In combat, the bad guys shoot at you, and sooner or later, they will hit your aircraft. We call that *taking battle damage* and that causes emergencies, probably three or four at the same time. If you're good at handling emergency procedures, you'll live to tell about it. Otherwise—'' He shrugged, not ending the thought. ''It's all part of the challenge.''

Brian turned to the photograph. ''I'm going to the Air Force Academy and fly fighters.''

''So I've heard. But it's a challenge just to get into the Academy and—''

''My mom can get me in,'' Brian said, interrupting him.

''Don't interrupt,'' Sarah scolded. ''It's impolite.''

''I'm sorry, sir.'' Like all teenagers, he had to explain himself. ''Sometimes I get excited and forget.'' He studied the photograph on the wall. ''But I really want to go to the Air Force Academy.''

Bender nodded, understanding. He could remember when he had said the same words. These were good kids, well mannered and respectful. And they definitely had minds of their own. ''Your mother can get you an appointment to a service academy,'' he explained, ''if you've got the grades. Once there, you're on your own, and if you can't cut it, you're out. But remember, not every cadet qualifies for pilot training. Then once you make it to pilot training, the selection process starts all over again and only the top students get an assignment to fighters. It's a tough program from beginning to end and nobody gives you a thing.''

Brian turned to the photograph and touched it, wanting to be part of it. ''I can do it.''

''Tell you what,'' Bender said. ''I'll bring in an old F-16 Dash One, that's the basic flight manual for an airplane. It will give you an idea of what you've got to study.''

''Yeah,'' Brian said, ''I'd like that.''

''Mom doesn't like stuff like that,'' Sarah said.

Brian stood up. ''Ah, she knows I read stuff like that all the time.'' He shifted his weight from foot to foot. ''Thanks. I gotta go—homework. Grams won't let me do anything until I get it done.''

The two kids left his office. ''See,'' Sarah said, her voice echoing down the hall, ''I told you he'd talk to you.''

Sanford stood in his doorway, speaking into the whisper mike under his sleeve. ''Merlin and Magic Two are on their way upstairs.''

"The names fit," Bender said.

Sanford nodded. "Do they come down here often?"

"It's the first time I've met Brian. Sarah is down here about every other day. We talk a lot." A rueful look crossed his face as he remembered how he and Laurie used to talk.

"General, we heard how you went to the mat with Shaw. You saved our butts. Thanks."

"I was the one who caused the problem," Bender said. "The Secret Service is not a praetorian guard isolating a Roman emperor from his subjects."

"It's too bad Shaw doesn't know that. Watch your backside, General. Thanks again." He disappeared down the hall.

Turner was in the small study off her bedroom nestled down for the evening and surrounded by work. Maura entered quietly and sat down in the comfortable over-stuffed chair near the fire. "I love it when the fire's going," Maura said.

"Humm," Turner replied. "How are the kids?"

"Sarah's in bed. Brian's reading some Air Force manual on airplanes."

"Where did he get that?"

"General Bender gave it to him."

Turner slowly removed her reading glasses and looked into the fire. "I'm not sure if I like that. How did he meet Robert?"

"Sarah introduced them. She talks to him quite a bit."

"She shouldn't be bothering the poor man," Turner said. "He's got enough to do without being bothered by children."

"He doesn't mind," Maura replied. Silence. "Why don't you let him go?" There was no reply. "He's the only person on your staff who doesn't want to be here, and he is a very unhappy man."

Turner picked up her glasses and resumed reading. "I need him in the White House."

"Maddy,"—a long pause—"he's very attractive. Please don't do anything foolish."

"Mother," Turner snapped, "I'm not a schoolgirl with a stupid crush on an older man."

"You're going to be forty-six next month," Maura reminded her. "And he's not that much older. How old is he?"

"I'm not sure." That was a lie, she knew exactly how old he was. "Fifty," she confessed. "Besides, he's married." She paused and thought. She did owe her mother an explanation. "The White House isolates a president. It also intimidates the people around me. But at the same time, they are infected by the power that is here and they become arrogant and demanding. They will do anything to stay here and crawl up the power curve. But they are afraid to tell me bad news in case I'll get angry and fire them. There are only four people who tell me the unvarnished truth and give me a window to the outside: you, William, Bender, and Patrick."

"Shaw!" Maura exclaimed. "I don't trust that man."

"Well, you do have to ask him a straight question," Turner replied. "Let me ask you a straight question. Who should I choose as my vice president?"

Maura didn't hesitate. "Sam Kennett. He saved Philadelphia when he was mayor and look what he's done as governor."

"Pennsylvania is an anchor state," Turner added. "But he's not on Patrick's short list."

"Tell Shaw to add his name," Maura said.

The butler poured a cup of coffee as Turner started her early morning routine. "William, what do you think of Governor Kennett?"

"They say he's a good man and turned Philadelphia around."

"I asked for *your* opinion, William."

"I know, ma'am. But he was awfully hard on people of color and sent a lot of them to jail."

"That was when he was mayor and cleaning up the streets and the city government. He also sent quite a few whites to jail. He's brought jobs by the thousands into the state since he's been governor."

"He has been a good governor," William said. "I'll

give him that, and he is popular. Will there be anything else?'' Turner shook her head, and he withdrew. Outside, William hurried down the corridor with as much dignity as he could muster. This was not the morning he wanted to run into Shaw.

Shaw and Jackie entered the study at exactly eight o'clock. Everything went smoothly until he handed her the day's action list. ''I've selected who I want for vice president,'' she told him. ''Sam Kennett.'' Jackie smiled and made a note.

Shaw dropped his chin on his chest and scratched his head. Kennett was young, incredibly honest by Shaw's standards, energetic, and an accomplished politician with national ambitions. He knew how to play the game and had a political base he would bring with him to the White House. In short, he was the last man Shaw wanted as vice president. ''I hadn't considered him.'' It was a true statement.

''I want to reach out to him,'' Turner said. ''Invite him to the White House.''

''We need to check him out first. You don't need any mistresses hiding in the woodwork.''

''He came through a brutal election,'' Turner said. ''They picked him apart and couldn't find a thing.''

''We'll check him out, Mizz President, and set up a meeting.'' He rose to leave.

''And, Patrick, they won't find any lithium this time.''

''I don't expect they will.'' That also was a true statement. But he would run a full court press on Kennett.

The East China Sea

The two dark gray Strike Eagles punched through the overcast, scudding across the East China Sea, and climbed into the clear, dazzling sky. ''Take the lead,'' the instructor pilot in the right F–15E radioed when they leveled off at 24,000 feet.

In the backseat of the left F-15E, Laurie glanced at the four video displays in front of her. Her fingers automatically danced around the edge of the third scope, pushing at the menu buttons, and called up the HUD, the pilot's head-up display. The multipurpose color display blinked, and she was seeing exactly what her pilot, Chris Leland, saw as he looked through his HUD. He was in the air-to-air mode with the gun selected. Now it was time to quit playing with the giant video game that made up her world in the backseat and return to the basics of air combat.

She twisted in her seat to keep the IP's aircraft in sight as Chris Leland shoved the throttles up and surged into the lead. "Padlocked," she told him. For the next few minutes, she would not take her eyes off the other aircraft. "Relax," she told Chris. "Jink-outs are a piece of cake." She watched as the IP's aircraft maneuvered to their six o'clock position and decreased the range to a guns-firing solution.

"Laurie," the IP called over the radio, "you call it."

She clicked the radio transmit button twice in acknowledgment. Because the intercom was always hot, she and Chris could talk normally. "Do a $2g$ break to the left when I make the bandit call, then come back hard to the right with about 4 g's. Just keep it up, short, hard, heading and altitude changes to break the bandit's tracking solution and stagnate him back there." It was all basic fighter maneuvers. In combat, any bandit who hung around too long trying to get off a gun shot behind a hard jinking F-15 was in for a nasty surprise when the F-15 either reversed into him or he got jumped by the F-15's wingman. But for now, there was no wingman to help them out, and it was a chance to sharpen Chris Leland's skills and build his confidence in his new weapon system officer.

"The poor son of a bitch won't know what happened to him," Chris told her.

She didn't like the tone of his voice. After two flights, she was having serious doubts about the pilot's overconfidence. "OK, he's almost in position," Laurie said. Then, over the radio as if she were talking to a wingman, "Chris! Break left! Bandit, six o'clock, half a mile, closing." Laurie was twisted around to her left and braced for a sharp turn in the same direction. Instead, Chris jinked hard to the right, loading the Strike Eagle with over 6 g's. Her head banged into the canopy, momentarily stunning her.

She fought the *g*s, trying to twist back to the right and regain a visual on the bandit. At the same time, she felt the afterburners kick in and the nose come down as they entered a split-S, a nose-low vertical turn. *What the hell?* she thought. A split-S was a good maneuver for defeating a rear-quarter threat when the bandit's range was beyond a mile. But they didn't have a mile.

Her head was up, and all she saw was gray as they blasted through the clouds going straight down. Her altimeter was a blur as it unwound, and she glanced at the altitude box in the HUD. They were through 16,000 feet and passing Mach 1.2. "Pull!" Laurie shouted as she reached for the stick. But they were still in afterburners and generating a horrendous *g* load as the pilot tried to bring the nose up. The dive shallowed out and the *g* read-out in the lower lefthand corner of the HUD increased to nine. Bitchin' Betty, the computer-activated woman's voice in the Overload Warning System, bitched at them. "Warning! Over *g*! Warning! Over *g*!"

"The throttles," Chris yelled. "They're stuck! Help me!" They had to get it out of afterburner or they would rip the wings off pulling out—if they didn't black out first. Laurie's vision started to pull in at the edges, grayout, as the *g*'s increased. Now she was looking down a tunnel. She reached for the throttles, fighting the *g*s and the encroaching blackness. Sweat poured down her face, stinging her eyes. Automatically, she tensed her abdomen muscles, harder than she had ever done before, helping her *g* suit keep her blood from pooling in the lower part of her body.

The IP's voice came over the radio, loud and urgent. "Pull out! Pull out!"

They were through the overcast, and all she could see was blue-gray ocean. Her fingers were on the throttles, but she couldn't get her hand over them. She was on the edge of unconsciousness when she felt the *g* relax. Chris had blacked out and released the pressure on the stick. Now they were going straight down again.

She grabbed a fist full of throttles and pulled. They were frozen. At the same time, she pulled hard on the stick and the *g*'s were back, pushing her to the edge of darkness, as the Strike Eagle shallowed its dive. For a split second, she considered ejecting. But at their speed, they were out of the ejection envelope, and the air blast would crush their chests. They were dead.

Her body got the message, and adrenaline coursed through her. She jerked at the throttles and felt something give. The throttles snapped out of afterburner. The F-15's nose came up and pointed at the sky. But their sink rate was still over 4,000 feet a minute, and the ocean was rushing at them. Laurie shoved the throttles full forward into afterburner, never releasing the pressure on the stick. She was aware of being surrounded in gray when she heard a loud "Oh, shit!" over the radio. It was the IP.

Then they were flying again, and she felt Chris's hand on the stick. He was conscious. "I got it," he said.

"Shit-oh-dear," the IP said over the radio. "I thought you'd bought it. I lost you in your rooster tail." The gray Laurie had experienced a few moments before had been ocean spray kicked up when she had jammed the throttles into afterburner to blast them into an upward vector. It had been a close thing, and they had almost died in the fifteen seconds following her bandit call.

She was agonizingly aware that she had wet her pants. *When did I do that?* she wondered.

"Fire light on number 1," Chris radioed as he shut down the left engine. "We're losing hydraulic pressure: PC-1 and utility A are gone."

Laurie called up the Overload Warning System display on her left-hand display screen to see how many g's they had pulled. Her heart raced when she saw the 13.2 appear under the ACC column. She was surprised they had only damaged one engine and two hydraulic systems. She grabbed the checklist she sat on so it wouldn't fly around the cockpit when they maneuvered but was still handy when she needed it. It was damp from her urine. She flipped to the emergency section to reconfirm what she already knew: no brakes nor nose gear steering and they would have to blow the gear down.

"You ever taken the barrier before?" the IP asked. The barrier was a cable stretched across the approach end of the runway that the F-15 could catch with its tailhook, much like a carrier landing.

"Negative," Chris answered.

"Hey, guys," Laurie said, "this is not fun."

Okinawa, Japan

Martini was in his car, stopped on the taxiway, waiting for them. His critical eye missed nothing as the F-15 landed 400 feet short of the cable and then jerked to a stop when its hook snagged the wire. He grunted in satisfaction. It had been a good single-engine approach and landing with a barrier arrestment. The F-15's one good engine spun down as crew chiefs hurried to disengage the cable from the tailhook and tow the F-15 clear of the runway. He watched Laurie follow Leland down the crew ladder and snorted when he saw the dark stains on her backside. He knew what had happened.

"Get changed and meet us in debrief," he muttered. He motioned for Chris to get into the pickup truck he was driving.

Laurie walked into one of the squadron's small debriefing rooms twenty minutes later. She was wearing a fresh flight suit and had taken a quick shower. Martini was sitting at the table with her squadron commander, the IP from the flight, and Chris Leland. The videotape from the mission was on the VCR, and the IP was explaining what had happened.

"After Captain Bender called bandit, Captain Leland rolled to the right and buried the nose, starting a split-S maneuver to reverse back into me. At the same time, he stoked his afterburners. Why, I don't know."

"To gain some separation," Chris said. "But I couldn't pull it out of afterburner. The throttles were jammed."

"Which got you going down, though the Mach, and in an over-g situation," the IP replied. Chris nodded, a forlorn look on his face. The rest of the tape played out.

Martini drummed his fingers on the table as he made a decision. There was no doubt that Chris had gotten way too aggressive and that Laurie had saved them. "I want to talk to these two T-bones alone," he growled. The room rapidly emptied, leaving Chris and Laurie behind. The door closed. "Leland, Maintenance had better find something wrong with the throttles or your ass is grass. The only thing you'll be flying is a commode and the only stick you'll ever see in your right hand is your pecker."

He took a breath, gaining steam. "Maintenance tells me you pulled thirteen gs on the pullout. That calls for a major over-g inspection—takes two days. You caused a lot of good people a piss pot full of work, and you two are going to help Maintenance empty that pot. And Leland, you had better pray they find something wrong."

"They will, sir," Laurie predicted. "What then?"

"You'll get one more chance," Martini said. "Now get your asses over to Maintenance and do some real work—for a change." Chris darted out of the room, glad to escape. Martini's voice stopped Laurie. "You did good out there, Captain."

"Sir, he still needs an IP in the backseat."

"Why?"

"He's inconsistent. We were lucky today that I could handle it."

"I need every pilot, wizzo, crew chief, you name it, I can get," Martini admitted. "If you're right about the throttles, he gets one more chance—with you in his pit."

"Why kill a perfectly good wizzo?" she asked.

"Because I'm an equal opportunity employer."

Master Sergeant Ralph Contreraz, the production supervisor, barreled into the maintenance hangar late Sunday afternoon. Contreraz was the stereotype of the grizzled old master sergeant portrayed by TV and the movies. But there were a few exceptions. He had never smoked in his life, only drank an occasional beer, and never gambled for money. He claimed he was in a game with much higher stakes and throwing money around was for fools who needed a life. The last was a lesson he had learned when he was an F-16 crew chief with the Thunderbirds at Nellis Air Force Base near Las Vegas, Nevada.

He checked his watch: the over-g inspection was right on time. He collared the tech sergeant in charge of the inspection. The tech showed him what they had just found in the front cockpit, and they talked briefly. Contreraz was not given to long conversations. "Fuckin' A," Contreraz grumbled. He had never forsworn profanity and considered it a rare art form when used right. "OK, I'll take care of it." Then, "How's she doing?"

"Captain Bender?" the tech sergeant answered. "Not bad. She's worked one troop into the ground and is with Alvie. She learns quick."

Contreraz joined Alvie, a staff sergeant, and Laurie under the F-15E. He watched approvingly as she counted the tools they had been using during the inspection. Satisfied that all were accounted for and none left inside the airframe, she buttoned up the inspection panel. They came out from under the aircraft. "We found this in the linkage," Contreraz said. He handed her a badly bent metal ballpoint pen.

"Fuckin' FOD," she muttered. FOD—foreign object damage—had almost killed them. Someone had dropped the pen in the cockpit, and when they had maneuvered the jet in flight, it had fallen into the throttle quadrant and jammed the throttle in the afterburner position. "Murphy's Law is alive and well," she said.

"You were damn lucky," Contreraz said. He pointed to the marks on the casing. "It looks like you had a leverage advantage from the backseat and were able to break it free. The crew chiefs should have found it when they did the preflight and checked the cockpits."

She examined the expensive silver pen. "It wasn't their fault. This belongs to Chris." Contreraz nodded his thanks. Now he wouldn't have to crunch heads. "I'll tell him," Laurie said. She looked around. "Where did he go?"

"He left over an hour ago," Contreraz said.

Laurie exhaled sharply. "He should still be here."

"Well, I appreciate you helping," Contreraz said.

"I only got in the way," she replied. "Give me a tool and I'll do something stupid with it."

Contreraz laughed. "That's not what I heard. We're finished here, captain. Just the paperwork left to do."

"Thanks, I'm out'a here."

Contreraz watched her leave. *Martini knows what he's got there,* he decided. For a moment he was back at Nellis Air Force Base in Nevada, a young three-striper serving as a crew chief on the Thunderbirds. And a Captain David "Mafia" Martini was flying his jet.

Bob Ryan glanced at his watch when he heard Laurie come in. It was twelve-thirty Sunday afternoon. He heard the refrigerator close and the pop of a Coke can being opened. "Where you been?" he called.

Laurie came through, still wearing her flight suit, and sat beside him on the couch. "What'cha reading?" she asked, glancing at the book in his lap.

"Herman Wouk's *The Caine Mutiny*."

"That's a pretty old book," she said, cuddling against him.

"It's about what happens when the captain of a ship cracks up under pressure. The officers under him mutinied to save the ship."

"That's the Navy for you," she said.

He put his arm around her, responding to the tone in her voice. "Things got pretty rough out there?" he asked. He felt her head nod against his chest. He listened without comment as she told him about the flight, the debrief with Martini, and the long hours spent going through the inspection with Maintenance.

"Why did Martini make you do that?" he asked.

She shrugged. "Probably so we'd know the problems we caused for Maintenance. It was an object lesson so we wouldn't do it again." She finished the story and told him about the pen. "I'm on the schedule to fly with Chris tomorrow."

"Are you worried?" he asked.

Her soft "Yes" surprised him. Normally, she came home in overdrive after an exciting day, aggressive and eager for sex. But this was her first true experience facing death, and she was not reacting as he had expected. All the clinical studies and literature he had read on the subject described a different reaction from the men who had been in extreme danger in combat and knew they would be facing it again in the near future. Most of them experienced an overpowering need to get drunk and have sex, not necessarily in that order. It was the hormones sending a message to procreate in the face of death and destruction.

But Laurie was not a man, and she needed to be cuddled and find refuge in a safe nest. And better yet, it was his nest. *My God!* he thought. *I'm as basic and primitive about this as a Neanderthal.* "When are you going to make an honest man out of me?" he asked.

Laurie cuddled to his chest. "How soon can we find a chaplain?" She pulled back from him and touched his cheek. "If we get married, I'm going to resign my commission."

"Come on, Laurie, this is the twenty-first century. There's no reason for you to give up your career."

She smiled and cuddled back on his chest, completely captivating him. "Bob, I want to have a bundle of kids. Raising them is a full-time job. I'll worry about my career later—when they have a future."

He stroked her hair. "It's a deal."

"Good," she whispered. "Let's get started."

6 ⟋

Washington, D.C.

The summons to the Oval Office came late Friday afternoon on the ninth of November. *She's been president 83 days,* Bender calculated, *17 days shy of 100.* For some reason, 100 was a magical benchmark, and Shaw was building to it like a Superbowl. Bender hated to admit it, but Shaw was an excellent manager, one of the best he had ever seen, and things were running smoothly in the White House.

The big, hot-button issues were under control. Sam Kennett's confirmation as vice president was moving smoothly through the Senate, and the Chinese were still making the appropriate sounds in the Far East, calming their neighbors after the takeover of Taiwan. As a consequence, the press was muted in its criticism of Turner as Shaw pushed her administration to the 100-day mark.

But for Bender, it only meant 17 more days in purgatory.

Turner's secretary ushered him right in, and he was surprised that the ever-present Shaw was not in his usual position at the end of a couch. Turner came right to the point. "Robert, I understand the Thunderbirds are performing at Andrews on Sunday."

"Yes, ma'am. It's the last show of the season before they go home." Actually, they would do a postseason show the next weekend. It was for their families who hadn't seen them in seven months and for the biannual Thunderbird reunion held every other November—a reunion he and Nancy would miss again.

"Brian would love to see them," Turner said. "Could you take him? He is fascinated with airplanes—" Bender's warm smile stopped her in midsentence. It was the first time she could recall seeing him smile.

"My pleasure. I was going anyway." He paused, thinking. "Why don't you and Sarah come along, too?"

Turner returned his smile. "I would love a day out with Brian and Sarah, but my schedule—" Again, she did not complete the sentence.

"You're a workaholic, Madam President. You need a break."

"I'm afraid that's not possible," she replied, still smiling. "Please work out the details with the Military Office." He was excused.

"Of course, ma'am." He left and headed for the Military Office in the East Wing to arrange the details for Brian's trip to Andrews.

Turner leaned back in her chair and closed her eyes. She was tired. Then she leaned forward and picked up her phone. "Jackie, tell Mr. Shaw I want to clear Sunday's schedule."

Andrews Air Force Base, Maryland

Bender and Nancy were waiting by the reviewing stand when the presidential motorcade drove across the ramp at Andrews Air Force Base. "Does the president's son warrant a five-car motorcade?" she asked.

He shook his head slowly. "Nope. The family usually travels in a single car with a backup van for security. This is an informal or unannounced visit by the president."

"You didn't tell me she was coming."

"I didn't know she was," he replied. He stepped forward when the second limousine in line stopped in front of the reviewing stand. The brigadier general commanding Andrews hurried down the steps, stunned by the president's sudden arrival. "Sorry, Al," Bender told him. "It was my understanding that only her son was coming. I'll let you do the honors." The brigadier beamed. One of his duties was to meet and escort the president whenever she departed or arrived on *Air Force One*. But this was his first chance to interact socially with her.

Madeline Turner stepped out followed by Brian, Sarah, and Maura. Bender made the introductions and turned the family over to the brigadier who escorted them onto the reviewing stand. "Hi, Brian," he called. "Ready to get your eyes watered?"

Both Turner and Nancy watched the two as they talked. It was obvious that they liked each other. "Your son is a good-looking young man," Nancy said.

"He takes after his father," Turner said, studying the small woman. She had often wondered what type of woman Bender had married, and Nancy did not fit the image she had conjured in her mind. She focused on her son, struck by the way he mimicked Bender's stance and gestures. Even the way he talked sounded the same.

Sarah took her mother's hand. "I introduced them," she said. "They talk a lot. Brian wants to go to the Air Force Academy and fly fighters like he did." Turner hushed her so she could hear what they were saying.

"Sir," Brian said, "where's the best place to see the show?"

Bender pointed to a panel truck parked sideways in midfield next to the runway. "About there. The truck marks the center of the show box. That's where everything is supposed to come together."

"Can we watch it from there?" Brian asked.

Bender laughed. "No way." He thought for a moment. "There's a camera crew out there. We can watch the take-off with them."

Brian looked at his mother. "Mom?"

"It's perfectly safe," Bender explained.

Turner made her decision. "I'll go with you, Maura, you and Sarah can stay here if you want. We'll be right back."

Bender almost laughed when the Secret Service detail surrounding Turner realized what was happening. But she was off the platform before they could protest. "Let's go,'' she called, getting into one of the Secret Service's white sport-utility trucks. Behind her, the scramble was on as agents piled into their cars and frantic radio calls were made.

Bender and Brian joined her, and they drove out to the runway. Again, Turner led the way and got out to stand by the panel truck that marked the center of the show box. Her security detail was right behind and spread out. ''I bet they're screwing themselves into the ground,'' Brian told Bender.

''They are spinning up,'' Bender allowed. ''But it's a hard job to keep your mother safe.''

The Thunderbirds were taxiing out and lining up on the runway. Bender kept up a running dialogue, telling Brian what was happening. ''They've changed the takeoff sequence,'' he said. ''I liked the old way better when the diamond formation rolled first.'' Finally, the show was on, and a loud crack echoed over them as the lead F-16 stroked its afterburner and thundered down the runway, coming directly at them. Four seconds later, the second F-16 rolled. Then the four-ship diamond formation was rolling, their wings only a few feet apart.

The first F-16 was over them in full afterburner, reaching for the skies. Then the second passed over, the noise washing over them, building. Bender looked at Turner. She was facing into the four jets as they lifted free of the ground. They passed over, lower than the first two, and the force of their engines pounded at her, shaking her to the core. Suddenly, it was quiet, the silence as deafening as the noise.

''My God,'' she whispered, her face flushed. ''I didn't know. The noise, the power, it's overwhelming. It must be like riding the whirlwind.'' She stopped and looked at Bender, understanding. ''It's the power in those beasts caged and controlled—that's the attraction, isn't it?''

Bender didn't answer. ''We've got to hurry to clear the box,'' he said. ''Otherwise, no show.''

This time, Brian led his mother back to the truck. ''Mom, I gotta do that,'' he told her. She stared at Bender, her face unreadable.

*   *   *

Brian lowered himself into the F-16's cockpit. The seat was still warm from the pilot, the right wingman, who had just finished the show. The seat seemed to reach up and pull him in, enveloping him like a glove. He leaned back, surprised that the seat was tilted back thirty degrees. He sat there for a moment, taking it all in. A sense of purpose swept over him, and he had never felt so sure of anything in his fourteen years. This was where he wanted to be.

The stick was not between his knees but mounted on the right console. He reached for the side stick, barely touching it. Then he grabbed it, feeling more confident as he stroked its four buttons and trigger with his thumb and forefinger. It felt so natural, and the jet became a physical extension of his very being. His left hand naturally fell on the throttle, and again, his fingers brushed its six buttons. Now the fingers on both hands were moving, playing with the controls on the stick and throttle. What had Bender said? It was like playing the piccolo.

He tried to make sense out of the displays, gauges, and switches that filled the cockpit. He wasn't intimidated by their complexity, and there was no doubt that, someday, he would fly an aircraft like this one. He looked for Bender but couldn't see him. "Where did General Bender go?" he asked the crew chief standing on the maintenance stand that had been pushed up to the cockpit.

"Down there," the sergeant said, pointing to the large crowd of spectators who were milling around the jets. Brian raised himself out of the cockpit and saw Bender kneeling by a small boy in a wheelchair. "I never met a Thunderbird who could pass by a kid in a wheelchair," the sergeant said. Brian settled back into the seat and listened as the crew chief ran through the cockpit familiarization drill.

On the ground, Bender gestured toward the F-16. "Have you ever sat in a cockpit?" he asked the boy. A shy shake of the head answered him. Bender looked at his mother. "Can I take him up there?" She smiled and told him it was OK. Bender scooped the boy into his arms and carried him up the stairs of the maintenance stand.

"Time's up, Brian," Bender called. Brian wanted to spend more time in the seat and hesitated. "Scoot," Bender said, his voice all business. Brian scampered out of the cockpit. Bender sat the boy on the canopy rail and then lowered him into the seat while Brian held back, a little peeved at playing second fiddle to some stranger. He waited impatiently until Bender lifted the boy out and followed them down the steps.

"I want to fly one of those," the boy said when he was back in his wheelchair.

"Who knows?" Bender replied. "It takes a lot of work and you've got to have perfect eyesight."

"I don't think my eyes are so good," the boy said.

"You can still fly in other airplanes," Bender told him. "Say, I got to go, but I enjoyed talking to you."

"Thank you," the boy said very solemnly. His mother reached out and touched Bender's arm. She spoke quietly and Bender nodded.

"Come on, Brian," he said. "Time to find your mother." They headed for the waiting staff car that would take them to the reception where Turner was meeting the Thunderbirds.

"Why did you spend so much time with that kid?" Brian asked. "You don't even know him, and he'll never fly a fighter."

"He's dying of leukemia—maybe another month. Brian, you and I got lots of days like this one in front of us. I wanted to help give him this one."

"Mom," Brian called, charging through the crowd in the Officers' Club. Turner turned and smiled at the enthusiasm in his voice. "I got to sit in the cockpit—it fits like it was made for me. The crew chief told me all about it. You should see those jets, they look brand-new. General Bender told me this is the last year the Thunderbirds are flying the F-16. They're gonna get F-22 Raptors next year. I'm gonna be a Thunderbird, Mom."

Turner stared at her son when she heard the same certainty, the same stubbornness, that had made his father such a force in her life. A cold dread swept through her at the image of Brian as a Thunderbird sweeping low over a crowd, the ground rushing at him, and billowing flames consuming him. *I won't let the military kill my son*, she told herself. Suddenly, she wanted to leave Andrews and escape all that it represented. She turned to the brigadier escorting her, not remembering his name. "General, I want to thank you for your hospitality. I know how much trouble an impromptu visit causes."

"It was our pleasure, Madam President. I hope you'll come again."

Maura, Brian, and Sarah preceded her to the waiting limousine, and she entered last, settling into the seat beside her mother. "That was nice," Maura said. "I really enjoyed it, and Brian is certainly excited." Turner didn't answer.

"Mom thinks airplanes are too dangerous," Sarah said.

"I need to speak to Robert about that," Turner said.

The brigadier general broke into a big smile as the presidential motorcade drove away, heading for the main gate. "Yes," he whispered sotto voce. He gathered his staff around him. "We looked good today, folks." He headed back into the reception, searching for Bender. He wanted to thank Bender for standing aside and giving him the chance to shine in front of the president.

He grabbed a beer and twisted off the top. Bender's love of a good brew was well known. He saw Bender and took a long pull at the bottle as he joined him.

Bender sipped at the glass of dark ale he was drinking. "Al, how long have you been wearing a star?" he asked.

"Three months," the brigadier replied.

"I like beer with the best of the troops," Bender said. "But you are in command and not in a beer joint shooting pool. Get a glass." He spun around and walked away, looking for Nancy.

"Ah, shit," the brigadier moaned. The rumors about Bender's uptight personality were true.

Nancy found him. "Been chewing on the brigadier?" she asked. "I thought he did very well."

"Did the president see him with a beer bottle?"

"No," Nancy replied. She took his hand. "Lighten up, Robert." She saw a chef wheel out a cart with a big cake decorated with a Thunderbird motif. "Come on," she murmured, "let's go." She knew what was coming.

Bender went rigid as the Thunderbirds clustered around

the cake for the cutting. The right wingman stepped forward, and Nancy gave Bender's hand a hard squeeze. "We really should go," she whispered. He didn't move.

The right wingman thanked the crowd surrounding them, and his right hand flashed down in a karate chop, cutting the cake. "Hi-yah!" he shouted.

"Let's go," Bender said. The cake cutting was a tradition he hated, and if he ever gained his fourth star and commanded ACC, it would be a dead tradition.

They walked in silence to the car. "I spent quite a bit of time talking to the president," she finally said.

"I'm almost afraid to ask what about," he replied.

"Oh, mostly what mothers talk about. She didn't know we had a daughter in the Air Force." No answer. "Damn," Nancy fumed, "why are you always the great stone face? You wouldn't say shit if your mouth was full of it." She used profanity to get his attention.

"What's the problem?" he mumbled, now listening.

"Act like a human around her. It will help. Women feel better when there's a personal touch."

"She's my commander in chief," Bender replied. "We're not friends."

Nancy sighed, doubting that her husband would ever understand. She changed the subject. "She's much more attractive in person."

"Is she?"

Nancy pulled into herself and thought, recalling the day's events. She knew her husband only too well and wasn't worried in the least that Madeline Turner was attracted to him. Many women were. But she was worried that his career would come to an abrupt halt if he didn't get out of the White House and back into the mainstream of the Air Force.

The Pentagon

"Sorry to break into your Sunday," General Wayne Charles, the Air Force chief of staff said when Bender entered his office. "You made good time getting here."

Bender shrugged off his overcoat. It was early Sunday

morning after Thanksgiving, and Washington's streets were deserted. "Not much traffic out there at five in the morning."

"Let's go talk to the chiefs," Charles said. He motioned to the door and led the way to the Tank, the conference room on the second floor where the Joint Chiefs of Staff met. "The chairman is chewing nails," Charles warned him.

Overmeyer scowled at them when they entered. Like the last time Bender had been there on Black Wednesday, the Joint Chiefs were all assembled. *What now?* he wondered. Charles motioned him to a chair against the far wall. But before he could sit, the secretary of defense, John Weaver Elkins, came through the door, and the generals and lone admiral all stood. Elkins was a slender, mild-mannered Ph.D. and reminded Bender of a librarian. "Gentlemen," Elkins began, "I take it you have all heard about Korea?" Judging by the nods and silence, Bender assumed he was the only one who hadn't. But the question had not been directed at him. They all sat down.

"Well," Elkins continued, "it looks like the Chinese and South Koreans are going to make a joint announcement tomorrow morning."

The South Koreans! Bender thought. *An announcement of what?*

"General Bender," Elkins said, "exactly how will the White House react?"

"Sorry, sir," Bender replied, "I'm not current on the situation."

Overmeyer leaned forward and stared at him. "The Chinese and South Koreans are going to sign a mutual defense and economic assistance pact Monday."

This is the first I've heard about that! Bender thought. "The announcement will coincide with Turner's first 100 days as president," he said. "It will definitely embarrass the White House coming out of the blue like that."

"It's a surprise for all of us," Overmeyer said. "Fuckin' CIA. The boys in the basement cottoned on to it late last night. That's the only reason we know about it."

"Then the CIA hasn't got a clue?" the chief of Naval Operations asked.

"Apparently not," Overmeyer said. "There has been no mention in the President's Daily Brief, and the CIA has been hovering over the Chinese like vultures since the Taiwan fiasco."

What's going on here? Bender thought. *This should be no big deal. The chairman or the secretary only has to pick up the secure phone and call the Oval Office. They've got direct access. Or do they? Has Shaw been at work again?*

He was aware that all eyes were on him. "General Bender," Elkins said, "we want you to tell the president. Today."

Bender had to stifle a "Why me?" He forced a calm into his voice he didn't feel. "I'm operating in the dark here."

Elkins stood and paced the floor like a college professor giving a lecture, slow and deliberate. "In spite of many problems, the Chinese have successfully absorbed Hong Kong after taking over in 1997. They now have control of Taiwan, securing that problem area as well. By concluding a defense agreement with South Korea, their northern flank on the Pacific is secure, and they are free to directly challenge Japan and us for regional domination. The Chinese believe we are a paper tiger led by a weak and indecisive woman. I agree with them on the last part of their assessment. By announcing the pact on the president's 100th day in office, it will be a symbolic slap in the face. The world will look to us for leadership, but they will only find confusion. Which is one of the object lessons the Chinese wish to make." He sat down as if that explained everything.

"I still don't understand why I should be the one to tell her," Bender protested.

Overmeyer snorted. "Because she'll listen to you. She takes one look at me and the wall goes up."

"And the same for me," Elkins said.

Bender looked around the room. "And the rest of the story?"

Elkins stood up. "Thank you, gentlemen." The generals all stood as he left the room.

"General Charles will fill in the blank spots," Over-meyer said, following Elkins out. The meeting was over.

Back in Charles's office, Bender let his anger show. "I don't like this, General."

Charles lifted an eyebrow at Bender's rare show of emotion. "Why?"

"The DCI, the secretary, the chairman, all have direct access to the president. It's their job to tell her news like this, not mine."

"Your job is exactly what we say it is," Charles said. "Sit down and listen to a few basic facts of life. One, Turner issued a presidential directive terminating the boys in the basement. Two, we're doing that. But you don't shut down Intelligence operations like that on the spur of the moment. It takes months, even years, and their pipeline is still open. But how many politicians understand that? Three, she's going to ask for the source of your information. Four, you are going to tell her the truth. Five, she'll listen when you tell her that we are shutting the boys down."

"She'd believe Dr. Elkins or General Overmeyer," Bender said.

"We seriously doubt that," Charles replied. "I'm going to turn you over to the boys and let them fill in the details."

Bender gathered up his overcoat and left, heading for the third level of the basement. He spent the next hour talking to an Army colonel who hadn't worn a uniform in six years or shaved in three. Then he was in the parking lot, walking toward his car. He allowed himself a rare mental outburst of profanity. *Fuck me!* He thought. There was no doubt in his mind that he was caught in a bureaucratic brawl between the Pentagon, the CIA, and the White House. It was only a matter of time before Congress got involved and turned it into a full-scale shooting match.

And no one would be taking prisoners.

Washington, D.C.

The aide on duty in Shaw's office dropped the Sunday morning edition of the *Washington Post* when Bender appeared in front of him. He listened without comment as Bender asked to speak to the president. A long silence. "What does this concern?" the aide finally asked.

"A matter of national security," Bender answered.

"Please be more specific."

"It involves China and South Korea."

The aide picked up the newspaper. Bender was too low on the feeding chain to have anything of earth-shaking importance. "It can wait until Monday."

"Let me speak to Mr. Shaw."

"He's not to be disturbed," the aide said, turning a page.

"Sorry to disturb *you,*" Bender said. He walked quickly back to his office, his anger and frustration building. He was up against the power game in Washington that was based on three pillars: money, information, and access. Shaw's aide had just demonstrated his power by denying Bender access to the president and her chief of staff. In the past, Bender had always come running whenever she or Shaw whistled. But now, when he wanted to reverse the process, the door was firmly closed. In short, he had no access and no power. That didn't bother him, but telling Overmeyer that he had failed did. He checked his watch: 8:10 in the morning. He couldn't put it off much longer.

He sat down and studied the framed photo of the Thunderbirds on the wall of his office. As usual, it did its magic and his frustration and anger faded to a more manageable level.

"Hi," Sarah Turner said. She was standing in the doorway, wearing a pretty dress.

"What brings you down here?" Bender asked.

"Things," she replied, sitting in the lone chair. "I don't want to go to church. It's so boring. Why are you working on Sunday?"

For a moment, he considered using Sarah to access Turner, but just as quickly, he discarded the idea. He felt his face blush. *What's the matter with you?* he thought, ashamed that he had even considered it.

"Why is your face turning red?" the little girl asked.

"My parents made me go to church when I was your age, too. I hated it until I started watching the people around me. There was a woman who always cried at the same time every Sunday and an old man who took money out of the collection plate.''

"No kidding?"

Bender smiled. "No kidding." She bounced off the chair and out the door. "See you," she sang.

Wayne Adams, the Secret Service agent Shaw had almost fired along with Chuck Sanford, appeared at his door. He looked up the hall after Sarah and spoke into his whisper mike, passing her on. "General, I want to thank you for what you did. You saved our jobs."

"I was the one who caused the problem."

"Still," Adams replied, "not many people around here would take Shaw on." He paused. "Rumor says you want to speak to the president."

"That's a true statement," Bender replied. "But I can't reach Shaw." His voice filled with sarcasm. "He can't be disturbed."

"He's getting his Sunday morning blow job," Adams said. He waited for Bender to ask who the lucky lady was, and when the general said nothing, he jotted a name and number down on a piece of paper. "Try an end run around Shaw. But you didn't get this from me." Bender glanced at the name, and when he looked up Adams was gone. He dialed the number.

The phone was picked up on the first ring. "Kennett here," the vice president said.

Wayne Adams and Chuck Sanford were talking in room W-16, the Secret Service command post, when the west gate reported that Shaw had blasted through. "He's got the pedal to the metal," the uniformed guard reported. "You better have a valet meet him to park his car."

"No way I'm gonna miss this," Adams said. "Where's Magic?"

"In her private study in the residence," Sanford replied. He joined Adams as they hurried out of the command post, which was directly below the Oval Office. They split up and were in position to monitor Shaw's progress through the White House. Adams spoke into his whisper mike. "Now there's a man about ready to bust a hemorrhoid."

"Or have a stroke," Sanford replied.

"There's always hope."

Shaw didn't see Sanford at the far end of the hall when he knocked on the door to Turner's study on the second floor. He took a deep breath, forcing himself to calm down. Nothing on his face or in his voice betrayed what was beneath the surface when he opened the door. "Mizz President," he said, "you're going to work us all into an early grave." *How did Bender get in here?* he wondered. *Bad mistake, buddy boy. Not going through Patrick Shaw will cost you.*

He made a tactical assessment of the small room. Turner was sitting in her usual place on the left couch with Bender at the far end. He bridled at the sight of Sam Kennett sitting in *his* position directly opposite her. Sam Kennett was a young-looking forty-two-year-old. He had medium-length sandy brown hair, blue eyes, and a lean and athletic body. What had Shaw's companion from last night called Kennett? A studmuffin? *Too bad he's not,* Shaw thought. *It might give me some leverage.*

He poured himself a cup of coffee, suddenly aware that the girl's heavy perfume was still on him. An inner alarm warned him that this was not going to be a good Sunday.

"I'm meeting with the National Security Council in thirty minutes," Turner told him.

Shaw sat down next to Kennett, dumped his chin on his chest, and stuck out his lower lip—his Winston Churchill pout. "I wasn't aware of any crisis in the brewing."

"Robert," Turner said.

Bender quickly repeated what he knew about the impending Chinese–South Korean pact. *Fuck-a-duck,* Shaw moaned to himself. *Why hadn't the CIA caught it?* He had some scores to settle with the DCI over that. "Our friends at Langley seem to have let us down on this one," he said. "How did you learn about it?"

"Through the Pentagon's special operations and intelligence units," Bender answered.

"The crazies in the basement," Shaw muttered. "I thought we put those boys out of business."

"They are phasing down," Bender said. "But it takes time."

Shaw snorted. "Bullshit."

"At this point," the vice president said, "we have no reason to disbelieve what the Pentagon is doing. Let's stay focused on the immediate problem." Shaw glanced at the vice president and did not respond. "We need to send the Chinese a message," Kennett continued. "We must make it very clear that we will not tolerate this type of behavior in the Far East."

"It is complicated by the Beijing Pact," Turner said.

Kennett shot a worried look at Shaw, then Bender. "I'm not familiar with that."

"Robert," Turner said. Again, Bender explained what he knew about the deal the late President Roberts had cut with the Chinese over Taiwan. Shaw filled in the details and how he had the secretary of state's and national security advisor's resignation and confessions in his safe.

"Oh, my God," Kennett muttered. "We're in real trouble."

"How's that?" Shaw asked.

"The Chinese are doing a Mau-Mau on us," Kennett replied. Shaw's head jerked up. The allusion to the Mau-Mau uprising in Kenya in the late 1950s with its attendant bloodshed was a political metaphor he understood. He had done it many times to the opposition. "The moment we seriously oppose the Chinese," Kennett continued, "they will tell the world about the pact. There goes what's left of our credibility, and we will be in the political fight of our lives with Congress for selling out Taiwan."

"What do you mean by 'what's left of our credibility'?" Turner asked.

Kennett stood and walked to the window. "Most nations believe we are retreating into isolationism, concerned with domestic issues at the expense of our international obligations." He paused for effect. "And I agree."

The boy has a terminal case of stupids, Shaw thought. *Maddy won't stand for that kind of talk. He'll talk himself right into a hangin'.*

"What do you suggest I do?" Turner asked. The tone

of her voice was flat and noncommittal, totally devoid of emotion.

"Take the Beijing Pact away from the Chinese," Kennett replied, "and scare the hell out of South Korea."

"Easily said," Shaw mumbled.

A smile flickered across Kennett's mouth. "When you're losing—leak. First, date and release Murchison's and Rawlings's letters of resignation. Then leak the 'real' reason, the Beijing Pact, to the press. But do it quick, in time for the evening news. If we do it soon enough, *60 Minutes* might even have time to jump on it."

"Too obvious," Shaw said. "It'll backfire in our faces."

Kennett shook his head. "Not if I know Murchison. He'll try to justify the role he played in the agreement, claiming it was a significant step toward world peace and security, the high point of Roberts's short administration. No reporter will take that at face value and will figure Murchison is trying to make himself look good. So when some reporter comes to us for verification, we tell the truth. We found out about the pact long after the fact—too late to do anything about it. The reporter figures that Murchison is using the press to save what's left of his reputation, and we end up looking like the good guys. Meanwhile, the CIA slips the South Koreans a copy of the Beijing Pact. They won't be too hot to sign on the dotted line when they see China is slicing them off like Taiwan."

Shaw begrudgingly admitted he was in the presence of a master. He laughed. "And we Mau-Mau the Chinese."

"You'll need more than that to discourage the Chinese," Bender said. They all looked at him. "The Chinese practice *Realpolitik* with a vengeance. Everything they do is based on calculations of power and national interest. Right now they believe we are a paper tiger, so why should they change direction when all we do is talk? We need to send them a message that we mean business."

"And how do you suggest I do that, Robert?" Turner asked.

Well, well, Mr. General, Shaw thought. *You stepped in it this time.*

"Talk to Dr. Elkins and General Overmeyer about your military options," Bender answered.

"Such as?" Turner asked.

"You can increase the state and stage of alert on the Pacific Rim," Bender replied. "Or you can increase the DEFCON here. Or start joint military exercises with Japan."

"Thank you, Robert," Turner said. "That will be all." The room was silent until he left. "Whose line were we hearing there?" she asked.

"Probably Overmeyer's," Shaw told her. "The chairman hates you and thinks you haven't got a clue."

"Really?" Turner replied, her anger flaring. Then it was gone. "Well, I have a clue for him. There is no way that I will take this country into a war over this issue."

"Madam President," Kennett said, "I agree with General Bender and think you should explore all available options. But do it through the NSC. The secretary of defense is a member and Overmeyer is an advisor. They will be heard." It was time for the meeting with the National Security Council.

"Patrick," Turner said, "find a reporter—one who is not known as being friendly."

"I've got just the one," Shaw assured her. He escorted Turner and Kennett to the Cabinet Room where the NSC was meeting. Then he ambled back to his office. *Liz Gordon will be most appreciative,* he thought. *And yes indeed, Mr. General Robert Bender is going to learn about fucking with old Patrick.* It was going to be a good Sunday after all.

7 🖝

Okinawa, Japan

Brigadier General David Martini glared at the message, then at Lieutenant Colonel Peter Townly, the chief of his Intelligence section. "I'm getting sick and tired of these messages, Pete. Especially at oh-dark-thirty early Monday morning."

"It's not my fault," Townly declared. "I just decode them."

"So why do they want us"—Martini read from the message—"to 'immediately commence an unannounced wartime readiness exercise to last five days'? What the hell is going on?"

"Best guess? For some reason, the NMCC"—National Military Command Center—"wants to send a message to the Chinese. We're the messenger."

Martini smothered what he really wanted to say about sending messages. "Why the Chinese?"

Townly thought for a moment. "Why the secrecy and the backdoor communications? Tasking for an exercise should have come out of Headquarters PACAF"—Pacific Air Forces—"at Hickam. Look at the addresses on the message. Besides CINC PACAF and CINC PAC, you're the only other recipient. Sorry, General, but the NMCC wants us to get someone's attention. And the only someone I can think of are the Chinese."

"According to the DIA's latest Intel summary," Martini said, "all is sweetness and light with the Chinese."

"That was the official line, sir. Have you seen the Sunday news from the States?" Martini had but said nothing. "Well," the lieutenant colonel explained, "Liz Gordon on CNC broke the story about the sellout of Taiwan. Needless to say, the press has gone into a feeding frenzy. I think this is all related."

Martini was far from being slow and had come to the same conclusion for the same reasons long before Townly. But at four o'clock in the morning, he wanted confirmation that his brain was awake. He worked the problem. Whatever message Washington wanted to send to the Chinese, it was very low key and guaranteed not to upset them. "What do you think of this so-called message we're supposed to be sending, Pete?" Now he was testing his intelligence officer, getting his measure.

"One wing in the forward area conducting an unannounced wartime readiness exercise? Not much, sir."

Martini humphed and reread the decoded message. "Well, this is about as official as marching orders can get." He walked out of the Intelligence vault and into the command post, which was in the same building. He made his way to the Control Cab overlooking the main floor. "This is an exercise," he told the on-duty controller. "Condition Scarlet has just been declared." The controller gulped. Condition Scarlet meant an attack was expected within six hours. She turned to the communications console in front of her and started the alert.

Between telephone calls, she said, "I'll have to notify PACAF when the exercise started."

Martini glanced at the master clock on the wall. "Make it fifteen minutes ago, 0400 local time. We're already behind the power curve." He stomped out of the command post because there was little he could do until the battle staff reported in.

"Thanks a bunch, General," the controller muttered.

Outside, Martini headed for the Security Police shack to see if his cops could meet their post out and have the base fully guarded within ninety minutes. A chief master sergeant was already on duty when he arrived, and the police were streaming through the armory, checking out their weapons. They were off to a good start. His next stop was Munitions. The first dollies with Mark-82 500-pound bombs and AIM-9 air-to-air missiles were already moving toward the flight line for a weapons loadout.

He drove slowly down the flight line, past the hardened shelters that housed his F-15Es. Not too much action yet, but he could sense the building momentum. He stopped and got out of his staff car when he saw Master Sergeant Ralph Contreraz. "How's it going?" he asked.

Contreraz didn't immediately answer. "I'll have six of my jets uploaded and ready to launch in three hours. We should be able to generate six more aircraft two hours later. We'll need another three hours to generate the last six. The other two are down for maintenance." Martini grunted, not totally satisfied with the answer. But he knew Contreraz was giving him a rock hard commitment. "My people live all over the island," Contreraz explained. "It takes time for them all to get here."

Martini's personal radio squawked at him. He was needed in the command post. "Make it happen," Martini told Contreraz. He drove to the command post, which was now alive with people arriving in various states of sleep.

The major in charge of the command post met him at the entry point. "Sir, you've got a call from CINC PACAF on the secure line. I've chased everyone out of the Battle Cab, and you can take it in there." The Battle Cab was the glassed-in commanders booth overlooking the main floor of the command post opposite the Control Cab.

Martini sat down and took a deep breath before turning the key to the secure telephone to activate its encryption circuits. CINC PACAF, the commander in chief of Pacific Air Forces, was his immediate boss and responsible for the air arm of U.S. Pacific Unified Defense Command. "Martini here," he said.

The tinny distortion of the secure telephone did little to modify the anger of the four-star general on the other end. "Mafia, I just came out of a meeting with CINC PAC." CINC PAC was the admiral in command of Pacific Unified Defense Command and CINC PACAF's boss. "The Chinese and South Koreans are getting ready to sign a mutual defense treaty today and want to embarrass the White House.''

''That won't be hard to do,'' Martini replied.

The general ignored him. ''We need to send them a message to cease and desist that type of crap. But the only overt response we're allowed to make is your readiness exercise. The president doesn't want to 'antagonize the Chinese and make the situation worse.' She's going to pursue it through the State Department.''

''That will impress the Chinese,'' Martini said.

''In a pig's ass. I want you to pull out all the stops on this exercise. Stir up the locals, get the media looking at you. Let the Chinese know we're still out there and looking at them.''

''And I'm to do all this in five days?''

''Give it your best shot.'' The line went dead. Martini had his unofficial marching orders.

Lieutenant Colonel Pete Townly saw him lay down the phone and stuck his head through the Battle Cab's door. ''Going for broke on the exercise?''

Martini glared at the Intelligence officer. ''Townly, go do something productive and quit harassing my ass.'' *I'm going to have to get that son of a bitch promoted,* he thought.

Laurie Bender was feeling grubby and hadn't taken a shower in three days. Her pilot, Chris Leland, had a distinct aroma about him, and she suspected that she was fairly ripe herself. ''When are they gonna let up?'' Chris moaned.

''The rumor mill says today is the last day of the exercise,'' she replied. Martini had deliberately spread the rumor as he escalated the exercise to its climax.

''God, I hope so. Can you believe it? Living in a hardened shelter with an F-15? If I ever see another MRE, I'll puke.'' An MRE, meal ready to eat, was the replacement for the old C-ration and lived up to its reputation as ''meal rejected by Ethiopians.''

Laurie wandered over to the big blast doors that had been rolled back for the fuel truck that was refueling their jet. The sound of gunfire echoed down the ramp. ''Intruders!'' Laurie shouted. They had been through this exercise before. She helped the pumper disconnect the fuel hose while Chris ran for the door controls. The gunfire was drawing closer. A shadowy figure darted behind the aircraft bunker across from them. It was a sergeant from the Japanese Self-Defense Force base at Naha on the southern end of the island. The Japanese had entered the exercise on day 2 and had thrown a series of intruders at the base, adding to the realism of the exercise and testing the base's defenses.

The pumper drove the truck into the bunker as the big doors slowly rolled closed. Just before they were sealed in, a blue hand grenade rolled through the gap. Laurie threw herself on the dummy grenade. ''Ka-blooie!'' she shouted. She looked up, smiling. ''I'm dead.''

A sharp rap at the entrance door on the left side of the shelter echoed through the revetment. ''Exercise team!'' a voice shouted. Chris opened the door and two umpires, an American captain and a Japanese lieutenant, stepped through. Martini was right behind them. He was haggard with fatigue.

''Status,'' Martini snapped.

''Captain Bender threw herself on the grenade,'' Chris told him.

The two umpires conferred and decided that she had saved the other personnel in the shelter and the aircraft from damage. But she was dead. ''Great,'' Laurie said, thinking about the shower that was waiting for her.

Martini picked up the blue practice grenade. ''It looks like a dud to me,'' he growled. ''I'm undeading you. We're surging for a max effort and going to launch everything we got.''

''Ending with a bang?'' Laurie quipped.

''The biggest one we can manage,'' Martini said. Then he was gone.

''Shouldn't the general be in the command post?'' Laurie asked. ''Not out on the line.''

The captain on the exercise team shook his head. ''Only if he's alive. General Martini exercised out half of the commanders on base. He was the first to go.''

''Who's running the show?'' Chris asked.

"The second echelon," the captain answered. "The general has the dead guys out haunting the base, seeing how their troops are doing. He's leading the pack and has been all over the place kicking butt and taking names. He fired a major in the motor pool for not dispersing his vehicles. He's an absolute madman."

"It has been most instructive," the Japanese lieutenant said. The two officers left, closing the door behind them.

"Beagle One, this is Dogpatch. You're scrambled to high CAP Alpha-Three, angels two-four."

Chris acknowledged the call from the command post. "Beagle One scrambling now." He disconnected the long cord that plugged them into a land line to the command post. He pulled the handle for the jet fuel starter, and a high-pitched shriek filled the bunker as the right engine came to life.

"This should be it," Laurie told him as she lowered the canopy.

"Where the hell is Alpha-Three," he asked. Laurie called up the moving map display on her number 2 scope. Alpha-Three was a CAP (combat air patrol) point north of the island. Their job was to climb to 24,000 feet, orbit at the CAP, and shoot down any hostile aircraft that came their way. "Where the hell is our wingman?" he asked. Normally, two aircraft manned a CAP and another aircraft should have been scrambled with them.

"Probably exercised out by the umpires," Laurie said. They taxied for runway 5 right maintaining radio silence, barely able to see the taxi path in the fading light. A sergeant guided them past a fuel truck parked on the taxiway. A large red tag indicated it had been destroyed in a simulated air raid. "I got to admit," she said, "this exercise has been a real ballbuster."

They halted at the end of the runway check area and a team of two crew chiefs and two weapons specialists materialized out of a dugout for the EOR check. The crew chiefs gave the aircraft one last inspection, checking for hydraulic leaks, cut tires, or loose panels. A weapons specialist ran out from under the aircraft holding up the safety streamers from the practice air-to-air missile they were carrying. He gave them a thumbs-up: They were good to go. A green light flashed at them from the glass cupola on top of the small trailer that served as the backup for the main control tower. They taxied onto the right runway of Kadena's two parallel runways, and the runway lights flashed on so they could take off. Chris stroked the afterburners and they climbed into the darkening sky.

"So what the hell do we do now?" Chris asked.

"Go to the CAP point and hold until we hit bingo fuel or get recalled. There is no way we'll be hit with a stresser this late in the exercise. The boss knows we're all tired and wants to end it with us all in one piece."

She was wrong and Vice Squad, a Marine ground-controlled intercept radar site, immediately paired them against a bogie, an unknown aircraft. The F-15's APG-70 radar did its magic, and they easily found the aircraft 50 miles to the north of their position. Chris turned into the aircraft to close for an intercept. Almost immediately, they were called off. "Damn," he muttered. "I hate turning JP-5 into noise."

"It was an airliner anyway," Laurie told him. They were required to stay well clear of all commercial traffic.

They returned to their CAP point, entered a race track pattern, and bored holes in the sky for another hour. "Damn!" Chris moaned. "I think we're the only jet still up here."

Laurie shared his frustration. "Let's talk to Dogpatch and find out what's happening." She switched radio frequency to the command post and made the call. "Dogpatch, Beagle One."

"Go ahead, Beagle One."

"When can we expect recovery?"

"Beagle One, be advised the runways are closed for an emergency."

"Both runways?" Chris protested.

Dogpatch sensed the pilot's frustration and answered, "The nose gear of a KC-135 collapsed on landing, and the aircraft skidded across the grass onto the other runway. We're clearing the debris now and runway 5 left should be open shortly."

"This one sounds for real," Laurie told her pilot.

"Shit!"

Seventy minutes later they finally received clearance to recover at home plate. Chris nosed the Strike Eagle over into a high-speed descent and pushed the airspeed up against the Mach. It was a classic case of get-home-itis. "We got all the time in the world," Laurie cautioned. "Let's do it right."

"No pro-blem-o," Chris answered. He throttled back and called the tower for clearance.

"You're cleared for an overhead recovery, report initial," the tower answered. Ahead of them they could see the base lit up like a Christmas tree.

"What the fuck," he muttered. "How long has the fuckin' exercise been over?" He overflew the point four miles short of the runway and made the radio call. "Beagle One, initial now."

"Report the break," the tower answered. It was developing into a standard overhead recovery where the aircraft overflew the end of the runway at 1,500 feet and pitched out, circling to land.

"In the break," Chris radioed as he pitched out to the right. But it was in the wrong direction. They were landing on the left runway and should have pitched out to the left. He was tired.

The tower caught the mistake immediately. "Continue," the controller transmitted. "No one else is in the pattern. Cleared to land runway 5 left. Check gear down and locked."

"Cleared to land," Chris repeated. "Three in the green."

"Push it up," Laurie said, "we're a bit slow."

Chris didn't answer and turned final. But he was tired and overshot final, rolling them out well to the left of centerline. He started to correct back as they slowed still more. The F-15's nose came up as the angle of attack increased. Laurie glanced at the airspeed. "Let's go around," she said, not liking the way the approach was developing.

"No fucking pro-blem-o," Chris muttered, determined to salvage the approach after screwing up the break. He cross-controlled the jet by feeding in right aileron and opposite rudder to get lined up on the runway.

"Chris," Laurie repeated, "go around."

At the same time, the supervisor of flying, the pilot who monitored all flying in the tower, came on the radio. "Beagle One, go around." Even in the dark, he could see Chris had blown the approach.

Chris jammed the throttles forward. The left engine did as commanded and started to spin up. But the rear compressor variable vanes on the right engine failed and a massive dam of air built up in front of the compressor blades, causing a compressor stall. A loud bang filled the cockpit as the engine tried to clear the stall and sort itself out.

The jet yawed into the stalled engine. Because of the high nose-up attitude, slow airspeed, and cross-control, it rolled to the right into the dead engine. Chris and Laurie yelled "Eject!" in perfect unison. Laurie jerked at the ejection handles on the side of her seat. The canopy blew off, and her seat went up the rails with an 11-g kick.

But the F-15 had rolled past the vertical, and she was on a downward trajectory as the seat's rocket pack ignited. Chris was still coming up the rails when the F-15 hit the ground and fireballed. The drogue chute in Laurie's seat had not deployed when she hit the ground, bounced into the air, and then skidded over 300 yards before slamming into the wire cyclone fence that surrounded the base.

David Martini was alone in his office when his vice commander, a full colonel, entered. Martini stood up and paced the floor, warning the colonel it was going to be a very short meeting. "You're the acting president of the SIB until whoever they appoint as the permanent president gets here." The SIB, Safety Investigation Board, was the panel that would investigate the accident. "Get cracking. Find out what the hell went wrong. I don't want to see you until the permanent board is in place and you've turned everything over to them."

"Yes, sir," the colonel replied.

"One more thing," Martini said. "Captain Leland was a marginal pilot and still flying because of my decision.

Make sure the board is aware of that fact and that it is part of the investigation.''

The colonel was speechless. Martini was admitting to the SIB that supervisory error may have been the cause of the accident. If that was true, Martini's career was as dead as the pilot. "This is no time to fall on your sword and do push-ups,'' the colonel said.

Martini banged his fist down on his desk. Hard. "If the buck belongs here, it stops here.''

"I understand, sir,'' the colonel said. He saluted and turned to leave.

"George,'' Martini said, stopping him, "I want the truth.'' The colonel nodded and left. Martini sank into his chair and hunched over his desk, leaning on his elbows and massaging his bruised fist as he stared at the wall.

Washington, D.C.

"General Bender,'' the White House usher said, looking around the small basement office. He wondered how anyone could survive in such a dank dungeon. But he assumed that Bender, like everyone else in the White House, would tolerate any discomfort to say they worked in the executive mansion. "The president has requested that you join her in the Oval Office.''

Why the formality? Bender thought. Normally, a secretary gave him a call and he was on his way. He followed the usher up the stairs and waited while he knocked and opened the door to the Oval Office. The moment he entered, he sensed something was wrong. The president immediately stood up and came around her desk. "Please,'' she said, gesturing toward one of the couches opposite her desk. She sat down next to him.

"Robert, I'm afraid there's bad news.'' She looked at him, and her eyes filled with tears. "General Charles called a few moments ago—your daughter has been in an accident.''

Bender knew. Laurie was dead. Laurie, his only child. He nodded dumbly as Turner's words echoed through him, confirming his daughter's death. A dark chasm spread before him. He half heard her words as he fought for his balance, swaying on the edge of the dark void. Slowly, he regained his composure and stepped back from the edge. What had she said? "Please excuse me, Madam President, I didn't hear—" His words trailed off. He felt her hand on top of his.

"Robert, I'm so sorry. If there is anything I can do."

Suddenly, he had to know. It was a compelling need that had to be satisfied. "Do you know what happened?"

"Only that it was an aircraft accident during an exercise being conducted at Kadena Air Base." She stopped, searching for the words to explain, to comfort. "Robert, I"—again she hesitated, determined to take the weight— "I approved that exercise. If I had known your daughter was there—" Her words trailed off. What would she have done? Would she have made a different decision?

For a moment, her words did not make sense, and her hand burned as it lay on his. He looked at her, finally hearing the pain in her voice. "What happened was not your fault," he said. "It's one of the risks we take. I've"—his voice started to fade, then more strongly— "I've had to tell three wives that their husbands had been killed"—he worked to keep his voice steady—"in the line of duty." Then he broke down and buried his head in his hands. He wanted to speak, but the words wouldn't come. He pulled out his handkerchief and rubbed his eyes, fighting the tears.

"It's all right," Turner said.

Her words snapped at him like a whip. It was not all right. He regained control. "Thank you for your concern, Madam President." He stood up. "I need to tell my wife."

She stood with him. "I meant it when I asked if there was anything I could do."

"Perhaps if Laurie could be buried here—in Arlington."

"Of course," she said. She walked with him to the door. She wanted to say more, but the words weren't there. She watched him leave, his back ramrod stiff as he marched down the hall. She closed the door and returned to her desk. But instead of sitting, she stared out the window at the pin oak planted by Dwight Eisenhower. "Oh, Robert," she whispered. "I am so sorry."

Arlington, Virginia

Bender drove slowly into Arlington National Cemetery and parked at the southern end of the visitor's center parking lot. They could have driven to the chapel, but Nancy understood his need to walk. The bitterly cold December wind that had cleared the sky whipped at them as they made their way down McClellan Drive.

It had been twelve days since the crash and the demands of bringing Laurie home, going through the lockstep of gathering the family, and making the necessary arrangements had buffered them from their sorrow. Nancy had cried at first, little more than a few tears gently dried with a handkerchief, then a rigid control snapped into place and she was the general's wife, doing what had to be done. She would save her grief for later.

"Remember the first time we came here?" Nancy asked. "Laurie wanted to see President Kennedy's grave."

"It was for a school assignment," Bender said. "She ended up writing about silence."

She slipped her arm in his. This was an old story, one they found comforting in the retelling. "Silence is what she saw."

"She always did have a funny way of looking at things," he said. "Sometimes, I really despaired, wondering if she would ever get her act together. Finally, I just accepted it."

"Laurie had her act together, you just didn't realize it."

"I know that—now," he admitted.

"She so wanted to be like you," Nancy said. "Remember when you used to come home with the Thunderbirds at the end of the show season? And how the families would all go out to meet you?"

"I remember the short skirts you used to wear."

"What did you expect me to wear? I had been a widow for seven months while you were on the road and wanted your undivided attention."

"You always were the worst of the Thunderbrides."

She took his hand. "I was a Thunderbroad and don't you forget it." He looked up at the sky and remembered. "Remember how Laurie would run out and jump into your arms?"

"It was like being hit with a bowling ball."

"And she always insisted on carrying your hangup bag."

"It was too big for her."

"And how she ended up dragging it across the parking lot?"

"I remember," he said, the ache retreating one more step.

They entered the chapel and walked down to the front, sitting on the opposite side of the aisle from the honor guard of officers assigned to Arlington. The chapel filled and the crowd spilled outside, shivering in the cold wind. The chaplain entered through a side door and stood at the head of the casket. "Welcome, friends," he began.

The service played out with the formal, predictable routine that Bender found comforting. Then the pallbearers carried the flag-draped casket to the waiting caisson that would carry Laurie to her grave. Bender and Nancy walked behind as the funeral cortege made its way to the far side of the cemetery. As they approached the grave site, five black limousines approached from the other direction and stopped. Men in dark overcoats were spreading out quickly on the outskirts, moving through the white rows of crosses.

"Robert?" Nancy whispered.

"I didn't know she was coming," he told her.

He was surprised when General Charles stepped forward and opened the door of the second limousine. Madeline Turner stepped out, and Charles escorted her to the open grave. She stood quietly as the casket was placed over the grave. The wind whipped at her hair, stinging her, but she didn't move, suffering in the cold with them.

Again, the ordered, predictable routine of the interment service helped Bender make it through. The pallbearers were standing rigidly at attention on both sides of the casket when he heard the sound of approaching jets. Three

F-15s from the First Fighter Wing at Langley, Virginia, approached from the south in a perfect missing-man formation. General Charles looked up and saluted the fighters as they flew past. Bender glanced at the president, wondering if she was aware of what the formation symbolized. He hoped so.

The flag was lifted from the coffin and folded with precision. Then Turner stepped forward and stood for a moment at the head of the casket. With slow, deliberate solemnity, the sergeant smoothed the flag, his hands caressing the triangular fold before he handed it to her. She cradled the flag in her arms as she took the few steps to Bender and Nancy. She stopped in front of Nancy.

"On behalf of a grateful nation and your president, please accept this as a small tribute for your daughter's sacrifice." Turner handed the flag to Nancy and the two women stood there, their hands touching as the firing squad fired three volleys over the grave. The haunting refrain of taps echoed down the wind. It was over.

"Thank you, Mrs. President," Nancy said. Turner looked away and Bender caught the traces of tears at the corners of her eyes. Was she crying or was it just the wind? He and Nancy stood there as the mourners dispersed, returning to what was left of the day.

They were alone with their daughter for the last time. "The missing-man formation," Nancy said. "I remember when you did that."

"Only when I flew with the Thunderbirds," he said.

"We were happy then."

"But I was gone most of the time."

She took his hand and looked at him. "We were happy then," she repeated. "The three of us." She buried her face in his chest and cried as he held her in his arms.

PART TWO
BLOCKADE

Madeline O'Keith Turner is learning the rules of the game. Her recovery after the Gwen Anderson fiasco by nominating Sam Kennett for vice president was masterful, and she adroitly sidestepped the startling revelations about the Taiwan sellout to the Chinese. But it is time for a reality check in that part of the world. China is an empire and empires make their own rules.

ELIZABETH GORDON
CNC-TV News

8 ⟋

Okinawa, Japan

The two men walked through the hangar, picking their way through the wreckage that had been carefully collected and laid out in a pattern that resembled an F-15. The president of the Safety Investigating Board, a colonel, clasped his hands behind his back and did most of the talking. The investigation of the crash was finished, and the meeting with Martini was a courtesy, a verbal summary of the report he had just signed. "There were two causes of the accident. One was pilot error."

"I expected that," Martini grumbled. He had served on too many accident boards to avoid the grim truth that pilot error was the most common, direct cause of accidents.

"The other cause was a mechanical malfunction. The rear compressor variable vanes in the right engine failed at the worst possible time."

"I thought they failed to the safe position," Martini said.

"They do. But until the system sorts itself out, a massive dam of air builds up in front of the compressor, which takes a few seconds to clear—seconds they didn't have. They were slow, high AOA, in uncoordinated flight, and too damn low to the ground."

Martini's head came up. This was the first he had heard about the jet being in uncoordinated flight. There was only one way that could happen. "Are you sure Leland was cross-controlling the jet?" Martini asked.

The colonel probed among the remains of the right engine, the one that had stalled. "We modeled the crash in your simulator."

"How close can a simulator come to the real thing?"

It was a fair question, and the colonel was slow to answer. "We took the civilian contractors who run the sim up for a ride in an F-15E. They came back and fine-tuned the simulator for us. They came damn close. The only way we could get the sim to roll under the same conditions, with a compressor stall, was when it was being cross-controlled with a high AOA. Six pilots tried it with the same results."

"Were any of them able to recover?" Martini asked.

The colonel mumbled the word *no* and shook his head. "I tried it myself. God, it happens fast. I'm surprised Captain Bender was able to initiate ejection. We flew that approach over 100 times in the sim where the pilot overshoots and cross-controls to save the landing. Without a compressor stall, the pilot could salvage the approach. When we did it the other way 'round, compressor stall with no cross-control, they recovered every time."

"So you're telling me it took the two occurring in conjunction to cause the accident."

"It's all in the mishap report," the colonel said. "It was a unanimous vote for the primary cause: pilot error combined with a mechanical malfunction. You'll have your copy today." They moved into the section where the cockpit had been reassembled. Martini touched the ACES-II ejection seat that had not burned—Laurie's seat. The area in the cushions where the seat and back pad joined was stained dark with dried blood. "Blunt massive trauma," the colonel said. "Her spine collapsed on impact."

The colonel took a deep breath. He and Martini were old friends. "Mafia, there's a contributing factor. It was a unanimous vote. Supervisory error."

Martini nodded in agreement. He had no trouble accepting bad news. It was good news that he didn't trust. "I should have grounded Leland."

"Or at least kept him with an instructor pilot," the colonel added. "You've got another problem. Your flight surgeon, Captain Ryan, knew a great deal about your decision to team Leland with Bender. He testified that after the over-g incident, you ordered her to continue flying with Leland. She asked you, 'Why kill a perfectly good wizzo?' and you responded, 'Because I'm an equal opportunity employer.' Nothing damning in itself, but when combined with the accident, it makes you look bad. We voted to exclude his testimony from the mishap report when we learned he was engaged to Captain Bender—emotional stress, we figured."

"It's the truth," Martini growled. "Include it."

"Reworking the report will keep us on the island at least another day," the colonel protested.

"You got anything better to do?"

Washington, D.C.

Saturday, December 15. The date burned into Patrick Flannery Shaw, branding him forever. He would remember it like his parents remembered JFK's assassination and his grandparents, December 7, 1941. It was the day when the handwriting appeared on the wall, the veil was parted, and Armageddon occurred. The situation was so desperate that he was thinking in biblical terms, a hangover from the countless hours he spent as an altar boy in New Orleans where the parish priest had made an unknown, yet indelible impression.

Shaw had spent his entire adult life in politics and could not even breathe outside the corridors of power. He wasn't in it for money, and although he had tweaked the system enough to keep him off the streets, politics satisfied a much more basic need. By picking up the phone, people reacted to his will and did things that he was incapable of doing. It was everything to him, all he was, all he had. It gave him control.

December 15 was the day he started to lose it.

His fingers beat a relentless tattoo on his desk, an outward sign of his agitation. What were Maddy Turner's exact words? He couldn't remember he had been so shocked. But she wanted one Lieutenant General Robert Edward Bender to join her kitchen cabinet. It was her support group that met once or twice a week to discuss whatever was bothering her. Originally, it was made up of Maura O'Keith, Richard Parrish, the secretary of the treasury, and Noreen Coker, an African-American congresswoman from Los Angeles.

Occasionally, they asked Shaw to join them when they needed his particular take on a knotty problem. Until recently, that had not been a problem because Maura was a nobody and the other two were political lightweights easily controlled. But then Sam Kennett, a loose cannon who owed Shaw nothing, had been asked to join. Now Turner wanted Bender. Two loose cannons with access to the president added up to disaster on his political abacus.

Although Kennett was beyond his control, perhaps Bender was another story. He opened his private safe and fished out the file his staff had recently compiled on the general. There wasn't much, and the incurable optimism that marked his personality took a heavy blow. Bender was fifty years old, born April 1, 1951. His father had graduated from West Point in 1950, married in July of the same year, and shipped out for Korea two months later. He was killed in December. Almost nine months to the day after his parents were married, Robert Edward was born to the still grieving widow.

Bender's mother had eventually remarried, and he had spent an uneventful early life in Sacramento, California. There was no hint of the usual teenage pranks or misdeeds contrived to drive parents up the nearest wall. He had played football in high school, become an Eagle Scout, and graduated at the top of his class in 1969. There was not even a hint of one antiwar demonstration or experimentation with marijuana. He had gone directly into the Air Force Academy and, again, played football. He graduated number 2 in the class of 1973, missing the Vietnam War.

He had met the eighteen-year-old Nancy Beth Orren while a first classman at the Academy, courted her relentlessly, and they were married two days after he pinned on his second lieutenant's bars in June of 1973. Nine months later, Laurie Ann was born.

Shaw took some hope in that Bender was descended from a lusty lot who procreated at the earliest possible moment. But there were no other children and no hint of sexual impropriety. Damn! Shaw raged. How could a man do business with someone like that? Bender had gone to pilot training, flew F-16s, had a two-year tour as a Thunderbird, and moved up the rank structure, making early promotion to lieutenant colonel and then colonel. He was the commander of an F-15 wing during the 1990–1991 Gulf War and had shot down an Iraqi MiG-29 in what was described as the most aggressive and hair-raising encounter of the entire war. *Well,* Shaw thought, *the Iraqis had at least one good pilot. But apparently, Bender was better.*

After that, Bender's career had skyrocketed, and he moved through a variety of headquarters slots, commanded the test pilot school at Edwards Air Force Base, made brigadier general at an early age, and seemed to never slow down.

Come on, Shaw thought. *There's got to be something. The guy has got to have a chink in his armor. What or where is it?* He thought about the man he knew, the unbending Bender. He chuckled inwardly at his play on words. Maybe there was a way to bend him—if the temptation was right. He picked up the phone and dialed a number in the Pentagon. "What have you got on the crash that killed Captain Laurie Bender?" he asked.

Bender came through the west gate of the White House at the usual time the Monday after Laurie's funeral. He walked up the drive with a small group of workers. Although all of them worked for other government agencies and were, supposedly, only assigned to the White House for special projects, Bender had seen them so often that he knew each by sight. They often talked, and it struck him how much they had in common. All of them worked there temporarily and it was not the be-all and end-all of their existence, not like so many others who came and went with each change of administration.

"Only eight more days until Christmas," a gardener said. "Then we get to take it all down."

"It must get pretty routine," Bender replied. A nod answered him. *Eight days to Christmas,* Bender thought. *Eight more miserable days.* He would give it until the first of the year, he decided. Then he would be gone, one way or the other.

He was surprised to see his office door open. Then he saw two skinny legs in black leggings swinging back and forth from the only chair. Sarah was waiting for him. "School's out?" he asked as he came in.

"Yeah, I guess so," Sarah replied. She slipped off the chair and handed him an oversized homemade envelope. She looked up at him and then darted out the door. He glanced at the envelope. "To General and Mrs. Bender" was written on the front in a childish scrawl. He broke the seal and pulled out a handmade card. On the front was a finger painting of long, narrow green, yellow, and gold leaves with white flowers on top. Inside, Sarah had written, "We're so sorry." She and Brian had signed it.

It was a card that Nancy needed to see.

"General," a seductive voice called. It was one of Shaw's gorgeous assistants. "The chief of staff would like to see you in his office."

Bender checked his watch. It was three minutes after seven. "I didn't know he came to work this early," Bender replied. There was no reply, and he followed the young woman up the stairs.

"Close the door," Shaw said when Bender entered his large corner office. He waved at a chair. "The president," Shaw began, "wants you to join her kitchen cabinet."

"I'm the wrong man," Bender protested. "General Overmeyer is not going to approve—"

"What Overmeyer approves of," Shaw muttered, "is not the issue. First meeting's this morning, eight-thirty. The president's private study in the residence. Be there."

"Will that be all?" Bender asked.

Shaw's fingers drummed his desk. *Was this the time?* He decided to chance it. "I saw the preliminary report on the accident," Shaw said. "It didn't say much."

"They never do," Bender replied.

"I've heard," Shaw said, carefully watching Bender, "through the grapevine that accident investigators often cover up what really happened to save some asshole's career."

"It's been known to happen," Bender conceded. He made no attempt to explain how a previous Air Force chief of staff called the Buzzard had solved that problem with a vengeance. The Buzzard had simply held everyone to a higher standard—the commanders, the investigators, everyone. Those who couldn't meet the new standard found themselves on the outside as civilians looking in.

"It must be terrible knowing there's a chance of the accident being covered up, especially when your child was a victim."

Was Laurie a victim? Bender wondered. He had to step back from that pit. To look into it was too threatening, too close to chaos. "She knew the risks," he finally said.

He's thinking about it, Shaw decided. He made his voice gentle. "General, if there's a cover-up, we can fix it. No one needs to get away with killing your daughter."

An icy cold gripped Bender. He knew what Shaw was offering—vengeance. It was his for the taking.

"What do you know about this guy Martini?" Shaw asked, dangling the bait. "I hear they call him Mafia. That doesn't sound good."

So that's the offering, Bender thought. *A wing commander's career for my daughter's life.* What did he know about Martini? Not much. Only that he had been a Thunderbird and had flown right wing. "Without seeing the final report," he said, "anything on my part would be pure speculation."

"If you want, I can get you a copy of the Safety Investigation Board's mishap report."

So he knows the right terminology, Bender thought. He stared at Shaw for a moment before nodding his head and leaving.

Shaw watched him disappear out the door. He went back to work, humming a tuneless melody.

"I hope you all know Robert Bender," Turner said, introducing him to the small group. To be sure, she went around the room, introducing her kitchen cabinet. The two women and two men were seated comfortably in her private study drinking coffee and only Richard Parrish, the secretary of the treasury, stood up. They shook hands. "And of course, you and Maura have already met."

Sam Kennett stretched his hand out. "Good to have you aboard." They shook hands, and Bender felt reassured by his firm grip and steady look. His instincts told him that Kennett was a man he could trust.

Noreen Coker gave him a warm and friendly smile. The African-American representative was a big woman, over six feet tall and weighed 285 pounds. The tight dark red outfit she was wearing did little to streamline her bulk. "Honey, it's a good thing I'm a married woman," she said. "Otherwise, you wouldn't be safe."

"Noreen," Turner said, "behave yourself. Don't be fooled by the act, Robert. Noreen is not what she seems."

The strident black activist, inner-city facade, that Coker presented for public consumption slipped away. Underneath was an educated woman with a future in national politics. "General, we need to hear from the military. Don't be afraid to speak out. Otherwise, there's no good reason for you being here. You give us balance."

Bender sat in one of the straight-back chairs at the end of the facing couches. William, the butler, offered him a cup of coffee and then withdrew. At first, he thought he was caught in a coffee klatch, but the conversation turned serious the moment Turner mentioned tax reform. Maura said little as the group hammered the issue and created a philosophical framework. It was obvious that they were not in agreement, yet all respected the others' opinions. He was amazed how rapidly Turner pulled it all together. She knew how to run a meeting.

"Sam, I want you to take the lead on this. Work with Richard and put together a policy team. It's time to get it on paper. I want something concrete for the staff to chew on, say, right after the new year."

"That's asking a lot," Parrish said. "But we should have a point of departure by then."

The meeting was rapidly drawing to a close. "Well, child," Noreen Coker said to Bender, "why haven't we heard from you? Don't go telling me that you're in over your head.''

"When it comes to taxes," Bender said, "I am. But I can tell you, you're in for the political fight of your lives."

"We didn't know this?" Coker scoffed. "And it's 'us,' child, not 'you' who are in this." Bender felt his face blush. "Now don't go playing the innocent virgin."

"You, we," he corrected, "need to know the opposition early on. In military terms, it's called a *threat estimate*. What have they got, who have they got, and where have they got it? Who's going to lead the fight against us? What intelligence do we have on them? What are their weaknesses? What are their strengths? How will they attack?"

Turner had never approached politics from a military point of view, but she saw the logic. "Who should be working this part of the problem?"

Bender thought for a moment. "Mrs. Coker and Mr. Shaw."

Coker's laugh filled the room. "Me in bed with Shaw? Oh, Lord, what would my mother think?" She shook her head. "Well, this is Washington—it had to happen sooner or later."

"Senator Leland," Shaw said, "may I introduce Lieutenant General Robert Bender." The two men shook hands and sat down in Shaw's office, which had been stripped of all Christmas and New Year decorations. "I apologize for the delay, Senator. We'll be going in to the president in a few minutes."

"It's quite all right, Patrick," John Leland said. His voice had the rich rolling tones of an accomplished orator, and he possessed the full head of gray hair and jowly cheeks the public expected of one of the most influential senators in Washington, D.C. John Leland's political career in Washington stretched over thirty years, and he was widely regarded as the city's leading rainmaker. With a few well-chosen phone calls, he could change the political weather of the capital overnight and blow whatever legislation he wanted through the Senate. Because Leland was the chairman of the Armed Services Committee and the acknowledged leader of the opposition party, Shaw always made the appropriate groveling sounds whenever Leland called and kept the door to the Oval Office wide open.

The senator studied Bender for a moment. "This was a very unhappy Christmas for my family," he said. "I was saddened to learn that we have both suffered a deep personal loss. Chris was my nephew."

"Yes, I know," Bender replied. "Thank you for your concern. You have my deepest sympathy, and please extend our condolences to Captain Leland's family."

"General, have you had a chance to read the accident report?" The senator's voice had gone flat.

Bender shook his head, wondering what had happened to Shaw's promise to get him a copy. He shot a look at Shaw. There was no reaction. "I am concerned about the veracity of this report," Leland said. Before Bender could reply, Alice Fay announced the president was ready for them, and the three men walked into the Oval Office.

After the usual exchange of New Year's greetings, Leland came right to the point of his visit. He snapped open his briefcase and extracted a thick document printed on oversized paper with a green cover. "Madam President, have you read the accident report?"

"No, I haven't," Turner replied. "Patrick, Robert, have either of you?"

Shaw shook his head. Actually, he had read it the night before, and his copy was in his office at home, where it would stay.

"No, ma'am," Bender answered. "This is the first time I've seen it. Senator, may I?" Leland handed Bender the report, and he quickly thumbed through to the relevant findings. "As I expected, pilot error combined with a mechanical failure."

Leland ignored him and focused on Turner. "Madam President, forgive me, but my staff has fully digested this report and claim that it is a cover-up by the Air Force."

"Robert?" Turner asked.

"I've just seen the report," Bender said. "I need to read it before I can—"

"Did you know your daughter was pregnant?" Leland demanded. "What was she doing flying?"

Leland's words drove a cold spike into Bender, ripping and tearing at his emotions. He felt his heart race, and he forced himself to breathe. "Your daughter was pregnant" rang in his mind, drowning out everything else. How could he tell Nancy, especially after going through Christmas without Laurie? But he would have to. Their relationship was too deep and trusting for him to hide it from her. "Please give me a few moments," he finally managed.

"I understand," Leland said kindly. He and Turner exchanged a few words, circling in on the reason for the senator's visit.

Bender forced his mind to focus and buried his emotions. He would keep them there, forever hidden. While they talked, he turned to the front of the document and read the names of the officers who were on the board. He only knew the president by reputation. No problem there. Then he quickly scanned the document, looking for the telltale omissions and phrases that announced a cover-up was in play. Nothing. He scanned through the appendixes and slowed to read the flight surgeon's testimony. Then he read the hard part: the cause of death.

"At first glance," he finally said, "it appears to be very straightforward."

"Are you sure?" Shaw asked from his end of the room. "It was your daughter they killed."

"*They* didn't kill Laurie or Chris," Bender said. "Pilot error in conjunction with a mechanical failure killed them."

"Chris was a good pilot," Leland said.

Bender's mental alarm went off. He had lost his situational awareness and should have caught the signals earlier. Was his own grief getting in the way of doing his job? "I would have been very proud if I had a nephew who flew fighters," he ventured.

"I followed Chris's career very closely," Leland said. "That's why I know he was an excellent pilot."

Bender flipped through the report, gaining time to think. He read the appendix that detailed Chris's and Laurie's training. All the pieces were there. He wanted to ask the senator how he knew Chris was a good pilot. Had he ever flown with him? Leland's words came at him in bunches.

". . . Chris was an accomplished pilot . . . There was no pilot error involved . . . I am fully aware of maintenance and contracting problems . . . an airplane with known problems."

Bender's warning system was now in full alarm. He had commanded a wing of F-15s and flown over 500 hours in the jet. "What problems?" he asked, almost conversationally. "The Eagle is an old aircraft and is a well-known commodity. It doesn't have any problems that I know of."

Leland ignored him. "Madam President, Chris was a victim of military incompetence and bungling. How can I tell his parents that his death will go unpunished?"

Bender was reading the report and listening at the same time, not the best way to carry on a discussion with a U.S. senator. "Sir, I want to know the truth of the matter as much as you do. But so far, I haven't found anything in this report that suggests a cover-up."

Leland gave him a cold look. "I want this man Martini relieved from duty and court-martialed."

Turner moved from her desk and sat beside the senator. She placed her hand on his. "We will find the truth. I promise you." They exchanged the customary words ending the meeting, and Shaw escorted the senator to his waiting limousine.

Turner leaned back against the edge of her desk and crossed her arms and ankles. "Well, Robert? What do you think?"

"I've seen it before, Madam President."

"Must you be so formal? Robert?"

"I'm sorry, Mrs. President, but it's my nature. I'm much more comfortable—"

She nodded. "You were saying?"

"It *is* very hard to accept the death of a loved one, especially a young and healthy son or daughter. It's natural for Chris Leland's family to believe he was a victim. And if there's a victim, there's got to be someone who was responsible."

"Was he a victim?" she asked, coming to the heart of the matter.

"Yes."

Turner was shocked by the answer. "I know it's hard

for you to criticize the Air Force," she said, "especially in front of a senator."

"You have to know how to read the report," he told her. "It lays it all out." He paused, fighting to regain his composure. *This is Laurie you're talking about,* he thought. "The primary cause of the accident was pilot error in combination with a mechanical malfunction. Both had to happen simultaneously for the crash to occur." He hesitated. This conversation was tearing him apart. "That's a fact, pure and simple. There is a contributing factor: supervisory error."

"Is this part of the cover-up?" Turner asked. She was like a bulldog, unable to let go of the idea.

He shook his head. "There was no cover-up."

"Then what is there?" she asked.

"Senator Leland trying to unload his guilt. He desperately wants to do an 'off me, on you.' "

"Guilt for what?"

"For Chris Leland being there in the first place." The look on her face was ample warning that she did not understand and that he was on dangerous ground. "Chris Leland was a victim of the system. What did the senator say? 'I followed his career very closely.' The Air Force plays politics like any government agency and if a senator, who happens to be the chairman of the Armed Services Committee, is interested in a nephew's career, that kid is going to get every break in the book." He handed her the mishap report and pointed to Leland's training record. "Chris was a below average pilot who was carried through the system because of the senator's political influence."

Turner was with him. "So this supervisory error was Martini caving in to political pressure."

Bender nodded. "Indirectly, yes. Leland may have been below average, but he was qualified to fly the jet. So when a decision had to be made, he got the benefit of the doubt—every single time because of his uncle. If Chris had been totally unfit, it would have been an easy decision. But he wasn't."

"Then Martini should be court-martialed."

"For what? For living with the sins of the system? I would have done the same thing if I was pressed for pilots.

And Martini was. He had been in command ninety-three days at the time of the accident and had inherited a weak pilot because of circumstances beyond his control. He knew it, addressed the problem, and had teamed Leland with one of his strongest backseaters.''

"Who was your daughter," Turner murmured. "How did the senator know she was expecting? Is that in the report?''

"I folded the corner of the page. It's near the bottom.''

Turner found the page and read how the autopsy revealed Laurie Bender was two to three weeks pregnant. "She probably didn't even know," Turner said. She returned to her chair, putting the wide expanse of her desk between them. "Maybe Martini should be court-martialed. Perhaps I need to send every commander in the armed services a message not to play at politics.''

"Should you be impeached for Roberts's sellout of Taiwan?" Turner stared at him, shocked by his words. No one, not even Maura or Shaw spoke that frankly to her. Not now, now that she was the president. "Tell the chairman," Bender urged. "Let General Overmeyer fix the problem. That's what he's hired for.''

Turner's face clouded over. "I can hardly believe what I'm hearing. Overmeyer won't change a thing, and you're defending the system.''

"I trust the system," he said. "And until I know otherwise, I trust the people making it work.''

"Even Martini?''

He nodded. "Even Martini.''

Turner exploded. "This is your daughter we're talking about! She and Chris were sacrificed to the system. Hasn't that sunk in? Your daughter is dead. Haven't you got the picture yet?''

Bender stared at her. Hard. He had the picture. "The page that I marked—turn to the next page—at the bottom.'' He waited while she read. Her face paled. It was the clinical description of how Laurie Bender had died. "I know what blunt massive trauma means." His voice cracked. "I've seen it." She could only look at him. He was a man on the edge, fighting for control. "Is there anything else, ma'am.'' He was begging to be excused.

"No. Thank you, General Bender." After he had left, she sat down and spun around to gaze out the window. "Not my son," she said to no one. "Not while I'm president."

Shaw knocked at the door and entered. "Cabinet meeting in ten minutes, Mizz President."

"Patrick, I'd like to know a little more about General Bender's service record."

It was late Sunday afternoon and the snowstorm that had descended out of Canada had frozen the capital in a miserable, raw, half-light. High winds and ice had knocked out the power to much of the city, and emergency crews were fighting a losing battle to restore basic services. But the lights in the White House had blinked only twice before the emergency generators had kicked in, sparing the inhabitants of the executive mansion from the problems swirling around them.

Patrick Shaw wasn't so lucky, and when the Watergate complex lost power, his condominium turned quickly into a cold storage locker. Feeling chivalrous, not to mention frozen, he bundled up his young female companion and headed for his office in the White House. Lacking a chauffeur, he drove and barely made the three-quarters-of-a-mile journey down H Street. As he expected, the West Wing was mostly deserted.

With a fresh pot of hot coffee delivered from the kitchen and his companion curled up on a couch, he had time to thaw and do some serious thinking about tax reform. Too many legislators and lobbyists were getting wind of Turner's plans to reform the system, and the signals coming from the Hill worried him. No matter which way he cut the deal, Madeline Turner was rushing headlong into disaster and taking him with her. His thoughts turned away from tax reform when his companion sent him another, much more basic signal when she shrugged off her panties and kicked them on his desk. "Lock the door, darlin'," he muttered as the phone rang.

It was the president. "Patrick, I knew you'd be here. I'm in my study. Why don't you come up? Let's talk taxes."

It was a command he couldn't ignore no matter how much the lower regions of his body protested. The president needs a distraction, he decided. He pulled Bender's file from his safe and added the videotape and thin report a contact in the Pentagon had sent him. He lumped it all together with his thick folder on tax reform. "Put your clothes back on, darlin'." He smiled and dropped her panties in a desk drawer. "A souvenir of your first visit. Now, I'll be a while, so don't you go starting without me." He closed the door behind him and ambled down the colonnade that led to the mansion, considering his next move. He knocked on the door of the president's study and was mildly surprised when Brian opened the door. He knew how he would play it.

He settled into his usual spot. "I've got somethin' you might like to see before we get started, Mizz President. I've been rummaging around in the Bender attic. Pretty interesting stuff. Turns out he's a roarin', snortin' top gun. A certified aerial assassin." Brian perked up and moved away from the football game he was watching on television. He sat beside his mother and listened. "Did you know he shot down a MiG in the Persian Gulf War?" Shaw didn't wait for an answer. "Pretty impressive stuff. I've got the videotape from the mission."

"Mom, can I see it?" Brian asked.

"I don't think so," Turner answered.

"Mom," he begged, "I've seen stuff like this before."

Reluctantly, she gave in and let him play the tape. It wasn't what she expected. After a brief title identifying the pilot, date, time, and place, the Iraqi skyscape flashed onto the screen. They were seeing what Bender saw through his HUD at 18,000 feet on a cloudy day. Brian interpreted the symbology on the screen. "It's sorta like an F-16's," he said.

"Bolo flight," a woman's voice said. "Four bandits. Snap vector three-six-zero, bearing three-zero-zero at thirty-five, on the deck, heading zero-eight-five, speed four-eight-five. You are cleared to engage. Repeat, you are cleared to engage."

Bender's voice answered as the picture on the screen swirled and the ground rushed at them. "Rog, Phoenix.

Bolo's engaged." Nothing in his voice indicated he was heading into a fight at 800 miles an hour and descending toward the ground at over 10,000 feet a minute.

Brian crouched in front of the TV and told them what was happening. "Phoenix is an AWACS, a radar plane, ordering him to go after four MiGs 35 miles away."

"Arm 'em up," Bender radioed.

"Reb, I've got a problem," Bender's wingman answered. "I've got a CAS light."

"Who's Reb?" Turner asked.

"That's Bender's personal call sign," Shaw said. "I think it stands for his initials."

Again, Bender's cool voice came over the radio. "You're cleared to home plate. Phoenix, copy all?"

The woman's voice answered, much more rapid than Bender's. "Copy all, Reb. Are you still engaged?"

"Roger that," Bender answered. "Contact ten o'clock, 20 miles, four bandits." He had a radar paint on the bandits.

"Contact is your target," the AWACS replied.

"Judy," Bender transmitted, telling the AWACS that he was taking over the intercept.

"He's taking on four all alone!" Brian yelled. The TV screen filled with hills and rocks as Bender descended below the MiGs. He was so low that it looked like he was going to hit the ground. "He's below 100 feet!" He pointed to the vertical airspeed bar in Bender's HUD. "He's going over 500 miles an hour!"

They could hear Bender's breathing, much louder now but still regular, controlled, and rhythmic. "Tallyho," he transmitted. The symbology on the HUD flashed indicating he had a radar lock-on. "Fox One," Bender said. The smoke trail of an air-to-air radar missile leaped out in front of him, tracing an arc through the sky toward a fast-moving dot.

"He's fired a missile!" Brian shouted.

"Calm down," Turner said. She caught herself. Her voice was much more rapid and edgy than Bender's on the videotape.

"Radar broke lock," Bender radioed. "Missile's ballistic." The picture turned topsy-turvy as Bender turned into the bandits and sliced head-on through their formation. The nose of his aircraft pitched up as he reversed back into the fight. "Fulcrums," Bender shouted.

"They're MiG-29s," Brian shouted, jumping up and down. The MiG-29 bore a striking resemblance to an F-15 but was about the same size of an F-16.

"Brian!" his mother said, stopping the tape. "Calm down."

"But a MiG-29 is better than an F-15!" the boy shouted.

Shaw's easy laugh broke the tension. "Hey, good buddy, this happened eleven years ago. We know he made it."

"Oh, yeah," Brian said, a sheepish look on his face. "Can I see the rest of it?" Without waiting for permission, he hit the play button.

The picture was back, the radios deafening as the AWACS directed other fighters into the fight. "Strangle the chatter," Bender shouted. The commotion on the radios tapered off. The picture on the TV again filled with terrain as a dark shape flashed by in front of Bender's jet, passing from left to right. He had avoided a midair collision by inches. "Coming back to the left," he radioed, his voice heavy and laboring as he fought the g's. "Fox Two!" he shouted. Again, the TV screen recorded the action as the smoke trail of an infrared-guided missile streaked out in front of the F-15. But he was too low, and the missile hit the ground. "Fuck!" Bender shouted.

"Well, I'll be," Shaw allowed. "He does know the F word."

The screen twisted and spun as he rolled his jet, turned to the right, and started jinking. "Bandit, at my six," Bender radioed, trying to shake off the MiG that was behind him. The picture stabilized for a brief second as another MiG filled his HUD. Bender was in the saddle and tracking for a gunshot. "Fox Three," he shouted as he came off and pulled up into a tight loop, trying to shake the MiG that was still on his tail.

"He's too low!" Brian shouted. He turned his face away from the TV and looked at his mother. The tension was overwhelming and he couldn't bear to watch.

"You wanted to see this," Turner said, unable to take her eyes off the screen. She heard Bender grunt as he fought the *g*'s and turned the tight loop into an Immelmann. He rolled out on top, 1,000 feet above the ground, and jinked to the left before again diving. He was on the tale of another MiG, this one down on the deck and trying desperately to escape from the fight. "Fox Two," he said, a little calmer than before. He had a much better shot this time, and no one was on his tail. The MiG was in a shallow turn to the right as the AIM-9 missile tracked. The doomed pilot must have seen the missile coming and tightened up his turn, rolling past the vertical. He ejected just as the missile exploded.

The HUD's videotape recorded the ejection seat as it shot out of the inverted aircraft, heading straight for the ground. A puff of dirt marked the spot where it hit as Bender flew over barely fifty feet above the ground. "Splash one bandit," Bender transmitted, his voice still staccato-quick. "Phoenix, any more trade?"

"Negative trade," the woman controller onboard the AWACS answered. "I hold the two bandits in Iran. Do not pursue. Repeat, do not pursue."

"What happened to the third guy?" another F-15 pilot asked, anxious to enter the fight. There was no answer as the videotape played out.

Brian hit the reverse button, playing the tape backward. "That was great!" he said.

Turner folded her arms. "Where did you learn all that?" she asked her son.

"General Bender," Brian answered. "He likes talking about flying and real stuff."

She turned to Shaw. "He seems so decent, so rational, civilized. What kind of man is he?"

Shaw shrugged an answer. "I don't know."

9 ⟍

Washington, D.C.

Robert Bender was shoveling snow off his driveway Sunday evening when the second wave of the storm hit. He kept shoveling as the snow kept falling, and it became a personal challenge. Finally, he gave up and leaned on the handle of the shovel, defeated. He was worried. Nancy was working a volunteer shift at the hospital downtown, and he didn't like the thought of her being stranded in the inner city. He thought about his options and allowed a little smile. This was the type of challenge he enjoyed. Within minutes, he had tire chains on the rear wheels of his four-wheel-drive Ford Explorer.

He glanced outside at the blowing snow and remembered the winter they had spent at Offutt Air Force Base outside of Omaha, Nebraska. He rummaged through the boxes in the basement until he found another set of tire chains and mounted them on the front wheels. After throwing a shovel, two blankets, a survival kit, and a thermos of hot soup in the Explorer, he called Nancy on his cellular phone. "How's business?" he asked.

"It's not," she answered. "We're snowed in and the patients are snowed out."

"I'll come and get you," he said.

She laughed. "Robert to the rescue! You've been itching for a chance to use the Explorer, but I'll be OK here.

144

Why don't you wait until morning when the roads are clear?''

"No problem," he said. "I'm on my way. I'll call if I get stuck."

She wished he would stay home, but after twenty-eight years of marriage, she knew what he was like. "Be careful," she cautioned.

With chains mounted on all four wheels, the Explorer turned into a tank and he made good time crossing the Capitol Street Bridge. The real battle started when he hit the city streets, but by plowing down the center, he maintained a slow progress. Twice, he pushed stalled cars out of the way and, once, detoured down a sidewalk. He was thoroughly enjoying himself until the heart of the storm moved over the city and stalled. The wind rocked the truck, and snow piled against the windshield wipers, dragging them to a slow beat.

He paused to fix his position by using a GPS (global positioning system) receiver he had added to the Explorer's survival kit. He was eight blocks from the hospital. A hard knocking at his window startled him. A hand scraped the snow back and a frost-encrusted face appeared, shouting at him. It was an African-American woman, and her words were jumbled, incoherent, and filled with panic. "What do you want?" he shouted back. An inner alarm went off, warning him that trouble was inches away. More shouting, the words still senseless. He started to inch forward when the words finally made sense.

"My man . . . got's to get t'hospital."

Bender did not make a conscious decision; it was simply a part of him, the result of years of experience making choices and being responsible for others. He opened the door. "Where is he?"

"Over d'ere." She pointed to a car that had broadsided a parked car. The wind blew his hat away when he opened the back door. A man was doubled up in pain on the backseat.

"What's the matter?" he shouted, dragging the semiconscious man out.

"Don' know," the woman answered. "He jus' doubles up."

"Scrape the windshield while I get him in the car," he ordered. The woman climbed on the Explorer's hood and pulled the heavy snow off the windshield with her bare hands. "Let's go!" he shouted. She moved slowly, the cold numbing her, and crawled in the rear seat. Bender was thankful for the blast of heavy warm air coming from the heater, keeping the threat of hypothermia at bay. He called ahead on the cellular phone, and a medical team was waiting for them at the emergency dock.

Free of his charges, he bulldozed his way into the parking lot and abandoned the Explorer in what looked like a parking spot. He jammed on a knit watch cap, pulled up his hood, and waded through the snow back to the hospital. Nancy was waiting for him by the entrance to the emergency department. She gave him the look that had captivated him the first time they met. "Nanook of the North," she said, "mushing to the rescue." She nodded at a woman huddled over a cup of coffee and wrapped in a blanket. "You saved her husband. He has acute appendicitis." She led the way down the hall to her cubicle. "Not much business tonight. It's been this way all afternoon." She locked his coat and snow boots in her locker. "Come on, I'll give you a tour." She gave him a smile he hadn't seen in weeks.

He followed her through the hospital, responding to the tone in her voice while he tried to absorb everything she was saying. Her enthusiasm was infectious, and he was certain the dark days following Laurie's death were behind them. Even the pain from learning their daughter had been pregnant had slipped into the dark recesses of memory. But he could sense something was different between them.

Her pager bleeped, and she walked hurriedly back to her office. "It's Shalandra, one of my patients. We've got her on an experimental vaccine program that eases the craving and dependency on cocaine. But to work, we have to keep her off coke. Unfortunately, she's caught up in an abusive relationship and can't get out of it." He listened while Nancy talked to the woman on the phone. "Did you call the police? . . . They probably didn't come because of the snow. . . . If you can get here, we can take care of you. . . . Get out if you think he's going to kill you. . . . No, Shalandra. There's no way I can pick you up.''

"I'll go get her," Bender said.

Nancy put her hand over the phone. "It's too dangerous out there. The police have to bring them in.''

"I saw a cop in the cafeteria," he said. "I can drive if she goes with me.''

She shook her head. "It's a war zone out there, even now.''

"Maybe inside, but not in the streets, not in this weather. Tell Shalandra if she can get outside, we'll pick her up.''

Nancy looked at her husband. He would never change. "Be careful.''

"Turn here," Patrolwoman Elena Murphy said, pointing to the left. Murphy was a tall and slender African-American, made bulky by the heavy anorak she was wearing. He plowed through the snow barely able to see the middle of the road. "This is the last time I listen to some dumb-ass white man," she grumbled.

He shot a glance at her. "Murphy, I think you'd do this with or without me.''

She ignored him and pointed to a four-story building. "Over there, beside those steps." He pulled to the right, and a small figure materialized out of the blowing snow. It was Shalandra. She tried to run, but the snow was too heavy and dragged at her shoes. She stumbled and fell.

Murphy was out of the car and moving toward her when Bender heard a man shout, his anger carrying over the wind. "What'cha doin', bitch?" Two shots rang out, and Murphy went down. Then Bender saw the shooter—a big, shadowy hulk of a man—stumble down the steps of the building and head for the two figures lying in the snow. He pulled at the slide of the pistol he was carrying and screamed, his obscenities broken by the wind. ". . . don' fuck wid me! . . . I'm a mean mutha fucka!" Again, he pulled at the slide, trying to clear a jam. He crouched on the sidewalk behind a parked snow-covered car and worked at the pistol.

Bender didn't hesitate. He gunned the Explorer and

cranked the steering wheel hard to the right. The chains bit into the snow, and the truck skidded around, heading directly for the car where the shooter was hiding. He saw the man's head bob up from the opposite side of the car and disappear. Bender rammed into the side of the car and pushed it up onto the sidewalk. The shrieking and tearing of metal drowned out whatever human cry might have been there. He backed away in time to see Murphy struggle to her feet. She was pulling the much smaller Shalandra with her. Bender reached across and opened the front passenger door while Murphy shoved Shalandra into the rear seat. She was a wisp of a girl, her face bloodied and bruised, and was holding a blood-soaked rag to her right ear. Then Murphy was in the car and they were moving again.

"I thought you were dead," he said.

"That's why we wear vests," Murphy told him. "Damn, this is brand-new." She fingered two bullet holes in her anorak. They would have been lethal if she had not been wearing a bullet-proof vest. "I ought'a make you pay for this."

"If you can give me directions back to the hospital, it's a deal."

Murphy gave him a disgusted look. "You know we did this for a fourteen-year-old nigger hooker?"

"Does it matter what she was?"

Murphy didn't answer at first. Then, "You really a general?"

"That's what they tell me."

She shook her head. "This is the last time I listen to some dumb-ass white man."

Bender allowed a tight smile. "I've heard that line before, Murphy."

Nancy sipped at her coffee. "You're becoming some sort of hero around here."

Bender leaned back in his chair, stretched out his long legs, and took in the hospital's deserted cafeteria. It was after midnight, and the police had left after an hour of intense questioning. "I can tell from the admiring audience. Are you ready to go home?"

She looked at him. "Yes. No."

He smiled. "Sounds like we got a problem with decisions."

She reached out and touched the top of his hand. It was a warm and loving gesture that meant she wanted to have a serious talk. "Are you still thinking of retiring?" A nod answered her question. "The hospital has offered me a full-time job as a counselor."

"And you want to take it," he said. It wasn't a question. He knew his wife too well.

"I can make a difference here," she said. They looked at each other. All the pain she had been hiding was back, there for him to see. "This is how I'm hanging on," she told him.

"I know. But I'm a fish out of water in this town." He humphed. "Actually, I'm more like a beached whale about to be rendered for oil. We've got to get out of here."

She clenched his hand, and they looked at each other. "I want to stay."

The signals were all there, and for the first time in their marriage, they were on opposite tracks. "Let's go home," he said.

Okinawa, Japan

An observer can see it all from Habu Hill, the grassy bluff that overlooks the runways at Kadena. In front of Habu Hill, to the north, the concrete expanse of the parallel runways stretches almost two miles from left to right. Most of the activity on the flight line takes place east of the hill, around the hardened aircraft shelters, the long flow-through shelter, hangars, and buildings where the three F-15 squadrons are located. To the west, less than a mile away, the East China Sea shimmers in the sun. Across the runways, on the north side of the base, are another set of buildings, hangars, and a vast concrete parking ramp, now mostly deserted.

A small plaque on Habu Hill tells how it was named in honor of the SR-71 reconnaissance jet that flew missions out of Kadena until it was retired from service in

1990. On Okinawa, the twin-engined SR-71 Blackbird had earned the name Habu after the deadly black cobra that inhabits the island and bears such a strong resemblance to the spy plane.

But no observer was standing on Habu Hill that breezy morning on Tuesday, January 8, when a black stiletto-shaped apparition appeared on final approach over the East China Sea and touched down on runway 5 right. A bright reddish-orange drag chute billowed behind the long dark shadow as the supersonic aircraft slowed to a crawl and then stopped. The jet dropped its drag chute on the runway and taxied into the old Little Creek hangar on the north side of the base.

A Habu, the last of the three SR-71s that had been returned to service, had come home and was safe in its nest.

A hunch-shouldered Air Force captain who rarely saw the light of day met Brigadier General Martini at the entrance of the building less than fifty yards from the Habu's hangar. No plaque or sign identified the building or gave any hint of its function, and even Martini did not know the exact nature of the intelligence that was produced inside. The captain was about to give him his first clue. "The imagery is coming out of the processor now," the captain explained. He led the way through a set of double security doors and into a large room. They stood in front of a projection screen as the high-resolution film scrolled out of the processing unit.

"Only the SR-71 can give us this quick a response time," the captain said, "and nothing matches its quality." He froze a frame and gave a low whistle. "Son of a bitch. Will you look at that." He fast-forwarded to another frame. "General, this is not good. The PLA never stood down after positioning in front of Taiwan last August." He pointed to the ships in the harbor at Fuchow on the mainland opposite Taiwan and counted. "Now they've brought in five, six, seven more surface combatants."

Again, the machine whirred, and this time the captain froze on the frame of an air base near Taipei on Taiwan. "They've almost doubled the aircraft deployed in the forward area opposite us." He slowed down and mumbled to himself as he scanned a supply dump. He hit the rewind button. "General, we've got to get this to Omaha ASAP."

"What are we looking at?" Martini asked.

"A quantum jump in their offensive capability," the captain said. "Offhand, I'd say we're getting a definite signal about their intentions."

Martini left the building and drove along Perimeter Road, around the west end of the runway, past Habu Hill, and back to his headquarters. Away from the flight line, the base turned into a community with neatly manicured lawns and pristine buildings. Martini drove slowly, fully aware that he was in command of a $6 billion operation and responsible for 7,300 airmen and over 11,000 family members. It was a large and complex air base and a happy one. But he was not a happy man. Every instinct told him to bring his base to a wartime footing. But what if he was misreading the signals? He didn't pursue that line of reasoning, for if he was wrong, there would be 1,000 coroners presiding at the inquest of his career.

But what were the consequences if he didn't act? Fortunately, he also knew the answer to that question. And for all this, he was paid $87,000 a year.

Washington, D.C.

The newspaper was on Bender's desk when he came to work that same Tuesday. The story on page 3 was circled in red and related how one Lieutenant General Robert Bender and Patrolwoman Elena Murphy had rescued a fourteen-year-old African-American prostitute off the streets at the height of the snowstorm. The girl, whose name was being withheld because of her age, had been mauled by her pimp. The pimp had tried to cut off her right ear before she escaped. The pimp had chased her and fired two shots at Patrolwoman Murphy, striking her in the chest. Fortunately, Murphy was wearing a bullet-proof vest and his 9-millimeter automatic had jammed. Bender had used his vehicle as a battering ram and crushed the pimp under a parked car. Patrolwoman Murphy claimed Bender had saved their lives by his quick action. The pimp's frozen body was found the next morning under the car, the gun still in his hand. Ballistics matched the gun with the two slugs taken from Murphy's vest. No charges were being filed in the incident.

He grudgingly gave the reporter high marks for getting the story absolutely right. But it wasn't the way he wanted to make the news.

"Sir, may I come in?" Brian Turner asked. He was standing in the doorway, shifting his weight from one foot to the other, the F-16 manual under his arm.

"Sure," Bender said, waving the boy inside.

Brian struggled with his emotions and searched for the right words. The man in front of him did not meet the stereotypes demanded by television, the movies, and his friends. "I saw the article in the newspaper. It says you killed a man."

Bender studied the fourteen-year-old before answering. "He was trying to shoot the people I was with, Brian. I didn't have a choice."

"I, ah, I," Brian stammered. Bender waited patiently, not rushing the boy. "What did you think about? I mean—" Brian's voice trailed off. He didn't know what he meant, only that he needed to talk about it.

"I didn't have time to think about it," Bender said.

"What if you had made a mistake or if his gun hadn't jammed?"

Bender gave a little shrug. "I don't know. We live with a lot of uncertainties in life. We just have to do the best we can at the time."

"I wish I had been there."

"Why?"

"Nothing ever happens around here," he mumbled. "People only talk all the time." He dropped the F-16 manual on the desk. "Is a MiG-29 better than an F-15?"

He's seen the videotape, Bender thought. He shook his head. "It's a serious threat for an F-15, but no, it's not better." He pointed at the manual. "You can keep that."

"Mom told me to return it. Thanks anyway." He spun around and darted out the door. Bender leaned back in his chair. Had he overstepped his bounds with Brian?

The phone rang, demanding his attention. It was Alice

Fay, Shaw's secretary. "The kitchen cabinet is meeting in twenty minutes," she told him. "Oh, General, we are very proud of you."

"Thanks, Mrs. Raskin. But I just happened to be there." He hung up. *I should have said that to Brian,* he thought.

Madeline O'Keith Turner looked up from her spot on the couch when Bender came through the door of her private study. She was glad he was the first one to arrive and smiled. "Coffee?" She watched him as he moved over to the tea cart. *A fascinating man,* she thought. She had never met anyone like him. He was intelligent and civilized and did not match her image of the military robot. Yet he was part of a system that she hated and feared as a mother. He could kill another human being without a second thought and order other men, maybe even her son, to sacrifice their lives in battle.

Can I ever understand men like you? she wondered.

The vice president and Noreen Coker came in. "Sam," the congresswoman said, "sooner or later you're going to realize big is beautiful."

"In your case," Kennett replied, "I've known it for years." Richard Parrish, the secretary of the treasury, and Maura O'Keith were right behind them, completing Turner's kitchen cabinet.

"Before we talk taxes," Turner said, "I've been wondering about the military." The group listened while they poured coffee and settled down. "What exactly do they mean when they say, 'mean and lean?' "

The question was for Bender, and they all waited for him to answer. "Basically, it means having a better tooth-to-tail ratio where combat power, the teeth, grows in relation to the support base, the tail."

"A man of few words," Coker murmured. "What determines the size of the teeth?"

"The threat," Bender replied.

"Which has definitely decreased," Parrish added.

"It has changed," Bender admitted.

"I want to make the military more lean and mean," Turner said. "How do I get their attention and shake them up?"

"Well, Madam President," Parrish said, "you certainly shook them up with your defense budget cuts."

"Was thirty percent in two years enough?" Turner asked.

"Becoming lean and mean doesn't necessarily equate to cutting costs," Bender replied. "Talk to General Overmeyer about it."

"Overmeyer," Turner said, shaking her head. "You've got to get his attention first. Otherwise, he won't listen to a damn thing."

Before Bender could protest, Maura intervened. "Maddy, we need to talk about taxes. That's much more important."

Turner nodded. "You're right. So where are we?"

"Madam President," Kennett said, "it might be a good idea if we heard about the downside of tax reform."

"Mrs. President," Coker said, "I agree. I've been working with Patrick about our legislative strategy, and you should hear what he has to say before we go on." Turner nodded and Kennett made the telephone call, summoning Shaw to the study. Four minutes later, Patrick Shaw was standing in the doorway, out of breath and his face flushed from the quick walk from the West Wing.

"I know you have some reservations about reforming the tax system," Turner said.

" 'Some reservations' hardly describes it," Coker said.

The look on Shaw's face reminded Bender of a repentant schoolboy who was caught smoking in the boy's restroom. Or in Shaw's case, the girl's restroom. "Sorry, Mizz President," Shaw muttered. "But I keep asking, Who does it buy for you?"

"I don't intend to *buy* anyone with it," the president replied.

"Then don't do it."

"Mr. Shaw," Maura said softly, "have you ever tried to raise a family on the minimum wage? You can't do it."

Bender saw Turner's head nod at her mother's gentle words and realized why she was part of the small group. Maura was Turner's lodestone, her moral compass. Maura tied her to the millions of people who survived from paycheck to paycheck, hoping for the break that never came, believing in the politicians who promised them a better life.

"Patrick," Turner said, exasperated, "we've been over this before. It's the right thing to do."

"Mizz President, when I shoot craps, I don't want any loaded dice in the game."

"Only when you're doing the rollin', honey," Coker scoffed, her black, inner-city accent heavy and staccato-sharp.

Shaw shook his head. "I only gamble when I think—when I know—the percentages are in my favor. Ask yourself, What are the percentages?"

"We're talking politics, Patrick, not gambling," Turner reminded him.

"It works the same. Roll the dice on tax reform and who does it bring to your side? So it's the right thing to do for the average working American. You ever met one? What does one look like? You start using words like *fair* and *average* and you've already lost."

"Most people think *fair* and *average* are important," Maura said.

Again, Shaw shook his big head. "Everyone else is average. Me and mine are special, better than the schmuck next door. And fair? I want what's due me and screw fair."

Turner came to her feet and paced back and forth, wearing a path in the carpet. "It's still the right thing to do. By restructuring the tax system, we can give working men and women the jobs they need."

Shaw warmed to the subject. He was on his home turf, sure and competent. "OK, let's roll the dice and see what it takes to play the game. Now, you got a lot of people who buy themselves a piece of the action with healthy campaign contributions whenever an election comes around. Every one of them will be putting the hard squeeze on to get a special break. OK, Mizz President, first we got to handle the gaspers and wheezers."

"Gaspers and wheezers?" Bender asked.

"The gray and green crowd," Parrish answered. "Gray hair and green money. We know a lot about them over at Treasury."

"The trouble with the gaspers," Shaw continued, "is that they're organized, and Lord, do they vote. Get 'em angry enough, and they'll vote our ass out of office. These are also the same voters who lived through Watergate and are running as hard as hell to stay ahead of the grim reaper. So, if they really get pissed, why wait for the next election? Words like *impeachment* start to get whispered in the hallowed halls of Congress. So they get a category all their own with a lower rate—or maybe no rate at all.

"OK, now the unions want a piece of the action. After all, they vote, too, not to mention all the stuff they give you under the table that lets you stay within finance laws at election time. So they get their little tickle. Now the doors to the stable are wide open and the stampede is on. Who from the Fortune 500 is going to be next in line? In my bravest moment—"

"Which occurred August 3, 1969," Noreen Coker muttered.

"—I can't even think about what the petroleum companies will do. It won't be pleasant when some of their more public-spirited baby-boomer executives send you a message. I can see it now, miles of honking cars lined up for gas. What about small businesses? The suppository of the American dream."

"I think he meant *repository,*" Parrish said in a stage whisper.

"He meant *suppository,*" Coker replied. "A small business campaign contribution is a contradiction in terms. He can't get any money out of them."

Shaw was in full gallop, the bit between his teeth. "Or what about the blacks? The Hispanics? Or the angry white male? How about the guy who plants 1,000 acres of corn and can only survive if he gets a break on taxes? I haven't even got to the bankers. And what about all those pesky foreign investors who invest their money in the good old U. S. of A. because of the current tax structure? They may not vote, but they know how to buy congressmen. And congressmen come cheap these days."

Patrick Flannery Shaw stood in front of his president, his head tilted to one side, his clothes a disheveled wreck. He made his last appeal. "Madam President, you help everyone and you help no one. But worst of all, you don't help yourself. Everybody is willing to talk tax reform, but no one wants it to happen. Least of all, with respect, you.''

"You're wrong, Patrick," Turner replied. "I do want it to happen."

Shaw nodded, a rueful look on his face. He had had his day in court and lost. Was it time to cut his losses? "Anything else I can do?"

Turner shook her head and Shaw left, thinking about his next phone call. "Well," Turner said, "we have our work cut out for us. Sam, I want you to take the lead on this. Use my staff and give it your highest priority. It's time to find out who our friends and enemies really are."

The meeting was over, and Bender was the first out the door while Noreen Coker held back. "I think you're on the right track with Defense," she said. "But the generals I know won't listen to any woman who talks about a lean and mean military. At least, not until you get their attention. And Shaw was right about running into stiff resistance on tax reform. We need to bug the opposition."

"Any suggestions how I can do all that?" Turner asked.

Coker nodded and sat down.

10

Washington, D.C.

Bender came through the west gate the Wednesday morning after the snowstorm at exactly seven o'clock. Many of the temporary workers who seemed to be permanently assigned to the White House were returning after a two-day break with pay thanks to the storm. They all recognized him, and a gardener waved. "Saw you in the newspaper, General. No way I'd go into that part of town."

"You got more guts than me," another worker said.

"Hell of a way to make page 3," an electrician called.

Bender grinned. He had come to like the rough comradery they shared every morning. "I just happened to be there," he replied. That set off a chorus of rude comments about the fickle finger of fate.

The gate guard stopped him. "Alice Fay called. You're wanted in Mr. Shaw's office—like soonest." Bender thanked him and walked as quickly as he could over the well-sanded walk that led to the West Wing.

Before Alice Fay could take his overcoat, Shaw's voice boomed from inside his office. "Say, boy, glad you hustled your body in so right smart." Bender's spine prickled at Shaw's use of the word *boy,* but he said nothing and went in. Alice Fay gave him an encouraging look and closed the door behind him. "I just got a call from Overmeyer," Shaw said, fingering a message. "It seems the

DIA issued a WATCHCON III effective 12:00 Greenwich mean time.''

Bender glanced at his watch: 7:12 local time. The WATCHCON had been in effect for twelve minutes. *Why are you sitting on this?* he thought. *I'm not the guy you should be talking to.*

"Then this shows up in the message center," Shaw muttered, handing him the message. "What the hell is a WATCHCON III anyway?''

"A WATCHCON," Bender explained, "is a notice issued by the Defense Intelligence Agency's National Military Intelligence Center in the Pentagon. It goes out to all our forces. Think of it as a war warning to prevent another Pearl Harbor. The III is the lowest level.''

"Which means?" Shaw asked. Bender didn't answer and read the message.

Chinese naval forces opposite Japan have reached task force level and continue to be augmented. Both increased air and ground assets observed in place in northern Taiwan. The necessary logistic structure is assessed to be in place in sufficient quantities and operational. These forces are positioned to bring pressure against Japan and can commence operations at any time with minimal warning. The most logical objectives are the island chains, including Okinawa, near Taiwan. DIA continues to monitor the situation.

"It means," Bender finally replied, "that you notify the president and activate the Situation Room. It's time to call in your heavy hitters, the DCI, the secretary of defense, the new secretary of state, General Overmeyer, the national security advisor—''

"We ain't got a national security advisor," Shaw interrupted. "Remember?''

"His staff is still in place. I'd suggest you call in whoever is running the show over here.''

Shaw fingered the message as he reread it. "If the situation was serious, the NIO would be over here breaking the gawddamn door down.'' The NIO was the CIA's national intelligence officer for warning. The NIO had a small staff whose job was to guard against a sneak attack on the United States. Since the collapse of the Soviet Union in December of 1991, there wasn't much to guard against. "He'd be waving a warning of attack message with some percentage he pulled out of thin air or more likely his ass." Shaw decided it was payback time. *Don't make end runs around old Patrick,* he thought. Nothing in his voice or look betrayed what he was really thinking. "Who you kiddin'? You know, I know, the whole gawddamn Pentagon knows, this WATCHCON message has nothin' to do with China."

A cold fear gripped Bender. For some reason, Shaw refused to take the warning seriously. The alerting system, with its built-in redundancy, that had been so carefully created during the Cold War to prevent another Pearl Harbor was falling apart. He leaned across Shaw's desk, his hands gripping the edge, knuckles white. He had to get Shaw's attention. "The DIA may be overreacting to what they are seeing, they may even be dead wrong, but they are not diddling with the system. We don't play games with war warnings."

"Sure," Shaw answered. Unconsciously, he reacted to Bender and scooted his chair back, trying to put some distance between him and the general. For a moment, he seriously considered hitting the duress button under his desk with his right knee. The alarm would bring five or six Secret Service agents with guns drawn to his rescue. *What the hell!* he thought. *Why am I afraid of this guy? He can't do anything to me.*

Shaw's ego demanded he crush this nobody general. "You haven't seen the directive President Turner sent over to your bosses yesterday afternoon. I expected some dirt-dumb reaction and told her so. But this one really takes the prize. Tell your bosses to get their act together." He threw the latest presidential directive at Bender, hoping it would be enough to get him to back off.

Bender picked up the directive and read. "Damn," he muttered. Then he leaned back across the desk and pulled out all the stops. "Notify the president and activate the Situation Room." His voice carried an authority that even Shaw couldn't ignore. "Now."

Shaw picked up his telephone and punched at a number. "Activate the Sit Room," he grumbled into the phone, still not convinced. He rattled off a list of the individuals he wanted to respond. Bender felt the knot in his stomach loosen when Shaw named Secretary of Defense Elkins and Overmeyer. "I'll tell the president, myself," Shaw muttered. He stood up to leave.

"Tell me something, Shaw. What would you have done if I had *not* been here?" Bender's words whipped at the chief of staff, and he didn't expect an answer. He had to make a point that Shaw would never forget. "A WATCHCON III can go on for days, even weeks. But if it goes to a II, you can damn well bet a I is not far behind. And you had better be ready by then because someone, somewhere, is about to give a war in the very near future. And I guarantee you, if they give a war, they will come."

Shaw started salvage operations on his battered ego. No one had spoken like that to him in years. "Gen'ral"—his southern drawl was back in place, heavy and threatening—"obviously you put a hole lot'a faith in the DIA's alerting system. You had better be right about this or your ass is dog meat."

"It doesn't matter if I'm right or wrong," Bender shot back. "You honor the threat in this business."

What the hell does that mean? Shaw wondered as he headed for the president's quarters.

The basement corridors under the West Wing were filled with uniforms and suits as aides and key staff members milled around, ready to be of instant service to their bosses in the Situation Room. Bender's extra chair had disappeared out of his office hours ago, and twice, an admiral had asked to use his phone in private. When the admiral appeared the third time with an aide carrying a secure telephone, Bender turned his office over without a word and closed the door as he left.

He pushed his way through the crowded, but strangely quiet corridor. Every man and woman was waiting with a mixture of excitement and apprehension. Being near the decision makers in a crisis was thrilling, but it also carried the unspoken burden of responsibility. "Bob," General Charles called, "hold on."

"I didn't know you were here, sir. You could have used my office. I turned it over to the webfoots."

"The Navy is jumping through it's ass on this one," Charles replied. "Give 'em all the help you can." He looked around. "We need to talk. Let's try the White House mess. We can find a corner." Bender led the way to the dining room were the staff ate and found a table off to the side. "I just came out of the Situation Room," Charles told him. "I was called in because there was some discussion on replacing Martini. What do you think?"

Bender considered his answer. By rights, he should have been outside the decision loop on that question. So why was Charles asking him? Was he being given an inside track because he was in the White House? "I've never met Martini," Bender said, "so I assume you're referring to the accident report." Charles nodded an answer. "Other than the accident, has he screwed up?" This time a shake of the head from Charles. A waiter stopped by their table and they ordered an early lunch.

Bender made his decision. "This is no time to start firing wing commanders."

Charles allowed a tight smile. "That's what I told them." He leaned back in his chair. "I talked briefly to the chairman during a break. He didn't say much, but he finally has a dialogue going with the president. He credits you with it." Charles leaned forward and dropped his voice. "You're in her kitchen cabinet. Where is she coming from?"

There it was. Bender had the answer to his question as to why Charles had taken him into his confidence about Martini. Suddenly, he wasn't hungry and he wanted out of this conversation. "Sorry, chief. I'm only valuable to the president if she trusts me to keep my mouth shut."

Charles gave him a blank stare. "Perhaps," he said, "she wants you to leak information to us. Maybe that's the reason you're there."

I'll have to ask her, Bender thought. But Charles was

waiting for a reply. "Sir, she is my commander in chief and I am bound by presidential privilege. But I'm not going to—" He cut his words off in midstream, ashamed for justifying what was right.

"Not going to do what?" Charles asked. Surprisingly, he was not angry.

What's going on here? Bender asked himself. "I'm not going to short-circuit the chairman."

That seemed to satisfy Charles, and they ate in silence. "How was the WATCHCON III handled when it came into the White House?" Charles asked when they finished the meal. They were on safe ground, and Bender quickly related how he had spurred Shaw into action. "I suspected you had a hand in it," Charles said, "when I heard Shaw use your favorite phrase."

"What favorite phrase?" Bender asked. He didn't know he had one. He made a mental note to check with Nancy.

"Honor the threat," Charles replied. "But the CIA's national intelligence officer for warning has a different take on this and is downplaying China's intentions. He won't even issue a minimal warning of attack. He claims that the Chinese are posturing to shake Japan's economic tree and this is all show and no go, like everything else since they took over Hong Kong."

An uncomfortable suspicion demanded Bender's attention. Had Shaw been right after all? Had Overmeyer deliberately used the WATCHCON message to force a dialogue with the president? "Who determined the activate time for the WATCHCON III?" he asked.

"The chairman," Charles answered.

"Which was about the time Shaw and I arrive at the White House every morning."

Charles gave him a thoughtful look. "Well, the chairman did have a certain dynamic in mind."

"You can tell him he got it right, but Shaw is pissed."

"Why should he be upset?" Charles asked.

"Because I had to beat him up to get any action. He thinks Overmeyer issued the WATCHCON to retaliate for the directive Turner laid on us yesterday."

"Shaw is dumber than a can of rocks," Charles muttered. "Of course, the chairman is upset about the directive. Hell, we're all upset. But we can live with it—until the next president is elected. We've survived other hostile administrations, we'll outlast this one." He stood up to leave. "Look, I know how you feel about the Thunderbirds. They mean a lot to all of us."

The basement and the Situation Room were deserted when Bender descended the stairs. The crisis was over for now or had been relegated to another level. He sat in his office and stared at the photo on the wall. His commander in chief, by presidential directive, had disbanded all military aerial demonstration teams and most of the honor guards in the name of lean and mean. Only the Third U.S. Infantry Unit, the Old Guard, which guarded the Tomb of the Unknowns, and the United States Marine Band had been spared.

Why are you doing this to us? he raged to himself.

Okinawa, Japan

About the time most of the bureaucrats in Washington, D.C., were leaving work that same Wednesday afternoon, newly promoted Major Robert Ryan, Jr., M.D., was waking up. He checked his watch: 5:30 in the morning. Good. He had six hours to spend on his project before reporting for duty at the clinic. *Working the late shift will work out fine,* he thought, *and give me plenty of time to work on the Personnel Reliability Program.* "What a waste of time," he muttered aloud. Ryan got out of bed and studied the photo of Laurie by his bedside. He missed her more than he could ever have imagined.

His desk was laid out for work, the outline completed, his research notes arranged, and the reference books annotated. It was time. He switched on his computer and called up a new file on his word processing program. He stared at the screen, willing the words to appear. But it was painful. *What would Laurie have done?* he asked himself. Her voice was there, still with him. "Quit being a prima donna and sweat!" Slowly, he typed:

The Degradation of Rationality:
A Case Study of the Dysfunctional
Military Commander Under Stress

*The subject of this study is the authoritarian person-
ality under stress. It is based on an extended observation of a forty-eight-year-old Caucasian male in
command of the largest operational Air Force combat wing outside the continental United States.*

Satisfied with this opening, Ryan leaned back in his chair
and reread his outline. All of the professional buzzwords
were covered: low self-esteem (an absolute in the current
world of psychology), childhood abuse, and, best of all,
multiple-personality disorder.

The more Ryan read, the more he convinced himself
that his diagnosis of Martini was accurate. But he had to
get inside Martini's decision-making process to gather the
anecdotal evidence necessary to sustain his theory. *The
answer is so obvious,* he thought. The commander of the
Medical Group always sent a representative to the battle
staff when the command post was activated for exercises.
Without exception, the officer always complained of nothing to do except listen to Martini and the other colonels
talk. So why not him?

Washington, D.C.

The message light on the answering machine was flashing when Bender arrived home that Wednesday night. It
was Nancy. "Dinner's in the oven and should be cooking.
I'll be home around seven, set the kitchen table for three.
We've got a house guest."

House guest? he thought. *Nancy hadn't mentioned it
before she went to work at the hospital. It must be a friend
or acquaintance if we're eating in the kitchen.* He changed
into casual clothes and set the table as she asked. At exactly seven o'clock, Nancy walked in with Shalandra. The
thin bandage covering the stitches in the girl's right ear
was hardly noticeable, and she was wearing clean jeans

and a new sweatshirt. Bender was stunned by the change and how young she looked. Shalandra's eyes widened when she saw him and turned into large brown pools of surprise. Nancy had assumed Shalandra knew who her husband was, but the girl had not made the connection until she actually saw him.

"It's OK," Nancy said. "He won't hurt you." Shalandra stared at him and said nothing. "The bathroom is through there," Nancy said, pointing the girl down the hall. Before Shalandra could move, Nancy held out her hand for Shalandra's handbag. Without a word, Shalandra handed it over and headed for the bathroom while Nancy dumped the contents of the bag on the counter.

"What are you doing?" Bender asked.

"Searching for drugs," Nancy said.

"I mean, is this wise? Bringing her here."

Nancy stuffed the contents back into the bag and breathed a sigh of relief. "She's clean." She turned to face her husband. "She was released from the hospital today and has nowhere to go. I'm trying to get her into child protective services to find a good foster home. It's only for tonight, and she'll be gone in the morning."

"But in our own home?" he protested. "There must be temporary facilities somewhere."

Nancy shook her head. "The snowstorm screwed up everything. If I send her home, she'll be doped up and back on the streets in an hour. She's a pretty girl and still free of AIDS. How much longer will that last?"

"I'll pay for a hotel room."

"She doesn't need a room," Nancy said. "She needs people who care." She reached up and touched his face. "She's very passive and not dangerous at all. You don't know what a big step it was for her to call for help and get way from her uncle."

"Was he the pimp?"

Nancy nodded. "All the men in her life are either pimps, drug pushers, in jail, or a customer. For her, a relationship with a man means abuse, physical, emotional, sexual abuse. This may be her only chance, and I don't want to lose it. If you're really upset, I'll check us both into a hotel. But I'd rather stay here."

Bender gave in. "I hope this isn't an on-going requirement now that you're getting paid." He made a mental note to set the security alarm in the hall outside the guest room after Shalandra went to bed.

Nancy reached out and touched his cheek. "I know this goes against all good sense. It won't happen again. It's just—just that—it's the way I'm holding on right now."

Bender smiled, breaking the tension between them. "You'll pay for this, woman." He saw Shalandra staring at them from the doorway. "Welcome to our home," he told her.

Nancy said, "He won't hurt you, Shalandra. You can trust him."

"I hope you ladies are hungry," he said, holding a chair for Nancy. Shalandra looked at him for a moment and then sank back into the hall.

"It's OK," Nancy called. "You can eat with us." Slowly, the girl emerged from the shadows and came into the kitchen, her eyes still full of fear and apprehension.

This is not good, Bender told himself. *Nancy knows better.*

Late that evening, Turner curled up on the couch in her private study. Two attaché cases were open on the floor beside her and the TV was on, tuned to CNC-TV. The fire crackled and sent out a warm glow as she burrowed in for a hard night's work. A discreet knock at the door broke her concentration, and she laid the speech she was editing aside. "Come," she said. *When did I start saying that?* she wondered. *It doesn't sound like me.*

Jackie Winters, her personal assistant, peeked in. "Is there anything you need before I leave, Mrs. President?"

"No, I'm fine," she said, smiling. "Jackie, do you have a significant other waiting for you?" A shy look and tentative shake of the head answered her. For a moment, Turner considered asking Jackie to sit and chat for a few minutes if she wasn't in a hurry to go home. But a request from the most powerful person in the world carried an imperative that could not be refused by a normal human being, and Turner knew that would be intruding. She smiled. "Thank you, Jackie."

"Good night, Mrs. President." Jackie quietly closed the door, leaving Madeline O'Keith Turner alone.

"Gawd, Jessica," Shaw moaned, "what a day." He pushed off his shoes and sank into the deep leather of the couch in his Watergate condominium. "We got the CIA yelling at the DIA about China, and not one of those shit-for-brains speaks the language." The young woman smiled at him and padded barefoot over to the bar to fix him a drink. Jessica's bare legs flashed in the soft light, and he felt the beginnings of an erection. She moved with the grace of a dancer, and her blond hair hid her face when she looked down to mix his Jack Daniels and water. She held the drink up to the light to check its color. It was perfect. She tossed her hair back and gave him a radiant smile. "Come here, darlin'," he said huskily.

He watched as she shed the last of her clothes, dropping her panties near the bar. She walked slowly toward him, her hips swaying to an inner music. He didn't mind one bit that she was not a natural blonde and half his age as long as she was there, with him. She handed him the drink and dragged her fingernails along the back of his hand, arousing him even more. Then she moved away and settled into the corner of the couch. She drew her legs up, knees together, and stretched her arms out, resting her right arm on the back of the couch and the left one on the padded arm. She tossed her hair back.

Shaw was ready, but Jessica wanted to talk. She had a soft, cultured voice. Bryn Mawr, if he remembered right. He enjoyed the conversation, discussing the finer aspects of computer polling that could instantly take the pulse of the American electorate. He savored the moment. How many men had sat next to a beautiful naked woman and carried on an intelligent conversation while sipping the perfect drink? He tried to think of something impressive to say about the way the White House's computer programs interacted with local polling stations. He gave up.

"Darlin', I was a history major because my professors thought computers were an illegitimate cross between al-chemy and voodoo. Truth to tell, messin' around with the polls is more simple than shoveling shit in Louisiana. Just get the best results money can buy.''

Jessica's mouth pulled into a little pout as she looked at his crotch. His blood pressure went up thirty points. ''Actually,'' she murmured, ''I'm more interested in attitude formation. Computer polling only confirms if you're doing it right. And you do it very right. What's your secret? You always know which buttons to push, with exactly the right people at the right time and place.'' She gave him an enticing smile and glanced at his crotch again. ''I can predict an emerging trend but—'' She stopped in midsentence and came across the couch, slipping her hand inside his shirt, stroking his nipples. Her lips brushed his ear. ''But you're the one who makes it happen,'' she whispered.

Shaw wasn't sure how they made it to his bed or how she had undressed him so fast. But she was there, riding him, her legs clamped to his side. She laughed when he came so quickly. ''We're not done,'' she murmured. To his amazement, she was wickedly, delightfully, perversely right.

The phone started ringing at five o'clock the next morning. It was three hours earlier in California and according to the caller, a superior court judge, whose appointment Shaw had sponsored and rammed down the throat of the governor, had been caught with a pregnant hooker in the backseat of his car in an alley behind the courthouse doing his own ramming. The arresting officers reported that the hooker's lips were definitely encircling the judge's judicial pogo stick at the moment of apprehension.

A delightful aroma from the kitchen momentarily distracted Shaw. ''What's that I smell cookin'?'' Jessica answered him with a wicked laugh.

The caller assumed Shaw was talking to him. ''You want us to fry the bastard?''

Shaw thought for a moment. He could still kill the story. ''Throw him to the hyenas and let him explain it to his wife.'' He dropped the phone in its cradle and homed in on the tantalizing smells coming from the kitchen. ''Oh, Lord,'' he mumbled, ''what more could a man want?'' He hadn't felt so good in weeks and Henry Kissinger's words about power being the only true aphrodisiac flitted through his mind. *You got it wrong, Henry,* he thought. *The only true aphrodisiac is a young, long-legged girl with her legs wrapped around you in bed.*

For the young woman who had been squirming under his big belly and doing the cooking, it was the power.

Okinawa, Japan

The Habu's mission was simple in the extreme: overfly dangerously hostile territory and take pictures. But in the Habu's world of strategic reconnaissance, the simple things are always hard. The Habu itself started life in 1959 when Lockheed won the contract for building the A-12. Originally, the A-12 was designed as a follow-on for the U-2 spy plane, and by 1964, the single-seat A-12 had evolved into the twin-place SR-71. Thirty-two of "Kelly" Johnson's Blackbirds rolled out of Lockheed's Skunk Works before production ceased in 1967. After an early series of eleven crashes, the SR-71 settled down to a productive life and only one more was lost in 1989. Then, in the face of mounting mission costs, satellite reconnaissance, and the need for an expensive technical upgrade, the SR-71 was retired from service in 1990. But nothing ever replaced it, not satellites, the still-flying U-2R, nor the much vaunted top-secret Aurora. Finally, after sitting out most of the 1990s, the Air Force pulled this Habu out of its storage hangar at Palmdale, California.

Unfortunately, the people and the expertise that had kept the incredibly complex aircraft flying had been lost. It took time to relearn the old skills. Although this particular SR-71A had seen less than 3,000 hours total flying time, it was four years older than its thirty-two-year-old test pilot, Greg Stein. At twenty-eight, Dick Robards, the reconnaissance systems officer (RSO) in the backseat, was the youngest member of the team.

Greg had never intended to be a test pilot, he was planning for an extended retirement, but every flight in the SR-71 was an excursion into the unknown, rediscovering what had been lost or forgotten. Preeminent among the unknowns was how to contend with the cantankerous ways of the elegant, but elderly jet that was still the fastest and highest-flying operational aircraft in the world.

The mission started late Saturday morning, January 12, when the pilot and RSO suited up in their full-pressure suits complete with space helmets and moon boots. Exactly one hour before takeoff, they were driven to the Little Creek hangar on the north side of Kadena Air Base and began the lengthy process of strapping in and starting engines. It was impossible to simply "kick the tires and light the fires" of the Habu. At exactly 3 P.M. local time, Greg taxied the SR-71 onto the active runway, eased the throttles into max afterburner, and resumed his career as a test pilot.

The Habu headed south, into the South China Sea, where it rendezvoused with two KC-135 tankers at 25,000 feet. Greg slowed to 350 knots for the hookup. At that speed, the Habu becomes sluggish and is not a happy jet. Greg sweated freely in his pressure suit as he held the SR-71 on the tanker's boom for fifteen minutes. The fuel-hungry Habu sucked up 70,000 pounds, over 11,000 gallons, of JP-7 before it was satiated. After the boom was disconnected, Greg dropped away from the tanker, lowered the nose to pick up airspeed, and lit the afterburners. With the throttles pushed up to max, they climbed into an incredible cobalt blue sky. But Greg was too busy monitoring the climb, managing the fuel flow, and checking the engine instruments to notice. As usual, Dick had his head down, studying the scopes in front of him.

The flight plan called for them to turn over the northern end of Luzon in the Philippines and head toward Hong Kong at 80,000 feet and Mach 2.8. But before they reached the mainland, they turned to the northeast and headed for the Taiwan Strait, the channel that split the island of Taiwan and the Chinese mainland. Although their track was near the mainland, they were careful to stay over international waters.

"I've got two radars painting us," Dick said over the intercom.

"Anything cosmic?" Greg asked.

"Only your standard issue early-warning radars. They

know we're here." The RSO double-checked the defensive electronic systems. The programmable software the mission planners had fed into the system was guaranteed to defeat any electronic threat the Chinese might have had. But the mission planners hadn't counted on the Habu getting cranky. It started with a little tantrum, just enough to get Greg's attention.

"Hold on," the pilot said, "I've got a warning light." He scanned the annunciator panel with its forty-eight warning lights. "We got a bus-tie open." In itself, that was no problem. The relay that merged the electrical power coming from the generator on each engine into one common power source had flipped open. It just meant that one generator was out of phase or frequency with the other and they could proceed with the mission.

The defensive electronic systems scope in the rear cockpit lit up like a Christmas tree. "The entire fucking Chinese Air Force is looking at us," Dick groused from his office. "I got a bearing of six aircraft at twelve o'clock coming straight at us. They're probably going to try snap-ups." The hostile fighters being radar-vectored onto the Habu were at 40,000 feet, almost eight miles below the Habu, and strung out in a long line.

When the lead fighter had closed to thirty miles in front of the SR-71, the radar controller issued a command in Chinese that roughly translated as "go for the celestial squeezings." The Chinese pilot pulled back on his stick and zoomed, trading whatever airspeed he had for altitude, trying to get high enough to launch an air-to-air missile at the high-flying intruder. He didn't even come close. Then the next fighter in line repeated the maneuver with the same lack of success.

Even though the Habu was over international waters, the Chinese were willing to salvo missile after missile in the hope of getting a shoot-down. Under normal circumstances, that equated to wishful thinking. But if they were lucky, they would argue about the where and who got the bodies later.

Greg used the Habu's standard defensive tactic and went faster and higher. On the good side of the equation, they got better gas mileage. On the bad side, it increased the strain on the Habu, and it became more irritable. A mongoose going after a cobra instinctively understands the situation. But Greg Stein and Dick Robards were a little slower, and strange things can happen while flying at Mach 3.2 at 83,000 feet. They were literally flying faster than a speeding bullet when the right generator fell offline. "Right generator failure," Greg said over the intercom. The checklist told them they had to abort the mission. But where? They were still between the Chinese mainland and Taiwan.

The Habu solved the problem for them by failing the left generator. Normally, the emergency AC and DC power kicked in automatically, but the Habu was being difficult and the automatic relay did not close. Before Greg could hit the switch, manually activating standby electrical power, the fuel-boost pumps stopped pumping fuel to the engines. That caused a flameout, Habu dirty talk for big trouble. Without power, the SR-71 had the flying characteristics of a lump of coal. They were going to abort straight ahead.

They were descending through 60,000 feet and in the envelope where a fighter could engage them when Greg got one engine started and a generator back on-line. The defensive electronic systems started to stir with partial power. "We got a hostile lock-on!" Dick screamed. The RSO did something he rarely did in the backseat: He looked out his window. He wished he hadn't and totally blew his cool, which, in the world of strategic reconnaissance, is worse than dying. "Bandit! Ten o'clock on us! We're going to die!" The mission recorder system dutifully recorded his words for posterity and the mission debrief—if they had one.

"Shut up," Greg answered, his words labored and slow, "and die like a man. Do your job." The RSO did, and his fingers danced over the buttons of the defensive electronic system while Greg got the second engine relit. The Habu's second generator came on-line, the bus-tie closed, and the Habu coughed up a burst of electrical power. Finally, the defensive electronic system could do its job as designed and hit the attacker's radar with a barrage of electronic magic that told the Chinese pilot to do a physically impossible act. "Come on, baby," Greg coaxed, inching the throttles into max afterburner. "Let's go home."

The Habu responded, and they climbed into the sky, reaching 94,000 feet before Greg felt the need to level off. "Where are we?" he asked.

Dick recycled the inertial navigation system and updated the moving map display. "Abeam Fuchow," he answered.

"That's where we were supposed to go," Greg answered. He turned to the east, heading for Okinawa.

"Do you think we should slow down?" Dick asked. His airspeed indicator was reading Mach 3.6.

"Hell no," the pilot answered. "Did the cameras come on?"

The RSO checked the power and sensor control panel. "They're on now," he answered.

"I hope to hell they were on when they should have been," Greg said. He checked the fuel remaining and made an emergency radio call for a tanker to meet them as soon as possible.

Martini was on Perimeter Road when the SR-71 entered the landing pattern. He pulled into the parking lot on top of Habu Hill and, like any pilot, watched it land, critically bisecting the other pilot's performance. Like any commander, he felt a touch of relief when one of 'his' aircraft was safely recovered. Because it would be almost an hour before the 700-foot-long film from the bird's technical objective cameras started to come out of the processing unit, he decided to 'howdy' the pilot and RSO. He drove to the Physiological Support Division where they stripped off their pressure suits, the first step in a long mission debrief.

"How'd it go?" he asked Greg.

"Pretty much your standard mission," the pilot answered. "We had a small problem with the generators and got a flameout on both engines when we were in the straits. There were a few bandits around, trying to cause trouble, but it was a piece of cake."

"Right," Martini deadpanned. He knew.

The RSO grinned at them. "According to the mission recorder, we set a new speed and altitude record for a 2,000-nautical-mile flight."

"Sure," Greg muttered. "But who's going to know about it."

"The Chinese," Martini said. "Fast forward the mission recorder tape to the flameout."

An unhappy RSO did as Martini commanded, and he blushed brightly when they reached the part where he proclaimed their impending death. Greg stopped the tape and laughed. "We've been working on that line for weeks," he explained. "I never thought I'd have a chance to use it."

"Right," Martini deadpanned. He knew.

The film was coming out of the processing unit and Lieutenant Colonel Pete Townly, Martini's chief of Intelligence, was with the hunch-shouldered captain when Martini joined them. "Talk to me," Martini said.

"Great resolution," Townly said.

"The KA-102B may be an old camera," the captain explained, "but we're getting image resolution of less than two inches from 80,000 feet."

"Cut the bullshit," Martini growled. "What have you got?"

Townly and the captain exchanged worried glances. "I can't be sure until analysis and mensuration is complete," the captain said. "But I think the Chinese fleet has sortied out of Fuchow and is coming this way."

"How sure are you?" Martini asked. The captain gulped and didn't answer. He looked at Townly for help.

"Damn sure," Townly replied.

Martini nodded. He had no trouble accepting bad news. "You got a secure line to the command post?" The captain pointed to a STU-V, the latest version of a portable secure telephone, and Martini dialed his command post. "I'm declaring Condition Scarlet," he told the controller on duty. "This is not an exercise. Expect an attack within six hours."

"Sir," the controller protested, "an actual Condition Scarlet can only be declared by CINC PAC."

"Want'a bet?" Martini barked. "Do it. And make sure CINC PAC and the Pentagon knows about it in the next ten seconds." He banged the phone down and turned to

Townly and the captain. "Get this on the wires to Offutt and the DIA ASAP." He glanced at the wall clocks that were set to different times around the world. It was 5:10 Saturday afternoon on Okinawa and 3:10 Saturday morning in Washington, D.C. "I hope to hell someone's awake over there," he grumbled.

Okinawa, Japan

Bob Ryan collapsed on the floor of his BOQ and vowed never to play another Saturday afternoon game of touch football. The base league was the creation of a captain from the Security Police, Terrence Daguerre, who had played pro football at one time and delighted in maiming people. The phone rang, and Ryan groaned loudly as he collected what was left of his body and answered. It was a recall ordering all personnel to their duty stations. He went directly to the command post and found his seat in the glassed-in Battle Cab that overlooked the main floor. Besides the center position for Martini, there was a position at the long console for each of the group commanders who made up the Eighteenth Wing: Operations, Logistics, Support, Civil Engineer, and Medical.

Unlike the other group commanders, the commander of the Medical Group chose to send a representative, in this case Ryan, to the command post when the battle staff was activated. Ryan checked the bank of telephones in front of him and opened the black loose-leaf binder in front of him.

What the hell is an Emergency Actions book? Ryan thought. *Is this the book I'm supposed to read?* He glanced at the other commanders. Each had a similar book and was going through it, checking off action items as they made phone calls. Even Martini was reading his. Ryan

177

flipped to the first page of his book and read the first item: "Perform communications check." *This is stupid,* he thought. *The telephones are working.* He checked it off and went- on to the next item: "Determine state/stage of alert and notify Medical Center on secure telephone." *What a waste of time,* he thought. *The Med Center always knows what the state/stage of alert is during an exercise. This is so typical of the military—make work to keep people busy. Just like all the crap over the Personnel Reliability Program Martini dumped on me.*

He checked that item off. He ran through the rest of the checklist and closed the book. He took some satisfaction that he was the first finished. From his vantage point in the Battle Cab, Ryan could see every status board and position in the command post, including inside the glassed-in Control Cab against the opposite wall where the controllers manned a huge communications bank. He was fascinated by the purposeful activity on the main floor as people streamed into the command post, answering the recall to the Condition Scarlet. The Support Group commander sitting next to him finished his emergency action checklist.

"The general is going to be in a world of hurt if CINC PAC cancels Condition Scarlet on him," the colonel ventured. Ryan said he didn't understand. The colonel gave him a studied look, then forgave his ignorance because he was a doctor. "Martini declared Condition Scarlet on his own authority. He can't do that."

"So why did he do it?" Ryan asked.

"Who knows?" the colonel replied. "I guess he thought the base is coming under attack within six hours. That's what Scarlet is for: to get us hunkered down as quick as possible." Ryan nodded. This was the perfect place to study Martini in a stressful situation. The colonel glanced at the Emergency Actions Status board on the far wall. "Everyone but the Med Group is showing a green light," he told Ryan. "You had better build a fire under the Med Center before Martini builds one under you."

Ryan looked confused. "Oh, my God," the colonel muttered, "you haven't got a clue. What the hell was your boss thinking of?" He grabbed Ryan's secure phone and punched up the Med Center, updating them on the stage of alert. The colonel broke the connection and gave Ryan a quick lesson on how the Air Force went to war at the operational level. He worked his way through Ryan's Emergency Action book, demonstrating how it was Ryan's job to get the Medical Group configured to a wartime footing through a series of actions all directed from the command post. It was a revelation for the doctor, but unfortunately, it came too late.

"Major Ryan!" Martini bellowed. "What the hell is going on with the quacks? Everyone is in the green except them."

"Tell him the truth," the Support Group commander muttered.

Ryan gulped. "I was late in notifying them, sir."

Martini waved his hand, and the Battle Cab quickly emptied. Ryan wanted to sneak out with the four colonels, but Martini's hard look told him that he was the reason the cab had been emptied. Ryan was a post–baby boomer who had lived a charmed life, pampered by his parents, the school system, and even the Air Force because they needed doctors. He had never been held personally accountable for a screwup. It had always been the fault of the system or someone else. Like everyone else, Ryan was only a victim. Unfortunately, Martini did not subscribe to that philosophy.

"Ryan," Martini said when they were alone, "in a Condition Scarlet, we need every available second to get ready for an attack. When you did not understand what was happening, you should have asked for help. Because of your inaction, we have not used our time wisely. If we are attacked and the Med Center is caught unprepared, I will court-martial you and recommend that you be sentenced to Leavenworth. Count on it. Regardless of what happens, I will fire your boss for gross stupidity. He shouldn't have sent you here in the first place. Do you understand every word I have said?"

Martini had never suffered from a lack of credibility, and Ryan panicked. He withered under the general's intense stare and his head twisted from side to side, a trapped animal looking for a place to hide. He shot a furtive glance at the Emergency Actions Status board, willing the light beside the Med Center to change to green, anything to divert Martini's wrath. The light flashed from red to green, and for a brief moment, Ryan truly believed in guardian angels. "Sir," he said wildly gesturing at the board.

Martini never took his eyes off the doctor. "I'm waiting for an answer," he growled.

What was the question? Ryan couldn't remember, and his panic hit a record high. Then it came to him. "Yessir, I understand every word you said."

Martini's head turned slowly to look at the Emergency Actions Status board. "Good," he said. "It appears your court-martial has been put on hold for the time being. Now, give me one good reason why I should *not* fire your boss."

Ryan swallowed the bile that was rising in his throat. It was painfully obvious that Martini believed in personal accountability, and there would be no passing the buck. "Sir, because what happened here was my fault. I requested this assignment and told my boss that I was ready for it. He believed me and assigned me to be his representative on the battle staff."

"So you lied to him."

Ryan wanted to protest that he had not lied, only misunderstood what was required. An inner alarm warned him that was the wrong answer. "Yessir, I lied."

"Actually," Martini said, "you're probably suffering from the disease of the doctors."

"I'm not familiar with that particular condition, sir."

"It's delusional," Martini told him. "You think being a doctor makes you a genius in everything. Being a doctor simply makes you a doctor. Nothing else." He scanned the boards, concerned about the progress of the loadout on his F-15s. "You will work here until Condition Scarlet is canceled and it is safe to move around outside. Then I want someone here from the Med Center who has a clue."

Ryan nodded. "Sir, are you still going to fire my boss?"

"I'm still thinking about your answer," Martini replied. He gestured for the other colonels to return, and Ryan retreated back to his seat.

The Support Group commander was back in his seat next to Ryan. "Have a religious experience?" the colonel asked. There was no answer. "I happen to like your boss, so if you listen, I'll keep you out of trouble."

Unknown to Ryan, two senior NCOs in the Med Center had saved him from the wrath of Martini. After responding to the recall, no further messages had come from the command post. That worried the sergeants. Because they did not have access to the secure line to call Ryan in the command post and find out what was going on, they backdoored the information through a buddy NCO in the Security Police shack. The moment they discovered Condition Scarlet had been declared, they initiated the actions that Ryan should have started. When they finally got the official word from the command post, the Med Center was almost ready. It was the way sergeants took care of each other and a lesson Ryan would never learn.

Ryan sat in the command post and did a slow burn. *It is so obvious,* he thought, *even a child could figure it out.* Martini was trying to even the score because of his testimony to the Safety Investigation Board about the accident. He mentally composed a new section for his case study on Martini:

Ego and Fear: Operative Factors.

The egoistic roots of the dysfunctional commander are often manifested in the climate of fear and intimidation created by the subject. This is an essential step, for total subjugation to his will must be attained at all costs and never questioned, regardless of the rationality of his decision. In fact, the more irrational the decision, the stronger the need for unquestioning compliance.

Ryan smiled to himself, feeling much better. If the Condition Scarlet was canceled by CINC PAC, who would be getting court-martialed? Better yet, would the investigators be interested in the documented observations of a recognized expert about Martini's mental stability?

Washington, D.C.

The phone call came at 5:10 Saturday morning and woke Bender from a sound sleep. His response was automatic, honed from years of command, and he answered on the first ring. "Bender here," he said, instantly awake and alert.

It was the duty officer at the NMCC. "Sir, I'm glad I didn't wake you. General Charles said there is a message that requires your immediate attention."

Bender hated talking around a subject on an unsecure telephone. "Tell General Charles I'll see him in thirty minutes."

"Sir, it would be better if you went to your office."

The DIA has upgraded the WATCHCON III, Bender thought, *and no one at the White House is responding.* He moved quickly and was dressed and out the door without disturbing Nancy. He would shave later. He was backing out of the driveway when he saw a police car parked in front of his house, its engine idling.

Patrolwoman Elena Murphy unlimbered from the car and walked toward him. Bender rolled down his window. "Shalandra," Murphy said, pointing to the patrol car. "She ran away from her foster home and came to the hospital. She's not hurt and I was comin' off duty, so I brought her here."

He could see the girl sitting in the backseat. "It's OK. Ring the doorbell. My wife will help you."

Murphy shook her head. "She wants to talk to you."

Bender was stunned. He hadn't said a dozen words to Shalandra before she left on Thursday morning after spending one night. *Nancy should have never brought her here in the first place,* he thought. *This is her problem, and she'll have to handle it.* "I'm sorry, but there's an emergency. I've got to go." Murphy nodded and stepped back. She understood emergencies.

The early-morning traffic was very light, and he made it to the White House in less than twenty minutes. He cleared the west gate and walked quickly into the West Wing, surprised at the activity around him. The White House was responding this time, and he wasn't needed.

But lacking information, he went directly to Shaw's corner office. "Good morning, General Bender," Alice Fay said. "Mr. Shaw is expecting you. Please go right in."

"Glad you got the word," Shaw boomed from behind his desk.

"Not really," Bender answered. "What's happening?"

"The DIA has declared a WATCHCON I for the Far East," Shaw told him. "And the NIO agrees this time."

"Why the sudden change of heart by the CIA?" Bender asked. Shaw handed him the warning message.

A Chinese naval task force of thirty-eight (38) surface combatants centered on the Chairman Mao *aircraft carrier has sortied from its East Sea Fleet naval base at Fuchow. At its current speed and direction, the task force will reach Okinawa at approximately 2300 hours GMT (1800 hours EST) this date. National resources indicate that all PLA units in the Nanjing Military District and on Taiwan are at full alert. These military moves point toward hostile action by China. However, the intentions of the PRC are unknown, and this may only be an escalation in psychological pressure on the Japanese by Beijing.*

"How'd you like that last bit?" Shaw asked, not expecting an answer. "You got to give those boys credit for covering their backside."

"You've notified the president?" Bender asked.

"And activated the Sit Room," Shaw added. "She'll be there in a few minutes for a situation brief and the NSC is meeting at seven-thirty." Shaw grinned at him. "I do like to honor the threat."

Bender stared at him for a moment. "Have you?" Before Shaw could answer, he was out the door and headed for his office. The corridor outside the Situation Room was full of the same uniforms and suits as before. He pushed through the crowd to his office. Lacking anything to do, he retrieved his shaving kit, turned over his office to the admiral's aide who was already there with a secure telephone, and retreated to the locker room in the gym where he showered and shaved. *This is going to be one long day,* he told himself.

A White House usher was waiting for him when he came out of the locker room. General Overmeyer wanted to see him immediately. The usher's quick pace warned Bender that the crisis was reaching criticality, the moment a mass of fissionable material could sustain a chain reaction and explode. The chairman was pacing the floor of a small office, talking to the chief of Naval Operations and General Charles. "The president wants you to attend the NSC meeting," he gritted.

"Sir, there's no reason for me to be there. I've only seen the WATCHCON message and I'm totally out of the loop."

"Not any more, you're not," Overmeyer grumbled. He was chewing on an unlit cigar, turning it into a ragged stump. "Charles, get him up to speed." He paused, thinking. "Bender, if I give you the nod, speak up." He stomped out of the office, and Charles quickly filled Bender in on the situation.

Bender's stomach turned into an icy void. "Have we got a war on our hands?"

"It looks that way," Charles replied. "But the CIA and State are not so sure. I hope to hell they're right." Bender followed him into the packed Cabinet Room and found a seat against the back wall, opposite Madeline Turner's chair. He didn't have to wait long. The door opened, and everyone automatically stood when she entered. Shaw was right behind. Bender studied her, looking for clues. She was calm and poised, her hair brushed back and wearing little makeup. She was wearing a dark suit and walked with confidence. He was reminded of the time in the Situation Room when she had reacted with calm fortitude to the revelation that President Roberts had sold out Taiwan.

"Please be seated," she said, her voice matching her image. "We," she began, "must formulate a response to this crisis. But I want to make it very clear that I will not be the first president in this century to take our country into a needless war."

Or the first woman president, Bender mentally added. He listened as the discussion moved around the table. It was obvious that there was no agreement on how to respond. Those favoring a military response, led by Overmeyer, wanted to draw a line in the water, whereas those seeking a diplomatic solution, championed by Barnett Francis, the newly confirmed secretary of state, wanted to negotiate. It was rapidly coming to an impasse.

Bender glanced at Shaw and saw an extremely contented man. Why? Then it came to him. Shaw wanted a distraction to turn Turner away from tax reform. *The bastard!* he raged to himself. *He's more than willing to let a foreign threat build and rage out of control to save a political situation at home. That's why he ignored the first warnings. He doesn't give a damn about the price.*

For Bender, the price was measured in casualties. He forced himself to calm down. Not even Shaw was that cynical, he decided. Suddenly, his mental image of Shaw cleared, and the man stepped into full view. Shaw truly believed that tax reform was not in Turner's best interests and that he was saving the president from herself. But he was still Patrick Flannery Shaw, and if he couldn't convince the president, he would let events distract her. Shaw's initial reaction to the WATCHCON III had been based on an honest doubt and even Bender had found himself momentarily questioning Overmeyer's motives. In that moment, the murky fog that had swirled around Shaw was gone and Bender saw him for what he was: a politician no better or worse than any of the breed inhabiting the Capitol. Shaw was, without a doubt, more devious, certainly more lusty, but there were lines even he would not cross.

An angry voice caught Bender's attention. The DCI was on the attack. "That cowboy at Kadena is out of control. When he put the base on alert, he took our best option off the table. We might have been able to publicly ignore this while negotiating a resolution in secret."

"Are you saying," Shaw asked, "that he honored the threat when he shouldn't have?"

Barnett Francis spoke up. "Exactly. He sent the Chinese the message that we will overtly oppose their actions with force if need be. That is a message we did not want sent at this time."

Overmeyer started to speak, then stopped. He looked at Bender and nodded. "I think there's a basic misunderstanding here," Bender said. Everyone in the room looked at him, shocked that a nobody had the arrogance to contradict the secretary of state. Bender plunged ahead in the silence. "When General Martini put his base on alert and assumed a defensive posture, he was protecting his people. A commander never loses the right of self-defense. The Chinese understand that and expected it. If he launches armed aircraft to defend his base before he is attacked, then he is honoring the threat." The look on Overmeyer's face was ample warning that he had said the wrong thing.

Turner also saw Overmeyer's reaction. "Thank you, General Bender," she said.

A military aide from the communications room entered and handed Shaw two messages. He scanned them and looked up. "The Chinese fleet has changed direction to the southeast and is now headed toward the Yaeyama Islands. On their present heading, the vanguard will enter Japanese waters in less than two hours." He held up the second message. "And the Japanese ambassador requests an immediate audience with the president."

The CNO, chief of Naval Operations, stood and flashed a laser pointer at the big map at the far end of the room. A red pinpoint of light moved around the island chain 275 miles southwest of Okinawa. "The Yaeyama Islands are the southernmost part of Japanese territory," the admiral said. "The major island in the group is Iriomote Jima, which is about 100 miles from Taiwan. It appears Iriomote is their objective."

"Or," the DCI said, "as I have maintained, this is an exercise and they are turning around."

"General Overmeyer?" Turner asked, wanting his opinion.

"They may be turning," Overmeyer said. "A task force that size needs sea room to maneuver. We need to watch them."

"Am I correct in saying," Turner asked, "that there is no immediate threat to our people on Okinawa."

Overmeyer looked like he was about to explode. "Yes, ma'am. You are correct in saying that."

"How were the Chinese able to build a carrier task force so quickly that scares you all silly?" Turner asked.

The CNO answered her question. "They bought it. When the Soviet Union came apart, the *Yaryag,* an Admiral Kuznetsov class aircraft carrier, was eighty percent complete. The Russians sold it to the Chinese. That was bad enough, but the Russians also sold them ninety Su-27K Flanker aircraft to go with it."

Turner looked at Bender. "Robert, didn't you shoot down a Flanker?"

"No, ma'am. It was a Fulcrum, a MiG-29. The Fulcrum and the Flanker look very similar, but the Flanker is bigger and a match for the F-15."

Turner closed her eyes and leaned back in her chair. "What is the strongest possible message I can send the Chinese that we are in a defensive posture militarily?"

This was for Overmeyer. "Order a Condition Scarlet for the entire forward area in the Pacific and go to DEFCON FOUR." DEFCON FOUR, defensive condition 4, was the lowest level of increased defense readiness. It was also a signal that the United States was preparing to use its military.

"Barnett?" she asked.

The secretary of state stared at his hands. "Send an immediate message to the Chinese ambassador calling him to the State Department. I will protest to him in the strongest possible terms while you reassure the Japanese ambassador."

Turner made her decision. "Declare Condition Scarlet in the western Pacific and call in the ambassadors. But do not declare DEFCON FOUR. For the time being, I'll monitor developments from the Oval Office. Please stay available in case we need to reconvene. But under no circumstances do I want to make the situation worse than it already is. Any questions?"

Bender scribbled a brief message on a notepad, "What is the ROE?" and handed it to General Charles. The Air Force chief of staff glanced at it and shook his head, saying nothing. The meeting was over, and Turner walked out with Shaw, Secretary of Defense Elkins, Francis, and the DCI right behind her. Bender waited while Overmeyer and Charles spoke quietly with the chief of Naval Operations. He hoped they were discussing the rules of engagement. Charles motioned Bender to them.

"Sir," Bender said, "apparently I said the wrong thing in there."

Overmeyer stared at him. "You didn't."

What's going on? Bender wondered. *Everyone in the room saw your reaction.* "Shouldn't we have clarified the rules of engagement if the Chinese penetrate Japanese airspace or territorial waters?"

"Nothing needs to be clarified," Overmeyer said. "According to the treaty returning Okinawa to Japanese control, we reserve the right to defend our national assets if a hostile force penetrates Japanese territory or airspace."

"Sir," Bender said, "that treaty was signed over thirty years ago. I don't think the president understands the ROE."

"If she wants to know," Overmeyer muttered, "she only has to ask." He spun around and stomped out of the Cabinet Room.

"Don't worry," Charles said. "We'll clear it up after she meets with the Japanese ambassador."

"That might be leaving it a bit late," Bender protested. Charles did not answer. "Sir," Bender said, frustration eating at him, "what's going on? From the look on the chairman's face, I could have sworn I said the wrong thing about Martini."

"You said exactly what the chairman wanted to hear. But he knew Turner was looking at him. So he frowned, and she reacted the opposite. She accepted what you said."

Bender looked at the admiral. "Sir, with all due respect, what happened to the Navy? You should have been a big player in this."

The CNO's face turned beet red. 'This goes no further than right here. The *Nimitz* is in Yokohama, thirty hours away, and the *Reagan* near Singapore, three days away. Before you joined us, the president decided to withhold the Navy for now." His voice filled with bitterness. "Like the lady said, she doesn't want to make the situation worse than it is."

"Submarines?" Bender asked.

"Same story," the CNO answered.

"What have we been doing the last three days?" Bender asked.

A hard silence held the three men. "Not much," Charles finally answered.

Liz Gordon came out of the press briefing room, her quick stride snapping the fabric of her short skirt. The brief statement by the press secretary had been a waste of time, and her frustration was building. Ben, her cameraman, was waiting for her. "The network wants a package on the press secretary's briefing," he said. "What the hell is going down?"

"I wish I knew," she grumbled. "We either have a full-fledged crisis going or the fuckup of the century."

"Either way it makes for good news," Ben said. He handed her an overcoat and scarf. "Let's do an exterior." She followed him outside with two other reporters and their cameramen who were also working the latest crisis to hit the White House.

After checking her hair and makeup, she took the microphone. On impulse, she shook her head, giving her hair an unruly, hectic look that matched the situation. "Is the Far East about to explode?" she began. "No one seems to know. The facts are simple. A large Chinese fleet is sailing into the East China Sea on what may be a large military exercise or an incursion into Japanese waters. Veteran China watchers claim Beijing is only increasing the psychological pressure on the Japanese to break their economic stranglehold on Asian markets."

As arranged, she stopped for Paul Ferguson, the distinguished anchor in the studio to ask a question. "Liz, does the Pentagon support this view?"

"Paul, the Pentagon has been strangely silent. We are told they are very worried, and there has been talk of honoring the threat. But other than that, inactivity seems to be the watchword."

"What is the White House's reaction?" the anchor asked, his voice heavy with concern and carrying what insiders called *pompous-assed gravitas*.

"President Turner is meeting with the Japanese ambassador while the Chinese ambassador has been called to the State Department. Inside sources claim the secretary of state is delivering a strongly worded warning to the Chinese."

"But, Liz, do we have a crisis or is this simply a misunderstanding stemming from a military exercise?"

"Paul, that is the question that has not been answered. For now, we can only wait for further developments. This is Elizabeth Gordon, standing by at the White House."

"That's a good one," Ben said. He listened to the instructions coming from the network through his headset. "They want something more definitive or Fergy is going to start calling this the Counterfeit Crisis. What'cha think?"

"Premature," Liz replied. "There's more going down here than we know."

"Why not interview General Bender?" the cameraman suggested, remembering their interview from August. "We need an inside."

"The great stone face? We'd be lucky to get five words out of that bastard." *But Ben is right*, she thought, considering her options. A little smile played at her lips.

Okinawa, Japan

It was almost midnight on Okinawa, and the base had been in Condition Scarlet for six and a half hours. The Support Group commander sat down beside Martini in the Battle Cab. "How's the kid doing?" Martini asked.

"Ryan?" the colonel asked. A nod from Martini. "Damn good after you got his attention. He's a quick study and has been coordinating the Med Center's actions with the rest of the base. He's made some good changes and improved our response."

Martini grunted. Maybe he would let Ryan off the hook. After all, teaching was a major part of his job, and as long as Ryan was learning, they were making progress. But had any harm been done? He looked around the command post. It hummed with purposeful activity and seventy-two of his seventy-four jets were armed and ready to launch. The Security Police were fully augmented by support personnel and deployed in bunkers around the base. The disaster response teams were all in place, and Maintenance was moving critical equipment into the hardened aircraft shelters for protection. The motor pool had dispersed all its vehicles and was busy filling sandbags. He snorted, his way of showing relief. The 7,300 men and women under his command were ready.

But he was a worried man. He still had 11,000 family members and dependents on his base to protect. A perverse thought came to him. But the more he considered it, the less wrongheaded it seemed. He turned to the Support Group commander. "Chuck, what's your take on Major Ryan?"

"Smart as hell and ambitious. He did good work setting up the Personnel Reliability Program. He's got an ego problem and thinks he's smarter than everybody else. He's convinced that allows him to take shortcuts and manipulate the system. Definitely not a team player. Still, I see lots of potential there."

The Support Group commander's evaluation matched Martini's. "Your group," Martini said, "is responsible for NEO." NEO was the nonessential personnel evacuation operation. "I want Ryan to get involved. When he's up to speed, he takes it over."

The colonel shook his head. "He's going to love that can of worms."

The red phone in front of Martini buzzed. It was the senior controller in the Control Cab. "Sir, CINC PAC has declared Condition Scarlet for the western Pacific."

Martini leaned back in his chair and took a deep breath of relief. His superiors had agreed with him and he was off the hook. If they had returned the base to normal readiness, they would have relieved him of his command, maybe even court-martialed him. "Are there any changes to the standing ROE?" he asked.

"Negative, sir," the controller answered. "The ROE remains as published."

Martini broke the connection, and his fingers danced on the communications panel in front of him. He called up the air defense coordinator and the mission director on the main floor below him for a conference call. "Are we talking to Tac Ops at Naha?" he asked. The Japanese Self-Defense Force had two squadrons of F4Js at Naha that were responsible for the air defense of Okinawa. They were controlled by the Japanese Tactical Operations Center under the command of the Naha base commander.

"The hot line was activated when CINC PAC declared Condition Scarlet," the air defense coordinator told him.

"Good," Martini said. He told the mission director to put twelve jets on cockpit alert, twelve on fifteen-minute alert, and the rest on thirty-minute alert. He watched the status boards as twelve lights flicked to green indicating which hardened aircraft shelters had aircraft manned and ready to be airborne in less than five minutes. Twelve more lights changed to yellow; the pilots on fifteen-minute alert were ready to go. Now he could honor the threat.

He buzzed the Intelligence section. "Tell Townly I want an Intelligence update ASAP," he ordered. He broke that connection and looked down the long console. Ryan was staring at him, his mouth slightly open in surprise. The Support Group commander had just finished telling him what running the nonessential personnel evacuation operation involved.

Two minutes later, Lieutenant Colonel Pete Townly was in the Battle Cab with a briefing board under his arm. "Sir, this is the situation as of thirty minutes ago." He showed Martini the map that plotted the progress of the Chinese ships. "Our latest radar plot holds them 48 nautical miles due north of Iriomote Jima." Townly's face paled, but his voice was measured and calm. "That places them 250 nautical miles away from us, about ten hours steaming time, thirty-five minutes flying time."

Martini's red phone buzzed. "Sir," the air defense coordinator blurted, "Chinese aircraft have penetrated Japanese territory and Naha is launching their F-4s." From his position, Martini could see the young captain talking into his phone, his eyes wide with fear. He was on the edge of panic.

"Relax, son," Martini said. "If you panic, I panic, and that's not good. Just keep the information coming and we'll kick ass big time.'' The captain turned and looked up at him. Martini gave him an encouraging nod. He called the senior controller in the Control Cab. ''Use some of that cosmic gear you got and call CINC PAC,'' Martini said. ''Tell them the Japanese are launching F-4s from Naha and verify that the ROE is still the same.''

Martini saw the controller's head bend over the communications panel as his fingers danced on the keyboard in front of him. ''Sir,'' the controller said, ''CINC PAC confirms there is no change to the ROE.''

Martini turned to his Operations Group commander. ''Those F-4 drivers are pretty gutsy. It's for damn sure I wouldn't want to take on a Flanker in a Phantom.'' The Ops Group commander was of the same opinion. ''Maybe we can help,'' Martini said. ''Scramble the alert birds into blocking CAPs. Get them way out there, at least halfway to Iriomote. Bring the next twelve jets up to cockpit status. Then backfill them. Tell Tac Ops at Naha what we're doing and that we got four tankers available for airborne refueling if their F-4s need gas.''

Ryan felt his heart race as the command post responded to Martini's commands. *Martini is taking us into a war*, he thought. He fought the urge to run away and hide. But where could he find safety on an island 67 miles long?

Washington, D.C.

Out of boredom and with nothing to do, Bender retreated to the White House mess for coffee. He had nowhere else to go since his office was still occupied by the Navy and the halls outside the Situation Room were packed with experts from the Pentagon, the CIA, and the State Department. Everyone was ready to furnish instant information to his or her boss inside with the president and, if need be, label the other experts imbecilic idiots incapable of finding their own backside without enlightened guidance. *What a waste of time,* Bender thought, *playing games like this.* Still, he was all too aware of how the delicate mix of ego and personality drove policy and decisions. The lieutenant colonel who served as General Charles's aide rushed up to him. "Sir, you're needed in the Situation Room."

"What's the problem?" Bender asked. The lieutenant colonel shook his head—he didn't know. The two men walked quickly down the stairs to the basement. Charles was waiting for him outside the Situation Room and pulled him aside.

"The chairman is going to self-destruct," Charles told him. "Can you spread some oil on the waters?"

"Not without knowing what's going on," Bender replied.

"Apparently fighting has broken out between the Japanese and Chinese, and Martini has launched his jets. The DCI and secretary of state claim the situation is totally out of control.''

''It sounds like Martini has a clue,'' Bender said.

Charles shook his head. ''According to them, it's the military's fault. They want us to immediately disengage and are demanding Martini's head on a platter to show the Chinese we want to negotiate.''

''Stalwart fellows,'' Bender muttered.

''I'm going to justify bringing you in as a tactical expert who can shed some light on the situation. Stall for time until we can get a clearer picture.'' Bender nodded. ''You're on.'' Charles opened the door and they went in.

Overmeyer was standing beside a TV monitor displaying a situation map. ''Madam President,'' he said, glancing at Bender, ''do not tie General Martini's hands at this time. Let him defend his base. And I strongly urge you to order the aircraft carriers *Nimitz* and *Reagan* into the East China Sea.'' He sat down, his face flushed and his right fist a tight knot. Automatically, he reached for a cigar to worry but reconsidered and dropped the cigar on the table in front of him.

Turner stood up, her face pale and drawn. Bender could sense the tension between them. ''How many times have I said that I'm not going to make the situation worse than it is? I will not be drawn into a Gulf of Tonkin incident and overreact.'' A hard silence gripped the room. At the Air Force Academy, Bender had studied the August 1964 incident when North Vietnamese patrol boats reportedly attacked two U.S. destroyers in international waters off the coast of North Vietnam. In the confusion, Congress authorized presidential action which escalated the war. But was the lesson still the same? He didn't think so.

Charles broke the silence. ''Madam President, I'd like to hear General Bender's reaction to the situation.''

''Why him?'' the secretary of state asked. The memory of the last time Bender had intervened was still fresh.

''Because he's one of the best tacticians in the Air Force,'' Charles replied. He didn't wait for a reply. ''General Bender.''

Bender had used the few moments since he entered the

room to study the situation map on the TV screen. "This information is twenty-four minutes old," he began. "In the world of tactical operations, that's ancient history." He phoned the communications room for an update and asked for a force disposition on the second screen. The force disposition appeared first. "Oh, no," he whispered.

He looked at Turner. "The Chinese aircraft carrier, the *Chairman Mao,* is still in international waters off Iriomote Jima but twenty of its fighters have overflown Japanese territory. The Japanese have responded by launching sixteen F-4 fighters from Naha"—he checked his watch— "twenty-six minutes ago."

"We know all this," the secretary of state groused. "You're wasting our time."

Bender fixed him with a cold stare. "Why did the Chinese put up so many jets?" he asked. A blank look from the secretary. "They're the bait to draw the Japanese F-4s. But any engagement will take place over international waters."

"You mean the shooting hasn't started yet?" the DCI asked.

"If it's going to happen," Bender explained, "it will start in three or four minutes. The F-4 is an old aircraft and no match for the Flankers from the *Chairman Mao.* Plus, they will be low on fuel and will have to disengage very quickly."

"It's going to be a turkey shoot," Overmeyer grumbled.

"Not necessarily," Bender replied. "The Japanese are superb pilots and have an excellent antiship missile, the ASM-1. They'll go for the *Chairman Mao,* the only place the Flankers can land. It's going to get very interesting."

The look on Turner's face told him he had said the wrong thing. "Interesting?" she murmured. Then, more strongly, "People are going to die, General, and you only find that interesting?"

"Madam President," Bender replied, "we can help." When she did not reply, he pressed ahead. "Kadena has twelve F-15s airborne and established in CAP points between Okinawa and the Chinese." He pointed at the map on the TV. "Allow General Martini to move these CAP points closer to the action. I would suggest over the island of Miyako Jima.'' Miyako Jima was 100 miles east of Iriomote, closer to Okinawa, and had an airfield. "But let him decide where he can best position his fighters."

"I agree," the DCI said.

"Why?" Turner said, surprised by the DCI's sudden agreement.

"The National Security Agency has a listening post on Miyako Jima," the DCI admitted. "Right now, it's our primary source of intelligence. NSA has broken the Chinese codes, and thanks to Miyako Jima, we've got them wired for sound. We want to protect that source, Madam President."

Now it was Overmeyer's turn. "We have a GCI, a ground-controlled intercept site, on Miyako Jima. The GCI site is the cover for the listening post. But it is also giving us good information."

The situation map on the TV monitor flashed with an update. An air-to-air engagement was taking place twenty miles northeast of Iriomote over international waters as Bender had predicted. The room was silent as each person stared at the TV screen, willing it to change. But they could only wait. The passing minutes seemed like hours. The TV displaying the force disposition scrolled. The *Chairman Mao* was moving to the north, away from Iriomote. Only two F-4s were reported escaping to the east, heading toward Miyako Jima. The chief of Naval Operations finally spoke up. "The *Chairman Mao* is recovering its fighters. The engagement is over."

"Only two F-4s?" Turner asked. "What happened to the others?" She knew the answer. "Oh, no."

"Madam President," Overmeyer said, "we need a show of force. Let Martini move his CAPs further to the west and the *Chairman Mao* will head west, right back to China. The Chinese will not risk losing their only aircraft carrier if we show any backbone."

Wrong words, General! Bender raged to himself. *She doesn't think that way.*

Turner stood up. "Recall our F-15s. I will not make this situation any worse than it is." She walked out of the room. Shaw and her personal assistant, Jackie Winters, were waiting for her. "I want to speak to the Chinese ambassador," she told them. "Immediately."

"We crumpled," Overmeyer said, jamming the cigar in his mouth and chomping.

"I don't think she heard you," Bender said.

Okinawa, Japan

The red phone in front of Martini buzzed, demanding his attention. He picked it up, his eyes still riveted on the status board. The GCI site at Miyako Jima had reported only two of the Japanese F-4s had survived the engagement. Above all else, Martini was a fighter pilot and he raged with anger. He knew the Japanese pilots who had thrown their obsolete F-4s against a superior foe. He had met their commander, eaten with the pilots, drunk their whisky, and swapped the same old war stories that always started with "There I was . . ."

He hadn't joined the Air Force to sit on the sidelines when he could make a difference.

"Sir," the controller said, "we have been directed to recall all our aircraft. We are not to intervene."

Martini slammed the phone down into its wire cradle. The hook broke, and the receiver lay on the console, buzzing at him. He punched at the off button, and it went dead. He stifled an obscenity before it escaped. But his anger filled the Battle Cab. Ryan looked up from his end of the console. He had never seen a human being so angry. He jotted down the time and made a mental note to add it to his case study.

"Recall all our aircraft," Martini told the Operations Group commander. He slammed his fists down on the table, staring at the big status boards. "Get Townly in here. Maybe he's got a clue."

Peter Townly was standing in front of Martini two minutes later. He stared at the status boards, astounded that the F-15s were recovering. "Our side just got creamed, and we're recalling our aircraft? That's dumber than dirt."

"Tell me," Martini growled. "OK, whiz kid, what the hell is the rationale for all this?"

The Intelligence officer pulled into himself. He didn't have an answer. A sergeant ran out of the Intel vault and skidded to a halt at the glass door of the Battle Cab. He waved a message at Townly, frantic to get his attention. Townly opened the door. "The *Chairman Mao*," the sergeant blurted. "It's headed north, away from Iriomote."

Townly handed the message to Martini. "I think they're recovering their aircraft. We're not out of this yet."

"So you think they'll be back?" Martini asked.

"It's called salami tactics," Townly said. "They slice off a little at a time and then wait for our reaction. If I were advising the Chinese commander, I'd tell him that when the Americans recalled their aircraft, they blinked and may not be willing to defend Japan. Cut another slice and find out."

"Where the hell are the Navy's carriers?" Martini growled.

"I have no idea," Townly admitted. "The last I heard, the *Nimitz* was in Yokohama and the *Reagan* in Singapore. Both are too far away to be a factor if the Chinese move now."

"Thanks," Martini muttered. "See if I ask you a question again." The Operations Group commander snorted in half amusement, and the tension in the Battle Cab eased a notch. "Gentlemen," Martini said, "it looks like it is going to get very interesting around here. Start bedding down your troops for the long haul and make sure everyone gets a hot breakfast. Major Ryan, we can't implement NEO until cleared by CINC PAC. But we sure as hell can be ready when he does. As of now, you work for the Support Group commander full-time. Start making things happen."

"Sir, what about the other services?" Ryan asked. "All told, there must be 25,000 dependents and U.S. civilians on the island."

"Evacuate them, too," Martini replied.

Washington, D.C.

Bender was alone in the Situation Room. After the *Chairman Mao* was confirmed still heading north, away from Iriomote, Turner had taken her advisors, which now included Secretary of Defense Elkins and Overmeyer, back to the Oval Office. The Joint Chiefs had returned to the Pentagon and the basement halls rapidly emptied of the uniforms and suits who hovered like pilot fish around the big sharks. Turner had suggested that Bender stay behind to monitor developments from the Situation Room. In the White House, a president's suggestion is treated as holy writ and Bender found himself baby-sitting a bank of TV sets and reading messages.

At least it's something to do, he told himself. He picked up the hot line to the Communications Room down the hall and started asking questions. In short order, he discovered he had access to every Intelligence source available to the president. Between playing with the remote control and talking over the phone, he scrolled through a wealth of information on the monitors. *There's too much data here,* he decided. *How can anyone keep it all straight? Focus on basics,* he told himself. For him the key was the *Chairman Mao.*

There's a lesson here, he thought. *It shows what one aircraft carrier can do when it is used aggressively. Think objectives. What do the Chinese want out of this? What's the bottom line? Would I hazard my only carrier against a superior force? No. But I might use it to probe the reactions of a potential adversary.* He spoke into the phone, and a strategic estimate by the Rand Corporation in Santa Monica, California, scrolled onto a screen. There was no doubt in the author's mind that China wanted to drive a wedge between Japan and the United States and create an economic empire in the Far East.

The more Bender read, the more convinced he became that Okinawa was the key. His head hurt, and he needed to give his brain time to assimilate all that he had been reading. He closed his eyes and let his mind drift. It all snapped into place with a simplicity and clarity that left him reeling in shock. *The Chinese are testing us,* he thought. *They are going to peel us back like an onion until they hit resistance.* He jabbed at the hand control, and the left TV screen scrolled to a situation map. He picked up the phone. "I want to know immediately when the *Chairman Mao* turns to the east, toward Okinawa. It should happen any minute now.''

Shaw sat in a straight-back chair near the fireplace in the Oval Office, a yellow legal pad on his lap, his pen poised to take notes. *Come on, Maddy,* he thought, *do this one right.* Shaw sensed a deep-seated need in his country's collective psyche that demanded an enemy to hate. And if the world did not produce one, then the country turned inward and manufactured one. Fortunately, about every twenty years, a thug nation came along and saved the United States from itself. For Shaw, it was history repeating itself, and the president could ride it to reelection.

''Do the Chinese really expect me to believe this was all a mistake over a military exercise?'' she asked.

''Well, Madam President,'' Secretary of State Francis said, ''that is exactly what their ambassador is claiming. He is adamant: the *Chairman Mao* was in international waters at all times and only defending itself from hostile actions by the Japanese in international airspace. They were acting in self-defense the same as our forces did on Okinawa.''

''Did he make that comparison?'' Turner asked. ''Or is that your interpretation?''

''Those were his exact words, Madam President,'' Francis replied. ''Obviously, the Chinese are monitoring our reactions on Okinawa.''

Turner looked at the DCI. ''Exactly who has who wired for sound?'' There was no answer.

''It is the position of the Chinese,'' Francis continued, ''that they are the aggrieved party. The Japanese overreacted when a telephone call would have solved the whole problem.''

''Did anyone make that phone call?'' Turner asked.

''Not to our knowledge,'' the DCI replied.

''It was a probing action by the Chinese,'' Overmeyer said. He really wanted to say the Chinese were testing her resolve, but he had learned discretion.

''Are we in a position to negotiate?'' Turner asked.

''Of course,'' Francis replied.

Sam Kennett, the vice president, cleared his throat. "With all due respect, Madam President, negotiate what?"

The boy's got a head on his shoulders, Shaw thought. *Listen to him.* For Shaw, it was a simple matter. The Chinese were doing a Mau-Mau on the Japanese and the United States and needed to get their toes stepped on. Otherwise, they would keep right on doing it. It was an old lesson that people forgot at the first opportunity.

"I want to draft a letter to the Chinese premier, Lu Zoulin, protesting in the strongest possible terms," Turner said. "I want to negotiate a protocol for future naval exercises that will preclude this from happening again."

"Are you going to back up that protest with a show of force?" Overmeyer asked. "Putting two aircraft carriers into the East China Sea would get their attention."

"That is not necessary at this time," she answered. "The Chinese are rational actors and will respond accordingly."

It was the answer Overmeyer had expected, and he did not answer. He recalled a war game where he had caught the leaders of the opposing force exercising mirror imaging and projecting their own values and attitudes on him. He had stomped them. But this time, it was his president doing the mirror imaging.

The phone in front of Bender buzzed at the exact moment the TV screen flashed. "Sir," the voice said, "the *Chairman Mao* has turned to the east." The TV screen confirmed what the caller had said. "It may be reversing course."

"Don't bet your pension on it," Bender told him. He dropped the phone and hurried out the door. This was a message that had to be delivered in person so it could not be ignored. He trotted up the stairs and charged through the outer office to the Oval Office with a brisk "The president is expecting me." Wayne Adams, the Secret Service agent, was standing post and held the door open for him.

Turner looked up from behind her desk. "Yes, Robert?"

"The *Chairman Mao* has turned toward Okinawa," he told her.

"When did this happen?" the DCI asked.

"Less than five minutes ago," Bender answered.

"Premature," the DCI muttered. "It may be maneuvering."

"No, sir," Bender snapped. "It is not maneuvering. By now it is moving at flank speed directly toward Okinawa."

"The Chinese are not going to attack Okinawa," Francis replied, condescension dripping from every word.

Bender stood his ground. "They are not going to attack our forces on Okinawa. But they are going to challenge the Japanese."

The DCI scoffed. "How are they going to do that? How do they justify it?"

"The Japanese gave them the justification they needed at Iriomote," Bender said.

The DCI shook his head. "That won't wash."

The secretary of state was a very worried man. "If they show restraint and don't threaten our forces, the UN, Congress, might buy it. The Japanese are very unpopular."

"Gentlemen," Turner said, "reality check. Exactly *how* are the Chinese going to challenge the Japanese without involving us? Once I have an answer to that question, then I can proceed." No one answered her.

Bender's words cut through the silence. "With a blockade, Madam President."

"What makes them think they can get away with that?" she asked.

"Iriomote," Bender said. "They tested our resolve to defend Japanese territory and we failed." Everyone in the room knew the "we" he was talking about was Turner.

Turner came to her feet, her face flushed with anger. Bender braced for the reprimand that was on her lips. Instead, "I'm going to the Situation Room." He stood aside as she walked through the door. "You needn't come, Robert." Her advisors trooped out behind her.

Overmeyer paused to say something but only gave him a curt nod. Shaw was the last one out. "Well, boy, you stepped on the old foreskin this time. Gawd, that must hurt like hell."

13 ⟋

Okinawa, Japan

The sergeant walked onto the low stage at the front of the command post and paused in front of the big threat map that dominated the center of the status boards. Every head turned to watch him as he plotted the latest position of the Chinese fleet that was sailing directly toward Okinawa. Ryan felt his heart pound as the sergeant moved the red arrowhead closer to Okinawa and marked the time. *This is like a bad movie,* he thought. *This doesn't happen in real life. But there it is, heading straight for us. It's high noon on Sunday and there's no way out.*

The wing's vice commander was sitting in Martini's chair in the Battle Cab and, like Ryan, felt the danger bearing down on them. "Well, gentlemen," he said, his voice calm and matter-of-fact, "we do indeed have a problem. Major Ryan, please wake General Martini. Tell him we are now in missile range."

"Yes, sir," Ryan answered and headed for the small bunk room at the back of the command post. *How can he sleep at a time like this?* he wondered. Ryan had not seen a bed in over thirty-five hours and was dog tired. He knocked at the door and entered. Martini was sound asleep, and he nudged his shoulder. "Sir, you're wanted in the Battle Cab."

Martini stirred and rolled over. He blinked a few times

and then sat up. "I'll be right there." He turned on the light. "Status," he growled.

"The *Chairman Mao* is approximately seventy miles to the west, and we are now inside missile range," Ryan answered. "There has been no change in their air cover and they only have two helicopters on antisubmarine patrol."

"How do I look?" Martini said. Ryan was shocked by the question and didn't know how to answer. "Nervous ticks, shaking hands, weepy eyes," Martini muttered. "That type of thing. You're the doc, and your job is to keep me healthy." He paused. "A commander isn't worth shit if he's dead on his feet or falling apart from stress."

Ryan breathed an audible sigh of relief and gave him a quick visual check. "You look tired, but you're OK. Eat something and drink lots of water. Walk around if you can for exercise."

Martini nodded. "You look beat. Sack out for a while." He stood up and pointed at the cot. "It's called *hot bunking*." Ryan sat down as ordered and was asleep when Martini closed the door. Martini stepped into the Battle Cab and studied the status boards. "Are they going to come ashore?" he asked his vice commander.

"I hope not," the colonel answered. "No word from CINC PAC. We keep screaming for help and they keep saying 'Stand by.' "

Martini made his decision. "If they launch missiles, aircraft, or those ships come inside twelve miles, we scramble. Tell CINC PAC our intentions. I don't think they'll override us." The colonel picked up the phone and called the Control Cab while the Operations Group commander placed all his aircraft on five-minute alert. The phone buzzed, and the light from the radar early warning site flashed. Martini punched at the button, listened, and hung up. "The *Chairman Mao* is launching aircraft; judging by the speed and altitude, they're helicopters, much more than they need for antisubmarine patrol. Why the increase?"

He stood and leaned forward, his hands resting on the console. "Gentlemen, our bosses are not telling us what to do. It looks like we get to make our own decisions.

Launch eight jets into a base CAP for air defense, and I want the four E's that are carrying Popeyes airborne. We're going to give those bastards something to think about.'' The Popeye was a 3,000-pound medium-range standoff missile the United States had bought from Israel and adapted to the F-15E Strike Eagle. The Popeye's special warhead was equivalent to 750 pounds of high explosive and could sink a ship.

Martini settled into his chair and waited. "Hell of a way to fight a war," he groused to no one in particular. "Hey, anybody got an MRE? I'm hungry." A meal packet appeared in front of him, and he ate the food cold, surprised at how good it tasted. The seconds passed, dragging into minutes, turning into a half-hour.

The sergeant walked back onto the stage and paused in front of the threat map, his hands pressing his earphones against his head. He moved quickly and circled a small island sixty miles due west of the southern tip of Okinawa. The loudspeaker squawked. "Attention in the command post. The *Chairman Mao* has slowed and altered course to the south. Chinese helicopters are reported landing on Kumejima Island."

"Well, sir," the vice commander said, "we got an answer to your questions about them coming ashore and why all those helicopters."

"They just took another slice," Martini muttered. "Cancel the scramble. I'll be damned if I'll start a war over a rock in the East China Sea. Keep sixteen jets on five-minute alert and start cycling the crews into crewrest."

Major Bob Ryan was sound asleep in the bunk room.

Washington, D.C.

Madeline O'Keith Turner did not like what she was hearing. But Mazana Kamigami-Hazelton's soft voice kept hammering, pounding the president with velvet blows. Turner wished she was alone in the Situation Room with the NSC analyst and not surrounded by men: Sam Kennett, the secretaries of defense and state, the DCI, Shaw, and

Overmeyer. She glanced at the crusty general, surprised that he was not showing any I-told-you-so signs.

Hazelton paused to clear her throat before continuing. "Please excuse me, Madam President, but I'm not used to speaking." Shaw hurried to refill her water glass, and her graceful movements fascinated the men. Hazelton was a beautiful and petite Japanese-Hawaiian. Her clothes and the huge diamond in her engagement ring shouted money and influence, which went with the Hazelton name. But nothing could hide the fact that she was a brilliant analyst and not intimidated by her surroundings.

She set the glass down, ready to continue. "The Chinese have been ashore on Kumejima ten hours and are consolidating their position." She gestured gracefully at the bank of wall clocks behind her. It was eight o'clock Sunday morning in Washington, D.C., and ten o'clock that evening in Okinawa. "Although the picture is incomplete, the National Security Agency has intercepted and decoded enough message traffic to verify this was a well-planned probe of our resolve to defend the Japanese. The Chinese were monitoring the disposition of our naval forces and our reaction at Kadena Air Force Base. Whenever they saw a show of force on our part, they pursued an alternate course of action that had been planned well in advance."

The DCI struggled to hide his anger. This small wisp of a woman was telling the president the Chinese had played them like puppets. "Pure speculation, Mrs. Hazelton," he grumbled.

Hazelton arched an eyebrow, and her lips drew into a straight line—her way of asking "Is it?" Turner caught the unspoken question. "The *Chairman Mao*," Hazelton continued, "was in constant radio contact with Beijing and turned away from Iriomote five minutes after Kadena launched aircraft. From the message traffic, it is quite clear they interpreted this as support of the Japanese F-4s heading toward Iriomote. They then withdrew to the north to recover their aircraft and monitored our reaction to the aerial engagement.

"When we recalled our aircraft, there was another flurry of radio traffic and they advanced toward Okinawa, still monitoring our reaction. When Kadena again launched aircraft, there was another burst of message traffic. Again, they changed direction and occupied the island of Kumejima.''

Now it was the secretary of state's turn to be angry. "Exactly what are the Chinese doing, Mrs. Hazelton?''

"It's called salami tactics, Mr. Secretary.''

A monitor bleeped, and the words "Incoming message'' flashed on the screen. The room was deadly silent as the latest message the NSA had intercepted and decoded scrolled on the screen: The Chinese ambassador was instructed to present a carefully worded letter to the State Department that the People's Republic of China could not tolerate the unwarranted attack on the *Chairman Mao* in international waters. Therefore the PRC was forced to establish a peaceful blockade commencing at 1 P.M., Sunday, of the forces that committed the attack to preclude it from happening again.

"Peaceful blockade?'' Overmeyer snorted.

"Lord, love-a-duck,'' Shaw muttered. "Bender was right.''

"Madam President,'' Hazelton said, "please note that the Chinese do not specifically identify who committed this so-called violation of international waters.''

"Nothing in international law,'' the secretary of state said, "justifies this blockade.''

"The Chinese are making their own rules,'' Hazelton replied.

Turner stood up. "I want to meet with the National Security Council in thirty minutes.'' She headed for the door. "Sam, Mrs. Hazelton, Patrick, please come with me.''

The ever-present Jackie Winters, her personal assistant, was waiting in the corridor. "Your mother asked about the family dinner this afternoon.''

"Tell her I can't make it. I'll try to see them later this evening. And please have General Bender join us in the Oval Office.'' Jackie scurried off to make it happen. Kennett, Shaw, and Hazelton trailed after her into the Oval Office. "Please be seated, Mrs. Hazelton. Do you prefer to be called Mazana?''

"I prefer Mazie,'' Hazelton answered.

"Well, Mazie," Turner said, "the Chinese certainly made a fool out of me." Hazelton only looked at the president, her face an impassive mask. *She's not contradicting me,* Turner thought. The truth hurt more than she could imagine.

"Madam President," Kennett said, looking at Hazelton, "I think we've found your new national security advisor."

Turner considered the vice president's proposal. It felt right, and she trusted Kennett's instincts. But before she could answer, Hazelton shook her head. "Mrs. President, as much as I'm flattered, I was in that room. You saw how those men reacted to me. I'm too much of an unknown quantity for them to accept."

"You're right," Turner said. "We need to groom you under an acting national security advisor for a few months until you have the right amount of exposure. Are you interested?"

Hazelton considered her answer. "It all depends on who the interim national security advisor is."

"You're going to meet him in a few minutes," Turner said.

Shaw stifled an unspoken "Ah, shit." He mentally drove a knife into the vice president's back for proposing Hazelton in the first place and wondered how he could salvage the situation. A discrete knock at the door caught his attention. ·

Bender entered and sat down. *What now,* he thought.

It was late when Bender finally arrived home that same Sunday evening. He was still wearing the same clothes he had put on forty hours earlier and wanted nothing more than a beer, a hot shower, and a good night's sleep. The lights were still on, and he could hear Nancy talking in the family room. Was she on the phone or did they have guests? He stopped by the refrigerator and found a bottle of his favorite beer waiting for him with a glass. He ambled into the family room and froze. Shalandra was curled up on the couch by the fire thumbing through a magazine. *Why is she still here?* he groused to himself.

"Robert," Nancy said, "we've been waiting for you." He didn't reply and sat down. They would have to have a long talk about the girl when they were alone. Nancy gave him her I-know-what-you're-thinking look. "There were problems at the foster home," she said. "We'll have to get Shalandra into a new home tomorrow."

He allowed a noncommittal "I see."

Nancy shook her head. "Actually, you don't." She paused, waiting for Shalandra to speak. Nothing. "It's OK," Nancy urged. "He doesn't hit women."

The girl looked at him, her dark eyes full of worry. "'D' yo"—she hesitated, then regrouped—"do you remember what you said when Murphy called me a nigger hooker?" She fell silent. It was the longest string of coherent words Bender had heard her utter. Shalandra's eyes darted between him and Nancy.

Bender had to think for a moment. "As I recall, I said, 'Does it matter what she was?' "

"What'd you mean by that?"

"I meant a lot of things," Bender replied. "First of all, you were a person who needed help. But for me, the most important thing is what you are now and what you're trying to do with your life."

"Why did yo—you—run over my uncle?"

"He was trying to kill Murphy," Bender told her. "She was there because I had talked her into coming with me. I was responsible for her." He looked at his hands. Did Shalandra understand?

"Mizz Bender, I wanna go to bed now."

"Certainly, Shalandra. You know the way."

Bender took a sip of the beer and waited until they were alone. "Nancy," he said, "you know better than to get personally involved with a patient. And I do remember a promise being made."

"I know," she admitted. "But she ran away from the foster home Friday night when she was sexually molested."

He took a deep breath and exhaled loudly. "What is the matter with men?"

"It wasn't a man this time," Nancy told him. "She ran to the only shelter she trusted—the hospital. But there's more to it. You heard her question. Look at her. She's pretty and so vulnerable. She can be a beautiful, decent woman given half a chance."

"And you want to give her that chance."

Nancy nodded. "She's asking for help. Did you hear how she tries to speak properly? I talked to the admissions officer at the Georgetown Academy. He's very interested and wants to interview her tomorrow and conduct some tests."

"That's a school for rich kids," Bender protested. "Brian goes there. Think about that. The president's son. How many ambassadors, legislators, cabinet officers, you name it, send their kids there?"

"Do you know how many of them have worse drug problems than Shalandra?" Nancy asked. "Or how many have been abused? Or how many are failing miserably in school? The Academy has a residence program specifically designed to treat these children."

"And how expensive is it? Tuition, room, and board?"

"They have a scholarship program. But Shalandra will need a sponsor."

"You," Bender said.

"No. Us. It will cost us some money." She paused. "Quite a bit of money. Even with the scholarship, it will take over half of what I'm making at the hospital."

"Nancy, this is stupid. She has psychological problems that no therapy will ever solve. And what sort of games is she playing with us? If we start this, we can't walk away. We'll have to be in it for the long haul. But what if she can't adjust? What if she fails?"

"I don't want to walk away from her. I can do something here and make a difference." She worried her lower lip. "But if she's trying to use us or fails at the Academy, then I'll put her back into the system."

Bender heard the determination in her voice, and against his better judgment, he gave in. "I suppose she'll have to come here for the holidays," he said. She came out of her chair like a shot and was across the room, her arms around his neck. He groaned. "Just like a bowling ball."

"We'll make it work," she said. She kissed him on the cheek and nipped at his ear. "What's your news?"

He laughed. "I can't hide anything from you. Turner wants me to be her national security advisor."

Her arms tightened around his neck. "Did you accept?" He felt her heart beating with excitement. "I never thought—"

"It's only temporary while they groom a permanent advisor, Mazie Hazelton. She's a brilliant analyst on the National Security staff and deserves the job." He dropped his chin to his chest and stroked her hair. "I never expected anything like this." Bender was honest with himself and knew it was a rare opportunity, a chance to prove what he could really do and make a difference.

"If I take the job, I'll end up on the opposite side of the fence from Overmeyer and Charles and may even find myself telling them what to do." He shook his head. "I'm already on slippery ground with them, and I'd have to resign my commission." He told her about Charles wanting to know what was said in the kitchen cabinet and the way he had handled it. "If it was permanent, I'd do it in a heartbeat. But face it, I'm just a Ping-Pong ball being batted around the West Wing for her to play with."

Nancy drew back and studied her husband. "Robert, sometimes you are so dense—" She broke off in midsentence, amused by the look on his face. It was too bad she couldn't tell him the entire truth. "She trusts your advice."

Robert Bender gave his wife his don't-be-stupid humph. "She's on an ego trip," he muttered.

"All politicians are on an ego trip," Nancy replied. "Not a single one would score normal on a personality test."

"I promised her an answer tomorrow morning."

"Sleep on it," she murmured. "You'll do the right thing."

Jackie Winters hustled down the hall of the White House, leading Bender to the elevator. The president's personal aide reminded him of a fussy mouse, scurrying around a large kitchen, determined to get everything in order. She gave him a harried look. "The President wants to see you before she meets with Mr. Shaw at eight o'clock.'' The elevator doors swooshed open, and she darted inside. Before Bender could enter, Shaw joined them carrying the day's schedule and the PDB.

"Made up your mind?" he asked.

Bender decided that Turner should be the first to hear his decision and didn't answer. They rode in silence up to the second floor. Jackie broke the silence. "The president wants to meet with her kitchen cabinet at eight-thirty.''

"I've already slipped the staff meeting thirty minutes,'' Shaw said.

"What about the meeting with the NSC?" Jackie asked.

Bender split his attention as they resolved the changes to the president's schedule. *What will she say when I tell her I don't want the job?* he wondered. William, the butler, was retreating down the hall when they reached Turner's private study. "You go on in,'' Shaw said, following the butler.

What's that all about? Bender thought. Jackie answered without hearing the question. "Mr. Shaw is very concerned about what people discuss with the president when he's not around. It's something you'll have to get used to.'' Bender did not reply. Jackie knocked on the door and ushered him in.

"Good morning, Robert, Jackie,'' Turner said. Bender returned her greeting, worried that she looked so tired. He sat down on the couch opposite her. "Coffee?" she offered, still the thoughtful hostess. Jackie poured while he mentally rehearsed what he was going to say. The door from the bedroom burst open, and Sarah rushed through. She was dressed for school, and Maura O'Keith was right behind her.

The little girl pecked her mother on the cheek. "See you later.'' Then she kissed Bender on the cheek and was out the door.

"Kids,'' he muttered.

Maura was looking at him. "You're the first man she's kissed since her father died.''

Turner was silent until her mother had left. "Well, Robert, have you made up your mind?''

Suddenly, the pat answer he had been rehearsing disappeared. He was honest with himself and realized Sarah's peck on the cheek had thrown him for a loop. He changed his mind. "Madam President, there are some problems that need to be resolved first." Turner said nothing and waited for him to continue. "I have been approached by a member of the JCS asking what was discussed with your personal advisors. I refused to answer."

"What's the problem, Robert?"

"I cannot serve two masters. I would have to resign my commission to be your national security advisor."

"You don't have to resign your commission," Shaw said from the doorway. "We can arrange a leave of absence."

Bender twisted around at the sound of his voice. *When did he come in?* "Was it General Charles?" Turner asked.

Bender sensed they had come to the crossroads of their relationship and what happened now would determine how he functioned as her advisor. "Madam President, I would rather not answer that question. Suffice to say, the individual accepted my refusal to answer."

"Robert," she said, "I need your undivided loyalty. I do not expect you to betray the confidences shared with your friends, but can you stand up to the generals and implement my decisions?"

He thought about it. Standing up to Overmeyer and Charles would be hard. Could he do it? "Yes, ma'am, as long as I agree with your position, I can. If I do not agree, I will have to resign."

My, my, Shaw thought, *how noble.*

"Good," Turner said. "Let's proceed on that basis. For the time being, it would be best if you did not join with my private advisors but worked with my staff as the national security advisor should. That should take some of the pressure off." She gave him a pleasant smile. "Jackie, please introduce General Bender to his staff and help him move into his office."

Bender took that as a dismissal and left with Jackie. *Kicked upstairs,* he thought, *and barred from the inner sanctum.* Again, Jackie seemed to know what he was thinking. "May I suggest," she said, "that in the future you do not criticize the president in front of others."

"I assume you are referring to my remarks about the Chinese testing our resolve to defend Japanese territory."

"Your assumption is correct," Jackie answered.

So Turner got the message, he thought. *But why the sudden promotion to national security advisor?* Nancy's words from the night before about the president trusting him echoed in his mind. Another thought came to him. Jackie had not been present when he had criticized the president. He decided to pursue it a little further. "Did the president tell you to pass this on to me?" There was no answer to his question.

Shaw waited patiently while Turner read the PDB. She dropped the thin document in her lap and stared past him when she was finished. "Was General Bender right, Patrick? Did I crumble?"

Shaw snorted. "He had no call to say that, Mizz President. He overstepped his place."

"Did he?" She thought for a few moments. "Patrick, I'm not going to be a prisoner to this crisis, not like President Carter during the hostage crisis in Iran in 1980." She stood and paced the floor. "I want to send the message that foreign affairs do not drive my domestic policies. We are going full steam ahead on tax reform."

"Madam President," Shaw protested, "would that be wise"—he froze at the look on her face—"I, ah, I mean at this time."

Turner grabbed the small bell on the mantle and rang it. Hard. "Are you listening, Patrick?" The sudden silence was deafening. "The Chinese will not hold me hostage on this."

He gulped. "Yes, ma'am." He was rescued by a knock at the door. It was time for the meeting with her kitchen cabinet. Noreen Coker entered with Sam Kennett and Richard Parrish.

"Mrs. President," Coker said, "you seen the latest polls? We are hurtin'."

The two secretaries in the outer office stood up when Bender and Jackie entered the corner suite of the West Wing. They had heard the rumors about Bender's impending appointment, and first impressions did count. Normally, a national security advisor brought his own staff with him, but after talking with Alice Fay, Shaw's secretary, both women were hopeful that they might still have a job that evening. Jackie made the introductions. "Norma, Ella," Bender said, repeating their names as they shook hands, "I hope you're staying on board because I'm going to need all the help I can get."

The two women assured him they would be more than happy to work for him while they silently breathed a sigh of relief. "Please call Mrs. Hazelton and ask her to join me. Could someone clear out my old desk? And there's a framed photo on the wall that's mine." They were two very happy women as they hurried to do as he asked.

Mazie Hazelton paused when she walked into Bender's office. A brief pang of regret swept over her as she remembered the last time she had been there. Bender watched her, sensing what she was going through. "I understand you worked for Bill Carroll when he was the national security advisor," he said. "He was a good man."

She nodded slowly. "The last few weeks were terrible." Time had not diminished the horrible memory of Carroll's death from Lou Gehrig's disease.

"Mazie, what would he be doing right now?"

"Looking for a way to break the blockade while probing for a weakness."

"Any ideas what that might be?"

"Not yet, but I'll find it."

He checked his watch. "The National Security Council is meeting in a few minutes." He allowed a deep chuckle. "How about that? My first meeting and I haven't even met my staff yet. From now on, Mazie, you're my shadow. Don't be afraid to jerk me up short if I'm about to shoot my foot off."

Hazelton gave him a friendly look. "You do mix your metaphors, General. But I think I can do all that."

It was dark and snowing when Shaw finally escaped from the White House and drove into the Virginia countryside. He had no trouble following the directions and finding the narrow lane that wound through the hills. A county

snow plow was clearing the private road, the sure sign of
political clout. *Why am I doing this?* he asked himself for
perhaps the tenth time. But the first answer was still as
strong and compelling as before. Nothing could distract
Turner from her mad race to self-destruction over tax reform so he had to save himself. He hated going over to
the other side, but he didn't see any other way out of his
dilemma, not if he was to survive at the national level.

It had been an easy matter to reach out and make contact once he had made the decision. But the decision still
ate at him. He mentally rehearsed what he was bringing
to this meeting. He had to be decked out in all his political
finery if they were going to accept him on his terms.
Ahead of him, he could see the lights of the large farmhouse glowing on the hillside. He drove through the gate
and up the drive. A dark-suited young man was waiting
for him and opened the car's door. "This way, sir," the
aide said. Shaw did a mental double take when he realized
the young man was one of Senator Leland's staffers. *So
Leland's part of this,* he thought. *That means he's the
daddy rabbit.*

Automatically, Shaw resorted what he knew about the
senator. *Why is he out to get Maddy?* he wondered. *Is it
because of his nephew, Chris, who was killed with Bender's daughter in that crash on Okinawa? Maddy promised
she would investigate and do something. But thanks to
Bender, nothing has happened. That had to be part of it.*
Shaw felt better. He had one more card he could play.
But now that he was in the enemy's keep, their stronghold,
and about to do a Benedict Arnold, there was no margin
for mistakes. The aide held the door open, and he entered
the sumptuous study. *No going back now,* he thought.

"Good evening, Patrick," Leland said. "I think you
know most of these people." Shaw looked around the
room, and his ego took a sharp kick in the groin. Jessica,
his beautiful blond bedmate with the penchant for kinky
sex and great cooking, was there. He had been targeted.
"And I believe you have met Gwen." Shaw's big head
jerked around so he could see who Leland was talking
about. It was one of those rare times when he was at a
total loss for words. Gwen Anderson, the most strident

feminist in the capital, Turner's first choice to be vice president, the woman he had dismantled with the revelations about her bouts of depression and taking lithium, was sitting in a comfortable wing chair by the fire.

"Good evening, Patrick," she said, her voice under tight control.

"Mizz Anderson," he mumbled.

"Gwen," Leland said, "has proved to be invaluable with her insights into our flounder-in-chief's thinking."

Shaw did a quick recount of the room. The Senate and House majority leaders were there along with the Senate minority leader and two of the most powerful lobbyists on the Hill. Then it hit him, one-third of the group were women. Again, his political abacus clicked, and he subtracted the assumption that they were after Maddy Turner because she was a woman. For Shaw, politicians in the pursuit of power were first cousins to sharks in a feeding frenzy when there was blood in the water. These particular sharks scented a president who was too weak to guard her powers, prerogatives, and privileges, and they were going to take it all away from her. This had nothing to do with gender and was an old-fashioned grab for power. He was swimming in familiar waters.

"Gwen," Leland continued, "was against your joining us."

"I do hope you will prove useful," Anderson said.

Shaw sat down, his hands clasped between his knees. He knew what he was offering was more than enough to buy his way into the group. But by the same token, they had to accept it as sufficient payment because he knew who they were, and as the president's chief of staff, he had the power to hurt them. He began to talk, slowly at first, laying out the president's tax reform package. He was met by condescending nods. They were not impressed. When he got to the strategy he had formulated to get it passed, the nodding heads stopped. It was a masterful display of arm twisting, political bargaining, and, when all else failed, threats. Shaw knew where too many skeletons were buried and had the ammunition to make it a knock-down, take-no-prisoners brawl. He might have lost in the end, but it would have been a costly victory for the winners.

"How long have you known about our group?" Leland asked.

"For about two weeks," Shaw answered. "But I never told the president."

"Is there anything else you have for us?" Leland asked.

"She's afraid of a military confrontation with the Chinese and is going to roll over and play dead."

Leland stood and squared his shoulders. "If you can deliver on that," he said, "I do believe the lady is ours." For Shaw, Leland's voice and bearing conjured up the image of a vengeful prophet from the Old Testament.

"Damn," Liz Gordon muttered as she answered the insistent summons from the phone. It was the night door-man. "Goddamn it, Charlie," she snarled. He had standing orders to chase anyone away after 10 P.M. and should have known better than to disturb her so late on a Monday night. "It's almost midnight."

"Sorry, Miss Gordon," Charlie groveled, "but it's Mr. Shaw."

She clamped her hand over the mouthpiece. "Jeff, wake up. It's Shaw."

Jeff Bissell stirred. "Send the bastard away."

"I can't do that." She gestured him to silence. "Charlie, put him on the line."

"You said you weren't fucking him," Bissell growled.

"Shush," she hissed. "Patrick," she chimed, "what brings you here so late?" She listened. "Don't be silly, come right on up."

"Come right on up," Bissell mimicked crankily. "Is it going to be a threesome?"

"No. You're leaving. The back way. And be damned sure he doesn't see you."

"So you can fuck him in private."

"I'm not going to sleep with him," she said. "He doesn't know we're back together." She threw his clothes at him.

"Then put something on," he muttered as he headed for the kitchen and the utility entrance.

Liz had time to don a robe and to comb her hair before the front doorbell rang. She checked her appearance in the hall mirror, artfully loosened the robe, and fluffed her hair. She answered the bell on the second ring. "Why didn't you call?" she asked.

"I was on the cellular," he told her, shaking off his overcoat. Eavesdropping on a public official's cellular phone conversation was a highly illegal, but widely used practice by the Washington press corps. Liz's voice would have been instantly recognized and at least three reporters would have ambushed Shaw when he arrived at her apartment complex. "Don't worry," he told her, anticipating her next question, "I gave Charlie a healthy tip. He'll keep his mouth shut."

"Come on in," she said. "Drink?"

"Any good sour mash," he replied.

"With water?"

"Already too damn much water in it," he grumbled.

She recognized the signs and poured him a tumbler half full of a rich liquid amber whiskey. Her robe fell half open when she handed it to him. She had never seen him so depressed and for a moment thought he might be on the edge of a nervous breakdown. She quickly discarded the notion. This was Patrick Flannery Shaw, one of Washington's consummate actors. "Is it the China thing?"

"That's not the half of it," he grumbled. He didn't want to talk about China and only wanted company and a sympathetic ear. He deliberately changed the subject. "Why are the feminists so angry with the president?"

Play this one right, Liz cautioned herself, *he knows why.* She chose her words carefully. "They believe she is willing to compromise with the enemy. That makes her a traitor."

"Gawd," he moaned, "they can't be that stupid. Politics is compromise."

Liz shook her head, still playing the game, hoping she could get something useful out of him. "They're true believers. I think you need a good night's sleep. We can talk about it in the morning if it's still bothering you." She led him into the bedroom.

Jeff Bissell was parked in his car and saw the light in Liz's bedroom go off. He hit the steering wheel with his fist and reached for his phone. He knew a reporter who would be most grateful. Then he reconsidered, slipped the transmission into first gear, and drove slowly off. It was the price he paid for loving Liz Gordon.

The noise of running water punched through the shroud of sleep that held Shaw tight. He stretched, vaguely aware that it was morning. Morning! On the edge of panic, he fumbled for his watch. Ten minutes before five. He had plenty of time to reach the White House and be ready for whatever the new day would bring. "Don't worry," Liz said. "I wouldn't let you sleep in." She was standing in the bathroom door, her naked body glimmering in the soft light. She came back to bed, holding a long feather in her left hand. "I do hope you're up to this."

"Darlin'," he said, his voice low and husky, "we haven't got time for games this mornin'."

"Patrick Shaw," she fumed. "When you wake me out of a sound sleep at midnight, you had better be prepared to pay the price or I'll bite your balls off." She made a snapping sound with her teeth and rolled into bed, reaching for him.

He made a mock show of protecting his scrotum. "What are the stakes?"

"An inside?" she suggested.

"And if you lose," he said, "it's doggie style, on the roof, in the snow."

"Sounds like a chilling experience," she replied. "But I'm not going to lose." She went to work with the feather, trying to raise an erection. Nothing happened. After a few minutes, she looked at him, expecting to see his lopsided grin. But his eyes were wide with worry. "I must be losing my touch," she said, drawing her long fingernails up his flaccid penis. Still nothing. "I guess it's snow time," she said, rolling out of bed and reaching for her robe.

He got out of bed. "I'll have to take a snow check."

She waited as he dressed and helped him on with his overcoat. Then he was gone. She was making coffee when the phone rang, and as expected, it was Jeff Bissell. She listened for a few moments. "Absolutely nothing happened," she told him. "He only wanted to talk and get a good night's sleep. He's a lonely man."

14

Okinawa, Japan

Only the ruffling of pages punctuated the silence in the Battle Cab as Martini and his group commanders read their copies of the lengthy top secret message from headquarters CINC PAC. Pete Townly, the Intel officer, stood in a corner and read the message in bits and pieces as the Operations Group commander passed him pages of the detailed directive outlining how they were to respond to the blockade. Finally, Martini dropped his copy on the console in front of him and kicked back in his chair, his head against the back wall. "Supposedly, we've been blockaded for thirty-six hours," he said. "Your thoughts?"

His vice commander was the first to answer. "Some fuckin' blockade. All talk."

"At least the rules of engagement are unchanged, and we can still defend ourselves," the Operations Group commander added.

"What does it mean," the Logistics Group commander asked, "when they say 'Continue with preparations but do not disturb the local populace'?"

"It means," Martini grumped, "that the Japanese government is telling its people one thing, while our government tells us to get ready to fight."

"Does anybody back there have a clue what's going on?" the Support Group commander asked.

"They don't have the bad guys looking at them from 60 miles off shore," Martini replied. He gestured at Townly. "Pete, what's the latest status at Kumejima?"

Townly took a deep breath. "The Chinese have reinforced the island with approximately 10,000 combat troops, four batteries of antiship Silk Worm missiles and, at last count, thirty KS-1 surface-to-air missiles. They are digging bunkers and building aircraft revetments at the airstrip. But they got a fuel problem and are rigging fuel bladders. We calculate they will be able to start fighter operations within twenty-four hours. A Habu mission is scheduled for early tomorrow morning for an update."

"Where's the *Chairman Mao*?"

"At last report, it has withdrawn and is heading for Taiwan. But they left behind eighteen fast-attack craft armed with missiles and torpedoes along with four destroyers and six frigates, which all sport a damn good antisubmarine capability. It's safe to assume they have a few of their own submarines on patrol."

"They're not stupid," Martini grumbled. "They don't want to risk losing the *Chairman Mao* and have pulled it back before our carriers or submarines get here."

"Sir," Townly said, "I don't think the Navy will risk bringing a carrier inside the range of those Silk Worms on Kumejima."

"What's the range of a Silk Worm?" Martini asked.

"They've deployed the HY-5 version with a reported range of 1,000 nautical miles," Townly answered. "Until those missiles are neutralized, Navy air is forced into a standoff position, which seriously degrades their effectiveness." Martini stared at the Intel officer, challenging him to continue. "At this point, it appears that everyone is in a hold position and is waiting for the other side to fire the first shot."

Martini thought for a moment. "So they've got ships but no fighter cover. That means they can enforce the blockade at sea but not in the air. We have the right of self-defense, which means we have fighter cover, and have been told to continue with readiness preparations. To me, that means airlift." He looked around the Battle Cab.

"Any disagreements?" There were none. "Gentlemen, I think we have a window of opportunity here."

The Medical Group commander, Ryan's boss, shook his head. "The message also says to not make the situation worse than it already is."

Martini's blunt fingers drummed on the console. "We're not the ones who are going to make it worse. Besides, I think those bastards are too clever to shoot at us."

"But they will shoot at the Japanese," Townly reminded him.

Martini studied the airlift status board. He had two C-130 Hercules transports on base. "I think it's about time we establish a few ground rules of our own—before they can do anything about it. Ask for volunteers to fly a C-130 to Yokota." Yokota was the big U.S. Air Force Base 30 miles west of Tokyo.

The C-130 crew was waiting for Martini inside Intel's big walk-in vault. The aircraft commander was a junior captain and older than the copilot and navigator, the other two officers. The flight engineer was the oldest member of the crew, an ancient thirty-four-year-old tech sergeant. The youngest member was the loadmaster, a twenty-year-old mother who had just made airman first class. They all came to attention when Martini entered.

"I take it you all know what you've volunteered for?" he asked. He waited until each one acknowledged his question before continuing. "I want you to test this so-called blockade. Our latest Intelligence says the Chinese do not have the capability to intercept aircraft." He stared at them. "That could change at anytime, and you could be shot at. I want you to fly as high and as slow as you can to Yokota. Once there, expect to be sent right back." He looked at the loadmaster. *She's not much older than my daughter,* he thought. For a brief moment, he considered ordering her to stay behind. *Bullshit,* he told himself, *she volunteered for this.*

"Any questions?" he asked. They all shook their heads. "Good luck then." He walked out of the vault and back into the command post. He checked the time and ran the numbers. If the C-130 launched at 1300 hours and it took seven hours to fly to Yokota and back, the crew should be back on the ground at 2000 local time on Kadena, which was six o'clock Tuesday morning in Washington, D.C.

Martini allowed a short laugh, not much more than a bark. "Someone in Washington is going to have one hell of a surprise when they come to work." Now he had to wait, the curse of all commanders. The minutes dragged, giving him time to think about the young C-130 crew. He had only met them a few minutes ago and now he was ordering them to put their lives on the line. "Damn," he muttered. "The aircraft we're giving them to fly are older than they are."

"That's not our fault," the Operations Group commander replied. Martini did not answer and stared at the status boards as a sergeant posted the C-130's takeoff time. Ryan entered the Battle Cab to give his commanders a "how-goes-it" on NEO. He waited to be recognized, but Martini was still thinking about the four men and one woman flying the C-130. "What do you know about that C–130 crew?" he asked.

"Not much," the Operations Group commander replied. "They are stationed out of Dyess. The pilot is an Academy graduate. Apparently, the loadmaster's husband was killed in a motorcycle accident about a year ago. She's got a kid."

"If I'm wrong," Martini said, "I just made that kid an orphan." The Operations Group commander did not reply. "What the hell," Martini muttered. "She raised her hand and took the same oath as everyone else."

Martini's words cut into Ryan like a knife. It was another incident to add to his growing case book. *You are one mean-spirited son of a bitch,* he told himself.

"Major Ryan, how do we stand on NEO?" Martini asked.

"We are making progress, sir." Working on the nonessential personnel evacuation operation had taught him what the word *coordination* really meant. "At last count, we're dealing with over 26,000 people. That includes the Army, Marine, and Navy dependents, a big bunch of schoolteachers and civilian contractors. There are people coming out of the woodwork no one knew were here. That includes a guy that was listed as MIA in Vietnam."

"Did you arrest him?"

Ryan shook his head. "He's mentally disturbed, and we committed him to the hospital for observation and a physical exam."

"Other problems?"

"Our biggest problem is what to do with all the cars. So we've set up collection areas scattered around the different bases. We plan to call people in as airlift becomes available and use buses to get them to the flight line." Martini seemed satisfied with his answers, and Ryan screwed up his courage to ask the big question. "Sir, why am I involved with NEO? I'm a doctor and should be at the Med Center, doing what I'm trained for."

"Major," Martini replied, "there are going to be a lot of upset wives and children who will need reassuring and special care. I'm betting that a doctor is more attuned to their needs than your average bear. Case in point is the way you handled that crazy MIA."

But Ryan wouldn't let it go. "Sir, I must protest. I am a doctor. This is not what I should be doing."

"I heard you the first time," Martini said, his voice calm. He was the father, explaining the facts of life to an impetuous and willful teenager. "Your job is where I say it is. If you are unhappy, I suggest you write your congressman, see the chaplain, or file a complaint with IG. Dismissed."

Ryan jerked his head once in acknowledgment and beat a hasty retreat, his face a bright red. "Why so hard on the kid?" the Operations Group commander asked.

"That C-130 crew is willing to do their job. So should he." He humphed. "We're not a social welfare, all-hold-hands, feel-good, debating society. Once he learns that, he might turn into a halfway decent officer."

Rather than cool his heals in the command post, Martini drove around his base. All the signs that marked the life of a small community were gone, and it was eerily quiet. He passed the chapel as a small group came out from a worship service. They looked at him in silence as if they were holding their collective breath, waiting for the storm to hit. *I'm going to get you all out of here,* he told himself.

His car radio squawked: He was needed in the command post. He mashed the accelerator and switched on his emergency lights. His vice commander was waiting for him at the command post door. "Sir, the C-130 landed safely at Yokota, and CINC PAC has cleared us to continue with airlift operations. The C-130 is on its way back and more airlift is on its way."

The steel bonds of responsibility that held Martini tight eased their grip. "It's a beginning."

Washington, D.C.

At exactly six o'clock Tuesday morning, Shaw escorted Turner from her private study in the residence to the West Wing. Jackie Winters, her personal assistant, followed in lock step, determined to use every available second to ease the strain on her president. But Turner seemed distracted, not concerned with the mundane matters that made up Winters's world. *Maddy's showing the strain,* Shaw thought as they entered the Oval Office.

Seven of her key advisors were waiting for her. Only this time, Bender and Hazelton were among them. "Good morning, Madam President," Sam Kennett said. They all found seats as she stood in front of her desk. Shaw chose a chair against the back wall and tried to disappear. He made a mental entry for the secret journal he intended to keep: *Unless all the lessons of modern history were wrong, I knew this meeting marked the beginning of the internal breakdown that would lead to the end of Madeline Turner's effectiveness as a president.* He mulled the words over and rejected the idea of keeping a journal. He opened his notebook and waited for the meeting to start.

"I plan to address this crisis on three fronts," Turner began. "First, I want State to pursue a formal response through normal diplomatic channels and the United Nations. Second, I want the national security advisor to contact the Chinese secretly so we can talk behind the scenes. Third, I want an appropriate military response. The watchword will be *caution,* and I do not want to make this situation worse than it is by precipitating action. Finally, my presidency will not be held hostage to this crisis by the Chinese. We are going to get on with the business of running this country."

She looked around the room, stopping on the secretary of state. "What is the situation with the Japanese?"

"In a word, Madam President, chaos. They are waiting for our response."

She pointed at Secretary of Defense Elkins. "Until we can reach an agreement with the Japanese, I do not want any hotheaded reaction from Overmeyer."

Elkins looked very unhappy. "Understood, Madam President."

"It may have already occurred," the secretary of state said. "Apparently, the Air Force has challenged the blockade. They are flying airlift missions into Kadena."

Turner's head snapped up, and she fixed Elkins with a hard look. "Why wasn't I told about it immediately?"

Hazelton answered her. "We only learned of it a few minutes ago. General Martini—"

"I'm getting tired of constantly hearing that name," Turner interrupted.

"He is the commander on the cutting edge," Bender told her.

"As I understand the situation report," Hazelton continued, "Martini acted in accordance with the directives issued to all forces. He is ignoring the blockade and conducting regular airlift missions."

"At last report," Bender said, "the Chinese do not have the capability to enforce the blockade, at least in the air. Admittedly, that can change at any moment, and they may intercept or down one of our aircraft."

"I will not risk lives needlessly," Turner said. "I don't want this to happen again. From now on, I will personally approve every flight into and out of Okinawa."

Elkins's jaw muscles strained as he ground his teeth. "Madam President," he finally managed, "don't do that!" His outburst shocked the room into silence.

Bender spoke, his voice quiet and reasonable. "With all due respect, Madam President, that would be a mistake.

We learned the hard way in Vietnam that you cannot fight a war from the White House or, for that matter, from the Pentagon. We tell our commanders in the field what we want them to do and then give them the latitude and the means to do it.''

"Need I remind you," Turner said, "that I am trying to prevent a war.''

"Madam President," Hazelton said, "General Martini established a precedent we can exploit in future negotiations.''

"Just like the Berlin airlift when the Soviet Union blockaded Berlin in 1948," Bender added. "Not only does an air corridor offer us the means to resupply Okinawa, but we can evacuate dependents and civilians.'' From the look on Turner's face, he had made a telling point.

"How many dependents are there?" she asked.

"Approximately 25,000," Bender answered. "And every single one is a potential hostage.''

"I see," Turner replied. She made a decision. "For now, we will pursue this primarily on the diplomatic front. Robert, see what private channels you can open with the Chinese. Doctor Elkins, I want a detailed list of my military options. We will meet again at two this afternoon to review the situation.''

"What about the airlift?" Elkins asked.

Turner hesitated, a tick playing at the corner of her mouth. "Continue it for now. But don't put passengers at risk." Again, she hesitated. "Perhaps, if we can negotiate an air corridor like in Berlin, I'll order an evacuation. See what you can do." She pointed her pen at the vice president. "Sam, I want you to press ahead on tax reform.''

"Is that wise at this time?" Kennett wondered.

Turner fixed him with a steady gaze as she spoke. "As I said earlier, my administration will not be held hostage to this crisis.''

Well, Mr. Vice President, Shaw thought, *welcome to the wonderful world of Maddy Turner. She didn't listen to me, she won't listen to you.* "Mizz President," he said, "we need to prepare for the press briefing.''

Her advisors rapidly left while Shaw held back. Bender and Hazelton stood just inside the door, locked in a private conversation. They were a mismatched pair, the tall and lanky general bent over, listening to the short and petite analyst. *They make a damn good team,* Shaw decided. He glanced at Turner. She was looking at them, her face a blank mask. *Now what the hell is eatin' at her?* he thought.

"Madam President," Bender said, "may I suggest that your press secretary or I take this briefing?"

"Not a good idea," Shaw muttered under his breath for Turner alone to hear. "Maybe later when things settle down. For now, you must appear in charge."

"Thank you, Robert," Turner replied. "I really must do it this time."

A worried look spread across Hazelton's face, and she looked at Bender. She started to speak but thought better of it and walked out the door.

Shaw stood by the wall of the press briefing room with Bender and Hazelton. The chief of staff's eyes worked around the room, bisecting the reporters. But he was careful to avoid eye contact with Liz Gordon. *Four days into this crisis and they're already acting like sheep,* he thought. He listened as Turner fielded questions. He checked his watch, nine minutes into the briefing, and crossed his arms, anything to ease the cold chill he felt. Nothing was going to save Turner from what was coming, and he hated the knowing. All the joy of dealing with the unexpected surprises that made life in the Capitol so exciting was gone.

"Madam President," Liz Gordon said, "according to the leaders of the National Organization for Women, you have lost the support of the feminist movement, and they now regard you as a traitor to their cause."

Turner's head came up, and she shot a hard look at Shaw. They had not anticipated that question. "Liz, many of my sisters still believe that affirmative action is the answer. In reality, it is an idea whose time has come and gone. But what must remain in place is a commitment to equal opportunity. And equal opportunity starts with economic opportunity for everyone. To that end, I am sending to Congress legislation proposing a total overhaul of our tax system. Our goal is to promote productivity and create well-paid, meaningful jobs for anyone, regardless of race or sex, who wants to work.''

Again, the room erupted in questions. Shaw shook his head, his stomach churning. *Too bad, Maddy,* he thought. *You just scared the hell out of every CEO and stockholder in the United States and struck out with your strongest supporters. Hell, the feminists are no different from any other special interest group: They only wanted equal opportunity for themselves. You should have listened to old Patrick.*

Bender and Hazelton did not move when the press briefing finally reached a painful end. ''Not good,'' Bender said. ''I could have sidestepped that issue.''

Hazelton stared at Shaw's back as he left. She spoke slowly, ''Sir, I think this might be a good time to sit down with some of your senior analysts. May I suggest your office?''

''Let's do it,'' Bender said. They walked in silence and entered his office. Hazelton closed the door behind her. ''OK, Mazie, what's bugging you?''

''Liz Gordon's question,'' she answered. ''It sounded like a setup. There's a leak in the administration.''

''Any idea who?''

She frowned. ''It could be anyone, her advisors, a cabinet member, who knows?''

A picture of Norene Coker, the African-American congresswoman in Turner's kitchen cabinet, flashed in his mind's eye.

''Do you have someone in mind?'' Hazelton asked.

He shook his head. ''Yeah, but I don't know why.'' He settled into the chair behind his desk. Hazelton called for the analysts to join them while he studied a staff roster. He was shocked to learn that his staff occupied most of the third floor of the Executive Office Building across the street from the White House. Norma, the senior of his two secretaries, announced that two Secret Service agents, Chuck Stanford and Wayne Adams, were waiting to see him.

''We volunteered to serve on your detail,'' Stanford, the older of the two, said. Bender had been expecting increased protection because the national security advisor came under the Secret Service's umbrella.

"I hope you two like to run," Bender said. "That's what I do for exercise." No answer. *Why the silence?* he wondered. *Did I say something wrong? Why the tears?*

Sanford finally managed to say, "Our pleasure, sir."

"They ran with Bill Carroll when he was the national security advisor," she told him.

"That man could really pound the pavement," Sanford said.

"The heart attack detail," Adams muttered. "We must'a set a few records."

Bender grinned, breaking the sad remembrance of things past. "I'm not in Bill Carroll's league."

The light was on when Shaw entered the rear door of his condominium. Although he wasn't worried—security at the Watergate was top notch—he was puzzled. Perhaps the maid had left it on. He walked through the kitchen and paused. Jessica was curled up in the corner of the couch next to a fire. She tossed her blonde mane of hair when she saw him and smiled. "You are late," she said. "Are you hungry?" She stood up. She was wearing a short, off-white silk chemise and nothing else. "I can cook you an omelet."

"I ate at the White House." She sat back down and pulled her legs up. "Why are you here?" he asked.

"Senator Leland," she murmured. The senator's name opened many doors, including the one to his apartment, and explained why she was there. She was the messenger, the cutout between Shaw and what he had come to call the Group. She smiled. "Of course, people might get the wrong idea that you are settling down to serious monogamy. Can I get you a drink?" He nodded and sat down in an overstuffed chair, not bothering to shed his overcoat. Jessica padded across the floor and mixed his favorite drink. She held it up to the light to check the color. Satisfied she had it right, she set the drink down and dropped her chemise to the floor. Picking up the drink, she came back to him and sat in his lap.

"We need to talk," she whispered. "Are we on a monitor?"

A little nod. "A security video, no audio."

She nuzzled his ear. "The senator thought the press conference went well today. He wants you to keep feeding leaks to the press and play 'Deep Throat.' " Shaw cringed at her reference to the leak that kept the two *Washington Post* reporters on the trail of the Watergate cover-up. The reporters had named the leak after the porno movie of the same name, and Shaw didn't want to star in a remake of either episode. She told him how the Group was planning a series of demonstrations in the park across the street from the White House that would slowly build in intensity. Shaw was to counsel tolerance at first. But when the time was right, he was to clear the park with a show of force, the bigger the better.

"Can I see the videos?" she asked, smiling for the hidden camera. "We can do our own Deep Throat," she whispered.

"Some other time," he replied. He would destroy the videotapes after she left.

Jessica pushed his overcoat off and reached for his fly. She unzipped his pants and wiggled her bare bottom on his lap. No response. She stuck her tongue in his ear. "I must be losing my touch," she murmured.

Paris, France

"Don't expect this meeting to last more than fifteen minutes," Mazie Hazelton said.

Bender tried hard not to act like a tourist as the black Lincoln town car drove through the outskirts of Paris. He kept trying to get his bearings and orient himself. Finally, he picked up the phone and asked Chuck Sanford, who was sitting in the front passenger seat, where they were. The reply was a laconic "Near Versailles, General."

Bender sank back into the seat and tried to focus on what Hazelton was saying. But the so-called private negotiations the military attaché at the American embassy had set up with the Chinese were progressing with a speed that surprised him. "Mazie," he admitted, "this is pretty overwhelming for a boy from Sacramento, California."

"That's all part of the game," she told him. "The idea is to keep you off balance, and they will try anything to intimidate you. You've got one big factor in your favor: You are an unknown. So be noncommittal and say as little as possible."

"You've dealt with the Chinese before," Bender said. "Are they really inscrutable?"

"Not at all," she replied. "But they are very focused."

They turned off the main road and entered a tree-lined lane. Bender caught his first glimpse of the château when they crossed a low stone bridge. "Will you look at that?" he breathed.

"It's one of the Rothschild palaces," Hazelton told him. "The Chinese are overplaying this. Why?" Four Chinese in dark business suits were waiting for them when the Lincoln pulled up to the steps. The introductions were reserved and formal, and they were escorted to a small, but very luxurious room on the second floor. Hazelton motioned him to hold back, and she entered first. When she saw her counterpart enter from the opposite side of the room, she nodded and told Bender to enter on her cue. The moment the Chinese envoy appeared in his door, she motioned Bender forward. Both men stepped into the room simultaneously. "General Bender," she said, "may I introduce Wang Mocun, Chairman Lu Zoulin's special envoy."

The two men shook hands, taking the others' measure. Wang was two inches shorter than Bender but outweighed him by fifty pounds. His thin hair was plastered back against his skin, and he had a round face that bore a distinct resemblance to a young Mao Zedong. They sat down at a table on opposite sides and started the intricate opening moves that reminded Bender of a minuet. The fifteen minutes Hazelton had promised passed and grew into two hours. Although they were separated by different languages and cultures, Bender sensed he was up against a shrewd and very difficult opponent. How difficult became obvious when Wang concluded by speaking for over thirty minutes. Bender shot a questioning look at Hazelton when

Wang referred to the United States as a "crippled giant" and "a lost empire." Her face remained impassive, and she did not look up.

"I find your observations of my country worthy of an academic," Bender replied. "But surely more theoretical than practical."

"Okinawa is a very practical matter," Wang replied in English without waiting for a translation. "The correlation of forces is against you."

Bender may have been a novice at negotiations, but he knew when the gloves were off. "Ah, the dreaded 'correlation of forces.' We have heard that phrase before."

Wang's English was good enough for him to catch the sarcasm in Bender's reply. "Your society lacks the cohesion to resist it," Wang replied. "We do not wish to hurt any innocent Americans, so it would be in everyone's best interests to negotiate a settlement now—before events move out of control."

"I assure you, Minister Wang, that we can control events."

"That is doubtful under your current leadership."

"Do not underestimate the resolve of our president," Bender replied. He made the appropriate closing statements, and they were escorted back to the waiting Lincoln. They pulled away and did not talk until they reached the main road. "I blew that one," he said.

"Not at all," Hazelton replied. "The tone of Wang's speech was much more insulting than his words and the meaning was softened in translation. It was a calculated and deliberate insult."

"I didn't know you spoke Chinese."

"I'm considered fluent in Mandarin and Japanese," she replied.

"Does Wang know that?"

"Probably," she answered. "But he has another problem."

"Which is?"

"It is very complicated," she answered. "We asked for this meeting, which made us the supplicant. Naturally, they agreed to it. But the Chinese would have never been here unless they wanted something. They came out playing hardball and got nothing, not even a request for another meeting, and Wang has nothing to report to Beijing. I think they are pressing for a quick resolution and want these meetings more than we do. By forcing them to ask for the next meeting, we'll be in a much stronger bargaining position.''

Bender shook his head. ''I did all that?'' They rode in silence. Then, ''Mazie, when we were preparing, you said you would arrange for the next meeting with the Chinese.''

''True, but they didn't know that. We can increase the pressure by returning to Washington.''

''Sounds like a good idea,'' he replied. ''Let's do it.''

Washington, D.C.

Fresh snow had fallen on Friday night and covered Lafayette Park with a soft winter radiance. Workers were still clearing and sanding the walks at nine o'clock Saturday morning when a solitary figure crossed H Street and walked past the statue of General von Steuben. He was wearing a black cowboy hat with a small feather stuck in the silver-beaded headband. His dark hair was streaked with gray and braided into a thick pigtail, which hung down his back. A brightly colored blanket was wrapped around his shoulders and bulged in front, concealing his burden. The blanket almost reached to his heavy winter boots, and he walked with a quiet dignity that matched his craggy face.

A few workers followed his progress, but most ignored him as a policeman spoke into his radio, warning the Secret Service a ''possible'' might be approaching the White House. Part of the security apparatus surrounding the president started to move, focusing on the lone individual. Two other teams assumed he was a distraction, a feint for the real threat, and turned their attention elsewhere. An observer on the roof of the Treasury building on the east side of the White House followed his progress with a high-powered set of binoculars. When the possible approached Lafayette's statue in the southeast corner of the park, the observer radioed the sniper, who was carefully hidden from view, and ordered him into position.

The man stopped and gazed at the statue for a moment before turning to face Pennsylvania Avenue. Across the street, the White House was a mass of shadows and light in the early morning sun. The man stood there, not moving and gazed at the White House.

Ben, Liz Gordon's cameraman, found her in the press secretary's office drinking coffee with the secretary and five other reporters. He motioned her outside. "There's some crazy Indian who just turned himself into a statue in Lafayette Park. The network wants a news update with him in the background."

"We might as well," Gordon replied. "Nothing is happening around here." She retrieved her coat and scarf from her cubicle and followed Ben to the park. A small group of people were standing around the man, shifting from foot to foot, trying to keep warm. Ben moved around until he had the man, the statue, and the people framed in his viewfinder.

Gordon raised her head and looked into the lens of the Betacam. Behind her, the White House, fresh snow, and morning light created a sensational backdrop. "On this beautiful, crisp winter morning, the crisis in the East China Sea enters the second week as the White House reels with indecision. The Pentagon has adopted a wait-and-see strategy while it positions the aircraft carriers *Nimitz* and *Reagan* within striking distance of Okinawa. But for now, President Turner has chosen to pursue a diplomatic solution through the State Department. But the question most are asking is, Can the Japanese government survive this crisis if the United States does not directly intervene?

"Meanwhile, Madeline Turner is pursuing her dream of tax reform with the same intensity as Lyndon Baines Johnson when he created his version of the Great Society. But perhaps this lone sentinel standing in Lafayette Park"— Ben zoomed in on the man—"best captures the moment as we all wait to see what will develop."

"That's a good one," Ben said as he lowered his camera. Behind Gordon, the man shrugged off his blanket back to reveal a flat round drum. Ben raised his camera, framed the man in the viewfinder, and hit the record button. The sentinel stared at the White House, not really seeing it, and struck the drum once with a padded drumstick. The single note died away as the sound echoed across Pennsylvania Avenue.

PART THREE
COLLAPSE

The reins of political power are held lightly in Washington. As Madeline Turner has discovered, it is all too easy for the team to kick over the traces and rear out of control, threatening the driver and all in the wagon. Although she still holds the whip necessary to control the team, does she have the will or the skill to use it?

ELIZABETH GORDON
CNC-TV News

15 ⟅

Okinawa, Japan

It was Monday, January 21, the tenth day since the crisis started and the seventh day of the blockade, when Martini walked through the commissary with the Support Group commander. The people standing in line either scowled at them or turned away as they passed. "We're out of fresh milk products," the colonel told him. "We need more airlift, or it's going to get very tight in three weeks, four at the most."

"I thought we had more stockpiled," Martini said.

"Our estimates on consumption rates were wrong, and we've got problems with selling food on the black market. But there's also hoarding, and a lot of people are giving food to the Okinawans."

"We don't have a choice," Martini said. "Start rationing and crack down."

"The real answer, sir—"

"I know what the real answer is," Martini growled. "We need to implement NEO and get them out of here." He barreled out of the commissary and drove around his base. A semblance of life had returned and the schools were open, but many children were absent, at home with a parent awaiting the evacuation order. Frustrated, he spun the steering wheel and headed for the command post. He had to build a fire under someone and start moving people

243

off island. He keyed his radio. "Have Major Ryan meet me in the command post ASAP."

His vice commander was waiting in the command post with more bad news. "Sir, the local authorities are reporting food riots in Naha, and we've got a demonstration building at the main gate. It's serious this time. I don't think our cops can handle it."

Martini dropped into his chair in the Battle Cab and phoned the Marine brigade commander at nearby Camp Lester. "Jake, I've got a demonstration building at my front gate." He explained the problem and listened for a few moments before hanging up. "The Marines are sending a company to back up our Security Police. Position some of them close to the gate but keep them out of sight. We'll present a show of force if they mass for a breakthrough."

"What happens if they get on base?" a colonel asked.

Martini's fingers drummed the table. "Don't forget we're dealing with Japanese. They like to play by the rules." He turned to the base map on the wall behind him. "We'll treat it as a parade and block off Douglas Boulevard with vehicles, the Marines, whatever we got. We'll let 'em march through the gate and down Douglas until they reach Kuter Boulevard. Then it's a right turn down Kuter."

"And right out gate 2," his vice commander added. "But what if they don't play it our way?"

Ryan walked into the Battle Cab as Martini's fingers drummed the table. The doctor could feel the tension as everyone waited for Martini's answer. "What's happening?" he asked Pete Townly.

"We got a demonstration at the main gate. It may get ugly."

"If they start to loot or get on the flight line," Martini said, "the Security Police and the Marines are authorized to use deadly force."

Ryan could not credit what he was hearing. *You bloody bastard!* he thought. *There's got to be another answer.*

"Major Ryan," Martini said, "I've been told not to put dependents or civilians at risk. However, in my judgment, keeping people on Okinawa is becoming more dangerous than flying them out. For reasons beyond comprehension, CINC PAC has not declared NEO. But a C-141 is due in, and rather than let it fly out empty, I'm asking for volunteers who want to leave.''

"I'll volunteer,'' Townly called from behind Ryan.

"Not you, asshole,'' Martini grumbled. "Dependents and civilians only. Major Ryan, see if you can find 200 volunteers who want to leave. And Townly, since you want to be part of the action, you make sure they know the risks before they volunteer. OK, get cracking and make it happen.''

Ryan and Townly beat a hasty retreat out of the command post. "How dangerous is it?'' Ryan asked.

"Well, we're averaging fourteen flights a day, and no one has shot at them—yet.''

Ryan shook his head. "I can't believe he's so, so''— he hunted for the right word—"so cavalier with other people's lives. How can he do this?''

"Who's going to tell him no,'' Townly answered. "Besides, there's a lot of people who want to get out of here and are willing to risk it.''

Martini watched the two officers leave the command post. "I want an AWACS on station before the C-141 launches. When it does take off, I want four F-15s on runway alert. Any aircraft scrambling off Kumejima and heading towards the 141 is dog meat.''

"Why did you do that?'' Ryan asked Townly. They were sitting in a car as the C-141 StarLifter taxied out with its load of 223 passengers.

The Intelligence officer jotted down the time—7:50 P.M. "Why did I have all the passengers sign consent forms?'' he asked. Ryan nodded. "CYA,'' Townly said. "Cover your ass in case something happens. I had them acknowledge in writing they'd been briefed on the risks and were volunteers. If this turns into a piece of shit, there will be more politicians and lawyers breathing down our throats than you ever knew existed.'' He snapped a rubber band around the forms and dropped them in his briefcase. "Let's watch the takeoff from Habu Hill.''

Ryan drove around Perimeter Road and pulled into the

parking lot on top of the low hill overlooking the runway. "Isn't that an AWACS?" he asked, pointing at a gray E-3 Sentry lifting off the departure end of the runway. The highly modified Boeing 707 with its thirty-foot saucer-shaped antenna rotating slowly above the fuselage was an airborne warning and command system aircraft. The C-141 was still lumbering down the taxiway with its load of evacuees. The two officers watched as the C-141 taxied into place on the runway and held, awaiting a release time. "Somehow," Ryan said, his stomach churning, "I feel that I'm personally responsible for those people."

"We're all responsible," Townly told him. "I'm the guy doing the threat estimates the general is relying on."

Fifteen minutes after the AWACS had taken off, the cargo plane rolled down the runway and lifted into the clear night air. Four F-15s taxied out of their hardened shelters. "Martini didn't say anything about escorting the 141," Ryan said. They waited in silence as the fighters went through an end-of-runway check and taxied into position on the runway. But they didn't take off. "What the hell is going on?" Ryan muttered.

"It looks like they're on runway alert in case the AWACS calls for help," Townly explained. "Let's go to the command post and find out." Ryan slipped the car in gear, and they pulled out of the parking lot. Behind them, the four F-15s were taking off in full afterburner, zooming into the night sky. "Shit!" Townly shouted. "Go!"

The MCC, mission crew commander, on board the AWACS hovered behind her weapons controller, directing the four fighters that had just taken off from Kadena. She was standing in the weapons pit of the main cabin, her headset plugged into a long extension cord so she could roam behind the various radar consoles and pull the mission together. "What are we dealing with?" she asked.

"It looks like eighteen J-8s so far," the weapons controller answered. The air surveillance officer at the rear bank of consoles had tagged up the fighter aircraft as they launched from Kumejima. The J-8 was a Chinese-developed variant of the old Soviet MiG-21. But with two engines, an improved fire control system, provided by the

United States, and a combat range of 500 miles, it was a worrisome threat. She told the senior director to order more F-15s scrambled off Kadena as she studied the scope and weighed her options. The next four or five minutes were going to be critical.

"Major," the air surveillance officer said over the intercom, "they formed up like a pack of wolves and are heading for the C-141."

She keyed her intercom. "Retrograde now," she ordered. "Vector the 141 northeast at mil power. We'll turn with him." The AWACS was 40 miles north of the C-141 as the two aircraft turned away from the bandits. The pilots on both aircraft fire-walled the throttles and nosed over into long-range, high-speed descents, trading altitude for speed and running away from the bandits.

Again, the MCC ran the numbers, deciding how to commit the F-15s. Thankfully, she had a clearer picture now. The eighteen bandits were definitely going after the C-141 and were in a 60-mile tail chase, forming the base of an inverted triangle. The four F-15s were south of the bandits and the C-141, forming the apex of the triangle. She checked the relative speeds and mentally did the math. The bandits had a 250-knot overtake on the cargo plane, which meant it would take them fourteen minutes to close the gap. To get that speed, the J-8s had to be in afterburner, which quadrupled their fuel consumption. She felt better. The J-8s might have enough fuel to catch the C-141, but they would never make it back to Kumejima. Unless they were on a one-way mission. "Split the F-15s," she ordered. "Two fly cover for the 141 and engage the other two."

The weapons controller did not hesitate and radioed the F-15s. "Knife 1 and 2, you are paired against eighteen bandits, Snap two-eight-five degrees, range 45 nautical miles. Knife 3 and 4, rendezvous on the 141 and escort."

"Thanks a bunch," Knife 3 replied, his disappointment obvious.

"Knife 1 has multiple targets on the nose at 42 miles," the flight lead for the two fighters radioed.

"That is your target," the weapons controller said. "You are cleared to engage, repeat, cleared to engage."

"Cleared to engage," Knife 1 replied, his words machine-gun quick. "Two, take spacing."

The mission crew commander watched the scope as two F-15s split apart and headed for the bandits while the other two raced after the C-141. The senior director told her that twelve more F-15s were launching from Kadena and four more were taxiing out for runway alert. She told the weapons controller to sequence them into the flight behind the first two F-15s, which were now closing into AMRAAM missile range on the bandits. "The poor bastards," she muttered to herself. She wasn't talking about the F-15s.

On cue, Knives 1 and 2 radioed simultaneously, "FOX ONE." Their voices were a chorus of destruction as four of the air-to-air missiles streaked into the bandits. As the AMRAAM was a launch-and-leave missile, the F-15s were free to maneuver and could employ their AIM-9 Sidewinders from totally different aspects before they merged with the bandits. Again, the missile launch calls came almost in unison, "FOX TWO!" The MCC calculated when she would have to disengage the first two F-15s so the second wave of F-15s could enter the fight. "Tallyho!" Knife 1 radioed. He had a visual on at least one bandit. "It's a J-8. FOX THREE." He was using his gun. The radar scopes on board the AWACS turned into a furball as the two F-15s merged with bandits.

Because it was dark, Knives 1 and 2 made no attempt to turn on the bandits and enter a dogfight. They blew on through to reposition for another attack. The scopes on board the AWACS started to clear, and the bandits were all over the sky. But the MCC could only count thirteen of the red inverted Vs that symbolized the bandits. The first two F-15s had given a good account of themselves and were repositioning to reattack. "Knife 1 and 2," the weapons controller radioed, "twelve friendlies are inbound, four minutes out."

"This will be one pass, haul ass," Knife 1 replied.

Again the two F-15s attacked, but this time on widely separated targets. Whatever cohesion or direction the bandits had was totally lost and not one was still heading in the direction of the C-141. Knives 1 and 2 repeated the deadly ballet and called off. Only this time, there were only ten red inverted Vs on the radar scopes. "We may have an ace," the senior controller told the MCC.

"Start pairing up the second wave," the MCC said, determined to kill as many bandits as possible.

"Holy shit!" the weapons controller yelled over the intercom. One of the bandits had turned toward the C-141. He mashed the transmit button under his right foot. "Knife 3 and 4, you have a bandit on the deck at Mach 2, two-three-five degrees, 38 miles, on you. Kill, repeat, kill."

The two F-15s escorting the C-141 acknowledged the call and turned into the lone bandit streaking toward the C-141. "At Mach 2," the weapons controller said, "it ain't a J-8." The Chinese had snuck one of the Su-27 Flankers from the *Chairman Mao* onto Kumejima and hidden it among the J-8s going after the C-141. "It's a damn good thing you covered the 141," the weapons controller told the MCC.

The MCC could only listen as Knives 3 and 4 ran a head-on intercept into the Flanker. The lead F-15 locked it up on radar and fired an AMRAAM. But nothing happened. The Flanker's electronic countermeasures systems had defeated the AMRAAM, and they were still converging at over 2,000 miles per hour. "FOX TWO," Knife 3 transmitted when he fired a Sidewinder missile. Six seconds later, Knife 4 repeated the call and two of the deadly infrared-guided missiles were headed for the Flanker. The Chinese pilot saw the rocket plume of the first Sidewinder in the night and pulled up as he chopped his throttles. He rolled, buried the nose, and jammed the throttles full forward. The Sidewinder passed by overhead, missing him by over 500 feet. The second Sidewinder flew up his left intake and exploded.

"Vector the 141 for Yokota," the MCC said. Again, the AWACS crew made it happen as the second wave of F-15s sequenced into the fight in flights of two, and the cargo plane headed north to safety. The MCC noted the time of the engagement in her log and wrote the words "turkey shoot" in the remarks section.

Ryan followed Martini and Townly into the Twelfth Fighter Squadron for the mission debrief. The building was alive with shouts and laughter as the squadron celebrated their victory. The number 15 had been spray painted on a wall by some well-meaning tagger. Ryan pushed through the crowd, talking to the pilots. One of the female crew chiefs pressed against him and grabbed his buttocks as she planted a wet kiss on his lips. Her face was flushed with triumph. "It was my jet!" she shouted. "We got five!" Ryan smiled at her and tried to find Martini. He saw Townly duck into a briefing room and followed him.

Martini was sitting at the small table with two pilots, Knives 1 and 2. The videotape from the engagement that had been recorded through Knife 1's HUD was playing on the TV set. "Here's where I stuffed guy five," the pilot said. His voice was calm and controlled with no hint of the jubilation going on in the hall. "They weren't very good, sir. I only had to pull 4 gs to get behind him."

Martini nodded, agreeing with him, as the video showed a Chinese J-8 barely maneuvering inside the gun pipper reticle. A captain stuck his head inside the door. "Sir!" he shouted. "It's sixteen. We got sixteen."

Martini smiled and stood up. "Congratulations," he told the pilots.

"General," Knife 1 said, "it was too easy—a piece of cake." The pilot's face was sad and drawn, reminding Ryan of a repentant basset hound. Again, Martini agreed with him. He left the briefing room with Townly and Ryan still in tow.

"Now comes the hard part," Martini said.

What's so hard? Ryan asked himself. *You don't have to live with the knowledge that you killed five men.* A voice shouted that the C-141 had landed safely at Yokota. The heavy weight that had been grinding Ryan down was gone and he was soaring. Over 200 of his people were safe.

Washington, D.C.

A worried look crossed Maura O'Keith's face when Turner emerged from the dressing room off her bedroom. "You look tired, Maddy." She immediately regretted saying the words, but the crisis in the Far East was in its tenth day and taking a terrible toll on her daughter.

"I'm not a morning person," Turner replied irritably. "You know that, Mother." Maura heard the tension behind her words and said nothing. "Are they here yet?"

"They're waiting in the dining room," Maura replied. "I thought it would be nice to offer them breakfast as you're meeting so early."

"Thanks. I don't know what I'd do without you—or them." Turner led the way into the corridor. As usual, Jackie Winters, her personal assistant, was waiting for her in the hall, notebook in hand.

"Mrs. President, William Knowles is retiring and today is his last day."

"Knowles?" Turner asked, not putting a face to the name.

"William, the butler who normally serves you in the morning," Jackie explained.

"Oh, William," Turner said. "Ah, do whatever is normally done, and make sure I personally sign whatever—"

"Normally, it's a personal letter and a framed certificate," Jackie told her. They were at the door to the dining room. "And the dean of the Academy would like to speak to you about Brian."

"Maura will take care of that," Turner said as she entered the dining room. Jackie closed the door behind her president and waited in the hall while she met with her kitchen cabinet.

They were all clustered around one end of the table. "Lord, woman," Noreen Coker boomed, "I never get up before seven. At my age, anything earlier and my body sags for the rest of the day. And that's a lot of saggin'." She smiled. "There, Mrs. President, I feel better now." The tension momentarily broken, they sat down, and William rolled in a serving cart. For a few minutes the talk was light and witty as they ate. Turner sipped her coffee and listened, finding strength and certainty in her friends. She felt a sad reluctance to let it go when Sam Kennett turned to business and described the problems he was encountering in Congress over tax reform.

"For some reason, tax reform has touched a deep nerve

on the Hill and is stirring them up," he told her. "I've never seen anything like it. They're already organized and entrenched. Apparently, there is some big money behind them." He went on to list the legislators who were lining up against them and ended by suggesting they might want to put tax reform "on a back burner until the Far East settles down."

But Coker claimed it was too late. "The fat's in the fire, honey, and we got to cook it now. We back off, and they'll just have more time to get their ducks waddling down the street in order." Parrish, the secretary of the treasury, disagreed with her and supported Kennett. Turner listened to them for a few more moments before turning to the Far East. On this issue, they all agreed with Maura when she said that caution was better than dead American soldiers.

Turner smiled at William when he entered the room with a fresh carafe of coffee. "Jackie tells me you're retiring."

"Yes, ma'am, I am," he replied. The rumors flying through the White House staff were too strong for him to ignore, and he hoped she would ask him the right question. But she only wished him well and waited for him to leave before she resumed talking. *I'm so sorry, Mrs. President,* he thought as he closed the door, *them bastards are gonna destroy you and I can't watch that.*

Shaw brushed past and did not stop to grill him about what the president had said. William considered it the best gift he could have received on his last day. Shaw knocked twice on the door and pushed through. "Mizz President," he said, not waiting to be recognized, "there's been fighting off Okinawa involving our aircraft." Her face paled and she stood up. "No casualties on our side," he said, answering her unspoken question. "General Overmeyer will be here in fifteen minutes. I told him to go directly to the Situation Room."

"Is General Bender in his office?" she asked. Shaw nodded an answer. "Ask him to be there." She paused. She hated the windowless Situation Room with its severe military atmosphere. It was a subterranean cave of war, and she needed a place with sunlight and windows to the

outside world. "Patrick, we'll meet in the Oval Office."
Again, she waited until Shaw had left and the door was
closed. "I'm pressing ahead with tax reform," she told
her friends. "Not China, not anyone, is going to drive my
administration."

Hazelton was with Bender in his office when Shaw's
secretary called, telling him to meet the president in the
Oval Office. "This doesn't play right," Hazelton said.
"Why did the Chinese go after the first aircraft carrying
civilians?" She walked back and forth in his office. "General, I need time to check this out."

"How long will that take?" Bender asked.

"May I use your telephone?" Hazelton asked. Rather
than push the phone across the desk, he stood up and
motioned to his chair. She sat down and dialed a number.
"My contact in the National Security Agency," she told
him. In a few moments she was talking to the desk chief
in charge of monitoring communications in the Far East.
She turned the key on the side of the phone unit and
activated the encryption circuits. Bender listened, not fully
understanding the technical jargon. She broke the connection and stood up. "They've got something," she told
him. "Most of it hasn't been translated yet so they're
going to relay the raw intercepts to me in the communications center in the basement."

"That's a long way from the Oval Office," he said.
Speed and security requirements during a crisis dictated
the colocation of the Situation Room and the communications center.

"We're not time critical on this one," she told him.
"Besides, I can get anything important to you in three or
four minutes." Her lips pursed as she considered her next
words. "General, stall for time until I can fit all the pieces
together." She gave him a worried look and disappeared
into the corridor.

Turner sat in a rocking chair at the end of the facing
couches in the Oval Office as the DCI summarized events.
She rolled a pen between her fingers as he finished, disturbed by the incomplete picture before her. *Is it always*

like this? she thought. *I have to react to problems that are forced on me. And I have to make a decision based on too little information in too short a time. Time is the ultimate challenge and there's no second chance if I make a mistake. Why hasn't Robert said anything? He just sits there calmly making notes. Did the generals force this to happen? If they did, I'll court-martial them. But how do I do that? Patrick would know. Patrick. What do I do about him?*

"We were making progress on the diplomatic front until this happened," Secretary of State Francis said. "The United Nations Security Council is going to consider the matter Wednesday and we should have a full debate in the General Assembly next week."

"Need I remind the secretary," Overmeyer said, "that the Chinese initiated the attack, not us." He leaned forward, uncomfortable on the couch, and rested his elbows on his knees, his hands clasped together. "Madam President, how much more is it going to take to convince you to get tough? Evacuate our dependents from Okinawa immediately before they become hostages. Then use the Navy to break the blockade."

How many people will die if I follow that advice? Turner asked herself. An image of an Air Force general riding a horse and wearing a pearl-handled revolver flashed in front of her. "General Overmeyer, the timing of this attack bothers me. Did Martini deliberately put civilians at risk?"

Overmeyer was slow to answer. "He was acting within his directives, Madam President. Food riots are breaking out on Okinawa and we are experiencing shortages ourselves. Because cargo flights have been moving in and out on a regular basis without incident, he asked for volunteers who wanted to leave."

"Perhaps we should replace Martini with a more senior ranking officer," Turner said, "one more capable of judicious action." She stopped talking when Hazelton slipped into the room. She spoke quietly to Bender and handed him six pages of translated intercepts. *They have a good relationship,* Turner decided. She motioned to an empty chair beside Shaw. "Please join us." Hazelton looked surprised and sat down. Turner felt better with another woman in the room.

"Madam President," Bender said. "We were set up." He read off the series of messages and phone calls the NSA had intercepted. It was obvious the Chinese had been monitoring activity at Kadena and were waiting for the first evacuation aircraft. "It was an ambush," Bender said.

"Ridiculous," Francis scoffed. "That would only make matters worse. They know that."

"Do they?" Bender asked. "They launched those planes to destroy the C-141. Only the timely reaction by General Martini saved it from being shot down."

"Why," Turner asked, "do I get the impression that Martini is driving events?"

"He is not 'driving events,'" Bender replied. "He's on the front line. It's his job to constantly assess the threat and react quickly."

"Madam President," Hazelton said, "this was another probe by the Chinese. They will continue until you say, 'No more.' But by then, they hope to have significantly altered the power structure on the western rim of the Pacific."

"I don't believe that," Turner said.

Hazelton refused to give up. "Ask yourself this, Madam President: If the C-141 had been shot down and the Chinese claimed it was a terrible tragedy, would you have responded with force? Or would you have continued with negotiations?"

Madeline Turner felt her stomach churn. Every instinct told her to negotiate, but if Hazelton was correct, negotiations would only lead to more aggressive probes by the Chinese. "Perhaps," she finally said, "it would be best if Martini was replaced with a more senior general."

"Without increasing our forces on Okinawa," Bender said, "that would send the Chinese the wrong message. Commanding officers are replaced when they have failed or done something wrong. General Martini is not a cowboy. The selection process weeds them out by the time they reach flag rank. By replacing Martini, you are telling the Chinese that he did the wrong thing by defending the C-141."

"Can you be sure of that?" Turner asked.

"There is always a degree of uncertainty," Bender replied.

Turner looked around the room. "What do you suggest I do?"

Hazelton answered. "For the next twenty-four hours, nothing. Make them respond to this incident, not us."

Turner listened as the discussion went around the room. But the more she thought about it, the better she liked Hazelton's advice. It gave her the one thing she wanted most of all: time. Her decision made, she said, "For now, we wait. We'll reconvene this afternoon." The meeting over, the Oval Office rapidly emptied.

Outside, Overmeyer stopped Hazelton. "Mrs. Hazelton, I appreciate what you did in there. We could have said the same thing and she would not have listened to us."

"Are you suggesting," Hazelton said, "that she listened because I'm a woman?"

"Exactly so."

"You're wrong, sir," Hazelton said. "She may not have felt so isolated because another woman was in there, but if my advice proves wrong and we don't hear from the Chinese very soon, I'll never set foot in the White House again."

Two hours later, Turner received a phone call from Chairman Lu Zoulin asking that Bender meet with Wang Mocun in Paris to discuss issues of mutual concern. Mazie Hazelton was off the hook.

It was a "walk and talk" shoot as Liz walked through Lafayette Park. Ben was in front of her, walking backward, careful to keep the White House in the background. "In what may be the coldest winter on record, a hearty band of demonstrators has taken up residence here." Ben panned to the lone Native American sentinel standing with a heavy blanket wrapped around him, his drum on the ground beside him. A similarly dressed man took his place. "What you have just witnessed is the changing of the guard," Liz said, "which takes place every one to three hours, depending on the temperature and weather.

So far, no one has learned what these men wish to accomplish.

"Other demonstrators," Liz said, her breath misting in the cold air, "have joined them, their cause more obvious." Again, Ben panned the park and zoomed in on a small group of women carrying a series of signs proclaiming:

TURNCOAT TURNER
TURNOUT TURNER
MADDY, WE ARE YOUR FIRST CONSTITUENCY

The women saw Ben swing the Betacam on them and started chanting, "Maddy come home, Maddy come home." Ben gave her the cut sign and handed her a cellular phone. The network was calling. She spoke to her editor and nodded.

"Come on," she told Ben. He followed her to the lone drummer. When Ben was ready, she spoke into her microphone. "Excuse me, sir. Have you heard that our aircraft have engaged and shot down sixteen Chinese aircraft over the East China Sea?" She jammed the microphone into the drummer's face.

Without a word, he lifted the drum and looped its thick leather strap over a shoulder. He beat the drum with a slow cadence. Liz turned to face the camera. Behind her, the women were chanting, "No more wars, Maddy! No more wars!"

Liz's tip had been accurate, and she had the story. She spoke into her microphone. "In this unusual alliance, we may be seeing the birth of an antiwar movement." The sounding drum reached across Pennsylvania Avenue and wrapped around the White House.

16

Paris, France

"**H**ow's the jet lag?" Mazie Hazelton asked. It was late morning the next day and the hurried trip from Washington had been hectic.

"As long as I can stretch out and sleep," Bender answered, "it's not a problem."

"You're lucky," she said. "I lose my appetite, can't eat, can't sleep, and get edgy." She looked out the Lincoln's window as they left the city limits of Paris and drove to the chateaux where Wang Mocun was waiting. "I think we're expecting too much," she said. "We'll probably see a repeat of the last meeting so Wang can recover some face."

"So you don't think we can get them to recognize an air corridor?"

"Very doubtful," she answered. "But it would be a very positive step, which could lead to other breakthroughs."

"I'll see what I can do." They rode in silence until they reached the chateaux. The same group of dark-suited young men were waiting to escort them to the meeting room. As before, Bender entered from his side of the room at the same moment Wang entered from his. They both sat, and Bender spoke the required opening lines. But Wang wasn't reading from the same script and began a long monologue accusing the United States of unwarranted aggression. Bender listened while the translator murmured in his ear. Wang reached a resounding crescendo, paused, took a deep breath, and said, "The People's Republic of China awaits your apology, General Bender."

"You forgot to say 'Yankee air pirate,' " Bender said.

A flurry of Chinese broke out across the table, and he chanced a sideways glance at Hazelton. Her face was impassive, but her eyes were dancing with amusement. "We fail to understand the term *Yankee air pirate*," Wang replied.

"The North Vietnamese liked to call us that," Bender told him. "I will, of course, relay your comments to my government." He closed his folder and capped his pen.

"General Bender," Wang said, "it was our understanding that you were here to negotiate for your government, not relay messages."

"My discretionary powers match yours, and I can negotiate on matters of mutual concern. But I did not come here to listen to propaganda." He stood to leave. "It was our understanding that the air corridor between Okinawa and the Japanese mainland was a de facto arrangement because you did *not* mention it at our first meeting. We wish to avoid future misunderstandings of this nature. Please tell your government that we deeply regret this incident because it could have been avoided by a prompt and timely agreement here."

Wang's face paled. He had to produce results for his masters in Beijing if he was to survive, and Bender had him by the diplomatic short hairs. Bender instinctively understood and decided to jerk those hairs harder. "As you know, Minister Wang, I am a fighter pilot. I am deeply distressed when I see so many good men die in such a senseless manner. But, given what appears to be a fundamental misunderstanding, for us to continue here, I must present my government with a sign of your good intentions."

"What would you suggest?" Wang asked.

"I can initial an agreement that recognizes the security of all existing air corridors over international waters."

"Of course," Wang said, "that would include any de facto corridors into Okinawa." He allowed a little smile.

"And what would that gain my government, General Bender?"

Bender fixed Wang with the coldest look he could muster. "Our agreement not to embargo your commercial aircraft flying to and from international destinations."

"The international community will never allow that," Wang said.

"I merely wanted to suggest that an embargo is an option"—again, the cold look—"which we will consider." A hard silence ruled the room as the two men looked at each other.

"We will have an answer to you shortly," Wang finally said.

Who's the messenger service? Bender wondered. *Maybe it's time I make that point.* "Ah, yes," he said, his tone patronizing, "I see. I leave for Washington late tomorrow morning. If you do not have a reply by then, please forward your response through normal diplomatic channels."

The meeting was over, and Hazelton followed him out to the waiting limousine. She settled into the seat and was silent until they had left the chateau. "You really worked Wang over in there."

"Mazie, unless I am sadly mistaken, he was the one who came out swinging."

"His opening remarks were mostly pro forma, and when he ended by demanding an apology, you should have done the same. But you completely ignored him and bashed him silly with the biggest bat you could find."

"I see," he said. "So what did I do to our chances of negotiating an air corridor?"

"I don't know," she answered. "Wang is very upset, and there is no true quid pro quo. You offered not to do something we wouldn't have done in the first place."

"You mean the threat to embargo their commercial aircraft."

"Wang probably read it as an empty threat," Hazelton said.

"Then I screwed up in there."

"It's too early to tell. But you may have given Wang the leverage he needs to pry an agreement on the air corridor out of Beijing." She reached out and touched the top of his hand. "I love the 'Yankee air pirate' part." She lay back in the seat and dissolved in a fit of unladylike laughter. "The look on their faces!"

Bender managed a little smile. *What look?*

Andrews Air Force Base, Maryland

Bender stood by the forward door of the C-137C and waited for the boarding stairs to be pushed into position. He looked out the window of the old Boeing 707 that had once served as the original *Air Force One* and was surprised to see a White House staff car waiting behind the stairs. The chauffeur and a White House aide got out. "What's all this for?" he asked Hazelton.

"It goes with the job," she said. "You'll get used to it."

How true, he admitted to himself. The aircraft, limousines, VIP quarters, servants—all paid for by the public—had a powerful allure and were addictive. *The trappings of power,* he reminded himself. As a general, he was used to having staff cars and aides at his beck and call. But their function was to increase his efficiency, not pamper him. The Spartan side of his nature jolted him back to reality. *This is too much,* he told himself as an image of Shaw surrounded by his sycophants, young staffers, and gorgeous women flashed in front of him. This was not for him. "Mazie, you go on ahead." He walked forward to speak to the pilots and get in touch with the real world.

She was standing beside the limousine door, shivering in the cold, when he came down the steps. "Mazie, get in." He chided himself for not anticipating the dictates of protocol.

"Yes, sir," she said. "The bags are loaded and we can go." As protocol dictated, she entered first so he would be the first out. She spoke on the phone to the aide in the front seat. "President Turner is out of town building support for her tax proposals," she told Bender. "The secretary of state is waiting to meet with you." She extracted her leather-bound notebook from her briefcase, and they reviewed her notes, making good use of the time. The limousine drove directly to the State Department and pulled up at the basement entrance. Her husband was waiting for them.

Everything about Wentworth Hazelton shouted East Coast establishment: impeccable suit, old but well-brushed wingtip shoes, and his hair cut to the Kennedy image. He was in his early thirties, younger than Mazie, and considered one of the comers in the State Department. "Secretary Francis has been with the Chinese ambassador and is furious," he told her. "I don't know why, but it must be tied to Paris." He escorted them to the secretary's large and ornate office. "Be careful," he warned.

Nothing in Barnett Francis's words or actions betrayed his anger as they shook hands and tea was poured. Wentworth sat off to the side, his black Mont Blanc fountain pen poised over his notebook. "Well, General Bender," Francis finally said, coming to the reason for the hurried meeting. "We seem to be working at cross-purposes. Whenever I appear to be making headway with the Chinese, your talks in Paris get in the way. This must stop."

Bender did not reply as Francis cataloged his list of woes in negotiating with the Chinese.

"With all due respect," Bender said, "the Chinese want to negotiate while they whittle away at the Japanese. I am demanding a show of good faith to stop their salami tactics."

"I do not subscribe to the so-called salami tactics you are so enthralled with," Francis said. "The Chinese do have a valid historical basis for their actions. Taiwan was always part of China."

"But not Okinawa," Bender replied. "It was an independent kingdom until the Japanese annexed it by force in 1879."

"Considering the strong Chinese elements in Okinawan culture," Francis said, "the Chinese claim to Okinawa is not without merit." Francis droned on about peaceful accommodation between the two countries. Suddenly, Bender's head came up when he saw where Francis's long speech was leading. He glanced at Mazie's notepad.

"We got the air corridor" was written in big block letters.

"Mr. Secretary," Bender said, "I take it we have an air corridor."

"No," Francis replied. "But the president has received a message from Chairman Lu." Mazie Hazelton underlined the words on her notepad.

The dining room in the State Department was still full as the afternoon break for tea drew to a close. Bender sat across the table from Mazie and Wentworth wondering if he and Nancy had been the same at their age. The two were careful to maintain the formal, public dignity required by their professions when they were together, but underneath there was passion. The little touches of the hand, the veiled looks, the little smile at a twist of words, were all there. *Were we so obvious?* he wondered. "Why is Francis so angry about the air corridor?" he asked.

Wentworth answered. "Because State had nothing to do with it. You presented Secretary Francis with a done deal and you get all the credit. He merely takes care of the paperwork."

Bender shook his head in disgust. "Let him take the credit as long as we get the corridor."

"But it puts him in your camp," Wentworth replied. "State has split into two factions on this issue. One group is pro-Chinese and is pressing for negotiations while the pro-Japanese faction wants direct intervention."

"Many at Foggy Bottom," Mazie added, "are backing the Chinese because they are anti-Japanese and believe this can serve as an object lesson. The disagreement runs very deep and is bordering on the edge of internecine warfare."

"It sounds like department politics are driving our country's foreign policy," Bender said.

"That's the way most of our government works," Wentworth said. "Actually, the disagreement here is much worse than Mazie said. It is becoming quite bloody."

Bender looked around the room at the protodiplomats practicing their best manners. "I don't think anyone is in much danger," he replied. "I can't say the same about our people on Okinawa."

* * *

With the president out of town, the White House was in an automatic mode of operation. The day-to-day routines went on, the tourists were ushered through the state rooms with brisk efficiency, and the mansion hummed with activity. But it lacked the tension, the crackling movement, the lively spirit that flowed from the Oval Office. The announcement that the president was returning early sent a shot of adrenaline through the staff, and a hushed anticipation held them in place, waiting for her return.

For Bender, it was a chance to get some much needed exercise, and he went to the gym for some one-on-one basketball with Chuck Sanford, the older of the two Secret Service agents permanently assigned to his watch. The exercise felt good, and Sanford was playing to win, which Bender liked. Sweat flew off his face as he broke around Sanford and pressed into the basket. But Sanford cut him off and took the ball away from him in a very aggressive move. He took the ball out and pounded in for a clean shot, sinking the ball. "You're down by two," Sanford puffed. "You don't stand a chance now, General." He was right and rebounded the next shot to score again. They walked off the court where Brian was waiting, dressed in gym togs and bouncing a ball.

"Want to shoot some hoops?" Brian asked.

"Sure, why not?" Bender answered. "I've got some time." He nodded at Sanford who got the message and called Bender's secretary to slip his next appointment. They walked onto the court and Brian shot a few warm-ups. Bender took a shot and sank it. "How's school?"

"OK, I guess," Brian replied. Bender waited. It was obvious Brian wanted to talk. "Do you know a girl named Shalandra?"

"Yep," Bender answered. He sank another shot.

"She says you're going to adopt her."

"We're sponsoring her," Bender said. "I don't know if you can call that adoption." He sank another shot.

"That's good," Brian said. "One of my buddies says she's a whore and he's screwed her."

Bender missed the shot. "Guys talk," he said retrieving the ball. *Nine days,* he thought. *She lasted nine miserable days.* "That doesn't make her a whore," Bender told him. "Did your buddy give her money?" Brian shook his head. "Did you do it, too?"

Brian looked at him, his eyes pleading for understanding. Slowly, he shook his head. "But I wanted to. The other guys are calling me a faggot for not doing it."

Damn kids, Bender raged to himself. He wanted to tell Brian that they were trying to get at him because of his mother. "And they all had sex with her?"

"All of them say they did, but I don't believe them."

Bender forced a laugh. "You played it smart. Shalandra is a girl with lots of potential and lots of problems. If those guys who had intercourse with her thought she was a whore, they are dumber than a fence post for doing it"—he passed the ball to Brian, who took a shot— "which"—he continued, dribbling the ball after catching it on the rebound—"doesn't say too much about them." He broke to the outside and sank a long shot. "Have you told anyone else?" Again, the slow head shake in answer. "I'll take care of it." He fed Brian the ball and let him make a basket. "Pretty good. You going to try out for basketball?"

"I'm thinking about it."

"Do it," Bender said.

"Sir," Sanford called from the sidelines, "the president has arrived. Meeting in forty minutes."

"I'm on my way," Bender said. He let Brian make another basket, and they walked off the court. "You did the right thing, Brian. Save the sex for someone you love. You won't regret it."

General Overmeyer was waiting in the president's outer office with her key advisors when Bender walked in. The two men nodded at each other but stood apart, the sign of Bender's changed status in the White House. The office was brisk efficiency as staff members hustled in and out, bringing life to the office of the presidency. Turner's senior domestic advisor came out of the Oval Office with Shaw, locked in an intense conversation.

Bender's personal view of the White House was limited and focused on national security. He was only part of the activity, the business, the turmoil, focusing on the president. But he had commanded and served on enough staffs to recognize a good one when he saw it. All of his experience told him that Maddy Turner had placed her own stamp on the White House and made it her own. Jackie Winters opened the door to the Oval Office. "Gentlemen, you're on," she said.

Bender turned to one of the secretaries. "Please ask Mrs. Hazelton to join me immediately after the meeting." He was the last one to enter the office.

Hazelton was waiting for Bender when he returned to his office after the meeting with the president. He motioned for Norma and Ella, his two secretaries, to follow him. "Mrs. Hazelton and I are leaving for Paris," he told them. He ran through a list of things he wanted done. "Can you think of anything else?" he asked.

"It's your wife's birthday tomorrow, " Norma replied. "I can send flowers."

He reached into a desk drawer and pulled out a thin square box. "Can you get this wrapped and send it along with the flowers? Also, please call my wife. I need to see her before I leave." The two secretaries bustled out of the office to make it all happen. Norma was back in moments, telling him that Nancy was at the hospital with a patient and a message had been left for her. "I'll have to pack myself," he said, wishing he had a valet. "Mazie, I've got an uncomfortable itch that needs scratching. Why are the Chinese so eager to talk now and sign an agreement on an air corridor?"

Mazie didn't answer for a few moments. "I can only guess at this point. Perhaps, they want a done deal to solidify their position."

"We're missing something," Bender said. "We may give the store away if we're not careful." He leaned back in his chair, recalling what Turner had said in the meeting. Secretary Francis had briefed her on Lu Zoulin's message requesting they initial a secret agreement in Paris recognizing the safety of all international air traffic. *No clues there,* he thought. An inner alarm went off. Was this how the sellout on Taiwan went down? "Mazie, we're being suckered here. What are the Japanese doing?"

"Still trying to cobble together a coherent political response."

Bender stared into space. Then it came to him. "Find out what the Japanese Self-Defense Forces are doing. We have been so focused on the Chinese that we may have missed what the third party to this triangle is doing."

"I don't think the Japanese are willing to go it alone," she said.

"Let's find out if they've got the capability to act unilaterally," Bender replied. "Someone in the basement of the CIA or the DIA knows. If they don't, then the National Reconnaissance Office had better get a Keyhole satellite looking at them."

"The NRO isn't going to like that," she told him. "They had to reposition a satellite to cover Okinawa. Another orbit change is going to burn a lot of fuel."

Bender stood up to leave. "One way or the other, we need to know what the Japanese are doing before we talk to Wang in Paris. Get someone working on it. I'll meet you at the airport in two hours." He gave her his encouraging look and left.

"Nothing's impossible for the man who doesn't have to do it himself," Hazelton grumbled as she ran to her office.

The two secretaries exchanged glances after Bender and Hazelton had left. "What did he get her for her birthday?" Ella asked, eyeing the thin box.

"It's none of our business," Norma replied.

"He might have left the price tag on," Ella coaxed. "You know men."

Norma nodded in agreement and carefully opened the box. Inside was a black silk negligee. "Look at the label," she whispered, holding it up. It was a long, delicate creation from Christian Dior in Paris. It was both revealing and demure, somehow proper, but incredibly alluring. "He must have paid a fortune for it."

"I wouldn't be caught dead in that," Ella announced.

"You definitely don't want to be dead if he catches you wearing it," Norma replied. Ella sighed and agreed with her.

Bender was zipping his old, battered, Air Force issue, green hangup bag closed. It had traveled countless miles with him and belonged in a museum. But he kept the old bag out of sentiment, and it had been mended many times. "I got your message," Nancy said from the doorway. He looked up. Her face was flushed and excited from the hurried drive home.

"I'm going back to Paris," he told her. "I don't know when I'll be back, and we need to talk. I didn't want to do it on the phone." He sat on the edge of the bed and told her about Brian and Shalandra.

"Boys at that age are temporary sociopaths," she raged, walking up and down. "They are so damn immature and impulsive." She waved an arm as if fending off an invisible but irritating insect. "I don't believe it. Boys and sex!"

"It's in the genes," Bender said, surprised that she was so upset.

"Don't give me all that bullshit about the biological basis of behavior. Fourteen-year-old boys are immoral cretins driven by their gonads."

Bender almost said that she had just made the case for biology but thought better of it. He did say, "I tend to trust Brian on this one. You better check it out."

"Check what out?" she grumbled. "Some half-baked lies?" She looked at him, pleading. "Robert, you should see her. She looks so different in a school uniform, and for the first time, she's eating right."

"Check it out," he repeated. "I've got to go."

"I need to get back to the hospital," she said.

"Sorry I'm going to miss your birthday."

"It's not the first time," she reminded him. He picked up the hangup bag, remembering how Laurie had dragged it to the car so many years before.

Paris, France

Bender heard Hazelton's heels echoing down the embassy corridor long before she reached the door of his temporary office. He stood up, ready to leave for the meeting with the Chinese. "Come on in, Mazie," he called before she knocked.

"It's these heels," she said. "You heard me coming. I must sound like a herd of elephants.

"Actually, it's the perfume," he said.

"Right," she deadpanned. She dropped a folder on his desk stamped "TOP SECRET RUFF." "This just came in. You were right about the Japanese." He opened the folder. "Kagoshima Bay on southern Kyushu," she announced. "Three hundred and fifty nautical miles from Okinawa." He spread out a series of satellite photos on his desk that covered the southernmost of the main Japanese islands. "The analysts count sixteen destroyers, twenty-one frigates, and eighteen long-range patrol boats. All have a significant antiaircraft and antisubmarine capability and are capable of reaching Okinawa in fifteen hours. Another report indicates the Japanese are sending more surface combatants to Kagoshima."

"If I were Chinese and on Kumejima," he said, "I'd be worried."

"I think they are," Mazie said. "That's why they want to get us to the bargaining table before the Japanese sortie."

"Mazie, we need that air corridor so President Turner will allow us to evacuate our dependents before the shooting starts."

"We can get it," she said. "But what's the price?"

"Let's go find out," he replied.

The translator's words were a low hum in Bender's ear as he listened to the translation of Wang's long monologue. Although he didn't understand a word of Chinese, he had the tempo and cadences down, and the tone of the speech was conciliatory. Finally, it was his turn. "We appreciate Chairman Lu's generous consideration of our offer to guarantee the safety of international air traffic. I, of course, will relay his words to my president."

"It was my understanding," Wang said, "that you were here to initial an agreement between our governments."

Bender nodded gravely. "That is true, but I see no document in front of me, no concrete guarantees have been advanced, and although we are agreed in principle, we are apparently stumbling over details." Magically, a thin leather-bound document appeared that reminded Bender of the agreement that sold out Taiwan. He thumbed through it, his face a mask. The Chinese wanted de facto recognition of the Yaeyama chain, the islands nearest Taiwan that included Iriomote, in exchange for the air corridor.

"As you can see, General Bender," Wang said, "we will withdraw from Kumejima within sixty days once the Japanese enter into meaningful negotiations."

"President Turner will certainly want to study your, ah, proposal," Bender said. "But for now, our goals are more limited." On cue, Hazelton produced their version of an agreement. It was only two pages long and stated that the safety of all flights over international waters was guaranteed by the signing parties. "We consider this the first step," Bender said. "It is, above all else, an expression of our mutual goodwill, necessary for these talks to continue."

Wang's face paled, and the real haggling began. Near the end, Wang declared nothing more could be done. Bender forced a sad look across his face and said that they had done all they could at their level, the Paris talks were at an end, and perhaps they should refer the entire matter to the United Nations General Assembly. Five minutes later, they had Wang's initials on the two-page agreement. Hazelton looked at him with a new respect as they left for the drive back to Paris.

"This may be one of the fastest agreements ever negotiated," Bender said.

"It's a replay of the Taiwan scenario," she told him. "It worked once, and the Chinese are confident it will work again. This is the price they had to pay to keep us in secret negotiations."

"Do you think they'll honor it?"

"Until the shooting starts," she replied.

"We had better get our dependents out before that happens," he said.

Hazelton was silent until they reached the embassy. "General," she finally said, "you have made a personal enemy."

"Really? Who?"

"Wang. He can't handle you and is probably in deep

trouble with Beijing. They'll send another negotiator next time.''

"Will there be a next time?"

"Oh, yes," she answered.

Washington, D.C.

She's as tired as I am, Bender thought. It was early Saturday evening, and he was sitting in the Oval Office with Turner and her key advisors. He was aching after the flight back from Paris Friday night and the long discussions, security briefings, and meetings that had filled the morning and afternoon. Now it was time to make a decision. "Madam President," he said, "the bottom line is that we have a safe air corridor. We can use it to evacuate dependents and mount an airlift operation to resupply Okinawa much like the Berlin airlift.''

"But even you admit that we can't be sure how long the Chinese will honor the corridor," Turner said.

"Madam President," Secretary of Defense Elkins said, "we have demonstrated our resolve and capability to defend our aircraft. The Chinese won't challenge us again."

She chewed her bottom lip for a moment and then stopped, aware that the men were carefully watching her. "I wish I could be sure of that." Logic told her to exploit the window and get as many dependents off Okinawa as possible. But would that be signaling her intention to withdraw from Okinawa? Or would it serve as a signal that she intended to fight for the Japanese? She didn't want to do either. But more importantly, what if an aircraft was shot down? How many women and children would die because of a decision she made? Was this why she became president? To send innocent people to their deaths?

She glanced at the clock on her desk: 8:40 Saturday evening. She closed the folder on her desk and folded her hands over it. She had never felt less presidential than now, the very time when she needed to make a decision. They were waiting. "Gentlemen, start positioning aircraft. You'll have my decision in the morning." She stood and left the room, leaving the door open behind her. Jackie

Winters was waiting in the outer office, desperate to resolve some of the minor matters that plagued every president.

Turner tried to focus on what Winters was saying, but Elkins's voice cut through all else. "She can't make a decision."

Bender's voice in reply, "We don't need an immediate decision on this. Give her some time."

Robert doesn't need to defend me, she raged to herself. *I'm the president of the United States and Elkins works for me!* Her anger died as quickly as it had flared, and she walked out, the hapless Winters in tow. But she felt better. Robert understood her dilemma.

"Mrs. President," Winters said, "there is a problem at the Academy. Some of Brian's friends are having trouble with a scholarship student—a girl."

"Was Brian involved?" Turner asked. Winters told her he was only a bystander. "Let my mother take care of it for now."

The grandmother clock in the corner of Turner's private study chimed three times. The fire was slowly dying in the fireplace and she was curled up on a corner of the couch, staring into the embers. It was Sunday morning, January 27, the sixteenth day of the crisis, and she had not slept in twenty-one hours. Her mother entered quietly and sat down. "I thought you might have fallen asleep," Maura said. A shake of Turner's head. "Is it that bad?" Maura asked. She was deeply concerned about her daughter and had never seen her so tired and drawn. She had lost weight and her warmup suit was bagging on her slender frame. For a moment, Maura considered talking about the problems at Brian's school, but she decided against it.

Turner stood and walked to the fireplace. She touched the bell that had sat on her desk in the California senate. It seemed like an age ago. "It was much easier then," she murmured to herself. Then, more firmly, "They're asking me—" She stopped. No one was asking her to do anything. They were only presenting options. "I have to decide if I should evacuate military dependents out of Oki-

nawa or leave them there. There is a risk no matter what
I do.''

Maura knew her daughter. "And you don't want to be
responsible for the death of innocent people." Turner nodded. "I'm not an educated woman, Maddy. But I do know
the Bible teaches us that some of the flock must suffer for
the rest.''

"Unfortunately, the Bible does not tell us how to decide
who does the suffering.''

"If it must be done, trust your judgment. Don't be
afraid to sacrifice one or two if you can save many. But
fight for every one of them." She looked at her daughter.
"Is there going to be a war?''

"Not if I can help it," Turner replied. "Go to bed,
Mother.'' She walked out and headed for the Oval Office.
The uniformed Secret Service agent on duty looked up
and murmured into his whisper mike.

"Magic is moving.''

The lighted board in the Secret Service command post
directly below the Oval Office followed Turner as she left
the residence and walked through the colonnade to the
West Wing. The light indicating she was in the Oval Office flicked on. A telephone call was made and the cook
on duty in the kitchen brewed a fresh pot of coffee—just
in case. Turner did not sit at her desk but moved around
the office, finally stopping at the Kennedy rocker. She ran
her hand over the top, stroking the wood. She sat down
and leaned back, slowly rocking, and closed her eyes. *So
lonely,* she thought. *So lonely.*

17 ⟵

Okinawa, Japan

Staff Sergeant Lancey Coltrain was the junior command post controller on duty when the emergency action message from headquarters CINC PAC came in. She automatically noted the date and time: It was ten o'clock, Sunday evening, the sixteenth day of the crisis. The alphanumeric code came in a constant stream, but she copied it down in blocks of four, which was, in itself, part of the validation process. She flipped the decode book to the right page and decoded the message. "Thank God," she told her supervisor. She closed her eyes and took a deep breath while he confirmed her decode.

"It's a valid message," he said. "I'll tell the general. We are about to see the dust fly."

Sergeant Lancey Coltrain exhaled and sank back into her chair, her slender body shaking with relief. "It's about time." She was taking her children home.

Martini read the message without comment and turned to his staff. "CINC PAC has implemented NEO. Get Major Ryan in here and start hollering for aircraft." He huddled with his group commanders and calculated the number of flights it would take to airlift out 26,000 dependents. Their best guess was approximately 100 sorties at a rate of 20 a day. "I want to move them out faster if we can," he told them.

Eighteen minutes later, Major Robert Ryan skidded

through the door of the Battle Cab. In his haste to dress, he had buttoned his BDU shirt wrong and was trying to get the right button in the matching buttonhole. Martini told him CINC PAC had implemented NEO, and the first transport aircraft was expected to arrive in six hours. "I want at least 250 people on that aircraft and 250 more ready to go every hour after that."

Ryan gasped. He had set up an intricate timetable to gather dependents at collection points, bus them to one of three processing centers, and then move them to the flight line for loading on an airplane. The acceleration Martini demanded was going to create havoc. "Sir, we simply don't have the resources to move and process that many people that fast. I don't think we can do it."

"For Christ's sake!" Martini barked. "Quit waffling and try. If you can't do it, then get back to me and tell me what you need to make it happen. Got it?" Ryan nodded dumbly and beat a quick retreat out of the command post convinced that Martini had suffered a total breakdown in good judgment. *The man's irrational,* he told himself.

The seething anger Ryan harbored for Martini eased as the system he had created worked well, and when the first five buses departed for the flight line and the waiting C-17 Globemaster III, he felt ecstatic. *Martini be damned,* he thought. *I'm going to make this happen.* The phone call from the command post came six minutes later. It was Martini demanding to know why only 238 passengers were going out on the first aircraft. "Because, sir," Ryan shot back, "that's all it's got seats for."

"Get ten more on it. I don't care how you do it. Have them sit on each other's laps, put 'em on the flight deck." He broke the connection.

"Damn!" Ryan shouted, his voice cracking. Couldn't he do anything right? But he made it happen, and the C-17 launched on time with 248 passengers.

Later that day, the family of Master Sergeant Ralph Contreraz, an F-15 maintenance production supervisor, made their way through the processing line set up in the base gym. Ryan watched as Contreraz bulldozed his way through the crowd to say good-bye and hug his children.

"The house had better be clean and the dishes done when I get back," his wife threatened. She started to cry then drew herself up, stopping the tears. "I'm coming back as soon as I can."

"I hear you," the crusty old sergeant muttered. He kissed his wife and helped her and his three kids board the bus waiting to take them to the aircraft. *That's the same Contreraz who Laurie liked so much,* Ryan thought. Laurie had claimed he was the best NCO in Maintenance and, arguably, on the base.

Behind him, Ryan heard angry voices in the processing line. He sighed. Why wouldn't people cooperate? "No one is taking my kids away from me!" a woman's voice shouted. Ryan hurried over to the table to see if he could help. A staff sergeant who looked vaguely familiar was blocking the line. A three-year-old boy was clinging to her leg, and she held a fourteen-month-old toddler in her arms. Ryan tried to read her name tag, but the little girl was in the way. "You are?" he asked.

"Staff Sergeant Lancey Coltrain," the woman answered.

"You work in the command post?"

"That's right. This here shit-for-brains says I can't take my kids out of here."

"NEO is only for nonessential personnel and dependents," Ryan explained. "Command post personnel are considered essential. We'll assign a sponsor to escort your children."

"CINC PAC says I can take my kids out of here!" Lancey screamed. "I saw the fucking message, and nobody is going to stop me." She was on the edge of hysteria.

"Please calm down," Ryan soothed. He pointed to a nearby office. "Let's go over there where we can talk."

"I'm not getting out of line," Lancey cried. "And we're leaving. My husband works on F-15s. Only one of us has to stay."

Master Sergeant Contreraz was standing behind Ryan and shook his head in disgust. The major was blowing it. He knew Lancey's husband and had seen it all too often when a husband and wife were in the Air Force. They expected the service to give them special treatment because they were a family. Normally, the Air Force tried to be accommodating, but when push came to shove, the needs of the Air Force had to come first. This was one of those times. "Major, can I help?" he asked. "Sergeant Coltrain's husband works for me."

Lancey gave Contreraz a thankful look. He would explain it to the major. Instead, Contreraz asked, "Who's detailed to take care of her children?"

A junior high school P.E. teacher stepped forward and volunteered. She was a big woman with short hair and a pleasant face. She had spent twenty-six years in the Department of Defense Dependent Schools and loved her career, children, and the military. "I'm not going to let some old dike get her hands on my kids!" Lancey shouted.

Countless parent–teacher conferences had taught the teacher when to ignore an upset parent and held out her arms. The toddler came to her, finding a warm refuge. "You'll be fine with me," the teacher cooed. She easily balanced the child with one arm while she gave Lancey her card. "My stateside address and phone number is on the back. Give me your number, and I'll call you when I get your children with their grandparents. By the way, I've got two grown kids of my own and I'm a grandmother."

Lancey grabbed her child and walked quickly to the bus, dragging her son. "You're not authorized to go," Ryan blurted at her back. "We'll make sure your children are OK."

"She's lost it," Contreraz said. "You want her off the bus?" Ryan nodded an answer, and Contreraz followed Lancey onto the bus. Ryan could see them standing in the aisle as they talked. She shook her head, her hair flying back and forth, and kicked Contreraz in the leg. His bellowed shout of "You are not listening!" echoed out the door as he poked a finger at her forehead. "Get your goddamn ass off this bus! NOW!"

Lancey clambered off the bus, a red spot in the middle of her forehead. "He hit me!" she cried.

"That was a poke to get your attention," Contreraz said as he climbed down. "When I say move, you move."

Contreraz had a formidable reputation and the jagged,

raw emotion that had been driving Lancey was rapidly fading to worry. She managed a very weak, "Wait until my congressman hears about this."

"Major," Contreraz said, "tell the bus driver to move out and call the cops. This lady needs to go to jail." Coltrain's mouth fell open, and she started to cry.

Ryan was desperate. At least 300 people were watching, hearing every word, and murmuring among themselves. He had to regain control before they keyed off Coltrain and turned into an unruly mob. The decision was easy. "Get on the bus," he told Lancey. "You're going home." The crowd was eerily silent.

Contreraz stepped back and watched Lancey board. He stood in silence until the bus pulled away. "It doesn't make sense to keep her here," Ryan said, justifying his decision.

"She took the same oath you and I did," Contreraz shot back. "Who in the hell is gonna do her job? I can't. How about you?" The sergeant spun around and walked away, not waiting for an answer.

Been here, done this, Ryan decided as the group commanders filed out of the Battle Cab. Martini was going to have another piece of his anatomy for lunch. He checked his watch and changed the "lunch" to "dinner." *This is turning into a very long day,* he told himself.

"Letting Sergeant Coltrain fly out was the wrong decision," the general said. Nothing in his voice betrayed the anger boiling beneath the surface.

"I thought it best to diffuse the issue, sir." Martini was not impressed with his defense, and Ryan trotted out his main argument. "You can imagine what the press would do to us if they learned we had broken up a family."

Martini's fingers drummed the console. NEO was going well, and Ryan deserved full credit. Martini weighed that against the incident with Sergeant Coltrain. How much damage did he do to good order and discipline by letting her go? Why did this have to occur now when discipline meant survival. He considered replacing Ryan but discarded the idea. He couldn't spare anyone to take over Ryan's job, and for the most part, the doctor had done an outstanding job. He made his decision: Ryan was going to get another chance. "What the press thinks or does is not your concern." Martini fell into his teaching mode, and he wanted to explain the modern Air Force with all its strengths and weaknesses.

But he didn't have the time. Instead, he settled for some practical advice. "Your job is to make the system work within the existing rules. When Coltrain called the teacher a dike, you should have pulled her aside for immediate counseling on sexual harassment. That gives you time to call her immediate superior and get him involved. By then, you've got her isolated. Then call in the legal beagles. They'll put everything on hold, which is exactly what you want. Then you make an offer she can't refuse: Her children can fly out on the next plane while the mess that she started in the first place is straightened out. As a mother, what's she going to do? Keep her kids in jeopardy? She lets them fly out, gets put on report, and is ordered back to duty. Problem solved."

Ryan was shocked at Martini's cold-blooded manipulation of the rules and people. "What happens now?" he asked.

"She'll be met at Yokota when the plane lands and brought back under armed guard. I'll offer her the choice of confinement to barracks or return to duty while we start court-martial proceedings—absent without leave or failure to repair come to mind. If she gets the message, cooperates, and does her job, I'll drop the court-martial and offer her nonjudicial punishment instead—nothing more than fining her a couple of hundred bucks and reduction in grade. If she's got her attitude screwed on straight, I might even suspend the bust. Next time something like this happens, use your head."

Ryan saw a chance to shift the general's attention away from his blunder and told Martini about Contreraz poking Coltrain in the forehead. He conveniently omitted mentioning that Coltrain had kicked Contreraz first. "What do we do about that?" he asked.

"Contreraz knows better than that. How hard did he strike her?"

"I only saw a little redness," Ryan answered. "It went

away very quickly." He almost added that Coltrain was more rational after getting off the bus. But that would be admitting physical intimidation modified behavior and that, from his viewpoint as a physician and a psychiatrist, was a barbaric practice on a par with voodoo.

"You're the doctor," Martini said. "At least he got her off the bus quickly without anyone getting hurt. Who knows how she would've reacted if the cops had to drag her off." He allowed a tight smile. "I'll bet she was off that bus in a heartbeat."

"Yes, sir. She was."

Again, Martini's fingers drummed the console. "You should have followed Contreraz's advice, rolled the bus, and called the cops." More drumming on the table. "Still, he shouldn't have touched her. I'll talk to him."

Ryan suffered a total breakdown in judgment and refused to drop the subject. "Sir, that doesn't seem fair. You're going to court-martial Coltrain and only 'talk' to Contreraz."

Martini drilled Ryan with a cold look. Did the major have a clue? A good sergeant knew how and when to bully an airman when there was no time for the legal and civilized niceties of modern society. Martini tried one last time to reach Ryan. "Contreraz didn't cause the problem, and he got things moving in a very direct manner. Next time, listen to your NCOs. You'd be surprised how fast they can solve problems." He studied Ryan for a moment. "I hope you learned something from all this. Always remember that when the shooting starts, the rules change. Get back to work."

Ryan scurried out of the command post convinced that Martini was losing his grip on reality. *Who's been doing the shooting around here?* he asked himself.

Washington, D.C.

"Ben," Liz Gordon said to her cameraman, "can you tune out that damn drum?" They were in Lafayette Park shooting a package on the growing number of demonstrators flocking to join the lone drummer still beating his drum by Lafayette's statute. Ben fiddled with the sound controls and had her turn away from the drummer, her back a shield to the echoing beat. It helped, and the mob cooperated by waving their signs back and forth.

"Fireplug's in the crowd," Ben said.

"Are you surprised?" Liz replied. She searched the crowd until she found Quella O'Malley, the guru of demonstrators. O'Malley was a short, stocky woman with an outrageous sense of style and a talent for stirring up trouble. O'Malley always made good news, and the media loved her for her gushy flamboyance and bright clothes. In the newsrooms but never in public, they called her Fireplug. But not one reporter or editor suspected she was one of the highest-paid and most cynical troublemakers on the American scene. "Get a shot of her sign," Liz said. Ben stood on a bench and zoomed in on O'Malley. True to form, she was carrying a huge new sign declaring

FAMILIES COME FIRST

Ben panned the crowd, focused on Liz, and cued her to start talking. "The first break in the snowstorms that have battered this city has brought out a new wave of protesters on this bright Wednesday morning. This is the nineteenth day of what is now called the Counterfeit Crisis by Washington insiders, and tensions are subsiding as more and more dependents and U.S. civilians are evacuated from Okinawa. At the same time, a massive airlift, reminiscent of the Berlin airlift and Operation Provide Promise in Bosnia, is bringing much needed relief to Okinawa.

"The peace drummer and demonstrators for women's rights have been joined by a new group." Ben zoomed in on O'Malley's sign without showing her. "The concern for families is in response to the bizarre and grotesque report that a sergeant was forcibly separated from her children during the evacuation of dependents from Okinawa. So far, the White House and the Pentagon have refused to comment on the incident. This is Elizabeth Gordon, CNC-TV News, reporting live from the White House."

Ben lowered his Betacam. "Fireplug's comin' this way. You want to interview her?"

"Not this time," Liz replied. "Let's go." O'Malley glared at them as they hurried away. It was one more personal slight she added to her ever-growing list.

Turner walked out of the Cabinet Room and headed for the Oval Office. The vice president and Jackie Winters matched her pace while Shaw lingered behind. "You're behind schedule," Winters said. "You have ten minutes with your security advisors before leaving for the luncheon speech with the American Banker's Association. You're talking on tax reform—twenty minutes. The speech is ready and similar to the one you'll be giving tomorrow in Seattle."

"I'll review it on the way over," Turner said. She turned into the Oval Office. Bender, Secretary of Defense Elkins, and the DCI were waiting for her. Winters peeled off to her desk while Kennett and Shaw followed her in, closing the door. "Well, gentlemen," she said sitting down in the rocker by the couches, "is there any good news today?"

"No change," the DCI answered.

"This is the third day of the evacuation," Elkins said, "and we're ahead of schedule. Over 15,000 dependents have been flown out, and we should finish it off in another forty-eight hours."

"And the Coltrain incident?" Turner asked.

"We want to treat it as a routine breech of discipline," Elkins said. "If Coltrain will return to duty, Martini will drop the court-martial charges and slap her hands with a fine and demotion in rank. Unfortunately, Coltrain is being difficult and refuses to return to duty. She's going for the court-martial."

"She also claims she was physically abused by a senior NCO," Sam Kennett said.

"When is the military going to learn?" Turner demanded.

"According to witnesses," Bender said, "she boarded a bus for evacuees without permission. An NCO ordered her off, and she kicked him. He responded by poking a finger at her forehead and shouting. She got off."

"I suppose he outweighed her by 100 pounds," Turner said.

"She did not belong on the bus," Bender repeated. "And she was holding up the flight. The officer in charge of the evacuation should have never—"

Turner cut him off. "Why are we even discussing this?"

Sam Kennett answered her. "We're discussing this because someone is feeding the demonstrators and the press misinformation, and they choose to make a case out of it."

"This is getting out of hand, Mizz President," Shaw said. "We need to defuse it—now."

"Suggestions?" she asked. She listened until Jackie Winters appeared in the doorway holding a heavy top coat and scarf. Turner stood up, her decision made. "Have the Pentagon issue a press release announcing all charges against Sergeant Coltrain have been dropped, and she is being reunited with her children." The meeting was over, and the men stood while she left.

"Well," Kennett said, breaking the heavy silence, "that solved the problem."

"Did it?" Bender asked.

The East China Sea

Ryan leaned back into the red nylon webbing of the parachute jump seat and let the sound of the C-130's droning turboprop engines wash over him. *Friday morning,* he thought, *and we're almost home.* He pulled himself up and looked out the small round window above his head. The sun was up, and he could make out the dark mass of Yoron Island, north of Okinawa. He was returning from a medical air evacuation mission to Yakota Air Base in Japan and would be back in time to see the fifth and, hopefully, the last day of NEO. Not that it needed him at this point, because the entire operation was running like a well-oiled machine functioning on autopilot.

Increasingly, he had found himself at loose ends, and when a doctor had been needed to evacuate six litter-bound hospital patients to Yokota, Martini had told him to go on the mission and evaluate the Yokota end of the operation for an after-action report. "Sir," the loadmaster said, "please strap in. We'll be landing in a few minutes." Ryan straightened up and savored the moment. *One more day,* he thought. And he had made it happen.

Two busloads of dependents and civilians were waiting to board the C-130 when it taxied to a halt. Ryan waited with the nurse and sergeant who had accompanied him on the air evac while children scampered off the buses and ran up the rear ramp of the Hercules. Automatically, Ryan tallied the passenger manifests. Ninety-four more gone.

"Lucky bastards," the sergeant muttered. Ryan agreed with him, and they climbed on board an empty bus for the ride back. The C-130's engines were spinning up as they drove away. The bus driver followed Perimeter Road back to the main base and slowed when they reached Habu Hill. "Sir," the sergeant said, "can we see the C-130 take off?" Ryan nodded, and the bus driver pulled onto the overlook.

The C-130 Hercules taxiing out had been delivered to the Air Force by Lockheed in 1969. It had performed yeoman duty airlifting cargo and troops in Vietnam, the Grenada invasion in 1983, the invasion of Panama in 1989, the Gulf War in 1990, and the Bosnian peacekeeping mission in 1996. Over 40,000 hours of flying time were recorded in its log books, and it had served the Air Force well, far exceeding its designed lifespan.

But Ryan only knew that this particular Hercules had carried him and six patients to Japan, returned him to Okinawa on time, and was now flying ninety-four more people to safety. He climbed off the bus and stood by the guardrail. His eyes followed the C-130 as it rolled down the runway and lifted off on another routine mission into a gorgeous tropical morning. The Hercules climbed straight ahead to 500 feet over the East China Sea and turned out of the pattern.

That was when the C-130's left main wing spar snapped, the result of age and metal fatigue. It was a clean break between the number one and two engines. The prop on the outboard engine was still turning as the wing twisted away, taking the number one engine with it. Ryan stood transfixed as if his feet were nailed to the ground. The Hercules was in a flat left spin, and he heard one of the engines surge. The wing was still falling away. One engine sounded louder as the aircraft hit the water in a gigantic belly flop. A wall of water rose above the plane and crashed down, obscuring his view. His first rational thought told him they were OK and it was only a matter of getting everyone out before the Hercules sank. But all he could see was the tall vertical stabilizer riding above the water, like a shark fin framed by the rising sun.

He sank to his knees and tried to breathe. He couldn't.

Ryan knew the smell: ammonium carbonate and ammonia water—smelling salts. "Are you OK?" the nurse asked. Ryan shook his head, fending off the fog that was still there to claim him. He was lying on the ground next to the guardrail, the nurse and sergeant bent over him. He had passed out.

"The C-130?" he cracked, barely able to talk.

The nurse stared at him, at a loss for words to answer his question. She raised her right hand, still holding the smelling salts, and made a vague gesture at the water. Ryan struggled to his feet and held onto the guardrail. The water was smooth and clear of debris, as if the Hercules had never existed. He could hear sirens in the background and saw a small boat speeding toward the scene of the accident. "Why?" he muttered. Nothing made sense.

Martini was on the main floor of the command post huddled with the disaster response cell. This was their first real emergency, and he listened as they drove the wing's response to the accident. They were a well-trained team, but no exercise, no amount of training, could guarantee their reaction to the real thing. He could hear strain in their voices, but there was no panic. They were OK. He forced himself to move slowly and ambled over to the airlift coordination desk. It was their aircraft that had just crashed. A sergeant looked up at him, his face drawn and flushed. "Take a couple deep breaths," Martini said. "It helps."

The sergeant breathed deeply. "I'll be OK, sir."

"I know," Martini replied. He continued to move

slowly around the big room, taking the strain and leaving a wake of calm resolve behind him. Finally, he was in the Control Cab with the controllers. "Are all the messages sent?" he asked.

The senior controller answered. "Yes, sir." He hesitated. "Sir, Staff Sergeant Lancey Coltrain was on that C-130."

"Damn," Martini muttered. "Get me CINC PAC on the secure phone. I'll take it in the Battle Cab." He paused. "I want to speak to her husband's commander ASAP. And get Major Ryan in here on the double." The phone call to CINC PAC was a short one. Staff Sergeant Donald Coltrain would be escorting his wife's remains back to the States at the earliest possible moment.

Ryan walked onto the main floor of the command post a few minutes later. He was still shaking as he made his way to the Battle Cab and knocked on the glass door. Martini motioned him inside and poured a cup of coffee. "I don't know about you, but I need a cup of coffee." He pointed to a chair, and Ryan sat down. "Care for a cup?" Ryan gratefully accepted the cup of steaming brew the general handed him.

"I saw it," Ryan said. Martini gave a little nod and was silent as Ryan relived the crash. Both hands were clasped around his cup as he fought to tame the surging emotions that threatened to engulf him. He told Martini about the engines and the way they sounded.

Martini sketched a top view of a C-130 and drew a jagged line on the wing between the left engines. He circled the inboard engine. "It sounds like the pilot firewalled the throttle on the number two engine and feathered the two engines on the opposite wing. He was trying to use differential power to regain control. That's what kept them in a flat spin." There was respect in his voice. "He never gave up. Remember that."

"NEO was my operation," Ryan said. "It was my responsibility to get them out of here." His voice was shaking. "Ninety-four people are dead. Ninety-four."

Martini lowered his voice, and the hard-driving, caustic general was gone. "Ninety-nine, counting the crew. But don't lose perspective. Over 20,000 people are safe because of what you did. And what about those six patients you got to Yokota?''

"Any good medical team could have done that,'' Ryan said.

"But you did it. You made all that happen.''

The chief of the disaster response cell entered the cab. "General—'' He stopped, unable to go on. Like Ryan, he was on the edge, losing control. "Sir—'' Martini still waited, not about to push the man. Not now. Finally, he was able to say it. "Sir, there are no survivors. Sharks are in the water.''

Ryan gasped for breath, and he buried his head in his hands. "The tail, I saw the C-130's tail in the water. It was like a shark's fin.''

Martini's voice cut like a knife, hard and sharp. "That's bullshit. It was the tail of an aircraft. Nothing else.''

Ryan couldn't look at his commander. "Thirty-eight children were on board. I saw the manifest. I saw them get on.''

Martini picked up his phone and keyed the public address system. "May I have your attention.'' His voice resonated through the building, and every head in the command post turned toward him. "I've been told there are no survivors from the crash. You are going to hear some pretty ugly rumors, and some of them are going to be true. But don't give in to them, make yourself look past the rumors and search for the truth. So what is the truth of it? The truth is that we've been hit hard and in the one place we didn't expect. They got to our families, our loved ones. Don't buy the argument that this accident had nothing to do with those sons of bitches who are blockading us. Our families are in harm's way because of them. Never forget that. We've got a job to do. So let's do it.'' He punched off the loudspeaker and dropped the phone on the console.

The professional in Ryan kicked in, and he knew what Martini was doing. He was taking whatever guilt or exaggerated sense of responsibility his people may have assumed for the accident and placing it directly on the enemy. Martini studied him for a moment. "It was the enemy that killed them, Doctor. Not you, not material failure, not a senseless accident. And they created the situation, not us. Hopefully, that'll put some hate in your heart.''

Ryan tried to pull back from the black pit of despair that still yawned in front of him. "Why them?" he moaned. "Why them and not me? I just got off that plane. I had just flown on it.''

Hard experience had taught Martini the answer to Ryan's question. But could the doctor accept it? "Because you weren't there.''

Over the Midwest

Bender was stretched out and sleeping near the rear of *Air Force One*. It had been a long day, and they had been traveling since early Thursday morning. Now it was the same evening, and *Air Force One* was taking the president back to Washington, D.C. One of Shaw's pretty staff members nudged him awake and asked him to please join the chief of staff in the conference room. Bender stood up, adjusted his tie, and put on his coat. He would have preferred wearing a uniform, but as long as he was on a leave of absence and serving as the national security advisor to the president, he would wear a white shirt and tie with a dark suit. "This just came in," Shaw said, handing him a long message.

Bender fished his reading glasses out of his shirt pocket and read the message. The old, bitter taste was back. "Has the president been told?" he asked.

Shaw shook his head. "No. Perhaps it'd be best if you told her. She's in her stateroom.''

Bender did a mental time conversion as he selected the right words to tell the president about the crash. It had happened less that two hours ago, right after sunrise on Friday morning in Okinawa. *It's going to be a long night here,* he told himself. He went forward and knocked on the door. The entry light flashed green, he counted to three, then entered. Turner was reclining in one of the plush leather airline seats that faced each other beside a window. "Please close the door," she said. They were alone. He sat opposite her and leaned forward, his hands clasped between his knees. "Is it bad news, Robert?"

"Yes, Madam President, it is. A C-130 carrying ninety-four dependents and five crewmembers has crashed in Okinawa. There were thirty-eight children on board."

She leaned back in her chair and blinked away the tears. "Were there any survivors?"

"No, ma'am, there weren't." He stopped, unable to continue. *You are so beautiful,* he thought, *so frail and vulnerable.* He stiffened. She was also the president of the United States and his commander in chief. She had to be told. All of it. "The plane crashed immediately after take-off. Witnesses report the left outboard wing fell off. The pilot was able to maintain partial control and crashed into the sea." He hesitated and for a moment could not find the right words. He considered letting her read the message.

"Go on," she said. There was a slight catch in her voice, but her words were calm and resolute. "I've got to know the truth."

"The C-130 is a high-wing aircraft, and it immediately sank up to its wings and floated for a few minutes. Apparently, the loadmaster was able to get a number of survivors out through an overhead hatch and onto the wing. Then the aircraft sank. There were sharks in the water, and they went into a feeding frenzy."

"Oh, my God," she whispered. She bent forward and clasped her arms to her breast, hugging herself, their foreheads almost touching. "It was my decision, it was my orders that killed them." Slowly, she rocked back and forth. She stopped, looked up, and spread her hands apart in supplication. "What do I tell their families?"

She was shaking, and Bender reached out and touched her hand. The unbidden gesture was so out of character, so presumptuous, that he was shocked by his own temerity. Suddenly, their hands were clasped together. "You tell them the truth, Madam President."

"A personal phone call."

"Perhaps, after they've been told," Bender said. "After they've weathered the initial shock."

She stopped shaking but did not pull back from his touch. "I don't know if I can do it."

"Do you have a choice?" he replied.

"No, I suppose I don't." The catch in her voice was gone, but she still held on to him. He was all too aware of how warm and soft her hands felt in his. "It's the faces," she whispered, "the shattered families, the lost dreams—" Her voice trailed off. Then, "Robert, I'm the one responsible for their deaths."

"Madam President, you must do this."

"That's so easy for you to say."

"I've never had to bear the responsibility you carry, but I've had to tell families that their loved ones have been killed in the line of duty. I've had to share their grief, their pain. It's never easy." She drew back and sat upright, her fingers intertwined in her lap. "It's something most commanders have to live with."

"And I am their commander in chief," she said.

"Yes, ma'am, you are."

"I never really knew what that meant," she told him.

"No one can possibly know until they've been there," he replied.

"I doubt if I still fully understand what it means." She pressed the intercom button on the arm of her chair. "Patrick, will you please gather the reporters in the main lounge. I'm going to make an announcement about the crash."

"Mizz President," Shaw answered, "might'en we want to wait on this one?"

"Now, Patrick," she said breaking the connection. She leaned back in her chair and looked at Bender. After a few moments, she said, "Is there a chance of recovering bodies still inside the aircraft?"

"Yes, ma'am. A very good chance. There's one other thing I didn't mention and you need to know. Staff Sergeant Lancey Coltrain was on that plane."

"Weren't her children evacuated out earlier?"

"Yes, ma'am, they were. I believe they are already in the States."

Turner stood and walked to the door. Bender stood to follow her. "We will not mention the sharks until after all the bodies have been recovered and the investigation is complete." Her eyes were fixed on Bender's face. "Or is that too political for you?"

He shook his head. "No, ma'am. That's a kindness."

18 ◢

Washington, D.C.

Bender woke with a jerk, rolled over, and automatically checked the time. It was an old habit that died hard, and Nancy swore that she was going to cure him after he retired. "It's Saturday," she murmured, waking up. "It's Groundhog Day. Isn't this a national holiday for politicians? Don't you get the day off?"

"You're thinking of April First," he said.

She rolled over and cuddled against his back. "I still can't believe you held the president's hand," she said.

"I can hardly believe it myself," he replied. "It seemed the right thing to do at the time. It was pretty emotional."

"Speaking of emotional," she murmured, "I love the negligee." She moved and felt the silk slide up her thigh and fall away as she moved a leg against his. She felt him respond. Mornings were always good. The phone rang. "Damn," she muttered. He reached for the phone and listened without comment. She felt his back muscles tense, and she sighed. Nothing had changed, and he was charged with purpose, responding to some new crisis. She sat up and reached for her robe. "The world can get along without you for one day," she said.

He grunted and rolled out of bed. "That was the White House. The chairman has requested a meeting with the president this morning. I've got to be there."

"What's got under Tennyson's hide?" she asked.

"The same as usual, I suppose. Turner." He headed for the bathroom to shower and shave. "What's the story with Shalandra?"

There was a long pause before she answered. "I talked to her counselor at the Academy. "There are problems."

"With boys?" he asked.

"You know how boys are. One of the little bastards called her a black cunt, and she called him a white-assed honky cocksucker. Anyway, he ended up propositioning her."

"Did he know about her past?"

"No, of course not," Nancy answered. "But it got out of hand. She got his pants down and scratched his testicles. That ended it."

Bender finished dressing. "Was Brian involved?" he asked.

"Not really. He was hanging around when it started but left."

"He is the president's son," Bender reminded her. "We don't need trouble on that front."

"I know," Nancy replied. "But who always loses when some poor black kid gets in trouble with a rich, pampered white kid?"

"Who usually causes the trouble?" Bender asked.

"This wasn't Shalandra's fault," Nancy said.

"I don't think this is going to work."

"It will work, Robert. Give her half a chance."

"I've got to go. I'll call from the office."

"I'll be at the hospital." She felt like crying. The morning had started so well, only to crash. But the tension was back, and they were at cross-purposes. *What's happening to us?* she wondered.

Bender's staff car dropped him at the South Portico to the White House as another staff car pulled away. A dark-suited aide opened the door, and the sound of the drum echoing from Lafayette Park hammered at him. "How early does it start in the morning?" he asked.

"It never stops, sir," the aide replied. "It's worse on the north side. At least we've got the building between us.'' He motioned for Bender to enter. ''You can hardly hear it inside.''

''Has General Overmeyer arrived yet?''

''No, sir,'' the aide replied. ''He's due in fifteen minutes.''

The Marine standing guard saluted and opened the door for Bender to enter. Unconsciously, Bender looked at the corporal and gave her a cursory inspection. Her uniform and bearing were above reproach, but an instinct warned him that something was wrong. He stopped. ''Good morning, Corporal.''

As expected, the Marine became even more rigid, if that was possible, and she replied with a crisp, ''Good morning, sir.''

In that brief few seconds, Bender saw the slight tick playing at the corner of the corporal's left eye and heard the catch in her voice. ''How long have you been on duty?''

''Approximately one hour, sir.''

''Is the drum getting to you.''

''Negative, sir.''

''Personally,'' Bender said, ''I'd like to jam that drum up that guy's ass.''

''I'll be glad to assist the general, sir.''

''Good answer, Marine.'' Bender knew what was wrong. The incessant beating of the drum was ratcheting up the tension and putting people on edge—some quicker than others. He thought of it as combat fatigue and headed for the East Wing, where the first lady's offices were located. Like the rest of the White House, the East Wing was spotlessly maintained and ready for a white-glove inspection twenty-four hours a day. But without a first lady in residence, it was a dull and lifeless backwater concerned with the routine administration of the White House. He passed the first lady's offices and entered the Military Office. A Marine captain was sitting at a desk. ''Are you the duty officer?'' Bender asked.

The captain stood up. ''No, sir. Mr. Terry is on call at home on weekends.''

The irony of it all struck Bender: The duty officer was a civilian who wasn't even present. ''I would like to speak to General Thomas," he said. Thomas was the Army major general in charge of the Military Office.

The captain looked embarrassed. "Ah, General Thomas has been reassigned and Mr. Terry is now in charge."

For Bender, it was too much. "Rotate the outside guard detail every thirty minutes."

"Sir, I can't do that. Mr. Terry approves the guard schedule."

"Please call him," Bender said. The captain made the phone call and handed him the telephone. Bender explained the problem to a very irritated Terry, who claimed the schedule was firm for the weekend. He would review it Monday when he came to work. Bender gave his reply some thought before answering. "May I suggest you come down here, stand outside, and listen to that drum for an hour. You'll have a better appreciation of what your people are going through."

"General," Terry said, "they aren't my 'people.' Mind your own business, and I won't mind yours." He banged the phone down, breaking the connection.

"Leadership is a wonderful thing," Bender said. "Captain, Mr. Terry told me that you are *not* his people. Therefore, I'm giving you a direct order. Reschedule the guard change for every thirty minutes."

"Yes, sir. But what do I do about Mr. Terry?"

"Write a memo for the record documenting this conversation. I'll endorse it, and it will be on his desk waiting for him—when he comes to work Monday morning. May I make a suggestion?"

"Check on my people more often?" the captain asked.

Bender smiled. "You got it, Captain." He spun around and headed for Shaw's office in the West Wing.

Shaw listened without comment when Bender told him about changing the outside guard schedule. "I was only out there a few minutes," Bender said, "and that drum was very annoying. Can't we do something about it?"

Shaw's lips drew into a narrow line. "Saint Peter shit-a-brick, tell me about it. You can even hear it in here." The two men were silent, and the faint sound washed over them. "It's louder in the residence. That's why Maura and the kids are at Camp David for the weekend and staying

with the Kennetts during the week." He paused and listened. The drumbeat was much louder and more rapid.
"Damn, he's really got a war dance going now."

"Why was Terry appointed the head of the Military
Office?" Bender asked, changing the subject.

"Maddy feels the military has too strong a presence
around here and wants to soften the overall image."
Shaw's secretary buzzed him on the intercom and said that
the demonstrators in Lafayette Park were on TV. Shaw
grunted an obscenity and hit the remote, turning on the
TV set. The screen filled with a group of demonstrators
streaming into the park. Quella O'Malley paraded by, waving a new sign. "Don't give that bitch air time," Shaw
grumbled. But the TV cameraman zoomed in, giving
O'Malley national coverage.

STOP FEEDING FAMILIES TO THE SHARKS

"Damn," Shaw groaned. "How did she find out about
that?" Unfortunately, he knew the answer. "Come on,"
he said. "It's time we talk to Maddy and get ready for
the meeting with Overmeyer."

"Why did the chairman ask for the meeting?" Bender
asked.

"You haven't heard? Maddy stopped the evacuation."

Bender clamped a tight lid on his reply and followed
Shaw into the Oval office. Sam Kennett was there along
with Secretary of the Treasury Parrish and Congresswoman Noreen Coker. Only Maura O'Keith was missing
from Turner's kitchen cabinet. Coker patted the couch beside her. "Sit here, honey," she said to Bender. "You do
look good in that suit." Bender did as she asked, and
Shaw retreated to a chair at the end of the facing couches,
leaving one vacant for the missing Overmeyer. Bender
listened as they discussed the ongoing demonstration in
Lafayette Park. During quiet moments he could hear the
faint, but insistent beat of the drum.

"We need to do something about that damn drum,"
Parrish moaned.

"And about Fireplug O'Malley," Coker added. "Sam,

didn't you have some trouble with her when you were mayor of Philadelphia?''

"More than I care to remember," Kennett answered. They listened with amusement as he described how he had neutralized her with a heavy dose of behind-the-scenes humor. They were still laughing at his stories when Jackie Winters opened the door for Overmeyer.

The chairman entered with his usual ramrod style and sat down, uncomfortable to be in a room of civilians. He shot Bender a disapproving look and came right to the point. "Madam President, I must protest in the strongest possible terms your directive stopping the evacuation of dependents from Okinawa. There are less than 4,000 remaining."

"I will not put any more innocent lives at risk," Turner replied.

"Madam President," Overmeyer said, "the situation is still volatile. They are more at risk remaining there."

"Are they?" Turner replied. "The secretary of state is of a different opinion. He believes the crisis has peaked and is contained."

Bender's inner alarm went off. Was Secretary Francis cutting another deal with the Chinese? What else was going on that he didn't know about?

Overmeyer wouldn't let it go. "Madam President, at least give them the option of volunteering to leave. Do not make them hostages against their will." Everyone looked at him in shocked disbelief. The general had overstepped his bounds.

Turner stared at him, her face granite hard as the drumbeat grew louder in the background. "General Overmeyer," she finally said, her voice cold and sharp, "they are not hostages, and I am acting in their best interests. Do you have anything else?"

He stood to leave. "Madam President, I'm asking you to reconsider your decision."

"Thank you, General Overmeyer," Turner replied. "I will take your request under advisement." The general gave her a short nod and marched out, his back still ramrod stiff.

"There goes one very angry man," Kennett said when the door closed.

"What can he do about it?" Coker replied. "Hold a press conference?"

"Robert," Turner said, "you know the chairman. What do you think he'll do?"

Every head turned toward Bender as they waited for his answer. "I honestly don't know."

"Too bad he's not the resigning kind'a general," Shaw muttered.

Turner moved gently back and forth in her rocker. "Well, we shall see. Until then, how do we handle those demonstrators and defuse O'Malley? Apparently, she has a direct line into the White House. How else would she know about the sharks?"

"At last report, we've recovered over half the bodies," Bender said.

"Don't change your strategy now," Secretary Parrish said. "Keep calling the families. Hold a press conference, and if a reporter mentions the shark attacks, sidestep. Refuse to comment on rumors. Claim we're still recovering bodies and you're doing everything possible to protect the families from more pain and grief. Appeal to the reporter's sense of compassion."

"Reporters with a sense of compassion?" Coker scoffed. "You been smoking too much dope. Personally, I think the drummer is the real problem. We need to break his goddamn drum over his goddamn head."

"'Such stuff as dreams are made of,'" Shaw said, misquoting Shakespeare. "Not much we can do about it. No president, not even LBJ and Nixon at the height of the Vietnam War or Watergate, ever stopped a demonstration in the park. It's too politically risky. Best we just outlast the bastard."

"Sam," Turner said, "you've dealt with O'Malley before. Can you pull her teeth again?"

"Mizz President," Shaw called, "no need for the vice president to go gettin' his hands sullied. Let me take care of her."

It was a quiet dinner at one of Washington's premier restaurants. The atmosphere was intimate, the food and service world-class, the wine exquisite, the table yours for the night, the tab outrageous, and coverage in the social columns guaranteed. In short, it was the perfect place for a public liaison and in Shaw's case, to meet Jessica, his cutout to Senator Leland and the group. She reached across the table and stroked the top of Shaw's hand. The way she smiled sent the waiter's temperature up three degrees. The waiter desperately wanted to hear what she was saying and savor the way her mouth shaped the words. But it wasn't worth his job or the astronomical tip added to the bill. "The senator wants an incident with the demonstrators in Lafayette Park," she murmured for Shaw alone to hear.

"I'm going to need a good reason," he replied. "A damn good reason."

"You'll think of something," she cooed. "The senator suggested using O'Malley. He'd like that."

"I imagine there's a lot of things the senator would like, darlin'," Shaw muttered. *Like you in his bed,* he thought.

Jessica's fingernail doodled on the back of his hand. Again, the little smile for them alone. She knew what he was thinking. "He's very virile for a man his age." She saw the waiter watching them and leaned into Shaw. "The senator is worried about Kennett. Can you isolate him?" The tip of her tongue flicked across her upper lip, a promise of things to come later that night. The conversation was exciting her more than any romantic drivel.

"I can sprinkle some dust around. He may sneeze once or twice, but none of it will stick."

She took his hand in both of hers and turned it over. Slowly, she continued to draw little circles in his palm with a fingernail, her face radiant. "The senator says it's time. He's going to nail her hide to the wall."

"What a charming fellow," Shaw said. He pulled his hand back and reached for the wine. "I have to make a phone call."

Liz Gordon was waiting in Jeff Bissell's car when Shaw's limousine pulled up to the entrance elevator in the Watergate's garage. She watched as he got out and used his key to call for the elevator. The limousine pulled away as the elevator doors swooshed close behind him, a steel and aluminum curtain wrapping him in safety. Liz waited. The elevator doors opened, and Shaw stepped out. She started the car and pulled up. "I got your message," she said as he got in. "Where's the bimbo?"

"Does it matter?" Shaw replied. She drove slowly out the exit. "The children were rootin' around in the basement," he said. The "children" were his staff. "You know how kids are. They found some interesting mementos."

"Whose basement?" she asked.

He handed her a manila envelope. "Mr. Samuel Kennett's."

"Mr. Clean?" She pulled over, switched on the dome light, and dumped the contents in her lap. She quickly scanned the documents.

"Now don't go hyperventilating on me," he said, his southern accent back in place. "It does lead to some unexpected places."

"Absolutely fascinating."

"I thought you'd like it."

"Patrick, what can I say?"

"Strictly deep background, nonattribution."

"Of course," she replied. Then, "I hate being alone Sunday mornings."

"Unbelievable headache, darlin'. And tomorrow's gonna come too early."

"It's already tomorrow," she told him.

"Quella O'Malley is not news," Ben, Liz's cameraman, complained. It was late Sunday morning, and they were on the Mall with the Washington Monument towering behind them.

"She will be today," Liz replied. She checked her hair one last time. "Here she comes." The squat woman waddled across Constitution Avenue, challenging the light traffic. A line of people followed her, all carrying signs and chanting.

"Damn," Ben muttered. "She's bringing half the crowd from the park."

"Anything to get away from that drum," Liz said. O'Malley waved and marched up for her interview, the conquering hero leading her troops in a victory parade. "Good morning, Mrs. O'Malley," Liz called.

"It's Ms. Liz," O'Malley corrected. Ben hit the Beta-cam's record button and like most interviews with the feisty woman, they were off to a rocky start. Liz endured her comments about sacrificing innocent children to sharks and made a mental note to edit out that part of the interview. "We speak for the innocent and the poor who cannot speak for themselves," O'Malley proclaimed. "Without us there is no justice in this country."

"Speaking of justice, Ms. O'Malley, how long have you been a paid informer for the FBI?"

O'Malley laughed and followed the classic rules of politics: Never knuckle under, never justify, always attack. "I know I'm right when they resort to smear tactics." She turned to the crowd and raised an arm, pointing at the White House. "They claim we're working for the FBI," she shouted. "Come on, everybody. Get out your pay stubs and let's compare wages." A titter of amusement rippled through the crowd. "Equal pay for equal work!" The laughter grew louder, and O'Malley beamed with success.

"Reliable sources," Liz said, "claim you supplied the evidence that led to the Philadelphia Neighborhood Action Group being indicted for embezzlement and misuse of public funds."

Again, O'Malley laughed. But it rang with a forced resonance that jarred the crowd to silence. "Sam Kennett was mayor then. That bastard was always out to get me. How many times have I proven him to be a liar?"

Mistake! Liz thought. *You shouldn't have made the connection to Kennett.* "To be exact, Mrs. O'Malley, never." She handed O'Malley a folder. "These are extracts of your bank account in the Bahamas. They go back a number of years, and the deposits that are circled were made in your name by the Intercity Regional Planning Commission. The IRPC was an FBI sting operation working with Mayor Kennett to clean up Philadelphia."

O'Malley glanced at the contents of the folder and tore the pages to shreds. She was careful to stuff the remnants into her pockets. "Lies, total lies," she shouted. She turned to the crowd for support. "This is libel, Gordon, and you're going to hear from my lawyers."

"I think you mean slander," Liz corrected, "and truth has always been the defense to slander. I have more copies—in case your lawyers need them. By the way, some of the deposits are very recent. You're a wealthy woman, Mrs. O'Malley. And speaking of pay stubs, did you declare this income on your tax return?"

"Who the hell do you think you are?" O'Malley sneered. *"Sixty Minutes?"*

"No, Mrs. O'Malley. I'm Elizabeth Gordon, and this is CNC-TV News."

A rock arced out of the crowd and hit Liz in the back of the head knocking her to the ground. The action froze, and while everyone was focused on the reporter, Ben ejected the video cassette, jammed it into his coat, and slapped a blank cassette into the Betacam in case the crowd went for the camera. He stepped over Liz's prostrate form and panned the crowd, swinging the heavy camera back and forth like a club while he filmed them. Two men and a woman from the crowd rushed him, and he froze, certain he was going down next. But they skidded to a stop, turned, linked arms, and stood in front, a human barrier protecting Liz. "Is she OK?" the woman shouted.

Ben lowered his camera and bent down. Liz's eyes were open, and she was holding the back of her head. Her hand was bloodied, and she would need stitches. "Did you get it all?" she asked.

"Got it all," he replied.

"She's OK," the woman standing above them yelled to the crowd.

"Where's Fireplug?" Liz asked.

Ben stood and looked around. The crowd was dispersing, and Quella O'Malley was gone. "She's finished in this town," he promised, helping the reporter to her feet.

For Bender, coincidence was simply a matter of probability. He loved the mathematical formulas that quantified reality and predicted the odds of two or more objects or events converging in space and time. In real-world terms, it could be devastating, like when a fellow Thunderbird had experienced a bird strike during an airshow and crashed. But more often than not, it was a harmless encounter, like meeting the vice president in a Capitol elevator. "Been testifying before a committee?" Sam Kennett asked.

"Not this time," Bender replied. "I was bringing a group of Senate staff members up to speed on Okinawa. I heard the bell calling for the vote. How'd it go?"

Kennett had been shepherding a piece of legislation through the Senate and, as president of the Senate, had cast the tie-breaking vote. "We made a few more enemies," Kennett said. "But it's one more step toward tax reform." They rode the elevator in silence to the garage. "Ride back with me," Kennett offered. "We can compare notes." Bender accepted and told Chuck Sanford, the Secret Service agent waiting for him, to take his staff car back to the White House garage.

Sanford held the vice president's limousine door before joining the other agent, Wayne Adams, in Bender's staff car. "Join the procession," Sanford said. Adams fell in behind the vice president's limo and followed them out of the garage.

"Did you see Liz Gordon's interview with O'Malley last night?" Kennett asked. "Liz really did a number on her."

"It's satisfying when it happens to the bad guys," Bender said. "For a moment, I thought the mob was going berserk. I take it Liz wasn't hurt."

"She's fine," Kennett replied. "The mood of the crowd did take a strange twist. I've never seen anything like it. Those people are deeply opposed to our policies, but at the same time they're rooting for the president, probably because she's a woman. Right now, my gut feeling tells me sentiment is swinging in our direction."

"Too bad we can't help it along," Bender said.

The vice president thought for a few moments. "Maybe we can." He hit the intercom to the front seat. "Tom, drop us off at Lafayette Park. We're going to press the flesh."

A worried Secret Service agent turned around and looked at him. "Is that wise, Mr. Vice President?"

"No one shoots at a vice president," Kennett said. "It's a complete waste of ammo."

Sanford and Adams heard the radio call from the vice president's limousine reporting the unplanned stop at the park. "That's dumber than dirt," Adams complained. "Ranger knows better than that." Ranger was the code name the Secret Service had given the vice president.

"Move," Sanford ordered. "They're going to need backup. Double park. Over there." The two agents abandoned the staff car next to a traffic warden and sprinted across the street into the park. Their breath misted in the cold air, and their thick parkas blended with the crowd. Sanford spoke into the whisper mike under his sleeve cuff, reporting their position. They slowed and moved through the crowd, trying to blend in and not draw attention. Rather than close in on the vice president, they circled behind him as he moved slowly through the park. "Have you got the general in sight?" Sanford asked.

"Behind Ranger and to your left," Adams replied. "He's talking to some kids."

"Bender's a regular Pied Piper," Sanford said.

Both agents were scanning the crowd, taking the emotional pulse of the people around them. At the same time, they were looking for the misfit, the person who was slightly out of step, moving against the grain or hovering too close. While their antennae were finely tuned to the people around them, they had to remain cool and remote. The beating drum didn't help, and they could feel its insistent call to action. "The crowd's edgy," Adams said.

"We'll be OK if Ranger terminates now," Sanford said. On cue, Kennett turned and moved back toward Bender and the waiting limousine.

"Over there," Adams said. "Behind the general. The woman. Red and purple coat. Green knit cap. Dark hair. Short, heavyset." Both agents focused on Quella O'Malley, who was on the outskirts of the crowd, moving parallel to Kennett. She was staring at the vice president and was oblivious to the people around her. "She's lost it," Adams said. He walked quickly toward Bender, trying to close the distance without disturbing the people around him.

Sanford spoke into his whisper mike. "We've got a possible. Subject is Quella O'Malley. She's at Ranger's ten o'clock, twenty feet, moving with him. The general is between them. Ranger is approaching the general now." The six Secret Service agents in the park responded with precision and speed. Adams sprinted for Bender, who was still between O'Malley and Kennett. The four agents detailed to Kennett collapsed around him like a cocoon while Sanford raced for O'Malley. She saw Adams first when he was less than ten feet from Bender. She reached into her coat and pulled out an Army Colt .45-caliber automatic. She thumbed the hammer back and held the heavy weapon with both hands.

Adams barreled into Bender and knocked him to the ground. On the way down, Adams reached out and pulled an eleven-year-old boy under him as O'Malley pulled the trigger. The bullet hit Adams square in the back, shattered his spine, deflected slightly to the left, and tore into his aorta, completely severing the artery. The recoil knocked O'Malley back, and she jerked at the trigger a second time as two agents sandwiched the vice president with their bodies. Sanford crashed into her as she fired the third time. His left arm came up and struck the Colt in an upward motion. The bullet arced harmlessly over the White House and fell into the Potomac, over a mile away.

It was over, and the screaming crowd scattered like dry leaves rushing before the strong winter's wind. Three shots had been fired. The first bullet had killed a thirty-eight-year-old Secret Service agent, the second round hit Sam Kennett, and the third bullet was never found.

Later, forensic experts from the FBI testified that an incredible sequence of coincidences was involved. By knocking Bender to the ground, Adams had cleared a field of fire for O'Malley. The recoil from the first round had knocked O'Malley back, and she had almost dropped the gun before regaining her balance. Chuck Sanford was only a blur in her peripheral vision as she raised the gun in panic. She never remembered pulling the trigger the second time or hearing the gun fire. The bullet had ricocheted off the pavement and passed under the left arm of the agent who was at Kennett's back and had wrapped his arms around the vice president. The bullet struck the vice president's left arm just above the elbow. If O'Malley had fired a fraction of a second earlier, the bullet would have hit the agent's arm. If she had fired a fraction of a second later, Kennett would have been totally shielded. As it was, coincidence had opened a gap less than four inches square for less than a second when O'Malley's bullet was there.

A videotape shot by a bystander recorded Bender on his knees comforting an eleven-year-old boy before turning him over to his distraught parents. Then he slowly removed his topcoat and covered Wayne Adams, the agent who had taken the bullet for him. He stood erect, waiting for the paramedics to arrive. The cold wind tore at him as he stood guard. In the background, the wail of sirens blended with the beating drum as the vice president was rushed to a hospital.

Jackie Winters was on the cellular telephone as the five cars drew up to the entrance to the Bethesda Naval Medical Center. "The vice president is still in the operating room," she told Turner.

"I thought he was only hit in the arm," Turner replied.

"Apparently the bullet entered his chest," Winters said. "Mrs. Kennett is in the waiting room." She rattled off the personal details about Barbara Kennett and their children. "She's said to be very stable in a crisis."

"I wish I knew her better," Turner said as a Secret Service agent opened the car door. She trotted up the steps. Bender and Shaw were inside the main doors waiting for her. "Robert, are you OK?"

"I'm fine, Madam President." He fell in behind her as they headed for the waiting room. "I tried to contact Mrs. Adams, but a neighbor answered the phone and she refused to speak to me."

"I want to visit her as soon as possible," Turner said. "Patrick, please find out how Mrs. Adams is doing and help in any way we can." She stopped and removed her topcoat as Shaw returned to the limousine to make the call. "It's warm in here." Winters held up a small mirror, but Turner ignored her and entered the room where Barbara Kennett was keeping her lonely vigil.

Bender stepped inside and stood beside the door with Jackie as the two women embraced. *They are so different,* he thought. Barbara was a heavy-set, handsome woman in her early forties and lacked the glamorous image demanded by Washington politics. They sat and held hands as they talked. Only fragments of the conversation reached Bender, but he sensed they were sharing an inner strength, comforting each other, and growing stronger together. A doctor wearing green surgical scrubs entered the room and waited to be recognized. "How is he?" Barbara asked.

Again, Bender only heard a few words, but he could tell the news was bad. Barbara paled but did not flinch. "Thank you, Doctor," she said. "I need to speak to our children. They're waiting at home."

"Jackie," Turner said, "please stay with Mrs. Kennett." It was an unspoken order that the Kennett family was firmly under the presidential umbrella. Bender held the door for the two women to leave.

Shaw was outside, waiting for the right moment to enter. "Mizz President, the agent's wife, Mrs. Adams, is under sedation. There's more. O'Malley has been arrested and is in federal custody. She's been advised of her rights and refuses to talk to a lawyer. She says Sam Kennett is a fascist pig who needs to be rendered for shark bait, and this is all a conspiracy to get her for what happened in Philadelphia."

"We'll deal with her later," Turner said. "Get the DOJ involved and make sure her rights are fully protected. She's not walking on a technicality." She turned to the doctor. "I want to know the details," she said.

"Madam President," the doctor said, "I must warn you, it's very—gruesome." The doctor led her and the two men into an office and snapped the X rays onto the viewer. He handed her a set of Polaroid photos and spoke in a monotone. He pointed to the X ray of the vice president's left arm and described how the bullet had shattered the bone above the elbow before penetrating the left side of his chest. The bullet still had enough energy to shatter a rib before tearing into the left lung. Turner's hands were shaking and her face paled as he described in clinical detail the damage to the lung. "The bullet missed his heart by three millimeters but still caused major damage. We think we can save his lung, but he may lose his left arm. It's still touch and go."

"For saving his arm?" Turner asked.

"No, for saving his life."

"I can't believe one bullet did that much damage," she replied.

"It can," Bender said. He studied the X rays. "The bullet must have been flattened before it hit his arm. Was it a ricochet?"

"Very possible," the doctor allowed.

"Thank God," Bender said.

"Thank God?" Shaw said, his words harsh and clipped. "How can you be thankful for this?"

"A .45 at that range has an awesome amount of striking power," Bender said. "The bullet had to have lost some of its energy before hitting the vice president. Otherwise—" He did not finish the thought.

"Otherwise what?" Turner asked.

"Otherwise," the doctor replied, "the vice president would be dead."

"What are his chances of pulling through?" Bender asked.

"Not good," the doctor answered. "I estimate less than thirty percent."

Turner stepped back and stood beside the desk. The men looked at her, not knowing what to say or do. "One bullet," she said. "One gun in the hands of a demented"—she paused and her voice steadied—"in the hands of a lunatic. So much damage, a fine man, his family. My God, why do we do this to ourselves? How can I allow it?" She stared at them, demanding an answer they could not give. "O'Malley. Did she act alone or did she have help?"

"We don't know," Shaw replied.

Turner's face turned to granite. "Patrick, I want the park cleared. Tonight. Send the demonstrators home."

Bender waited for Shaw to protest. Even he understood that was not a wise move and had far-reaching political consequences. But Shaw was silent, giving thanks in his own way that he didn't have to force the incident that

Leland wanted. "Madam President," Bender finally said, "that might be a mistake."

"Doctor, please excuse us," Turner said. The doctor gathered up the X rays and photos and made a hasty exit. "Robert, you seem to forget I'm your president. You do not question me in front of others."

"Please accept my apologies, Madam President. I overstepped." *Why am I doing this?* he asked himself. A knock at the door kept him from saying more. The door cracked open and an aide passed a message to Shaw.

"Mizz President," Shaw said, his eyes fixed on the message in disbelief. "The Japanese fleet—at Kagoshima—it's sailed."

Okinawa, Japan

Lieutenant Colonel Peter Townly sounded like a bored economics professor lecturing a freshman class on basic supply and demand theory. But no college professor ever held his class the way Townly held the attention of the command post. The Intelligence officer knew he sounded like an intellectual ass, patronizing and artificial, but it was the only way he could control his panic. He kept looking into the Battle Cab, wondering what the men were saying in their glass cocoon. The red dot of his laser pointer shook as he highlighted the situation map projected on the screen behind him and his message was simple: A battle was coming their way, and this time, there would be no last-minute reprieve.

"At last report, the Japanese flotilla has divided into three columns and is advancing towards Okinawa in an arrowhead formation. Each column is made up of ten to twelve destroyers supported by approximately the same number of frigates. At least three submarines are reported operating in front of the flotilla. The Japanese have 168 fighters for air cover stationed at these bases." Townly's pointer circled three airfields on the southern part of Kyushu.

Martini grabbed the microphone plugged into his console. "What can the wing at Naha put up?" he barked. His words hung over the big room like an ominous cloud.

Townly's mouth felt like it was full of bitter cotton. "The Japanese have four operational F-4Js, sir."

Martini's fingers drummed the table in front of him. "And the PRC?"

"At last count the Chinese have committed over 30 attack submarines, 18 destroyers, 20 frigates, over 100 small fast-attack craft"—he gulped hard—"and the *Chairman Mao*."

"When?" Martini growled.

"The Japanese are well within range of the Silk Worm missiles on Kumejima and the vans of the two fleets should meet here"—he circled an area in the East China Sea 200 miles northwest of Okinawa—"in approximately four hours, 2000 hours tonight."

"Our Navy?" Martini asked. He was calming down.

"Their location and strength is unknown, sir. At last report, the president is withholding them."

Martini stood up. Nothing in his words or actions betrayed the frustration he felt. "Ladies and gentlemen, we are about to witness the biggest sea battle since World War II. Bring the base to full alert, divert all inbound airlift flights." He thought for a moment. Six transport aircraft were still on Kadena. "Get Major Ryan in here," he ordered. He motioned for his staff to vacate the Battle Cab and punched the secure hot line to headquarters CINC PAC in Honolulu. Within moments, he was speaking to both CINC PACAF and CINC PAC, the admiral in command of all U.S. forces in the Pacific. "Gentlemen, our side is about to get its butt kicked and I got six transports I need to fly out of here. Can I evacuate dependents?"

"Negative," the admiral answered. "No more evacuations by presidential order."

"What the hell do you want me to do?" Martini asked.

"The same as everyone else," the admiral replied. "Go to max readiness and wait. Besides, we think the Japanese have a slight edge."

"Sure," Martini replied. "And the Chinese don't have a nuclear capability either."

"Washington doesn't believe the Chinese will go nuclear over this," the admiral said.

"Washington will not be glowing in the dark if Washington is wrong,'' Martini said. "How about asking them to declare DEFCON TWO and giving the Chinese cause for pause?''

"I know what you're thinking,'' the admiral replied. The CIA had worked hard to feed the Chinese hints that the nuclear posture of the United States changed as the DEFCON increased. But neither the Chinese nor the Japanese knew that when DEFCON TWO was declared for the Far East, a limited number of tactical nuclear weapons were moved into the forward area. "The president will never allow that.''

"At least you can ask,'' Martini muttered. The admiral said he would talk to the National Military Command Center in the Pentagon and broke the connection.

Pete Townly was taking the stage again. He held a clipboard in one hand and was visibly shaking. He looked across the command post and into the Battle Cab. "Sir, the Chinese have launched ten Silk Worm missiles from Kumejima and four ships in the Japanese van have been hit. We have a report of one submarine being sunk. We don't know the nationality.''

The air defense coordinator keyed his microphone. "The Tactical Operation Center at Naha requests that we assume the air defense of Okinawa.''

"Gentlemen,'' Martini told his staff, "it seems the Japanese are going to drag us kicking and screaming into this.''

Major Bob Ryan rushed into the command post in time to hear Martini issue the order assuming responsibility for the air defense of the island. *What the hell is going on?* he wondered as he entered the Battle Cab. Martini came right to the point. "How many dependents are still left on the island?''

Ryan was ready with the answer. "Three thousand nine hundred seventy-six.''

"Children?''

"There are 286 left,'' Ryan answered. He checked his clipboard. "That does not include 209 teenagers. Most of them are volunteer helpers working at various jobs around the base.''

Martini swung around in his chair to face the base map on the wall behind him. He traced the huge munitions storage area on the north side·of the base. "This is the 400 MUNS storage area. All the bunkers in the western section are empty. Shelter all the remaining dependents and as many Okinawans as you can there."

Ryan looked puzzled. "Sir, isn't that the nuclear weapons storage area?"

"We haven't had nukes on Okinawa since 1972," Martini said.

"But it's in a weapons storage area. You can't put civilians there."

Again, Martini's fingers drummed the table, the sure sign he wanted a quick answer to the problem. *The major has a point,* he thought. His fingers stopped their relentless tattoo. The OSI, the Office of Special Investigations, had provided the solution to the problem in a recent briefing. The Chinese rightly assumed that the movement of weapons was a warning of attack and two OSI agents had detected a team of Chinese informers monitoring the weapons storage area. Martini snorted in satisfaction. He had a way to feed information to the bad guys. "We'll declare the area a civilian shelter. Light it up like a Christmas tree. The Chinese will get the message."

"But it's still next to a weapons complex, which is a legitimate military target," Ryan protested.

Martini allowed a short, hard laugh. It was little more than a bark. "You don't know much about nuclear storage bunkers, Major. Believe me, it's the safest place on the island. Make it happen."

Ryan darted out of the command post, convinced Martini was cracking up under the pressure. But none of the telltale signs of instability were visible, only his headlong, mad rush into war. And he was taking innocent civilians with him.

Washington, D.C.

Bender split his attention as the chief of Naval Operations briefed Turner on the battle developing in the East China Sea. As usual, Turner was ill at ease, uncomfortable with the masculine atmosphere of the Situation Room.

Why is she so nervous down here? he wondered. He chastised himself for mentally straying and focused on the CNO. *He's too technical, and she's missing the point,* he thought. "Admiral, please forgive me," Bender said, "but I'm losing the big picture in the details." A grateful look from Turner.

The admiral saw her expression, caught Bender's meaning, and used big arrows to explain the movement of the opposing fleets. Three big blue arrows represented the Japanese who were advancing to the south against one big red arrow, the Chinese, advancing to the north. "Because of the time difference," the admiral said, "it is eight o'clock Tuesday night in the East China Sea. All our reconnaissance platforms and sensors indicate the battle was started." He circled the area 200 miles northwest of Okinawa.

"Why are they fighting at night?" Turner asked.

"Because the Japanese timed their advance, hoping to engage at night," the admiral answered. He struggled to keep his explanation simple. "Their electronics are much better than the Chinese and that gives them a distinct advantage during the hours of darkness." Bender listened while he explained the battle in layman's, in this case, laywoman's, terms. He could sense Overmeyer's growing impatience. Finally, a TV screen scrolled with a current update. They all read in silence. The Silk Worm missiles had sunk four Japanese ships and badly damaged three others. At least three submarines had been destroyed by other submarines, but there was no confirmation as to nationality. Aircraft were launching from both the *Chairman Mao* and Kumejima in support of the Chinese fleet.

"The Japanese will also launch aircraft, Madam President," Overmeyer said.

"So what are they doing?" she asked.

"Going after each other's ships, Madam President," the admiral replied.

"Are our forces on Okinawa involved or threatened?" she asked.

"No, ma'am," Secretary of Defense Elkins answered.

"However," Overmeyer said, "the Japanese have relegated the air defense of Okinawa to us. There is a potential for our aircraft—''

Turner stood up. Her face was flushed with anger. "How did that happen without my permission?"

"Madam President," Overmeyer answered, "that is a standard operating procedure that was worked out years ago. It is a decision based on the threat and availability of aircraft and is made by the local commanders."

"Martini again," she muttered. "Let me make it very clear, we will not get involved in this battle unless the Chinese directly attack our people." She stared at Overmeyer to reinforce her point and sat down.

Overmeyer's face was beet red as he fought for control. He was about ready to explode. "Madam President, General Martini is responding to conditions as they develop. He is our man in the hot seat. He's not going to do anything stupid."

"I wish I could be sure of that," Turner replied.

"You can always relieve him of his command," the director of Central Intelligence said from his end of the table.

"We've been down this road before," Overmeyer said. "That would be disastrous at this time." He faced Turner. "Madam President, sooner of later, we will be drawn into this. I urge you, act now before it's too late. If nothing else, send a strong message to the Chinese to leave Okinawa alone."

"I will call Chairman Zoulin on the hot line," she said. Bender shook his head. "Robert, do you disagree?"

Be careful how you answer, Bender warned himself. "No, ma'am. I'm thinking about the timing of the call and wondering if he will listen to reason."

"He's always struck me as a reasonable man," she replied.

"Is he?" Bender asked. "Personally, I don't think he sees the world the way we do and he's going to keep on slicing away until he gets what he wants. Zoulin will respond to actions, not words."

"Exactly what actions do you suggest I take?" she asked.

Overmeyer shot Bender a look of thanks. It was the

question he wanted her to ask. "Declare DEFCON TWO for the western Pacific, wait twelve hours, and then call Zoulin," Overmeyer said. "Tell him you will cancel it the moment the fighting stops."

"Why will that convince him to leave Okinawa alone?" she asked.

"Because," Overmeyer explained, "the Chinese know we change our nuclear posture at DEFCON TWO. We deliberately let them see us seal our bases and recall personnel from leave. Their agents will report our boomers and support ships have all put to sea."

"Boomers?" Turner asked.

"Sorry, ma'am," Overmeyer replied. "Boomers are nuclear missile subs. It's enough to send the message that we are very serious."

"How serious?" she asked.

"Specifically, our ICBMs are targeted accordingly, and a military aide will always be in your immediate vicinity with the football." She paled at the thought of the soft black leather briefcase that contained the nuclear launch codes. "There is more," Overmeyer continued. "A small number of tactical nuclear weapons are moved into the forward area."

"Is that necessary?" Turner demanded.

"Only if you wish to retain all your options," Bender answered. The room was heavy with silence. *She can't make that decision,* Bender decided. *The thought of the hell and destruction that is at her fingertips, her's for the ordering, is beyond her.* The TV monitor bleeped and scrolled, breaking the silence. The Japanese had launched their last four aircraft from Naha Air Base on Okinawa. "There go eight good men into harm's way," the CNO said. "They won't be coming back."

"How can you be so sure?" Turner asked.

"Because they're going after the *Chairman Mao,*" the CNO answered.

"How can you be so cold-blooded?" she raged. "Is this some sort of game you play? The ultimate Super Bowl?"

"I assure you," Bender said, "this is no game." He sensed she was moving toward a decision. "Think back twenty-five days ago when this all started and the *Chair-*

man Mao was moving on Okinawa. We saw a definite pattern of behavior in response to our actions and the Chinese went out of their way not to engage us. Only once did they directly challenge us—''

''When they went after the first C-141 carrying dependents,'' Turner said, interrupting him.

''Exactly,'' Bender said. He almost called it the Turkey Shoot, but an inner voice warned him that would be wrong.

''And we monitored a quantum increase in their message traffic after that,'' the DCI added.

''Not to mention the concessions General Bender got out of Wang Mocun at Paris,'' Secretary Elkins said.

Turner came to her feet, her decision made.

Maura O'Keith shepherded Sarah into the dining room for breakfast. The ten-year-old flopped into a chair and reached for a glass of orange juice. She looked over the rim of the glass while she drank and studied her mother. ''You look tired, Mom.''

''I've been up all night,'' Turner replied.

''Because of Mr. Kennett?'' Sarah asked.

''That and some other problems,'' Turner said.

''How's Sam doing?'' Maura asked.

''There's a problem with infection, and he's still on the critical list,'' Turner said. Brian joined them, and Maura turned the talk to school and homework. For a few moments, Turner was a mother, concerned with the mundane matters that made life predictable and safe.

But Maura was also a mother and sensed that something was tearing at her daughter. She waited until Brian and Sarah had left for school. ''You can't go on like this,'' she said. ''You need to get more rest.''

''I know,'' Turner admitted. She sipped her coffee. ''I hate some of the things I have to do.''

''Why don't you get together with Noreen and Richard?'' Maura asked. Turner was always more at ease and confident after talking to her kitchen cabinet.

''Not this time.'' A long pause. ''I wish Sam were here.''

''Is his advice that valuable?''

"Yes. No." Turner felt she had to explain. "It's just that, well, I had to make a hard decision this morning. And, and, Sam and I feel the same way about things. Besides, I trust him."

"Who else do you trust?" Maura asked.

"Robert."

A wave of self-satisfaction washed over Maura. Her daughter had not mentioned one Patrick Flannery Shaw. "But you don't always follow the general's advice."

"He's a man, Mother."

Maura knew her daughter too well. She was bottled up and needed to talk before she could move forward. "Maddy, that doesn't sound like you. What's the matter?"

"If you look outside in the hall," Turner said, "you'll see a young navy lieutenant commander sitting there. He's very good looking. A black leather briefcase is chained to his wrist. Do you know what's in that bag, Mother?" Turner didn't wait for an answer. "The launch codes that can unleash a nuclear Armageddon. I'm the only one who can do it. He's there because I declared a defense condition, DEFCON TWO, that puts us on the road to total war."

Maura tried hard not to gasp. She failed. "Are we that close to war?"

Turner shook her head. "I don't think so. I had to do it because, because"—she searched for the right words—"it's like a game where the rules were made years ago and it's the only way we know how to play now. Mother, I entered politics to make a difference, to help people, not to destroy them."

"Maddy, if what you say is true, and only you can use the codes, what's the problem? Don't use them." She stared at her daughter. "It's so simple. Just don't use them."

Okinawa, Japan

Normally, the command post hummed with activity as phones rang and people moved about. But now, the main floor was quiet and the silence was only punctuated by an occasional phone call, always answered on the first ring. Then a low voice would mumble a few words before hanging up, restoring the silence. Martini was looking out the window of the Battle Cab and into the Control Cab as the two on-duty controllers grabbed pencils and bent over their console. He recognized the signs and waited. An emergency action message was coming in.

The loudspeaker crackled, and the senior controller's voice echoed over the big room. "Please direct your attention to the Alert Status board." Every head turned to the board on the left wall and Martini felt a surge of relief. The president had declared DEFCON TWO.

"At last," Martini muttered. A sergeant entered the cab with new emergency action books labeled TOP SECRET and passed them out. Martini and the group commanders each signed for their book before breaking the seal and starting the actions that brought the base one step closer to war. It was almost midnight when they finished. "Tell Major Ryan," Martini said, "that I want all the remaining dependents and civilians bedded down in the bunkers before sunrise." He turned his position over to his vice commander. "I'm going to take a look around," he told his staff, "and then sack out for a few hours. Do the same if you can."

He strapped on his sidearm and flak vest, called for an armed escort, and walked out into the night. A gentle warm breeze washed over him and he took a deep breath. Two Security Police were waiting for him. "Come on," he said. "Habu Hill." They got into a Humvee and drove onto Perimeter Road.

Again, the night breeze wrapped around Martini when he got out of the Humvee on top of Habu Hill. But this time, it carried the strong scent of the sea. He walked to the guardrail and looked around. Except for the square of bright lights in the munitions storage area where the dependents were being sheltered, his base was cloaked in darkness. A dull red glowed on the far horizon to the northwest. It held him as it faded. Then another glow mushroomed up before it too faded. He strained to listen. Nothing. *Two hundred miles away*, he thought.

"Is that the Japs and Chinks going at it?" one of the Security Police asked.

"The Japanese and Chinese," Martini corrected. "A lot of good men are dying out there."

He prayed silently. *Please, God, help me do this one right.*

Martini walked into the command post at exactly 7 A.M., Wednesday morning, February 6. It was the 26th day of the crisis, and he was rested, showered, and shaved. His vice commander updated him on the situation, flipped open the new emergency action book, and pointed to the one item that was still open. "The C-141 is due in from Guam in two hours."

Martini grunted and sat down. "You did good. Where the hell is Townly? I want an Intel update."

"Sir," came the answer, "Colonel Townly is at Habu Ops waiting for the SR-71 to land. It was scheduled to be over the battle area at first light and should be on the ground in ten minutes."

The SR-71 could not provide him real-time Intelligence, but it was close and he needed to see the Habu's film as it came out of the processor. "Whatever happened to Mohammed coming to the mountain?" Martini muttered, happy to have an excuse to see his base in daylight. He called for his escort and went outside in time to see the Habu land and turn off the runway.

Pete Townly and the hunch-shouldered captain were waiting for him when he entered the windowless building on the north side of the base. "The film should be coming out in a few minutes," Townly told him. He paced the floor as he waited for the first frames of the 700-foot-long film to emerge from the processor. It seemed like an eternity. The two Intelligence officers ignored him as they bent over the film, trying to make sense out of the imagery. Finally, they turned to him. "Sir," Townly said, "it's going to take a hell of a lot of work before we get this all sorted out. But right now, it looks pretty much like a draw."

"It seems like it's lasting a long time," Martini said.

"Based on this imagery," the captain said, "the ships

are maneuvering over a huge chunk of ocean. It's hit and run or shoot and scoot until one side starts to lose and withdraws."

Townly kept studying the imagery as it fed out of the processor. "Sir, we've got to get this to the analysts, but my butt keeps twitching on this one."

"Absolutely marvelous, Colonel," Martini growled. "An Intelligence estimate synchronized to a twitching asshole."

Suddenly, Townly became very agitated. "Sir, I need to get back to the Intel vault. I need to check some other sources." His voice trailed off, and he looked pleadingly at the general.

"Go," Martini barked. Townly grabbed his helmet and flak vest and ran from the room. Martini followed him out at a more relaxed pace. His escort was waiting with the message that the C-141 from Guam had landed safely and was offloading by the fuel cell building on the eastern side of the main ramp. "Let's go," he told his guards.

The Humvee drove up to the C-141 as the last two pallets of cargo rolled out the back of the C-141. Each pallet held two 600-gallon external fuel tanks. In combat, an F-15 carried one on its centerline and jettisoned it before engaging in combat. For all appearances, it was a normal supply operation, and the pallets were rolled onto a cargo loader and taken to the fuel cell building. Martini followed the cargo loader into the building and watched as the four disposable tanks were hung on the Vertical Tank Storage System, the VTSS. The VTSS consisted of three tracks that bore a striking resemblance to a storage rack in any dry cleaning shop. But these racks were on steroids and instead of holding clothing awaiting pickup, eighteen-foot-long drop tanks hung in orderly rows like aluminum gourds awaiting harvest.

Five blue buses packed with dependents drove up to the C-141. Ryan got off and marched over to Martini in time to see the building's big doors clank shut. *Why all the interest in drop tanks?* he wondered. "Sir," he said, catching the general's attention, "I've got 250 volunteers who want to fly out. All we need is your OK."

Martini pulled into himself and considered his options.

They had all been taken off the table, and he didn't have a choice. "I can't allow it without specific permission from the White House."

"All of them have been briefed, sir. They know the risk and have signed consent forms." Martini did not reply, but Ryan wouldn't let it go. "What the hell am I supposed to tell them?" the doctor said, waving his arm at the buses.

Do you think I like it any better than you? Martini raged to himself. But he was a subordinate officer. "Tell them exactly what I told you." Then he relented. "Tell them I'm doing everything I can to get them out." He spun around and climbed into the waiting Humvee. "Command post," he barked.

Ryan glared at the back of the Humvee as it sped away. "Son of a bitch!" he shouted to no one. Two security police in full battle dress with M-16s approached and told him to move away from the building.

Martini was still in a foul mood when he stomped into the command post. Pete Townly was waiting and recognized the symptoms immediately. A strong sense of self-preservation warned him to disappear, but he felt suicidal. "Sir, I've got something you need to see."

"Can it wait?" Martini growled.

"It's perishable, sir."

Martini stiffened. What did Townly have that made him so adamant? "This had better be good," he muttered, following him into the Intel vault. He was not disappointed, and four minutes later, he charged out of the vault and into the command post. His vice commander saw him coming and vacated his seat in the Battle Cab. Martini dropped his helmet and flak vest and flopped into the chair. "Gentlemen, Intel claims we have a window of opportunity. The battle is hanging by a hair and can go either way. Townly thinks that all we need to do is close the runway on Kumejima. That should deprive the Chinese of air cover and allow Japanese fighters to get within range of the Chinese fleet and use their standoff missiles. I believe him. But we got to act now."

He turned to his Operations Group commander. "I think our Strike Eagles can do it. Get the Forty-fourth working on a package while I see if I can get permission."

Washington, D.C.

Bender picked at his salad and pushed it aside. It was late Tuesday evening, and he was sitting in his office trying to think like a national security advisor. *Think big picture,* he told himself. Although he had a moral and intellectual view of the world order, he accepted that his job was to help Maddy Turner realize hers. But how did she see the world? He chastised himself for not knowing and never asking. And where did he get off thinking of the president of the United States as Maddy?

Out of frustration, he closed his eyes and concentrated on the battle in the East China Sea. *It's midnight here and two o'clock Wednesday afternoon there,* he calculated, *and they're still going at it.* The Jedis in the Pentagon, that elite group of wizards who looked into the future of warfare, had predicted that naval warfare would be the nautical cousin of modern land war—short and very exciting. But they were wrong. This was turning into a prolonged slugging match where maneuver and speed over a large piece of ocean was life. His secure phone rang, bringing him back to the moment and his cage.

It was Hazelton calling from the Situation Room. "CINC PAC wants to attack the Chinese airfield on Kumejima. He says it is urgent and wants an immediate answer. Mr. Shaw is here and won't disturb the president. He says she's exhausted and has left specific instructions not to intervene unless we are under direct attack."

Bender stood up and bit off the profanity that was forming on his lips. Instead, he slammed his left hand down on the desk, venting his frustration. The tips of his fingers caught the salad fork, and it flipped up, peppering his tie with salad dressing. "I'm on my way," he said. He rushed out of his office, dabbing at his tie with a napkin.

Hazelton was waiting for him at the door of the Situation Room. She handed him the hard copy of CINC PAC's message and waited while he read. "How do you read this?" Bender asked.

She walked him through the latest message traffic. "It all tracks. For the next ten to twelve hours, Kumejima is the key. If we can shut the airfield down, the Japanese can get in range of the Chinese fleet to use their standoff missiles. If we can also neutralize some of those Silk Worm missile batteries on Kumejima, it should be decisive. But the president needs to decide now.''

"Why can't it wait?" Shaw asked, his southern drawl thick and sweet. "They've been going at it for over twelve hours and don't seem to be doing much more than scarin' each other.''

"To be exact," Bender said, "they've been fighting for sixteen hours. That's a long time.'' He glanced at the TV monitor. "And six ships sunk, four burning or dead in the water, five submarines down, over thirty aircraft destroyed, is far beyond 'scarin' each other.' ''

"So why is it so damn important for us to get involved now?" Shaw demanded.

Bender chose to ignore him. "Contact the NMCC and see if General Overmeyer is available. We need to speak to him." He turned to Shaw. "Wake the president. We're going to need a decision.''

Shaw's face was unreadable. "This is the first chance she's had at some rest since Monday.'' He cocked his head to one side and looked at Bender's tie. "Have a nice dinner there?" Shaw smiled when he saw Bender's blush.

"Sir," Hazelton said, "General Overmeyer is on the line. I can put him on the loudspeaker.''

"Don't bother," Shaw said. "We all got our marching orders, and I'm not about to wake Maddy over some dumb-ass request from an admiral who wants his fifteen minutes of fame.''

Bender stepped between Shaw and the door. "Wake the president," he said, packing his voice with all the punch he could muster.

But Shaw had experienced it before and was not moved. "No.''

"Then I will," Bender said.

Shaw smiled. "You go on the second floor of the residence tonight and I'll have the Secret Service all over you like a pit bull on a French poodle in heat.''

Hazelton's eyes grew wide in the silence. It was more than two male egos butting heads for supremacy; it was a contest for power and who had access to the president of the United States. A grin flicked across Shaw's mouth before retreating into some dark hiding place deep inside his psyche. "Do believe me on this, son." Bender stood aside and let him pass. Hazelton dropped her eyes, afraid to look at Bender. He had lost.

"Sir," she said, "General Overmeyer is still on the line."

Bender hit the monitor button so she could hear the conversation and asked for his evaluation. "I concur with CINC PAC," Overmeyer said. "But we got to do it within the next few hours, preferably at night, before the Japanese have to withdraw for refueling and resupply. We need a decision. Now."

"I can't get to the president," Bender said.

"What the hell is going on over there?" Overmeyer demanded.

"I can't get past Shaw," Bender admitted.

"We won't get a chance like this again."

"I know," Bender said. "Look, we still have some time. Plan the strike and have everything ready to go. I'll try to get her permission in the morning when she's awake." He broke the connection and told Hazelton to go home. "I'll watch it," he said. "I hope we didn't miss the one chance we had to end this with a minimum of bloodshed."

"I think we did, sir." She picked up her bag and briefcase and left, leaving Bender alone in the Situation Room.

He collapsed into a chair and clasped his hands between his knees, his head bowed. "Sir," a military aide said, "we have an update on the battle." Bender knew he was tired and needed rest. But he had to do this. He looked up at the TV monitors and forced himself to concentrate as information from satellites, reconnaissance aircraft, over-the-horizon radars, and communication monitoring sites filtered in.

Maybe, he thought, *just maybe, we've got more than ten hours.* He knew what he had to do. "Colonel, I'm going to sack out in an office down the hall. I want you to wake me in four hours." He called a valet for a pillow and blanket and went to his old office, which was still unoccupied. Within minutes, he was stretched out on the floor and sound asleep.

Turner took her seat in the Situation Room at exactly 6:30 Wednesday morning. She looked rested and fresh after a good night's sleep and nodded at the men. "Good morning, gentlemen, I hope you have some good news for me."

"Not exactly, Madam President," Overmeyer said. He hit the remote control button and the TV monitors scrolled with the latest Intelligence reports as he briefed her. He finished by saying, "The battle has reached a critical point and could go either way within the next few hours. The key is Kumejima. If we can neutralize it, the Japanese can prevail."

"How do we do that?" she asked. Overmeyer outlined the strike that was planned and ready to launch on her command. "I see," she said.

"Twelve F-15E Strike Eagles are loaded and ready to launch at Kadena," Overmeyer repeated. "We need to hit Kumejima now, while the Japanese still have the capability to exploit the advantage."

"Have the Chinese threatened or attacked our people?" she asked. Overmeyer confirmed that the battle had not reached Okinawa. She turned to Bender. "Robert, how will the Chinese respond if we attack Kumejima?"

"Militarily," he answered, "they can't since they are preoccupied with the Japanese. I'd expect a great deal of diplomatic howling and saber rattling but little else."

"Can we be sure of that?" she asked.

"No, ma'am, we can't." This from Barnett Francis, the secretary of state. The DCI agreed with him.

"In that case," Turner said, "we will do nothing. This is not our war."

Overmeyer stiffened. "Madam President, I beg you to reconsider. We will be drawn into this conflict sooner or later. Better sooner and under our terms."

"My decision is final," she said. The meeting was over, and she walked out of the room.

Bender shook his head in frustration. "I'm going outside for some air," he said. He walked slowly up the stairs and into the Rose Garden, his head bent in frustration.

A gardener he recognized from what seemed years ago walked past. "Good morning, General."

"Good morning, Stan," he replied automatically. *Did I remember his name right?* Bender thought. The smile on the man's face told him he had. He clasped his hands behind his back and dropped his chin as he walked. *So close,* he thought, *so close.* But inaction, the failure to strike at an opportune moment, had guaranteed the deaths of countless more men. He couldn't make a difference when it counted. Was it time to quit?

Mazie Hazelton stepped out of the White House and walked quickly toward him. "General Bender," she called, "you're needed inside. General Overmeyer has resigned."

20

Washington, D.C.

Turner burst into the Oval Office and stood behind her desk, glaring at Bender. "That bastard," she said. "He's playing politics. His resignation couldn't have come at a worse time." She stared at her advisors, daring them to speak. Only Shaw had seen her in a rage and had sampled the gale-force intensity of her anger. The only safe course of action was to wait for the storm to blow through.

Bender accepted the challenge. "Madam President, he resigned because he disagreed with your decisions not to support the Japanese as, I might add, we have pledged in the past."

"He did it at the exact time I need the unqualified support of the military."

"You still have the full support of the military," Bender replied.

"So I have it now—when I didn't have it before?"

Now it was Bender's turn to be angry. But nothing in his voice betrayed the emotion he felt. "The Department of Defense has supported you and been as responsive to your will as any branch of your administration."

"Really," she spat. "As I recall, the only advice I received from the Pentagon was to act; we have a plan for this—implement it before it's too late. Pardon me? What makes a goddamned plan so sacrosanct? Why is speed everything?" Her anger whipped at Bender and he did not

327

answer. This was a side to Madeline Turner he had never suspected. He expected to see tears, but her eyes were a perfect reflection of the anger and determination in her voice. "I love the way the military works," she said. "Pass the buck up the chain of command until it stops at my desk. You're only good soldiers following orders. You're not the ones responsible for the lives of your people. I am."

"General Martini will be glad to learn that," Bender said in a low voice.

"What is that supposed to mean?" she demanded. "Are you trying to say a one-star general is—"

"What I'm saying, Madam President, is that a one-star general has repeatedly made the right decisions to protect his people while everybody else was sitting on their thumbs. He never hesitated to act nor has he tried to pass the so-called buck. There's one other thing, Madam President. He will do exactly what you tell him to do, he won't complain, and he won't go running to the press when it gets tough. He understands loyalty, which is something you can't say about everyone on your staff."

Shaw's head came up. *Where's Bender taking this?* he thought. *Does he know about the group? Have the Pentagon's boys in the basement been digging around in my closet? Or has Leland double-crossed me?* Shaw caught himself hyperventilating and forced his breathing to slow as he calculated the odds of Bender knowing that he had given Maddy up. *I've given her up,* he repeated to himself. He calmed. At best, Bender could only suspect. He had covered his tracks too well.

"Don't lecture me on loyalty," Turner said. Her anger was gone, and she sat down behind her desk. "So tell me, what do I do with Overmeyer? I don't need a public discussion of why he resigned, not at this time."

Secretary of Defense Elkins cleared his throat to gain her attention. "General Overmeyer is bound by the constraints of his office. He will remain at his desk and dispose of routine matters until you accept his resignation. Then he will be on terminal leave while his retirement orders are processed. During that time, he won't discuss it. Afterward, well, he will be free to go to the media or write a book.''

"They all want to write a book," Shaw muttered, sotto voce. "Throw him a bone, Mizz President. Issue a press release that you 'reluctantly accept his resignation.' Spread some bullshit around about him being 'a fine officer acting in what he believes are the best interests of the service.' I'll get the word to him that if he goes public anytime in the next twelve months, I'll serve him up like grilled chicken liver.''

"That would be a mistake," Bender said.

"We're playing in the major leagues here," Shaw replied. "There's a penalty when you rat on the president."

"More important," Turner said, "who replaces him?"

"I'll get a short list to you as soon as I can," Elkins said. "How far do you want me to go down the list?" The men waited for her answer. It was not unusual for a president to reach down the seniority list to find a chairman for the Joint Chiefs of Staff who was politically attuned to the administration.

"Go as low as you need to find a general who will support my policies," she told them.

"May I suggest," Bender said as Jackie Winters entered the office, "that Dr. Elkins start with the current Joint Chiefs?"

"Look lower," Turner snapped, cutting off any further discussion.

"Madam President, your next meeting is in three minutes," Jackie announced. "You are meeting with the Council of Economic Advisors and the chairman of the Federal Reserve Board to discuss tax reform."

"Thank you, Jackie," Turner said. She rose and left the room.

Liz Gordon stood in front of Lafayette's statue and raised her microphone when the Betacam's red light came on. "Lafayette Park is quiet now, the peace drummer and the demonstrators gone. But like the shot at Concord that was heard around the world, the echoes from the aftermath of the attempted assassination on Vice President Kennett are still being heard. Did President Turner violate the law when she cleared the park early Tuesday morning? Congress wants to know, and the Senate, at the urging of Senator John Leland, has initiated a full-scale investigation.''

She paused so a clip of Leland filmed earlier could be inserted in the studio. The senator was most eloquent in condemning Turner's violation of the demonstrator's constitutional rights and demanding the Department of Justice appoint an independent prosecutor. Ben, her cameraman, keyed her to continue. "Meanwhile, the crisis in the Far East took a new turn as General Tennyson Overmeyer, the chairman of the Joint Chiefs of Staff, tended his resignation early this morning. Reliable sources claim General Overmeyer resigned in protest over the president's handling of the crisis. Many insiders are privately asking the question, Has Madeline Turner lost her grip on the reins of power? This is Elizabeth Gordon, CNC-TV News, reporting from the White House.''

"That's a good one," Ben said, shutting off the camera. "Who are the insiders you mentioned?''

"I made it up. But it's a safe bet someone's asking the question.''

Shaw reverted to profanity when he couldn't find the private road that led to the farmhouse in the Virginia countryside. Shaw was good at many things, but not at navigating. Much of the snow had melted from his first visit and everything was different. He cursed fluently and wished he had kept the directions from his first visit. But that was a piece of paper he didn't want surfacing at the wrong time in the wrong hands. A black Jaguar convertible flashed by him going in the opposite direction and he caught a glimpse of a blond mane of hair. Once, that would have been a distraction but not now.

He peered into the night and tried to remember the directions from his first visit. *That was less than a month ago*, he moaned to himself, *and I can't remember a gawddamn thing*. Fast moving headlights approached from his rear and flashed. He pulled over to let the car pass. The same black Jaguar convertible pulled alongside and slowed. It was Jessica, his contact with the group. They stopped, and her window lowered. "Lost?" she asked.

He gave her his lopsided grin and followed her to the farmhouse. *How many other people saw me flailing around out here?* he wondered. One of Leland's dark-suited young aides opened his door and directed him into the house. He entered the same rustic den. But this time, the room was full of people. It was a council of war. "So this is the group," he said.

Leland stood up, and they shook hands, honorable enemies currently erstwhile allies, a convenience of politics. "I believe you know everyone here," the senator said.

Shaw froze. Sitting next to Gwen Anderson, the secretary of health and human services he had trashed in her bid to be vice president, was Dr. John Weaver Elkins, the secretary of defense. "Gawddamn," he muttered. "People are hopping from bed to bed so fast I can't tell who's buggering who without being there myself."

Leland stood by the fireplace. "In the last few months," he began, his words rolling with a sonorous finality, "we have seen our President sacrifice our nation on the altar of compromise, stupidity, and inaction." He paused for effect. "Not to mention her unconstitutional efforts at tax reform."

Heads nodded in agreement and a low mutter of "Traitor" echoed from the back of the room. *Someone's getting emotional,* Shaw thought.

Leland smiled. "Patience, my friends, patience. Our polls show her negatives are surging." Shaw came alert as Leland recapped the latest poll results. The senator was on Shaw's home turf, and he made a mental note to have his experts do some of their own probing. "Her trending," Leland continued, "is reaching the point when we can move, which is why we are all here. First, what is the vice president's condition?"

"He's still on the critical list," Shaw answered. "There's a problem with infection, and he may lose his left arm and a lung."

"So he is effectively sidelined," Leland said. "That opens a window of opportunity since we have stripped away most of her political base on the Hill. But we still need to isolate her within her own administration.''

''I can delay in finding a replacement for Overmeyer,'' Elkins said. ''Besides me, the chairman of the Joint Chiefs is her only other link to the Department of Defense.''

''Can you keep it that way?'' Leland asked.

''For a week, maybe ten days,'' Elkins replied.

''Excellent,'' Leland said. ''That is more than enough time. Now it becomes solely a question of character. Did you know her personal aide, Jackie Winters, is a lesbian?''

''That's never been a big secret,'' Shaw said. ''Winters has always been very discreet and has not been, ah, active in years.''

''You mean she doesn't have a lover,'' Gwen Anderson said.

''I didn't know anything about this,'' Elkins said. ''Had I known, I would have resigned immediately.''

''It looks like we're all resigning,'' Shaw muttered.

Anderson smiled at him. ''In our own way.''

Leland paced back and forth, excited with the prospects looming in the near future. ''We are so close, so close.'' He stopped and looked directly at Shaw. ''The public has the right to know their president consorts with the morally degenerate.''

Shaw almost laughed. Classifying the Jackie Winters he knew as a moral degenerate was the stuff of high comedy. She was a lonely middle-aged woman whose only life was her job. ''Her and Bender are in a race for tightest asshole of the year,'' he muttered. He savored the quip and would use it again. Then his political instincts kicked in. He had no qualms ''outing'' Winters but the truth had a way of ultimately backfiring on those who twisted it to their own purposes. In Shaw's world, the whole truth and blatant lies were equally bad and to be avoided. It was much safer to operate in the gray areas of subterfuge, misstatement, and misdirection. Let other people play with the truth. ''This can't come from me.''

''Are you afraid of the truth?'' Leland asked.

Damn right, Shaw thought. ''If I'm involved in any way,'' he replied, ''Maddy will know and fire me in a heartbeat. Count on it. You need me on the inside.'' He almost added a caution about not underestimating Maddy Turner but thought better of it. Leland might question his commitment.

"Who can she still rely on for support?" Leland asked.

"Her kitchen cabinet," Shaw said. He added a few legislators and cabinet members to the list. "All are lightweights."

"What about Bender?" Gwen Anderson asked.

"He's a nothing," Shaw said. "No political base, alienated from the generals, nothing."

"He's an unknown quantity," Anderson said. "He worries me."

"Patrick," Leland asked, "can you sideline him by this weekend?"

All of Shaw's alarms were sounding, warning him that events were moving at a rate beyond his control and he was only along for the ride. He hoped he was in the right wagon. "I can do that," he promised.

Leland drew himself up, and Shaw saw the vengeful prophet emerge. "One more incident, my friends. That's all we need to act. It is time to remove this woman and save our great nation." Shaw sank back into his chair as the group chorused its approval. Jessica looked at him, her eyes alive with excitement and lust.

Okinawa, Japan

Martini slowed when he drove past the Base Exchange. A large number of people, all wearing BDUs, helmets, and flak vests, were entering and leaving. Some were eating on the run while others carried packages. A teenage boy and girl in civilian clothes walked past. They were holding hands. He drove to his office in the headquarters building on the west side of the base. Much to his surprise, his civilian secretary was at work arranging piles of folders on a long table. "You'll never get caught up," she told him, eyeing the stacks of paperwork that marked the everyday world of the Air Force. Life was definitely returning to normal.

The chief of Kadena's Office of Special Investigations

detachment was waiting. He was a young-looking man dressed in civilian clothes and wearing a photographer's vest. "How closely are we being watched by the Chinese?" Martini asked.

"We've identified three separate teams," the OSI agent answered. He pulled out a large-scale map of southern Okinawa and circled three areas. "Each team is constantly on the move within its own area of responsibility. Between them, they are always positioned to monitor takeoffs and landings and any movement into or out of the munitions storage area. Sometimes we lose track of them. But they always resurface in a day or two." He paused. How much more should he tell the general? He took a deep breath. "We have also identified four Japanese agents monitoring us."

"Are you surprised?" Martini asked. There was no answer. "I want you to neutralize two of the Chinese teams but leave the one monitoring the munitions storage area in place."

"Do you want us to do it or turn it over to the Japanese?"

"Who would be more efficient?"

"The Japanese. They don't worry about legal niceties."

"Let the Japanese do it."

"They'll enjoy it, sir."

Major Bob Ryan was in his makeshift office in the old nuclear weapons maintenance building in the munitions storage area when he heard a commotion down the hall. He followed the sound back into the building, wondering what was going on. Two armed guards stopped him. "Sorry, sir," one said, "you need a Class A security badge and two-man control to go beyond this point." Ryan froze. From working on the Personnel Reliability Program, he knew Class A areas and two-man control meant nuclear weapons were involved in some way.

"This whole area is a civilian shelter," he protested.

"Not this part of the building," the guard said.

"Not to worry, Major," the other guard said. "We're moving the last of some equipment out of the storage vaults. The place will be all yours in a few minutes."

Two men wheeled out a cart loaded with tool boxes and testing equipment. Ryan felt the tension slip away.

Pete Townly was having a good day. He was rested and freshly showered and for the first time in three days, felt human. The big intelligence vault hummed with activity, but there was none of the panic that had marked the first two days of what CINC PAC was now calling The Battle of the East China Sea. The green door to the top-secret communications room swung open and a wide-eyed sergeant handed him a printout. Suddenly, the day got even better. He double-checked the time and date in the message: Saturday, February 9, 5:37 A.M. local time. The information was less than forty minutes old. He ran out of the vault and into the command post.

He burst into the Battle Cab without knocking. "Sir!" he blurted. Martini started to reprimand the Intelligence officer but thought better of it. "The Japanese," Townly said, his voice under more control, "sank the *Chairman Mao!*"

"It's about time," Martini grumbled. "Details?"

"It happened at 0537 this morning. Three Japanese submarines penetrated the screen around the *Chairman Mao* and got four direct torpedo hits. Blew her in half."

"What happened to the submarines?"

"Apparently, all were lost."

Martini placed his elbows on the console, folded his fingers together, and rested his head against his hands and thumbs. *The battle has been going on for three and a half days; eighty-two hours of hell,* he told himself. *Not for us, for them.* He closed his eyes and visualized the action. He looked up, his face drawn and sad. "Three submarines is a hell of a price to pay," he told Townly. "They're rewriting naval warfare out there and I hope our people are taking notes." He came erect and his fingers drummed the table. "My gut instincts tell me the Japanese are going to win this one—without any help from us. Townly, is your asshole still twitching?"

"Yes, sir," he answered. "But not as bad."

"What's it telling you?"

"We're not out of this one yet, General."

Washington, D.C.

The black and white image was frozen on the large screen in the Situation Room. It had a grainy, blurred quality that reminded Bender of a World War II newspaper photo he had seen of a burning ship. But this photo was less than two hours old. The DCI's voice droned over them, creating the intense irrationality of a dream. "Our satellites monitored a transmission from one of the *Mao*'s escort ships. They were downlinking a video of the sinking to Beijing." A series of still frames cycled on the screen depicting the agony of the dying aircraft carrier.

"How many men died?" Turner asked.

"Unknown at this time," the DCI answered. "The Chinese are much more blasé about casualties than we are. They consider human life an expendable resource. They place a much higher value on material assets, like the *Chairman Mao*."

"Is the battle over?" she asked.

"Both sides appear to be withdrawing, Madam President," the CNO replied. "But it is not a total disengagement. They'll fight again."

"When will they stop this madness?" she asked. It wasn't a question the men could answer. "I thought wars with heavy casualties were a thing of the past."

"That's a misconception from the Gulf War," Bender said. "When both sides are evenly matched in size and technology, modern warfare is a very bloody process."

Turner looked away from the screen. "We must stop this," she said. "It's Friday evening, gentlemen." She walked to the door. "This has been a difficult week, and you all deserve a rest and an evening with your families. We'll review this tomorrow morning."

Jackie Winters was waiting outside and escorted her to the Oval Office. "Madam President," Jackie said, "I need to speak to you in private."

Turner heard the pain in her voice and sat with her on a couch. She listened as Jackie related how she had been warned by a friend that the National Gay and Lesbian Network was going to publicly reveal that she was a homosexual. "Jackie, don't worry about it. You've always been a decent, caring, hardworking person, and your private life has never been a factor in our relationship. I'm not going to let it start now. After all, this is the twenty-first century."

"But the political climate is so hostile, so partisan and unforgiving—" Jackie's words trailed off. "I'm a problem you can't afford now. I'm going to resign."

"Jackie, you have done absolutely nothing wrong, and I'm not going to let you resign. That's all there is to it."

Ella, Bender's junior secretary, took the call from Shaw's office an hour later. Shaw wanted to see the national security advisor. She relayed the message to Bender and asked Norma, the senior secretary, why Shaw hadn't called Bender directly, the way he usually did. "There's trouble brewing," Norma predicted.

Bender walked into Shaw's office and remained standing. Shaw kicked back in his chair and twirled a letter opener between his fingers. "The president asked me to speak to you. Perhaps you recall that charming little conversation you had with her Wednesday morning?"

"When General Overmeyer resigned," Bender answered.

"Well done, son," Shaw said, his southern accent in place and patronizing. He saw Bender's jaw harden, and he instinctively pushed a little harder. "You do remember." Shaw couldn't help himself, it was simply part of his nature. "Son, sometimes I think you must suffer from a terminal case of the stupids."

Bender was tired, and Shaw had called him son once too often. Bender's anger flared. He considered jamming the letter opener up Shaw's ass—sideways. Instead, he became formally polite. "Mr. Shaw, may I request you please stop being so patronizing? I am not your son, which can be readily established by a simple DNA test as I am not genetically challenged. As to the stupids you mentioned, it seems to be contagious around here."

"You don't fit in here—" The look on Bender's face cut him off before he could add son.

"Well done, Mr. Shaw. You got the message."

At that moment, Shaw's hate for Bender burst free of

the hiding place where it had festered and grown. The general was a man he could never dominate or control. Shaw's face turned red and his eyes cold. All traces of his southern accent vanished. "You are the most arrogant, insubordinate bastard I have ever met."

"From you, I consider that a compliment."

Shaw did a mental fall back and regrouped. "As I was saying about Wednesday morning—"

"Are you having trouble staying focused, Mr. Shaw?"

You're not going to drive this conversation, Shaw thought. *I'm in control here.* "You seem to forget Maddy's your president," he blurted.

"I see. So the proper form of address is Maddy, not Madam President."

"You do not debate or criticize the president," Shaw said. He was ready for Bender's rejoinder, but the general only looked at him, his face a blank mask. "You have done that once too often and been warned about it."

"I do recall Miss Winters mentioning something like that," Bender said. "But then, I didn't know she spoke for the president."

"I do speak for the president," Shaw said.

"And you accuse me of being arrogant and insubordinate?" Bender held up his hand. Was it a cease fire? "Please, Mr. Shaw, tell me whatever it is you have to say without the histrionics. It's much more efficient."

"The president has asked for your resignation," Shaw lied. "You can cite irreconcilable differences."

"Ah, like a divorce."

Shaw rolled out his heavy artillery. "Your inability to work smoothly and properly communicate with the president is only part of the problem. There is also the matter of—what's her name? Shalandra?"

Nancy was cooking dinner when Bender arrived home that same Friday night. It was a familiar scene, one that he always found comforting. But there was a rushed, almost hectic, distracted rhythm to her movements. "About an hour," she said. Normally, he would have reached for a beer in the refrigerator and changed clothes. But there were things they had to discuss first. He sat on a stool by the breakfast bar. "This has not been a good day," she told him. "Shalandra ran away from school."

"I'm not surprised," he replied. His wife stopped and dropped the knife she was using. She arched an eyebrow, demanding an explanation. "Shaw told me about the problems she's been having at the Academy."

"The boys wouldn't leave her alone," Nancy said.

"So he said."

"Did you know two of the boys forced her into making a porno video?" Bender nodded his head in answer. "They found out about her past and wouldn't leave her alone," she said.

"How did they find out?"

Nancy picked up the knife and started dicing a green pepper for the salad. "Brian told them."

Bender looked at her in shock. "How did he know?" He berated himself for asking such a stupid question. Obviously, someone in the White House had told him. A grinning image of Shaw flashed in front of him. *That fucking son of a bitch!* Bender raged to himself. *You don't bring our families into this!*

"She never had a chance," Nancy told him. The bitter disappointment in her voice struck at him. "She never had a chance."

Bender wanted to tell her to pull back from Shalandra and regain her professional detachment. Nancy could only put a patch on the problems Shalandra carried and hope for the best. Instead, "I know you wanted to help her. But I don't think there was anything you could have done."

"I feel so angry, everything I did for that girl was for nothing. I couldn't change her. She's bound and determined that she's going to self-destruct no matter what I do. I could just shake her. Like I wanted to do when Laurie joined the Air Force." She heard herself and stopped. It was a moment of revelation. "I never wanted her to join the Air Force, but she was always your daughter. Why did I think I could change her or Shalandra?" Her words cut into him and the old hurt was back. Had they both wanted too much from their daughter? He reached out, wanting to touch his wife. But she moved away, her back to him so he wouldn't see her anger.

"You never cried, you know. Not once. I would have known." She turned and looked at him. "It's OK. I cried enough for both of us. Is helping Shalandra a way to avoid facing Laurie's death or transfer guilt? I don't know. Oh, I know all the terms, I've seen it in other people, why can't I see it in myself? But it doesn't matter now, does it? She's run away and is probably back in 'the life.' She'll probably turn up in an emergency room, ODed or beat up by her pimp or a john. They always do, you know." Tears rolled down her cheeks. "You don't see what prostitution and drugs do to women. I see it everyday. My God, she's only fourteen." She hacked at the chicken in front of her. "Why don't you change before dinner?"

He wanted to comfort his wife but didn't know what to say. He wasn't sure if she would let him. He retreated upstairs and out of habit flipped on the TV to the evening news. It was the usual listing of murder, mayhem, destruction, and insoluble problems. Then he heard it. A gay liberation group had made national headlines by claiming the president's personal assistant was a lesbian. *That's why Jackie wanted to speak privately to the president this afternoon,* he thought. She wanted to warn her.

He flipped the channel to Peter Whiteside, the dean of the White House correspondents. He was standing on the steps of the Capitol with Senator Leland. "Senator, in this day and age, does the issue of a lesbian on the president's staff even deserve our attention?"

"Normally," Leland replied, "I would agree with you. But this has been hidden for years. Why? What was the exact relationship between Winters and the president? What else is going on in the Turner White House and being covered up? These are questions that many Godfearing Americans are asking. They deserve complete and honest answers."

Bender shook his head in disgust, switched off the TV, and went downstairs. "Were you listening to the news?" Nancy asked.

"Yeah," he said. "I heard."

"Did you know Jackie was a lesbian?"

"No, but I didn't know her that well."

"What are you going to say to the press?"

"There's nothing to say. Turner's asked for my resignation. It's on Shaw's desk."

"Why didn't you tell me sooner?"

He shrugged. "I was waiting for the right time."

Another thought came to her. "Did Shalandra have anything to do with it?"

"It doesn't matter," he replied. "Let's get out of here for the weekend and find some bed and breakfast or country inn where they don't give a damn about Washington."

The tears were back. "Robert, are we going to make it?"

The night duty officer in the communications section of the White House took the call from the police. She did not hesitate and immediately called Shaw. As expected, he grumped at being so rudely awakened at 3:15 on Saturday morning. But it wasn't a message he could ignore. "Wake the president," he told the duty officer. "I'll be there in twenty minutes. He made it in fourteen and went directly to Turner's private study in the residence. He knocked twice, and Maura opened the door.

Turner was standing by the fireplace reading a note. She was wearing a dark blue robe, and her hair was brushed back. Shaw waited for her to speak as she gazed into the fire. *This is a picture worth a million votes,* he thought and, for a moment, considered calling in a photographer to capture the scene. But that would be counterproductive. "The police sent this over a few minutes ago," she said. "It's a copy." She handed him the note.

Dear Maddy,

Please forgive me but I've hurt you more than I can bear and can't go on. I will always love you.

The note was signed with Jackie's tight but small and very distinctive signature.

"They outed her," Turner said, "and she was afraid the public's reaction would drag me down." Then, more strongly, "We'd have weathered this."

"Where was she found?" he asked.

"She drove to a small park upstream on the Potomac and took sleeping pills," Maura said. "A park ranger on a security patrol found her."

Shaw reread the note. "Not good," he muttered. "Quite a few assholes are gonna say this proves she was your lover."

"Don't be stupid," Turner snapped.

"We all know the truth, Mizz President. But politics is all appearances. Let me sterilize her office."

"No," Turner said. "There's nothing to find. I want you to go down there and have the Secret Service seal the office. Call the FBI and stay there until the investigators arrive."

"I'm on my way," Shaw said.

"One more thing, Patrick," she said, stopping him. "I'm not going to allow anyone, I don't care who it is, to twist the truth to their own ends. The first one who does is going to find the full weight of the presidency dropped on them like a ton of bricks."

"That can be counterproductive, Mizz President."

"As long as they stick with the truth, Patrick, it's no problem."

"Yes, ma'am," he replied. "So we're playing hardball on this one."

"Not hardball," she said, "slash and burn."

The long walk to the West Wing gave Shaw time to tranquilize the worry that was consuming him. Unless all his political instincts were wrong, Leland was going to use Jackie's suicide to beat Maddy into final submission. But had Maddy lost the will to fight back? He didn't know. Had he backed the wrong side? He calculated he would know in less than forty-eight hours. He entered the office Jackie shared with the president's secretaries and used his handkerchief to open her desk drawers. He rifled through, careful not to disturb the neatly ordered contents. He picked up a Polaroid picture that seemed out of place. It was a photo of the farmhouse where he had met with Leland.

The worry that had been swirling around him turned into a fully developed tornado. What was this doing in Jackie's desk? If Maddy knew about Leland and the group, she knew about him. Or did she? Did he still have time to maneuver before he was discovered? *Breathe,* he told himself. He concentrated on breathing. *Saint-Peter-shit-a-brick!* he thought. *Do something!* He pocketed the photo, closed the drawer, and walked as calmly as he could to his own office.

He unlocked a desk drawer where the panties left by his companion of the snowstorm were safely tucked away. He shoved them into his pocket and returned to Jackie's office. Again, he used his handkerchief to open a drawer in Jackie's desk and dropped the panties in. With a little luck, forensic and DNA testing would prove the panties did not belong to Jackie. But that raised the double-barreled question of ownership and why were they there? A sex scandal in the White House was exactly what Leland wanted. He was careful not to disturb the desk and closed the drawer.

He opened the door and beckoned to the Secret Service agent on duty. "Seal this office. Don't let anyone in until the FBI gets here." He walked back to his office. He had to telephone Leland. But from where? Certainly not from the White House. It would have to wait until later.

21

Okinawa, Japan

Martini sensed the change the moment he entered the command post. It smelled different. Everyone was wearing a fresh uniform and the halls sparkled from a recent GI party. He walked across the main floor and heard the sound of guarded optimism in the conversations around him. The door to the Battle Cab was open and like the command post, it was squeaky clean. His staff was crowded inside for a meeting, and Pete Townly was waiting for him with a briefing board tucked under his left arm. "Good evening, General," he said. It was 7 P.M., Saturday, February 9, the twenty-ninth day of the crisis.

"What'cha got, Pete?" Martini asked. He listened as Townly recapped the current status of the battle. Both sides had withdrawn to lick their wounds, and the fighting was over.

"When will they go at it again?" the Operations Group commander asked.

"Not for a while," Townly replied. "Both have depleted their fuel and ammunition stocks. Combine that with their losses and I don't see any major action for some time. Judging by the way the Chinese are digging in on Kumejima, they are settling in for a long siege. There is another possibility: We may be next."

Martini probed for details on the island and stiffened when he saw the extent of the bunkering and fortifications nearing completion. His fingers drummed the table. "Ladies and gentlemen, I don't like this. I want to hunker down and be ready for a missile attack within the next forty-eight hours."

Major Bob Ryan was standing at the back of the cab. "General," he said, "the crowding in the shelters is creating problems. Many of them want to go home. I'm not sure how much longer I can sit on them."

"Tell them we don't have a choice," Martini replied. "I'm still pressing for their evacuation. Maybe the president will change her mind now." He turned to his Operations Group commander. "Start prepping a Strike Eagle and move it to the hardened shelter closest to the fuel cells building." His eyes swept over the men and women crowded around him. "Any questions?" There weren't any, and the meeting was over.

Why all the attention on one F-15? Ryan thought as he escaped outside. Out of curiosity, he drove across the ramp on his way back to the north side of the base. It was already dark and lights started to wink out as Kadena transitioned to blackout conditions. Finally, the only patch of light was the bright square around the civilian shelters. *It's like a beacon pointing the way to the base,* he thought. Then it too blinked out. Ryan reached for his night vision goggles and waited for his eyes to adjust before continuing. He drove slowly past the fuel cells building. Three times he saw guards, always in pairs, patrolling behind a rope barrier that created a sixty-foot-wide no-man's-land around the building.

"Holy shit," he muttered to himself. An image of a mushroom cloud over an island flashed in front of him. "There's no way—" But he had to be sure. He drove up to the entry control point, a break in the rope, and stopped. A pair of guards approached him and scanned him with a shielded flashlight.

"Sir, you need a class A security badge to proceed beyond this point."

His suspicions were confirmed, and he felt sick. There were nuclear weapons on Kadena under Martini's control. He was trapped on an island with a power freak.

Washington, D.C.

Shaw followed the butler down the second-floor corridor of the residence on Saturday morning. He checked his watch and at exactly eight o'clock knocked on the door. He counted to three and pushed through. "Good morning again, Mizz President," he said. He settled into his usual seat and handed her the day's schedule. It was the same routine, and it was business as normal. "I've freed up a block of time this afternoon for a press conference," he told her. "I want'a take the offensive on Jackie's suicide. Make the press come to us, and anything they find out on their own will be old news. I got the children working overtime on the polls." *And taking a good look at Leland's polls,* he mentally added.

"I want to drive public opinion on this one," Turner said, "not the other way around." Shaw handed her the President's Daily Brief and waited while she read. "Apparently, the Chinese and Japanese have exhausted themselves. This might be the perfect time to start a diplomatic offensive." Shaw made a note and handed her the day's action list. She scanned the page and froze at the last entry. Robert Bender had tended his resignation as her national security advisor. "Why didn't you tell me sooner?" she asked.

"I only saw the letter about an hour ago," Shaw replied. "He gave it to my secretary last night after I had left." He handed her the letter.

"Generals define loyalty in a most unique way," she said. "He recommends Mazie take over for him. Please call her as soon as possible."

"I already have," Shaw said. "She's in his office and is preparing for the meeting with your security advisors in twenty minutes."

"I want to meet the agent in charge of the FBI investigation looking into Jackie's death."

"He's still in Jackie's office," he told her. "They should be about finished." He followed her into the West Wing. "You need to select a new personal assistant."

"We'll take care of that next week," she replied.

The FBI agents were still inventorying Jackie's personal

filing cabinet when Turner and Shaw entered the outer room that guarded the inner sanctum of the Oval Office. Shaw made the introductions. The senior agent said that they were almost finished with Jackie's office and asked if someone could explain a few file folders. He shifted his weight uncomfortably from foot to foot. The rules dictated that he not reveal or discuss the findings of an investigation in progress. But this was the president of the United States, and he was deeply troubled by what he had found. "We did find one item in her desk that bothers me." He held up a plastic evidence bag containing the panties. "These don't fit the pattern we're seeing, not at all, which raises more questions than it answers."

The palms of Shaw's hands grew clammy. Had he made a mistake? But he was a practiced politician, and his face did not betray the worry that was eating at him. This was coming apart on him.

"Perhaps it would be better if we discussed this under the proper circumstances," Turner said. "I just wanted to say, you have my unqualified support. If anyone on my staff is not fully cooperative or interferes in any way, speak to Mr. Shaw. Please excuse me, but I have another meeting."

The DCI was standing between Elkins and Francis when she entered the Oval Office. "Patrick, please call Mazie," she said. Shaw hurried out to make the call. "Well, John," she said to Elkins, "without the chairman, we seem a much smaller group. When can I see that list?"

"Tuesday at the latest," Elkins replied. He hoped he could drag it out to appease Leland.

Shaw came back in and sat down. "Mazie's in the communications room. New message traffic coming in."

"Well, gentlemen," Turner said, "I take it you have all heard about General Bender's resignation? Mrs. Hazelton will be taking over his duties. Am I correct in assuming the Chinese and the Japanese are done fighting?"

"Yes, ma'am," the DCI answered. "The Chinese are reinforcing the island of Kumejima. But our analysts interpret this as a defensive measure."

"Barnett," she said, turning to the secretary of state,

"I want you to open a diplomatic offensive to bring Japan and China to the negotiating table." Barnett Francis was outlining his ideas on how to make it happen when Hazelton entered the room. Her face was flushed, and she was out of breath from running up the stairs.

"Madam President," she paused to catch her breath. "The Chinese are giving the Japanese an ultimatum." They stared at her in shocked silence as she related how the National Security Agency had intercepted and decoded a message from Beijing to their ambassador in Paris. The Chinese ambassador was to present the ultimatum to the Japanese ambassador in two hours. If the Japanese did not cease all hostile actions in the East China Sea and cede the five Yaeyama Islands, including Iriomote, as reparations and a sign of good will to the Chinese by midnight Sunday, Greenwich mean time, the Chinese government would be forced to undertake extreme measures.

"Damn," Shaw moaned. "These time zone differences drive me crazy. How many hours does that give us?"

"About forty hours," Hazelton replied. "The ultimatum expires at 7 P.M., Sunday, our time."

"Why the Yaeyama Islands," Turner asked, "and not Kumejima?"

"Kumejima is a bargaining chip," Hazelton said. "The Chinese think they can slice off the Yaeyamas because they have an historical claim that goes back 300 years and the islands are only 125 miles from Taiwan. This is also a way for Beijing to save face after losing the *Chairman Mao*."

"What do they mean by 'extreme measures'?" Turner asked. No one could answer her. "So what do we do?"

"There is very little we can do," Barnett Francis said. "This is between the Chinese and the Japanese. The Japanese will have to come to us."

"If we go to the Japanese," the DCI said, "the Chinese will know we've cracked their codes."

"Have we?" Turner asked.

"We can read anyone's mail we want," the DCI replied, "including Japan's. That's a secret we don't want compromised under any circumstances. Personally, I think the Chinese are bluffing to save face and the Japanese know it.''

''Both sides are very concerned with saving face,'' Hazelton said. ''I doubt if the Japanese will ask for help, not after what's happened.''

''Mizz President,'' Shaw said, ''we ought'a brief key members of Congress, watch how this plays out, and be ready to respond.''

Turner made her decision. ''Call them to the White House. But I want to make one thing perfectly clear. I will not fight over a few disputed rocks in the ocean, but I will if the Chinese threaten our people on Okinawa.'' The meeting was over, and Shaw held back as her security advisors left. ''Patrick, did you notice Dr. Elkins hardly said a thing?''

Shaw shrugged. ''Maybe he's run out of words or hung over.'' He checked her schedule. ''Some visiting firemen from Iowa are waiting to receive an award.'' He turned her over to the appointments secretary and ambled back to his office. Alice Fay, his secretary, handed him a message from Jessica. He made a big show of sitting on the edge of Alice's desk and dialing Jessica's number. ''It's me, darlin'. Dinner tonight?'' He grinned at her reply. ''It'll be jus' like old times,'' he said, breaking the connection.

He hoped it wasn't an idle boast.

The two black staff cars pulling up to the South Portico of the White House made a perfect background for Liz Gordon's TV newsbreak. ''A White House briefing today confirmed reports that the naval battle in the East China Sea is over. But in what should have been a moment of triumph for President Turner, the capital is alive with rumors surrounding the apparent suicide of the president's personal assistant, Jackie Winters.

''Key leaders from the Hill''—Ben zoomed in on the two black sedans—''have been summoned to the White House and a highly placed source maintains they are only being briefed on the Far East. Meanwhile, veteran White House observers claim a major crisis is brewing on this quiet Saturday afternoon. This is Liz Gordon, CNC-TV News, standing by at the White House."

Ben lowered the camera and wound up the microphone wire. "Any idea of what's going on?" he asked.

"I haven't got a clue," Liz replied. "But I think the shit is about to hit the fan."

Shaw sank back on the couch and stretched out. He felt like a whipped dog after the long day and wanted nothing more than a soak in a hot bath and collapse in bed. But there was still more work to do. "Nice idea, having dinner at your place."

Jessica came out of the kitchen holding two glasses of wine and wearing a filmy dark green creation that would guarantee cardiac arrest under most circumstances. "It's ready," she said, curling up on the couch beside him. "Besides, we can talk here." She gave him time to taste the wine. "The senator has convinced the Speaker of the House to start impeachment hearings next week." Her eyes glowed with excitement.

"Hot air and smoke," Shaw replied. "They haven't got anything. Maddy's just a political lightweight stumbling around in the dark. Hell, if that was unconstitutional, half our presidents and Supreme Court justices would have been impeached."

She led him to the dinner table and served up a coq au vin that would have sent a Frenchman happily to the guillotine. "The senator is aware of all that," she said. "But he thinks he can force her to resign. All he needs is the 'last straw.' "

Shaw told her about the panties the FBI had discovered in Jackie's desk. He did not mention how they had gotten there or the photo he had found. "Very embarrassing," he said, "but not incriminating."

"We move now, or it's not going to happen," she said. "Is there anything else?"

Shaw dropped his chin. It was ides of March time and he held the dagger that could take his Caesar down. "The Far East is going to blow up in her face."

Jessica came out of her seat like a cat and stood behind him, massaging his shoulders. "When?" she murmured.

"Seven P.M. tomorrow evening," he answered. He told her about the Chinese ultimatum.

"Are you sure?"

"My gut is sure." He spoke quietly, succumbing to the wine and rich food. His words excited her more than any aphrodisiac as he guided her through the logic of his arcane and dark world.

"You must be exhausted," she murmured. "Let me run you a hot bath." She led him into the bathroom and undressed him as the tub filled. He settled in and let the hot water flow over him as her silk peignoir slipped to the floor. She scrubbed him down and gently massaged his neck. Then she reached between his legs. Nothing. "You need a good night's rest," she whispered. She toweled him down and led him to her bed. He was asleep the moment his head hit the pillow. She sat on the edge of the bed and crossed her legs as she dialed a number. "It's tomorrow evening," she said. She listened for a moment. "Oh, yes, he's sure. I can't discuss it over the phone. Meet me in forty minutes." Again, she listened. "He won't miss me."

The gentle moan cut through Bender's subconscious and jolted him awake. It was Nancy. She was talking in her sleep, meaningless words from a tortured dream, as her breath came in ragged bursts. He reached out to touch her, to tell her he was there and that everything was fine. "We were happy then," she said, rolling over into a tight ball. He pulled his hand back and tried to sleep. But he was wide awake.

Finally, he got out of bed and pulled on one of the heavy terry cloth robes the inn provided. He stood by the window. The low, snow-covered hills were bathed in moonlight. *What a beautiful sight,* he thought. But it held no emotion, no passion for him. He moved across the room to the fireplace and quietly placed a log on the dying embers. He stood there and looked at his wife. *What's the matter?* he thought. *What's come between us?*

The log caught fire and came to life. The glow flickered on his face as he stared into the fire. *Why am I losing my wife?* he raged to himself. *Why can't I understand this?*

Nancy's words echoed through his mind and they were at Laurie's funeral at Arlington. "We were happy then." He felt the tears in his eyes. Slowly, he raised his chin, and his head came back. "We were happy then," he said aloud. The tears flowed down his cheeks, and he knew. He had never cried for his daughter. He had turned away from his loss and carefully walled it in with work and intellectual conceit: words on an accident report, the demands of his profession, the commitment to duty. And he had abandoned Nancy, the woman he loved, to her own grief.

His tears dried as the fire warmed his face. Could he change and salvage his marriage? He didn't know.

Mazie Kamigami Hazelton stood as the president left the Situation Room. The Sunday 1 P.M. briefing on the Far East had lasted less than ten minutes and the room rapidly emptied. Only Elkins, the secretary of defense, remained behind. "Dr. Elkins," she began, selecting her words with care, "I don't share your confidence that the Chinese and Japanese have exhausted themselves and the fighting is over."

He gave her the most patronizing look he could muster. "Mrs. Hazelton," he sighed, "I choose to believe the CIA and the national intelligence officer. After all, threat assessments and issuing war warnings are their responsibility."

"What is the National Military Intelligence Center's assessment?" she asked.

Hazelton was probing too hard, and Elkins wanted to end the conversation. "The same as mine. May I suggest you stop chasing shadows?" He tilted his head and gave her a brief nod, the high official bestowing his benediction on a flunky. But Hazelton was not intimidated and waited until he had left before reviewing the mass of information flowing into the Situation Room. She agreed with them that there was no danger to either the United States or Okinawa. At least, none that she could see. Maybe Bender or Overmeyer might see something. But what she didn't know.

Frustrated, she went to Shaw's office and waited ten

minutes before Alice Fay escorted her in. She came right to the point. "We're missing something and need to hear from the Pentagon."

"That's why Elkins is here," Shaw said.

"He's a civilian concerned with policy. The president needs to hear from the professionals."

"I don't think Maddy is putting much store in her generals these days," he said. "Never seen a bunch who could cut and run like them."

"Maybe they're trying to send her a message," Hazelton said.

"Are they now?" He twirled a letter opener between his fingers. "We got a game plan and we're following it," he said, dismissing her.

She walked quickly back to her new office. Only Norma, the senior secretary, was there. "Please contact General Bender," she said. "I need to speak to him. It's very urgent."

"I'll try," Norma promised, "but he's not answering his pager or cellular phone. I'll have someone check his quarters again."

Shaw checked his watch. It was 6:29 P.M. Sunday evening. His hands were moist as he knocked at the door of the family room. He entered and paused. It was a scene of domestic tranquility: Turner was playing a board game with Sarah while Brian did his homework. Maura was knitting by the fire. He would never see it again. "Mizz President," he said softly.

She looked at him, her face passive. "Any change?"

"No, ma'am." Patrick Flannery Shaw closed his eyes for a second. He couldn't put it off any longer. He hoped his voice wasn't shaking. "Ma'am, a delegation from the Hill is waiting to speak to you in the Cabinet Room."

"Really?" she replied. "This is most unusual." Members of Congress did not barge into the White House uninvited. "Under the circumstances, perhaps it would be best if I didn't meet—"

Shaw interrupted her. "Mizz President, you need to speak to them."

She sighed. "It's the ultimatum, isn't it?"

Shaw tried to put a good face on it. "You need to do some hand holdin', Mizz President."

"I suppose you're right." She stood. "I'll be right back, Mother."

Shaw escorted her downstairs, held the door to the Cabinet Room, and stood back to let her enter alone. No one in the packed room stood up. "Gentlemen," she said, taking her seat at the center of the long table. "How may I help you?"

Senator John Leland stood at the end of the table. "Mrs. Turner," he began. Her right eyebrow arched at his obvious blunder in protocol. "We are here on a matter of national crisis."

Her voice was ice. "Exactly what crisis are you referring to?"

"You are destroying the office of the presidency," he replied.

She looked around the room, skewering each man with a hard look. "Gentlemen, this meeting is over." She rose to leave.

"No, Mrs. Turner," Leland thundered, "this meeting is not over until you hear what we have to say."

"Listen to him," Shaw urged.

Turner spun around and gave him a quizzical look. Then, to Leland, "Make it quick."

"You have subverted the political process with your misguided attempts at tax reform," Leland said. "Your actions in Lafayette Park violated the very constitutional rights of the demonstrators you are sworn to protect. You have abandoned a valuable ally who we have sworn to defend. You sacrificed ninety-four innocent women and children in your vain attempt to evacuate dependents from Okinawa, and they were devoured by sharks." He drew himself up in righteous anger. "Now we have proof of illicit, outrageous, morally degenerate conduct on the part of your staff within the White House itself. How much more lies beneath the surface?"

"You left out the most serious charge," she said. "I'm a woman."

"For the good of the country," Leland said, "before you totally destroy the presidency, you must resign."

"And if I don't?"

"Then you will be impeached and removed from office."

"You're an idiot, Leland, leading a pack of fools."

My Gawd, Shaw thought, *she's standing up to them all alone.*

"Leave," Turner snapped, "before I have the Secret Service throw you out."

Shaw panicked. She would do it. "Mizz President, that would be a fatal mistake."

"Yes, Mrs. Turner," Leland bellowed, "please do that."

For a brief moment, they glared at each other from across the table. A sharp rap at the door echoed between them, and every head turned to the sound. The Navy lieutenant commander on duty in the communications room burst through the door and halted at the scene frozen in place before him. "Madam President!" he blurted. He paused as words escaped him. "Madam President, the Chinese have detonated a nuclear weapon in the East China Sea."

Leland reached for his pocket watch and snapped the lid open. The ultimatum had expired. "Mrs. Turner, you have brought the world to nuclear war. I can only repeat what Oliver Cromwell told the Long Parliament in 1653 when it was no longer fit to rule England." He drew himself up, a biblical prophet raised in fury. " 'You have sat too long here for any good you have been doing. . . . In the name of God, go!' "

PART FOUR
DEFEAT

Politicians like to slay distant dragons. It's much safer than doing battle with the home grown variety. But in dealing with dragons, there is one unchanging rule: You only get one chance and mistakes are fatal.

ELIZABETH GORDON
CNC-TV News

22

Washington, D.C.

Madeline Turner closed her eyes as the first tremor swept through her. Only the sound of deep breathing reached her. Was it hers or the men surrounding her in the Cabinet Room? The words were seared in her mind: "a nuclear weapon" . . . "In the name of God, go!" How many people had died because of her? How many more had she sentenced to a certain death? She felt the tears course down her cheeks, etching paths of burning pain. She had failed.

"How many casualties?" she asked the stunned Navy lieutenant commander.

Before he could answer, Shaw waved him to silence. "Mizz President," he said, "why don't you sit down?" Shaw motioned for the Navy officer to leave.

"We demand an answer," Leland said. His words were filled with triumph and vindication.

Turner didn't move. "I don't know what to say."

Leland sensed victory and swelled with importance. "A simple note, Mrs. Turner. Similar to Nixon's—"

Again, Shaw held up a hand. "We need a few moments alone gentlemen." He gently held her elbow and guided her out of the room.

Behind her, the men exploded with shouts, and she heard demands for a retaliatory nuclear strike on Beijing. A uniformed Secret Service guard closed the door behind them. The guard spoke into his whisper mike. "Magic is moving." Then he muttered a few more words.

"It's OK, Maddy," Shaw soothed. "It's OK." He led her to the Oval Office, and she collapsed on a couch. Shaw rang the kitchen for tea and sat beside her. "It'll be all right," he said. The door swung open, and Maura O'Keith entered. "Not now," Shaw said, "Not now." He jerked his head for her to leave.

Maura ignored him and sat beside her daughter. "I knew something was wrong," she said. "I just knew it." It was a lie. A Secret Service agent on duty in the residence had overheard the whispered radio calls and told her. Maura listened as her daughter told her of Leland's demands. "I'll call Noreen and Richard," Maura said, reaching for the phone.

"It's too late for her kitchen cabinet," Shaw said, taking the phone from her hand.

"She needs time and friends," Maura snapped.

"There is no time left," Shaw said.

Turner stood up. "I did nothing wrong, Patrick, nothing."

Maura turned to her daughter. "Don't do anything until I get back." She rushed from the room and ran up to the Secret Service agent on guard. "Where's Chuck Sanford?" she asked. The guard spoke into his mike and told her he was on duty at General Bender's quarters. "I need to speak to him." She ran downstairs to the Secret Service command post directly below the Oval Office. Within seconds, she was speaking to Sanford. "Tell the general his president is in trouble and needs him."

Nancy Bender answered the knock at the rear door. "What now?" she asked. "We're tired."

"I need to speak to the general," Chuck Sanford said. "It's important." She led him into the family room, where Bender was sitting by the fire. "General, Maura O'Keith called. The president is in trouble and needs your help."

Bender shook his head. "You haven't heard. She asked for my resignation. Now she wants my help? I'm not a Ping-Pong ball." He looked into the fire. "What's the problem."

"Sorry, General. You know I can't get involved. I'm just the messenger."

"Thanks, Chuck," Bender said, dismissing him.

Sanford had stood post for two presidents and guarded the ailing national security advisor, William Gibbons Carroll, when he was dying from ALS, Lou Gehrig's disease. He had seen his partner, Wayne Adams, take the bullet for Bender and he had always been loyal to his oath. *Come on, General,* he thought, *do the right thing.* But Bender didn't move. "General Bender," he said, stepping over the line and getting involved, "she is your president."

Nancy stood by the fire and folded her arms. "Do what you're going to do," she said. "Answer the goddamn call to duty. You always have. You always will."

Bender stood up. He wanted to hold her. "I don't have a choice," he said.

"They're using you," she called to his back.

Okinawa, Japan

Every head in the command post was turned toward the tech sergeant in the disaster response cell. Even Martini could only wait as the sergeant plotted the winds. Once, the sergeant asked for confirmation that it was a fifty-kiloton weapon, an airburst, and located 120 nautical miles to the southwest over the East China Sea. Then he resumed work. Finally, he double-checked his calculations. "We're seeing an unusual wind pattern for this time of year, and the winds are blowing out of the west," he announced. "But most of the fallout will miss us. The footprint is downwind, to the east, and only the northern edge of the fallout will touch us. We can expect the first measurable traces to reach us in three hours and twenty minutes. With a little luck, the winds will veer to the south and we'll be OK."

"We'll probably get nuked before that," Major Bob Ryan groaned.

Martini snorted. "Not hardly. If we were going to get hit, it would have happened by now." He stood up and studied his staff. "That's the only detonation we're going to see for a while. We've got three hours to hunker down and get our people undercover. Get decontamination centers set up and make sure everyone who goes outside has a dosimeter. Plan on burrowing in for a week, maybe two. It all depends on how dirty the bomb was and what the winds do. Go. Make it happen.'' He motioned for Ryan to stay behind.

"Major, it's OK to spout off in here. But you're going to have to be positive as all hell when you talk to your people in the shelters. Thank God, we've already got them undercover. It's not the end of the world and we're going to make it. That's your message, pure and simple. Got it?"

"Yes, sir," Ryan said, eager to escape. He threw Martini a salute and scurried out of the command post. *How can Martini be so sure there won't be any more?* he thought. *He had to know more than he was saying.* Another thought came to Ryan with such a clarity and force that it stopped him cold. He couldn't move. It all made sense. They had dropped the bomb, not the Chinese.

Washington, D.C.

Shaw jerked the letter out of the typewriter and walked into the Oval Office. "This will do," he said.

Turner looked up at him. Her eyes were filled with anger. "I'm not resigning."

"You don't have a choice," Shaw replied. "Your political base—"

"Fuck my political base. I'm the president of the United States, and I've done nothing wrong." She glared at him. "If you can't support me on that, then—" She didn't finish the sentence. "Call Noreen Coker and Richard Parrish. I want to see them now."

"But Mizz President," Shaw protested, "they're still waiting in the Cabinet Room."

"They can wait until hell freezes over."

Shaw turned to Maura. "Can you reason with her? She's going to be impeached if she doesn't resign."

"Then I guess she's going to be impeached," Maura answered.

The door opened, and Bender stood there, not entering.

Liz Gordon dropped a pillow over the phone and ignored its insistent ring. She reached down with both hands and guided Jeff Bissell's head as his tongue flicked at her navel and worked lower. "Don't stop," she moaned. He reached for the phone and handed her the receiver, never missing a lick. "Liz Gordon," she said, suddenly taking a sharp breath. She closed her eyes and listened. She reared up and bucked, knocking Bissell out of bed.

"What the—" he groaned, holding the left side of his head.

"Have Ben meet me at the east gate," she told the caller. "I'm on my way." She banged the receiver down and leaped out of bed. "Get dressed."

"My head," he moaned.

"Sorry," she said. "Reuters broke a story that someone exploded a nuke near Okinawa."

"Holy shit!" Bissell shouted as he reached for his trousers. They quickly dressed and ran for the elevator. Fortunately, Washington's Sunday evening traffic was light and no police car saw them speeding toward the White House. Bissell pulled up to the east gate where Ben, Liz's cameraman, was waiting. She jumped out of the car, and they processed through the gate. Bissell was a few steps behind them.

Ben handed her a computer printout as they hurried to the north side of the mansion. "That's all we know," he said.

"Look at all the staff cars," she panted as they ran.

"The guard said they've been here since six this evening," Ben told her. "General Bender arrived just before you did."

"Oh, my God," Liz said. "It must be true. Are we the first here?"

"As far as I know," Ben said. He handed Liz a microphone and framed her in the lens, the North Portico with its lighted chandeliers glowing in the background.

"The White House is alive with activity," she said, her

expression properly grave, "as unconfirmed reports of a nuclear explosion in the East China Sea keep growing. Staff cars and limousines from the Capitol have been streaming into the White House grounds since six this evening and General Robert Bender, President Turner's national security advisor, arrived moments ago."

She turned and looked at the White House. "It is ironic that the first president of this century and the first woman to hold this high office should be confronted with a nuclear Armageddon in the midst of her other political problems. This is truly a testing time for Madeline O'Keith Turner as the world shudders on the brink of war. This is Elizabeth Gordon, CNC-TV News, standing by at the White House." She lowered her microphone and continued to stare at the North Portico. Ben kept the Betacam rolling and zoomed in on her face, catching her disheveled, flustered, worried expression. "Do this one right, Maddy," she said, loud enough for the microphone to pick up.

"Perfect," Ben whispered. "Absolutely perfect." Then, more strongly, "You've never looked better. We're talking Emmy here, folks."

Jeff Bissell shook his head. "The well-laid look does it again."

Shaw's head twisted back and forth, first to Turner, then to Bender, then back again. *Sweet Jesus,* he thought, *what if he tells her I said she wanted him to resign? How do I get out of this one?* "General, we need you," he said, trying for damage control. "Can we all let bygones be bygones and I'll tear up that letter?"

"I do need you, Robert," Turner said.

Bender hovered in the doorway. He wanted to put conditions on his help, to ask her to stop ignoring her generals and admirals, to stop punishing the men and women who defended their country. But he couldn't. She was his commander in chief and like all the other superior officers he had served under, there were no conditions. "Please tear it up." He stepped inside and closed the door behind him.

"Patrick, please call Noreen and Richard and ask them to join me while I bring Robert up to date." Shaw waddled out of the room, hopeful that the letter of resignation was a dead issue, drowned in a sea of crisis. Turner quickly related how Leland's delegation had arrived demanding her resignation as the Chinese ultimatum expired. The report of the nuclear detonation had only given Leland another weapon to use against her.

Bender paced the room. "Who was there?" he asked. She listed everyone she could remember, including John Weaver Elkins, the secretary of defense. "But no generals or admirals?" She confirmed his guess. "Was the DCI there?"

Again, she shook her head. "When I left, they were demanding I launch a ballistic missile at Beijing."

"Those idiots," he muttered. "When it comes to nukes, they don't even know the right questions to ask. We don't go crazy just because of one detonation someplace."

"What are the right questions?"

"How many," he answered, "who, where, how big, and what do they have left?"

"As far as I know," she replied, "there was only one, somewhere over the ocean."

"Those fucking bastards," he growled, surprising her with his profanity. "A sel rel. The Chinese are using our own doctrine against us." He picked up the phone. "May I?" he asked. She nodded, and he asked the operator to put him in contact with the DCI.

"What's a sel rel?" she asked as they waited.

"A selective release. In a conflict where we're losing, our doctrine calls for us to detonate one small nuclear weapon as a way to tell the enemy we intend to cross the firebreak to nuclear warfare unless they back off. The Chinese are sending us that message."

A look of relief spread across her face. "Then I'm not committed to a nuclear war?"

"Not yet," he told her. "But first, we got to be sure it's a sel rel. That's why you need to speak to the DCI." He paused. "And the JCS."

"Can I trust the Joint Chiefs?" she asked.

"It's Elkins you can't trust. Believe me, no general or admiral I know will ever betray his oath." The DCI came on the line. "This is Bender. I take it you've heard. Why aren't you here?" He listened for a moment. "They're cooling their heels in the Cabinet Room and the president's name is Madeline O'Keith Turner. When can she expect you?'' He listened to the answer and broke the connection. ''The DCI is on his way.''

Turner came to her feet and lifted her chin as Shaw returned. ''Patrick, call the Joint Chiefs of Staff. Tell them to meet me in the Situation Room immediately.''

Maura closed her eyes and breathed in relief as Shaw beat a quick exit. Her daughter was back. She didn't know if she would survive as president, but she was her old self. Maura walked to the door. ''I'll check on the children,'' she said.

''Robert, please contact General Overmeyer.'' Bender did as she ordered and handed her the phone. ''General Overmeyer,'' she said, ''I need you. Will you please reconsider your resignation?'' She listened to his reply, never flinching. ''Thank you for being so honest,'' she finally said. ''And I understand and appreciate your position. Who among the JCS do you recommend as your replacement?'' Again, she listened. ''Thank you, General, I will offer him the chairmanship this evening.'' She dropped the phone into its cradle. ''He said the Air Force was always the most screwed up of the lot and recommended General Charles.''

''Wild Wayne is going to love that,'' Bender allowed. ''But he will serve you well.''

''Robert, I can handle those idiots in the Cabinet Room, but what about the JCS?''

''First, make sure you all know exactly what's happening. That's where the DCI and Intelligence comes in. Then ask for their inputs and listen to what they have to say. Finally, make a decision and tell them to implement it.''

''Is it really that simple?'' she asked, not expecting an answer.

''No, ma'am, it's not. But you're not going for a consensus, and don't be afraid to kick a few of their egos around if one or two of them get difficult. They understand that sort of thing.''

She looked worried. ''Robert, how do I respond to this selective release?''

"You've got many options, but high on the list is dropping one of our own."

"I'm not sure I can do that. How many people will I kill?" A single tear streaked her cheek.

Robert Bender understood a little more. His president cried in the presence of death. Before, he had always chalked it up as an emotional response, which it was. But there was more. Madeline Turner hated death, wanton killing, and senseless destruction with every ounce of passion in her. She hurt from frustration when she could not stop it, and she cried from the pain of knowing that every death she might have prevented diminished her. "Madeline Turner may not be able to make the decision to cross that firebreak," he replied, "but President Turner may have to."

"Sacrifice a few for the good of many," she whispered.

Shaw hurried into the room, his face flushed. "Mizz President, the Joint Chiefs are. arriving."

"Good. Tell General Charles I wish to speak to him in private first. Then I will meet with all of them in the Situation Room." Shaw nodded and left.

"Madam President," Bender said, "I need to get with my staff and sort out the details."

"I need to speak to the JCS in private. I'll call you when I'm ready." She stopped him at the door. "Robert, please stop by the Cabinet Room and tell Senator Leland and his buddies that I'm involved here and they'll have to leave. You don't have to be polite."

"My pleasure, ma'am." He stood aside for Shaw and General Charles to enter. He glanced back into the Oval Office and saw Turner stand up. Shaw gave him a cold look and closed the door. Bender walked quickly to the Cabinet Room and entered without knocking. He studied the men, committing their faces to memory. "The president," he said, "is engaged in a national emergency. You are no longer welcome in her house, and she wants you to leave. May I suggest you do so immediately?" He spun around and left.

Turner led the procession out of the Oval Office. "Patrick," she said, "please check the Cabinet Room, and if anyone is still there, have the Secret Service escort them out.'' Charles followed her to the Situation Room as Shaw hurried to the Cabinet Room. Senator Leland was pacing the hall outside when he arrived. ''Where the hell have you been?'' Leland demanded.

''She's meeting with the JCS.''

''I thought you had isolated her.''

''Bender got to her,'' Shaw replied.

Leland's face clouded. ''I'll have that bastard court-martialed.''

''Not as long as she's the president, you won't,'' Shaw said. ''I've never seen her like this. She's got the bit in her teeth, and I'm not so sure I can control her.''

''That bitch can't ignore us.''

Shaw shook his head. ''I've got to find out what's going on in the Sit Room. You better leave.'' He scurried away, leaving Leland smoldering in the hall. ''You poor son of a bitch,'' he muttered to himself, not thinking of Leland at all.

The Marine guard on duty outside the Situation Room saw Turner the moment she descended the stairs and came to attention. She waited until the president was six feet from the door and snapped it open. ''Do not let anyone enter until I say so,'' Turner said. ''And that includes Mr. Shaw.''

''Yes, ma'am,'' the Marine replied, her face stone hard. She closed the door, stood in front, and allowed a tight smile before reverting to the standard-issue look required for duty at the White House.

Shaw scurried up. ''Get out of the way,'' he muttered.

''The president has ordered that no one enter until further notice.''

''That order doesn't apply to me,'' Shaw snapped.

''You'll have to speak to the president about that,'' the Marine replied.

''How can I when you won't let me inside?''

''President's orders, Mr. Shaw.'' He reached for the door handle. ''Touch me or the door,'' the guard whispered, ''and I'll put you down.'' She added a mental *got that, asshole.* and smiled at him.

Inside, Madeline Turner stood at the head of the table.

"Gentlemen," she began, "General Overmeyer recommended that General Charles replace him as the chairman and General Charles has accepted my offer. If any of you cannot continue to serve me or General Charles, please leave now." The four generals and one admiral exchanged glances and were quick to agree. "Good," she said. "If this is, as I suspect, a selective release to intimidate me, the Chinese will deeply regret their actions. So what exactly are we dealing with and what are my options?"

The discussion was a long one. Finally, she held up a hand, ending it. "I need more information before I decide how to respond. In the interim, prepare to execute our own selective release."

"What is the target?" Charles asked.

She didn't hesitate "The same atoll."

"Overmeyer is going to hate himself for missing this," the chief of Naval Operations muttered to the commandant of the Marine Corps.

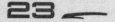

23

Okinawa, Japan

Major Bob Ryan cruised the flight line with Terrence Daguerre, the young captain from the Security Police. Daguerre was a tall, bony man who had a promising career as a professional quarterback until an injury ruined his passing arm. But he still played Saturday afternoon touch football, where he and Ryan had met. Ryan found Daguerre a fascinating subject for his study because he was a classic authoritarian personality.

"Our dosimeters never budged," Daguerre said.

"We were lucky," Ryan said. "The winds veered and the fallout never got here. The Disaster Response Teams have some very sensitive equipment, and they picked up a little radiation, about the same as you'd get from an X ray."

"That's why I've still got my men wearing full MOPP gear," Daguerre said. MOPP suits were the mission operative protection posture clothing worn to counter chemical, nuclear, and biological warfare. Although the men under his command were sweating in the restrictive gear, he had removed his gas mask and gloves while driving. He pulled up to a guard and rolled the car window down. "How's it going, airman?"

"Hot as hell," the guard replied, his voice muffled behind his gas mask.

"Keep drinking water," Daguerre told him.

"My canteen's dry, sir."

"That's why you got a radio," Daguerre replied. He rolled up the window, and they drove off. "Let's see if he's smart enough to use it," he grumbled.

"I understand you saw the fireball," Ryan said.

"Yes, sir," Daguerre replied. "Over there." He pointed to the southwest, over Habu Hill. "The horizon glowed, like a sunrise. But the sun was already up, and I knew immediately what it was." They drove slowly by the empty flow-through, the saw-tooth-roofed open bays where the F-15s parked during peacetime. It seemed like an age had passed since then. But Daguerre still had two guards patrolling the area, also in MOPP suits.

"The command post better sound the all clear, so we can get out of these suits or someone is going to collapse from heat prostration," Ryan said.

"Not until it's safe," Daguerre answered. "Besides, it's good training." Ahead of them, a Maintenance team was tugging an F-15E Strike Eagle down a taxiway. The Maintenance crews were wearing their normal BDUs and helmets. "Who's their supervisor?"

Ryan recognized Master Sergeant Ralph Contreraz, the Maintenance production supervisor who had thrown Lancey Coltrain off the bus. "That's him," he said, pointing out Contreraz.

Daguerre drove up to Contreraz and rolled his window down. "Sergeant," he called, "why are you moving around outside unprotected? The all clear hasn't been sounded. Get your people back into their MOPP suits."

"Sir, we're allowed to move outside for a limited time."

"I only want to hear a 'Yes, sir,' Sergeant."

"Yes, sir," Contreraz replied, standing back and saluting the captain.

They drove off. "Let's see what that insubordinate bastard does," Daguerre growled. They parked and watched the ground crew move the Strike Eagle to the fuel cells building. Guards inside the roped-off perimeter around the building lowered the rope barrier as the hangar doors cranked open. The F-15 was backed in, and the doors closed. The guards restrung the rope barrier and resumed their patrolling.

"What would happen if I crossed that rope?" Ryan asked.

"The guards had better shoot you," Daguerre said, "or I'll have their ass."

"Is that because they got nukes in there?" Ryan said in a low voice.

"That's need-to-know information," Daguerre said.

"What would you say," Ryan ventured, "if I told you that we exploded that nuclear weapon you saw and not the Chinese."

"I wouldn't be surprised."

"And if I said Martini was an egomaniac?"

"I can believe that," Daguerre answered.

"And if I said he's showing severe signs of instability and is breaking down under stress."

Daguerre looked straight ahead, never blinking. "You're the doctor."

Martini ordered the all clear at exactly noon on Monday, five hours after the explosion. Almost immediately, he felt the rush of fresh air as the outside air vents to the command post were thrown open, bypassing the heavy filters. His intercom buzzed at him and the light from Intelligence flashed. It was Townly. "The crews are here, sir," the Intelligence officer said.

Martini grunted one of his unintelligible answers and heaved his bulk out of his chair. "I need some exercise," he grumbled to no one in particular. He stretched, actually feeling pretty good. But he hated what he had to do. He stopped by the Control Cab and collared the chief of the command post. "I want you to brief the crews on the release procedures," he said. The lieutenant colonel was all self-importance, and he gathered up the messages, documents, and code books.

Townly met Martini and the lieutenant colonel at the door to the Intel vault and escorted them into the flight planning room. Two pilots and two weapon system officers were standing by the wall map. Martini gave them a crisp nod and sat down. "Please be seated," he said. He read the info sheet on the primary crew for the mission, Chet Woods and Ray Byers. Both were senior captains with over 500 hours of experience in the Strike Eagle. Martini remembered that Woods had been Laurie Bender's original pilot before he teamed her with Chris Leland. He was not familiar with Byers, but the name rang a bell. Then he made the connection. "Are you related to Sergeant Ray Byers?" Technical Sergeant Raymond A. Byers was both famous and infamous in the NCO ranks for being the only sergeant who qualified as being an ace, however unofficial.

"He's my father, sir."

Martini shook his head. "First, you are all volunteers, is that correct?" The four crewmembers told him they were. "Well, gentlemen, we have received an alert message to load and plan for a selective release mission."

They took the news without any sign of emotion. "Your job," Martini continued, "is to drop a small tactical nuke on the same target as the Chinese. Your aircraft has been prepped and moved to the fuel cells building, where a B-61 is being uploaded. Right now we are on a hold and awaiting a release. Hopefully, we'll never get a go. But if we do, I want you to smoke that target. Can you do that?" The four men all told him they could, and Chet Woods assured him the target would glow in the dark. "Very good," Martini said. He turned to the chief of the command post. "Colonel, they're all yours."

The lieutenant colonel in charge of the command post stood up and passed out the authenticators and code forms they needed. "Because we will not launch from an alert posture, you will be called to the command post and actually see the Quebec Zulu release message. This is critical because the permissive action link code is part of the message. Without the correct PAL code, you cannot unlock and arm the bomb."

"You mean to tell me," Chet Woods said, "that we've got bombs here and not the PAL codes?"

"That's the way the system works," Martini muttered. "Hell, they don't trust me with money, you don't think they're gonna trust me with a nuke?" The tension was broken, and the men laughed.

Byers asked why they were loading the bomb in the

fuel cells building, a soft shelter. "We got both the Chinese and the Japanese looking at the munitions storage area and the hardened shelters," Martini replied. "As far as they know, there are no nukes on the island, and the jet is in the fuel cells building for maintenance. Hopefully, we can surprise the shit out of both of 'em."

"Sir," Byers answered, "you're surprising the shit out of me."

"Are you up to this?" Martini asked.

"Sir, I wouldn't miss this for anything."

Martini had the men he was looking for.

Washington, D.C.

Ben pinned the back of Liz Gordon's blue blazer to accentuate her waistline before she sat down in the circle of leather chairs in the TV studio. She crossed her legs for maximum effect and adjusted the microphone on her lapel. She was ready for the round-table discussion. Two other political reporters joined her. At exactly 6:56 A.M., Paul Ferguson, CNC-TV's distinguished anchor, famed for his pompous-assed gravitas, stepped out of his dressing room, his makeup perfect, and joined them. At exactly seven o'clock, the director cued him to begin.

"Good morning, America. It is seven o'clock Monday morning and I am with three of my associates to investigate the nuclear detonation that occurred twelve hours ago in the East China Sea." He introduced the other three lesser lights with him in the studio, ending with Liz. "But first, hear this." They broke for three minutes of commercials.

After the commercials, Liz endured the next seven minutes listening to the three men pontificate on the crisis. It was obvious that Paul was winging it and the other two weren't much better. Twice, she tried to interject a few facts into the discussion, but Paul cut her off. Finally, she started talking and forced them into silence. "Paul, we are operating in the dark at this time. We only know a small nuclear device was detonated in the East China Sea and that a number of congressional leaders and high-ranking administration officials were at the White House before the explosion. Those are the facts, and everything else is idle speculation.''

''Are you suggesting that President Turner was expecting a nuclear attack?'' Paul asked.

''No, Fergy,'' she replied, using the nickname Paul hated, ''I'm not. And neither would anyone else in their right mind. Obviously, she was monitoring the crisis and talking to Congress.''

Paul Ferguson truly believed his words were transmitted to him over an ecclesiastical hot line from heaven. For Liz to even imply his questions ranked below the Ten Commandments was punishable by instant lightning strike. ''So what is the administration doing?'' he said, never losing his famed on-screen presence.

''I can't be sure,'' Liz answered, ''but I imagine they are examining their options, preparing a variety of responses, and opening lines of communication. But at this time, the best thing we can do for the American public is to stick to the facts and not speculate.''

The director called for a commercial break. ''You're not helping, Liz,'' he said when they were off camera.

''And you clowns haven't got a clue,'' she said. ''This is pure bullshit.''

''Liz,'' Ben called from behind the cameras, ''the White House has announced a press conference for eight o'clock.''

She stood up and unclipped her microphone. ''If you're going to group speculate''—she made it sound like a perversion—''do it after the press conference.''

The Oval Office was organized chaos as Maura touched up Turner's makeup. Her security advisors were clustered on the two couches and Shaw stood beside the door, funneling messages and other people in. ''Mizz President,'' Shaw said, ''don't talk to the media. Let Harry handle the press conference.''

''That would be a mistake,'' Turner replied. ''I'll keep it short and simple.''

''We haven't prepped you,'' Shaw protested. A runner

from the communications room handed him a message. Shaw glanced at it and handed it to the secretary of state.

"It's from Chairman Zoulin," Francis said. "He wants to resume the Paris talks immediately."

Turner stood up, and Maura adjusted a scarf around her neck. "I should think so. Robert, how soon can you and Mazie be in Paris?"

"Late this evening, Paris time," Bender replied. "We'll have to leave immediately."

"Very good," Turner replied. "Francis, wire Zoulin that Robert is on his way. Also, send the Chinese a strongly worded protest through normal channels. I want them in a crossruff. No matter what they do, they meet strength. We'll talk privately, but publicly, we're outraged. How do I reinforce that message?"

"You can declare a DEFCON ONE for the Far East," Charles replied.

Francis paled. "That's too strong a message. Call in the Japanese ambassador and issue a joint public announcement of mutual support."

"Do all of it," Turner said.

Shaw interrupted. "Mizz President, what are you going to do about Senator Leland?"

Turner was walking to the door. "Nothing." She stopped and looked at Charles. "When can you execute a selective release?"

"We have a tactical nuclear weapon ready at Kadena. The release codes are in the football."

Turner paled and closed her eyes. She took three quick breaths and straightened up. "I want no misunderstanding on this," she said. "I want a peaceful solution. I do not want to respond in kind. But this aggression must stop." She led the procession out the door.

Bender gathered up his papers to leave while Maura straightened Turner's desk. "I've never seen her like this," he said.

"It happens when she gets pushed too far," Maura replied. "Something snaps inside." She sat down beside him. "She can be very strong willed, but she hides it."

"Why?"

"Because I raised her that way," Maura said. "She was such a pretty little girl, and I wanted her to be nice."

Peter Whiteside, the dean of the press corps, was sitting in his normal seat in the small room used for press conferences. He automatically stood when Turner entered and was immediately struck by how calm and composed she looked. "Please be seated," Turner said as she stood beside the podium. She started by announcing General Charles as the acting chairman of the Joint Chiefs of Staff before turning to the nuclear explosion. "We are now confident the Chinese detonated a fifty-kiloton weapon at exactly 2400 hours Greenwich Mean Time, Sunday night. The explosion occurred over an atoll 120 nautical miles southwest of Okinawa in the East China Sea. We have reconnaissance aircraft on scene along with other national resources. The purpose of the detonation was to intimidate the Japanese into accepting a Chinese-dictated settlement in their dispute.

"We are protesting to the Chinese in the strongest possible terms. Further, our armed forces are at full alert and prepared to respond to any threat or attack."

"Will the Chinese launch missiles at us?" a reporter yelled.

The damn broke, and questions flooded over her. She raised her hand, bringing silence to the room. "I have time to answer only a few questions. To answer your question first, the Chinese do not have the capability to strike the United States."

She recognized another reporter. "Madam President, was the atoll uninhabited?"

Turner paused as an empty feeling claimed her. "There were a few Okinawan fishermen shacks on the island, and they were reported occupied at the time. We don't know the exact number." She worked around the room, allowing only one question from each reporter before moving on. Finally, she pointed at Peter Whiteside, giving him the final question.

"Madam President, did you have any warning that the Chinese were going to detonate a nuclear weapon?"

Turner fixed the reporter with a hard look. "None whatsoever. Thank you." She walked off the stage.

"Did you even consider the possibility?" Whiteside yelled at her back. There was no answer, and the reporters clamored to their feet.

Liz Gordon hurried outside and waited for Ben to join her with his Betacam. "A confident and forceful Maddy Turner left no doubt who was in charge," she said.

Near her, Peter Whiteside was talking into his microphone. "A badly shaken president fled from the hard questioning of the White House press corps this morning. Her lack of candor in answering many questions only reinforces the belief that a cover-up is in progress."

Nancy was waiting inside Base Operations at Andrews Air Force Base with a suitcase and a fresh change of clothes when the White House staff car arrived. Bender jumped out and hurried up to her. "I was worried you didn't get the message," he said. "I've got to fly to Paris."

"You need a valet," she told him. "I was at the morgue and just happened to check my messages when I came out."

Bender's head jerked around. "Morgue?"

"They found Shalandra." Nancy's voice was flat, without emotion. "Crushed skull. No suspects so far." He reached out and touched her cheek but she drew back. "There was nothing I could do to save her. Or anyone. It doesn't matter now."

A sergeant rushed up and grabbed his bag. "General, Mrs. Hazelton has arrived. The engines are running, and we've got clearance to take off."

"I'm coming," Bender said as Hazelton stood by the door waiting for him. He turned to Nancy. "It does matter," he said.

"You best go," she said. She was moving away from him.

"Nancy, I—" He couldn't bring himself to say how much he loved her and that he needed her more now than ever before. But he couldn't, not in public. "I'm very sorry about Shalandra," he managed.

"Really?" she replied, walking away.

*   *   *

Shaw sat at the end of the table in the Situation Room and doodled on his notepad, half listening to the conversation between Turner and her advisors. Reluctantly, he admitted that Charles was a good choice to replace Overmeyer, and they were communicating well. Or was it because she was willing to listen to him? "Why can't we use a cruise missile or a submarine-launched missile for our sel rel?" Turner asked.

"We can," Charles answered. "But not if you want to use a low-yield weapon. Most of our tactical nukes are out of the inventory, and we have a few selectable weapons with low yields, like the B-61, left. And it is air delivered."

"I want the lowest yield possible," she said. "That's of paramount importance."

"Then the B-61 is the only weapon we've got to do the job."

"Will the pilots be safe?"

"Probably," Charles answered. "I have the probabilities if you care to see them."

She shook her head. "I only need to know if you can do it."

"I can't give you an absolute assurance, but we have a high degree of confidence of putting a bomb on target."

The secure phone rang, and Shaw answered. It was Barnett Francis calling from the State Department. Shaw put him on the speaker. "The Chinese ambassador left a few moments ago," Francis said. "The meeting was not very productive, and they've rejected our protest."

"Are they posturing for public consumption or is this their real position?" Turner asked.

"I can't say at this time," Francis replied.

"They're stalling," Charles muttered.

"Keep the channels open," Turner told Francis, breaking the connection. She turned to her advisors. "I agree with General Charles. They're stalling to see how public opinion swings. But I'm not going to give them much time. I'm going to draft a personal letter to Zoulin and have Robert hand it to the Chinese in Paris. General Charles, when can the Air Force get it to him?"

Charles checked his watch. "If you can have it to us in two hours, it will be waiting for him when he wakes up."

"You'll have it inside an hour," she replied. "Well, there's not too much more we can do right now, so I want you all to resume your normal routines for the evening. Let the Chinese think we're not burning any midnight oil over this."

"We'll continue to issue hourly notices at the Pentagon," Charles said.

"Keep telling the media the military is at full alert," Turner said. "Reassure them with a few details so they'll know we are not worried." She stood up. The meeting was at an end. "We'll reconvene first thing tomorrow morning."

Shaw was the last to leave and went upstairs to his office. He spent an hour clearing his desk before calling for his limousine to take him home. Reluctantly, he admitted to himself that Maddy's decision to not act in haste was sound. But it had been over twenty-four hours, and the media was either howling for blood or predicting instant nuclear destruction. How much longer did they have?

He rode in silence, and the streets were eerily deserted as if everyone was seeking refuge from an approaching storm. Even the normal hustle in Watergate's parking garage was gone, and he rode the elevator alone. He unlocked the door to his condominium and caught the aroma of goulash cooking. Jessica was there.

"You're early," she said from the kitchen.

Shaw sighed. "What does Leland want now?"

"He wants to know what's going on."

"Maddy's handling the fuckin' crisis is what the fuck is going on."

"He's very upset. You assured him that it was going to blow up in her face."

"As I recall, it did."

"But not to our advantage," Jessica replied. "The senator is worried that unless we act now, we've lost a golden opportunity."

"Tell him to do what you always do in a situation like this."

"Which is?" she asked.

"When you're losing, leak."

24

Paris, France

Bender let the waiter take his half-eaten breakfast away and reached for his coffee cup. As usual, the service and food in the staff dining room of the American embassy was outstanding, and he savored the rich coffee. Mazie Hazelton came through the door and walked briskly up to his table. Jet lag was taking its toll on the petite and graceful woman, but she looked much better after a few hours rest. "A letter from the White House just arrived," she told him. "You're to deliver it personally to the Chinese as soon as possible." He set his cup down and followed her to their temporary office.

"It's eight-thirty now. How soon can you set up a meeting?"

"That's a problem," she admitted. "I've called the chateau but so far I'm only talking to the hired help and can't set up a meeting." She gave him a worried look. "I don't think they've got a negotiator here."

"What's going on?" he asked. "They were the ones who wanted to talk."

"For some reason," she replied, "the Chinese are stalling. They may be doing one of their periodic roundabouts in Beijing or they may be stalling to increase the pressure."

"They think Maddy will cave in, don't they?" *Stop calling the president Maddy,* he told himself.

"Probably," Mazie answered.

"I'll call the White House and tell them what's going on. I don't need to hang around Paris when I've—" He stopped in mid sentence, cutting his words off. He liked and trusted Mazie but could never discuss his personal problems with her. How could he admit to anyone that he and his wife were pulling apart? That he had to get back before it was too late and close the gap that had been growing between them ever since Laurie's death?

"I saw you speaking to your wife at Andrews," she said. Her eyes and words were full of concern.

She knows, he thought. *Why can women sense this sort of thing when men haven't got a clue? Or maybe it's me who hasn't got a clue.* "It's almost three in the morning in Washington," he told her. "Let's see who's awake at the White House."

Washington, D.C.

Jessica answered the phone beside the bed on the second ring and handed the receiver to Shaw. She rolled up against him as he listened and rubbed her breasts against his back. "No, don't wake her," Shaw said. "It can wait a few hours. Call her security advisors and have them in the Oval Office, no, make that the Situation Room, at six-thirty this morning. Make sure the DCI and secretary of state are there." He punched at the off button and dropped the phone on the floor. "Damn," he muttered, "I gotta go."

"So soon?" she asked, stroking his penis. No response.

"Sorry, Jess, but the Chinese are ruining my love life."

"Are you sure it's the Chinese?"

He ignored her question and rolled out of bed. "Tell Leland to get in bed with a reporter and play Deep Throat." He scooped up the phone and tossed it at her. "Why don't you wake him up?"

"It can wait," she told him. "I'll run your shower." She stood behind him and rubbed his shoulders. "It's going to be OK, don't worry." She kissed his back and walked into the bathroom. Suddenly, she turned and ran back to him, throwing her arms around his neck. She held onto him and buried her face against his neck, hoping he didn't see her tears.

"Now what brought all this on, child?"

The men watched as Turner paced the Situation Room. She reached the far end by the TV monitors and retraced her steps. "What's the Japanese response so far?" she asked.

"Confused," Barnett Francis answered. "But there is a growing war party and a demand for retaliation."

"Have the Chinese changed their military posture?" she asked.

"No, ma'am," the DCI answered. "No change on either side."

"Then why are the Chinese stalling?"

Secretary Francis answered. "They're betting the longer we go without responding with a show of force, the less likely one becomes." He took a deep breath and plunged ahead. "They may think you'll break and cave in if they can keep the pressure on long enough."

"Do they, now?" she replied. "I'm going to announce a complete freeze of all Chinese financial assets in the States and start discussions with our allies for an embargo."

"That should get their attention," Shaw said.

General Charles stared at his hands. "It may not be enough. A show of force may be the only thing that will convince them to back off."

Shaw shook his head. "I think you should pursue the Paris talks first."

"With whom?" Francis asked.

Turner sat down and penciled times on the notepad in front of her. "It's been thirty-six hours since the sel rel. How much more time do I have?" She listened as the men debated her question. Slowly, a consensus emerged that she would have to act very soon or she would lose all hope of taking the initiative. "What is the flying time from Paris to Beijing?" she asked.

"Approximately thirteen hours," Charles replied, "if

they can overfly Russia. They'll have to refuel somewhere, and that will add another hour or two.''

"Wire new instructions to Robert in Paris. I want him to fly to Beijing and personally deliver my letter to Lu Zoulin. He is to stress that this is the last chance for a return to normal relations. If he does not get a reply within six hours, he is to leave China immediately.''

Barnett Francis paled. ''Madam President, are you establishing a deadline?''

"I'm willing to give them another twenty-four hours.''

Charles de Gaulle Airport, France

The embassy staff car drove up to the waiting C-137, the specially modified Boeing 707 that had served as one of the original *Air Force One* aircraft. The Stratoliner was over forty years old but still gleamed in the sun like a new plane freshly delivered from the factory. Bender and Mazie got out as his suitcase was carried up the boarding stairs by the steward. "I still think I should go with you," Mazie said. "You'll need an interpreter.''

"The embassy can provide me with an interpreter," he told her. The look on her face said that was a poor excuse. "Mazie, we're only taking a basic crew of four because this may be a wasted trip. We haven't got diplomatic status or even clearance to enter Chinese airspace yet. I want you to stay here and try to open a channel with the Chinese. Hopefully, you can get us permission to land in China by the time we refuel in Novosibirsk. Then get back to Washington.''

She handed him his briefcase. "I don't trust Lu Zoulin, and Wang Mocun hates you. Be careful.''

He gave her his best grin. "I will." The worry on her face stopped him. "You really are concerned." She only looked at him. "Mazie, if you talk to my wife, tell her that I—'' He shook his head, not able to say what he felt. He turned and walked quickly up the stairs.

"That you need her," Mazie said, giving sound to the words he could not say. But he didn't hear her over the roar of a starting engine.

Washington, D.C.

Satisfaction took on a new meaning for Paul Ferguson as he sat down with Liz Gordon in CNC-TV's news studio. He had the ammunition, thanks to a leak from one of Leland's staff, to even the score with Gordon and once again demonstrate that he was the premier political commentator on the American scene, a power in his own right not to be trifled with. He clipped on his microphone and sat on his coattail, pulling out any wrinkles in his coat. He gave Liz the condescending look he reserved for newspaper reporters as he took his cue from the director. "Good afternoon, America. Elizabeth Gordon is back with me in the studio. Liz, is there any truth to the rumors flowing from Capitol Hill that many members of Congress are demanding Maddy Turner's impeachment?"

"Paul, as you know, we've been hearing these rumors for weeks as Congress splits along partisan lines. Knowledgeable insiders are saying this is part of Senator Leland's on-going feud with the president. Tax reform is at the heart of the issue because too many of Leland's supporters, all who have made large contributions to his election campaigns, will pay substantial tax penalties for accepting government subsidies."

Paul dropped his bombshell. "Then these rumors for impeachment have nothing to do with the fact that the president knew the nuclear attack was coming and did nothing to prevent it?"

"Paul, according to every responsible source I have talked to, this so-called fact you alluded to is a vicious rumor started to discredit the president." She upped the ante with a bigger bomb of her own. "What is unusual in this case is that the source of these rumors has been identified as a staff member working for Senator John Leland." She gave a silent thanks to Jeff Bissell.

Paul was furious. Gordon was taking the story away from him again, giving it her own twist. "I find it hard to believe that Senator Leland," he said, "who is our country's most respected elder statesmen, would be party to a deliberate lie."

Liz arched an eyebrow at him, questioning Paul's sanity.

It was a simple gesture that spoke more than words and ruined his credibility. And because they were live, it could not be edited out. "Right now, Paul, it's safe to say that partisan party politics is more important than the truth."

Paul hid his anger and turned toward the camera. "And now to other news."

The director motioned that they were clear. "Great reporting, Liz. Thanks for coming in." Everyone in the studio knew she would never share the same stage with Paul Ferguson again.

Shahe Air Base, China

The silver and blue C-137 taxied slowly past the long line of jet fighters parked near the end of the runway at the PLA air base sixty miles north of Beijing. Captain Rodney Davis, the copilot, raised his video camera to film the old jets. "Don't," Bender said. He pointed to the small truck they were following. "Someone in the follow-me is probably watching you."

"I've never seen a MiG-19 before," Davis said.

"The Chinese call them J6s," Bender explained. "They've still got over 3,000 of them." He counted thirty-seven of the jets as they taxied past. All looked in poor shape, in need of washing and paint. But they were all operational.

"The base seems very quiet," Tech Sergeant Otis Jenkins, the African-American flight engineer, said.

"It's lunchtime," Bender explained.

The pilot, Major Bill Courtland, laughed. "Very civilized." He hit the intercom button and called the steward. "Speaking of lunch, Larry, what'cha got?"

Master Sergeant Larry Burke's voice boomed over their headsets. "Lobster Newberg."

The follow-me truck slowed and stopped. A woman wearing a sloppy uniform jacket over a frilly blouse got out and guided them into a parking spot. She crossed her wrists above her head and made a cutting motion across her throat. Bill Courtland cut the engines as a boarding ramp was pushed up against the front entry hatch and a black staff car from the American embassy drove up. "I bet they've never seen an American plane here before," Courtland said.

"Oh, I imagine they have," Bender said, recalling how his predecessor and the former secretary of state had landed at the same base to sell out Taiwan. "Can we make it to Seoul in South Korea without refueling?"

Otis Jenkins, the flight engineer, checked the fuel gauges. "How far?"

"Eighty minutes flying time," the copilot, Rod Davis, answered.

"No sweat," Jenkins answered.

"Good," Bender replied. "File a clearance and be ready to take off the moment I get back."

The steward, Larry Burke, helped Bender on with his overcoat and handed him his scarf and gloves. Satisfied that his passenger was ready to meet the cold, he opened the hatch. An American was waiting at the base of the stairs. It was Mazie's husband, Wentworth Hazelton. "General Bender, glad to see you again." They shook hands, and he escorted Bender to the waiting staff car. "It's about an hour's drive to Beijing. We've got an escort and Chairman Lu is waiting for you."

"Mazie didn't tell me you were here," Bender said, recalling the time they had met at the State Department.

"We try to keep our professional lives separate from our private life," he answered.

"So you're one of the pro-Chinese faction," Bender said as they drove into Beijing.

"And Mazie is pro-Japanese," Wentworth said.

"That must make for some lively discussions at home."

Wentworth smiled. "It's the peace negotiations that make it worthwhile. I'll be your translator at the meeting with Chairman Lu. His English is perfect, but he pretends he doesn't speak a word." Wentworth opened his brief-case. "I need to update you on the current political status. There's a major power struggle going on between the hawks and the doves."

"Why haven't I heard about this before?" Bender demanded.

"It caught us totally off guard," Wentworth replied.

"Obviously, it has been brewing for some time, but it all surfaced in the last twelve hours. Because you'll be received by Lu Zoulin, we think he's currently on top. That's good, because we think he's one of the doves."

"This is really encouraging," Bender muttered. "You can't tell the players without a program. Who in the hell decided to go after Japan in the first place?"

"Lu Zoulin. But because of what's happening now, we suspect he did it to appease the hawks and relieve some of the domestic pressure he's been under. But apparently, the reaction of our forces on Okinawa surprised him. He may still be misjudging our intentions."

"That's why the president sent me here," Bender said.

Wentworth handed Bender a thin document. "Here's our current appreciation of the situation." They rode in silence as Bender read the latest analysis. "We're here," Wentworth said as the car pulled up to a large, nondescript building in the heart of Beijing.

An incredibly beautiful woman was waiting for them on the steps. She escorted them to a waiting room on the third floor where Hazelton introduced Bender. They chatted amiably in Mandarin for a few moments and then switched to English to include Bender. Finally, she led them into a large room. Wentworth stiffened but said nothing. Wang Mocun, the negotiator from Paris, was sitting next to Lu Zoulin.

Lu Zoulin spoke first, welcoming Bender. Wentworth murmured a translation, and Bender was sure he heard a conciliatory tone in Lu's voice. He replied with the customary courtesies and then handed the letter over. "President Turner is worried that peace is rapidly slipping away and may be forever lost if we don't reach a mutually agreeable solution in the very near future," he said. It was diplospeak for "time is running out and you had better get your act together or else."

Wang spoke in English without waiting for a translation. "Has Mrs. Turner set a deadline?"

Wentworth's face turned deathly white. They had jumped to hardball negotiations and bypassed the required niceties. "She has instructed me to deliver the letter and answer any questions you may have," Bender replied. "I am to wait until six this evening. Then I must return to Washington with or without a reply.''

"We will read the letter," Lu Zoulin said. The meeting was over, and their guide escorted them to a waiting room.

A whispered, very undiplomatic "Oh, shit" escaped from Wentworth when they were alone. "What's Wang doing here? He's the leader of the hawks."

I've got thirty minutes, Bender thought. He sipped at his tea and tried to relax in the low, heavy overstuffed chair the Chinese preferred. The waiting room was starkly functional, and books were stacked on shelves around the walls. A cold wind beat at the windows, but the room was warm and stuffy. He checked his watch again: Twenty-nine minutes left. Wentworth seemed totally at ease and unconcerned with the passage of time. "How much longer before we receive a reply?" Bender asked.

"I don't know what was in the letter," the younger man replied. "I imagine Lu and Wang are trying to arrive at a consensus."

The door opened, and the woman entered. "Please accept my apologies for the delay," she said. "You will have a reply to your president's letter in an hour."

Before Bender could answer, Wentworth spoke. "As you know, General Bender has been instructed by his president to return immediately with or without a reply. He cannot wait any longer."

"Surely an hour," she coaxed, "cannot be too long to wait on a matter of such importance. Perhaps you would like an early dinner?"

"I can wait until six o'clock," Bender said, "then I must leave." She bestowed a dazzling smile on them and left. "A very impressive and cool lady," Bender muttered.

"She's bait," Wentworth said.

"Not interested," Bender replied.

"Not for you, for me. No doubt, we'll meet again under very intimate circumstances."

They fell silent, and the minutes dragged. Finally, Bender stood to leave. He was returning empty-handed. Again, the door opened, and the woman appeared. This time she did not smile as she led them back to the office.

She turned and left, shutting the door behind her. Wang was seated alone behind the big desk. "Your Mrs. Turner is very naive," he said in English. "In her letter she urges a return to the status quo yet offers nothing in return."

"Except peace," Bender replied.

Wang ignored him. "We were expecting an accommodation similar to our agreement with President Roberts for the peaceful reversion of Taiwan. I am afraid you are here under false pretenses, General Bender, and have wasted our time."

Bender's face turned to granite. "Thank you for your hospitality. I will relay your observations to President Turner." Wang gave him a stony look and picked up a report on his desk. The exchange was over, and the woman met them at the door to take them to their waiting car.

Once they were safely inside and away from the building, Wentworth felt free to talk. "No one treats a special emissary from the president of the United States like that. I've got to report this to the ambassador, and you've got to get out of China immediately." He knocked on the window to the driver and told him to stop at the embassy. Just before he got out of the car, he sanitized Bender's briefcase, only leaving his passport. "I wish you had diplomatic status," he said. "I'm absolutely serious about getting out of China. Don't delay."

"What's going on?" Bender asked as Hazelton got out.

"A transfer of power, Chinese style," Wentworth answered. "Not even a Machiavelli or a Kissinger can predict what's going to happen next. Go." He ran past the Marine guard and into the embassy.

The driver made good time on the trip back to Shahe Air Base and drove directly up to the waiting C-137. Bender ran up the steps, and Larry Burke, the steward, closed the hatch. "You're late," Burke said. "We were getting worried."

Bender went forward to speak to the pilots as the engines came on line. Rod Davis, the copilot, was talking on the radios and getting answers in Chinese. "They were speaking English," he said.

"Son of a bitch!" Bill Courtland, the pilot, shouted. Outside, two trucks had stopped in front of the C-137 and blocked it from moving. A squad of soldiers was fanning out. "I don't think we're going to get clearance to taxi," Courtland muttered. He punched a number into the high-frequency radio to send a distress message. A loud, raw, rasping squeal flooded his headset, and he hit the off switch. "They're jamming the shit out of us. Shut 'em down," he told the flight engineer, Otis Jenkins.

Washington, D.C.

Madeline Turner leaned her head back into her chair and took a deep breath. The Oval Office vibrated with tension as her advisors sat transfixed, afraid to speak. The small carriage clock on her desk read exactly nine o'clock. She turned and looked out the window. It was an usually bright and clear morning. Wednesday, February 13, she thought. How will the historians record this date? What will they say fifty years from now? She felt old and very weary. "So they thought I had sent General Bender to sell out Okinawa."

Barnett Francis kept looking at the message from the embassy in Beijing hoping to find some good news. But there was none. "Wang Mocun did make specific reference to the reversion of Taiwan."

"I see," she said. "And there is no word on General Bender?"

"He was last reported on his way to the air base to board his plane," Francis replied. "He should be airborne by now."

"Have the Chinese changed their posture?" she asked.

"We are monitoring a sudden increase in communications traffic," the DCI answered. "They're using a new type of code, and it may take a few days, maybe a week, to break it."

"Madam President," General Charles said, "the fact that they are using a new code is a sign they are gearing up for more action."

"Can you be absolutely sure of that?" she asked, still looking out the window.

"No, ma'am," he answered.

"I see." She closed her eyes. "The atoll, where they dropped their bomb, I assume no one survived and it is uninhabited."

"As far as we know, yes. We are collecting all the data we can and may put a survey team ashore. It all depends on the level of radioactivity."

She made her decision and spun around to face them. "General Charles, the officer with the football?"

"He's in the outer office," Charles replied.

"Please ask him to come in."

Okinawa, Japan

The summons to the command post came just before midnight and woke Major Bob Ryan from a sound sleep. He dressed hurriedly and drove as fast as he could down the darkened streets. A sergeant was waiting for him when he came through the heavy blast doors and escorted him into the Intelligence vault where the battle staff was waiting. Martini entered a few minutes later and waved them all to seats. "Gentlemen," he began, "we have received a valid emergency action message ordering a selective release on the same atoll the Chinese nuked sixty-five hours ago."

"It's about time," the Operations Group commander growled.

Martini ignored him. "The primary and backup crews will be here in a few minutes to validate the Quebec Zulu release message and brief the mission. Keep the questions to a minimum." He turned to Ryan. "I want you to observe them for any signs of instability that might disqualify them from flying the mission." He looked around the room. "Okay, bring them in." The commander of the Forty-fourth Fighter Squadron opened the door and ushered the four captains into the vault.

Ryan listened in stunned horror as the briefing played out with the lockstep of an execution. He refused to believe he was in the room with sane, rational human beings, and nothing in Martini's voice or demeanor indicated he was about to take the world a step closer to a nuclear holocaust. Ryan focused on the primary pilot and weapons system officer who would fly the mission. Maybe, just maybe, they couldn't do it. Maybe he could declare one of them unfit and delay the mission from happening until cooler, more rational heads had a chance to reevaluate the situation. He studied Chet Woods, the pilot, looking for a telltale tick or sign of nervousness. Nothing. The captain was as solid as a rock and this was just another mission. Ray Byers, the WSO, was worse. He was treating it as an intellectual exercise on a par with a video game.

Maybe that was it, Ryan thought. He could claim Byers was exhibiting disassociative behavior and unfit to fly the mission. He glanced at the backup crew standing against the back wall and knew it was hopeless. Both men were eager to get the chance and prove they could fly the mission. *What kind of men are these?* he wondered.

Martini stood up. "Gentlemen, good luck." The briefing was over, and the vault rapidly emptied.

That took less than ten minutes, Ryan thought. Ten minutes to put the world on the road to total war. Pete Townly, the chief of Intelligence, wandered over to him.

"Nothing for us to do here," he said. "Why don't we go watch it from Habu Hill?"

"Will we be able to see the detonation from there?"

"At night?" Townly answered. "Oh, yeah."

The big doors of the fuel cells building rolled back, and a sirenlike wail rolled out of the darkened building as Woods pulled the jet fuel starter handle and the F-15E Strike Eagle's right engine came to life. Almost immediately, the left engine spun up. Outside, a guard dropped the rope barrier and the aircraft taxied out, a winged beast of prey free of its cage. A full complement of air-to-air missiles hung from under the wings and along the fuselage. A single bomb hung from the centerline. It was a sleek, shimmering dart, twelve feet long and weighing just over 700 pounds. The control dials inside the bomb had been set to the lowest yield, 10 kilotons, the equivalent of 10,000 tons of TNT, half the size of the first atomic bomb dropped on Hiroshima. By thermonuclear standards, it was a microcosm among giants.

The bright moonlight illuminated the taxipath and the pilot, Chet Woods, taxied quickly for runway 22 left. He turned onto the active and never slowed. He firewalled the throttles, and the dark gray raptor lifted into the clear night sky, its afterburners torching the night. The two men standing at the guardrail on Habu Hill looked straight ahead as the jet passed by at eye level, seventy-five feet off the deck. It held the runway heading as it disappeared to the southwest. ''That's as high as they'll get,'' Pete Townly said. Then he added, ''Until they toss the bomb.''

Chet Woods engaged the autopilot and rooted the airspeed on 480 knots as they raced for the target, 120 nautical miles from Kadena. In the backseat, Ray Byers kept glancing at the four video display scopes in front of him as he ran his checklist. He asked the pilot for verification of the permissive action link code. Chet's numbers agreed with his, and he dialed them into the PAL control box on the right-hand console. The light cycled from red to orange telling him the bomb was unlocked and could be armed.

Automatically, he checked the right-hand video scope where the radar warning and threat display was called up. The tactical electronic warfare system's highly sensitive antenna were only picking up the sweep of a friendly radar, and the threat audio was quiet. His hand hovered over the nuclear arming wafer switch next to the PAL control box. ''Nuclear consent switch,'' he said.

In the front cockpit, Woods broke the wire seal on the guarded switch, flipped the cover up, and moved the toggle switch to the up position. ''On,'' he replied, providing the two-man control that allowed the bomb to arm. Byers rotated the wafer switch to AIR for an airburst. He waited for the orange light to cycle to green. Nothing happened. He counted to ten and let out his breath when the light blinked to green. The bomb was armed.

''That took longer than I thought,'' he muttered. He hit the emission limit switch and the APG-70 radar came to life, sweeping the area in a mapping mode to update their position. The target was on the nose at sixty-five miles. ''Take it down,'' he said. Woods lowered the clearance limit on their terrain following radar to fifty feet, and the jet descended twenty-five feet. "Looks like a milk run," the WSO said. He hit the EMIS limit switch, and the powerful radar returned to standby. "Push it up, now." Woods inched the throttles forward and the Strike Eagle accelerated to 540 knots. Two minutes later, Byers hit the EMIS limit switch, and the radar came to life. Byers drove the radar crosshairs over the target and locked it up. The attack display in the pilot's HUD came alive, and they were in the primary delivery mode. But Byers was ready to cycle through three backup modes if anything went wrong.

Byers called the countdown. "Ready, ready, now!" The Strike Eagle was still on autopilot, and it pitched smoothly up into a sixty-degree climb. The weapons release computer had been programmed with the bomb's ballistics and was processing a wealth of information coming from the radar and inertial navigation system. At the precise moment when everything matched—airspeed, distance from the target, climb angle, speed, g loading, and altitude— the bomb separated cleanly from the F-15 and arced high into the air. "Bomb gone!" Byers yelled.

Woods flicked off the autopilot and took control for the escape maneuver. He jammed the throttles full forward and rolled the F-15 as he reversed course and slammed the nose toward the ocean, 2,000 feet below them. He leveled off at 400 feet and kept the throttles in full after-burner as they accelerated to Mach 1.6 and ran from the target. "She won't go any faster," he said. He engaged the autopilot, and both men lowered their gold visors that turned opaque in the flash of a nuclear explosion to save their eyesight.

The bomb arced over the top of its trajectory and headed down, straight for the small island that had been desig-nated as ground zero. A parachute twenty-four feet in di-ameter deployed out of the tail assembly as the bomb's radar came on, measuring the exact altitude above the target. At the precise altitude, the bomb would detonate for an air burst, and the fireball would never touch the surface.

Ray Byers counted down the seconds to detonation. "Ready, ready, ready—" Around them, stars were still visible in the night sky. In a few seconds, they would be blotted out by the incandescent light of a man-made sun. The men waited.

25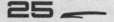

Okinawa, Japan

The two men stood in the dark on top of Habu Hill. Townly looked nervously to the southwest and then at his watch. "It was only fifteen minutes flying time," he muttered. "I guess we can't see it after all."

Ryan agreed with him. "A hundred and twenty miles is pretty far."

"They could've been shot down," Townly replied. He gestured aimlessly to the southwest.

"Let's go," Ryan said.

Townly checked his watch again. It was 1:35 A.M., five minutes past the time of detonation. "They might have taken battle damage. Let's wait a few minutes to see if they make it back." Each pulled into his own thoughts as the minutes passed. Townly heard the sound first, and his head came up. A jet was approaching from the southwest. The runway lights flicked on as both men strained to see into the night. A bright landing light pierced the night as a lone jet approached at 1,500 feet for an overhead recovery to land on 5 right. "That's them," Townly said, the tension broken. "Now we go." They got in the car and drove to the command post for the mission debriefing as the fighter circled to land.

Martini's fingers tapped the table in the Battle Cab as Woods and Byers debriefed the mission. When they were

396

done, his lips were compressed into a tight line. "Get an Op Rep III message on the wires," he told the lieutenant colonel in charge of the command post. "Major Ryan, please take them to the Med Center and take blood and urine samples. Then give them a quick physical." He held his hand up stopping any protests. "I don't expect to find anything, but we are going to be Monday morning quarterbacked to death on this one. Go. Get back here ASAP for a full deposition." The Op Rep III, or postmission operations report, was going to stir every headquarters in his chain of command.

"Impound the jet," he told the Operations Group commander. "Then get Master Sergeant Ralph Contreraz and his crew to go over it with a fine-tooth comb. Check every system, every rivet. If anything is wrong with that bird, I want to know." He paused and considered his next order. "Get the backup crew in here." The men sprang to action, and he stood up. He leaned on his arms, his hands flat against the table and looked out over the main floor of the command post. *You may have just given your last command,* he thought.

Washington, D.C.

General Wayne Charles sat in the Situation Room, his elbows on the table, holding his head in his hands. He had never felt so discouraged in his entire life. *I became the chairman of the JCS for this?* he thought. Slowly, he straightened and reread the Op Rep III message. He handed it to the DCI and waited as each of Madeline Turner's security advisors read the short message. There was no comment as it passed from hand to hand. Finally, it reached Secretary of State Francis.

"I never expected this," Francis muttered.

"Neither did I," the DCI added.

"There have always been problems in the nuclear stockpile," Charles told them. "That's why we did underground testing and recalls."

Francis was incredulous. "You recall nuclear weapons?"

"Of course," Charles replied. He looked at the master

clock on the wall. It was almost noon, Wednesday, February 13th. He couldn't put it off any longer and stood up. "I had better tell the president." Reluctantly, the other four men stood and followed him to the Oval Office.

Shaw was waiting for them and opened the door. "Mizz President," he said as he ushered them in.

Madeline Turner took off her glasses and leaned back in her chair. "Please be seated," she said. Only Shaw sat down.

Charles cleared his throat. "Madam President." He gulped. "The bomb—failed to—detonate." The president of the United States stared at him in disbelief.

"St. Peter shit-a-brick," Shaw muttered. "It was a dud?" Charles nodded, not knowing what to say. Shaw gave voice to what Turner was thinking. "You mean we spent how many gazillion dollars so when the chips are down you boys can't deliver?" He snorted. "Sumbitch."

Turner pulled her chair back to the desk and replaced her glasses. She folded her hands in front of her. What had Bender told her? Something about telling them what to do and not being afraid to kick a few egos around. "General Charles, how many coincidences must I accept? Fortunately, I'm not paranoid and given to believing in conspiracies. Otherwise, I would"—she paused—"well, let's just say no more coincidences or the results will be very unpleasant." She stood up. "Gentlemen, I'm going to lunch with my personal advisors, and in exactly one hour, I will be in the Situation Room. I want to know exactly what went wrong and what my options are." She studied the men standing in front of her. "I want the target area quarantined. Keep the Chinese guessing as long as possible. And find out what happened to General Bender." She walked from the room.

Okinawa, Japan

It was 3 A.M. when Ryan returned to the command post with the results of the urinalysis and blood tests. Much to his surprise, the colonels were not ricocheting off the walls and a cool calm ruled the main floor. He was directed to

Intelligence, where Martini was closeted with the Ops Group commander, the Forty-fourth Squadron commander, and Pete Townly. Master Sergeant Ralph Contreraz was also there, updating them on the inspection of the F-15 that had flown the mission.

"So far," Contreraz said, "she's as clean as a whistle. The weapons computer and release circuits test good. Not even a hiccup. The inertial nav system is right on. All told, one fine jet, good to go."

"Keep digging," Martini said, sounding very tired. He turned to Ryan. "How are the crews?"

"Absolutely clean," Ryan answered. He was struck by the dark circles around Martini's eyes. "Both are healthy as a horse."

"Any mental problems?" the Ops Group commander asked.

"Only the stress you'd expect," Ryan answered.

"We're going to give them a polygraph test about what happened on the mission," Martini said. "Since you head the Personnel Reliability Program, I want you and a legal beagle to be there."

"Sir," Ryan said, "those men are under a lot of stress and very upset about what happened. They need time to calm down and the results of any test this soon would be highly suspect. Based on my observations, I trust them implicitly."

Martini looked at his hands. He couldn't tell them that a certain general in the Pentagon had suffered a massive lapse of good judgment and had ordered the test. "We've got to validate what went wrong," he said. *How weak does that sound?* he thought.

"Sir," Ryan said, "I must protest in the strongest possible terms. I will not participate in a witch hunt."

"Put it in writing," Martini snapped. Then, more calmly, "Your protest will be included in the report. But you will be there during the polygraph. Dismissed." He spun around in his chair. Ryan threw a salute at his back and quick-stepped out of the room.

You miserable son of a bitch, Ryan thought. *You'll do anything to save your career. And that includes crucifying two innocent men.* Outside, he paused and breathed deeply, trying to fit everything together. *What's going on here?* he wondered. The more he thought about it, the more he worried about Martini. The man is coming apart, he decided. But did he want to cross the line from idle speculation to action? Maybe he would talk to his boss in the Med Center. He discarded that option almost immediately. The colonel was a good doctor but not much else. Then he considered the local IG, the inspector general, who handled complaints of wrongdoing. But the IG representative was the wing vice commander, one of Martini's ardent admirers. Ryan wondered if he was the only person on base who saw the general for what he really was.

A Security Police guard challenged him, and Ryan flashed his restricted area badge. "Is Captain Daguerre on duty?" he asked. The guard said that he was mobile in a patrol car. "Can he meet me?" Ryan asked. "I need to speak to him."

Captain Terrence Daguerre sat behind the wheel of his patrol car and listened as Ryan told him about the selective release mission and the bomb that failed to explode. "I suppose there's a reason why you're telling me all this," Daguerre said.

Ryan carefully selected his words, making sure they would push the right buttons with the rigid captain. "General Martini is breaking down under stress. As a doctor, I'm worried about his stability."

"How worried?" Daguerre asked.

"Worried enough," Ryan answered, "that he may not faithfully execute orders coming down from higher headquarters."

"Then he should be relieved of his command," Daguerre said.

"I don't even know who to tell about it," Ryan replied. "And what if I'm wrong?"

"Are you?" Daguerre asked.

"No, I'm not," Ryan replied, conviction in every word.

"If you can produce any hard evidence as to his instability," Daguerre said, "then you're talking to the right people. Otherwise, you're blowing smoke up my ass, and that pisses me off."

Ryan felt an urgent need to relieve himself. He forced a calm into his voice he didn't feel. "That's exactly why I'm talking to you. You've told me what I need to know."

Daguerre was a goose-stepping, anal-retentive authoritarian. He was also a good cop. "Look, Doc, we all got our doubts about the high rollers. That's normal. But normally, you keep them to yourself because it's a personal thing. Don't go messin' with the chain of command just because you hate Martini's guts."

"The evidence is there," Ryan promised.

Shahe Air Base, China

Tech Sergeant Otis Jenkins was stretched out half asleep in the copilot's seat on board the C-137 when the early-morning dark started to give way to the rising sun. The clock on the instrument panel was set to Greenwich mean time and read 21:45. He added eight hours. *Five forty-five*, he thought. He switched on the high-frequency radio, hoping he might be able to raise a friendly station and relay their status to the Air Force. Loud static filled his headset. "Damn," he muttered. They were still being jammed. He looked out the window. The night was yielding to the rising sun, and the vague shadows surrounding the Boeing formed into recognizable shapes. He sat upright in the seat. "Major Courtland!" he called. "You better come here."

Bill Courtland came forward, rubbing his eyes, still heavy with sleep. His tie was off and his shirt collar was open. "Oh, shitsky," he said. "Get the general. Where in the hell did they come from?" Parked on the ramp at his ten and two o'clock positions were two armored cars with their heavy machine guns pointed at the plane. Standing behind each gun was a helmeted gunner and loader.

"What's happening?" Bender asked as he came onto the flight deck. Without a word, Courtland stood aside and let him look out the thick glass windscreens. "This is going to get interesting," Bender said. "It might be a good idea if we all had a good breakfast and got cleaned up. Put on your class A blues." He moved back and headed for the galley, wishing he had packed a uniform.

Bender was still in the main stateroom's bathroom adjusting his tie when the sharp rap at the forward door echoed through the plane. He pulled on his suit coat and checked the full-length mirror one last time. He was as diplomatic looking as he could get. He walked briskly to the door, where the crew were standing. Without thinking, he checked them out. "Looking good," he said. He motioned to the flight engineer. "Jenkins, you open the door."

"Because I'm big and ugly?" the sergeant asked.

"Because you're black," Bender told him. "We're going to play every advantage we got." He told the men what he wanted done while the knocking grew louder.

Jenkins rotated the locking bar and opened the door. Four very surprised soldiers were standing at the head of the stairs. They saw Jenkins's big face and lowered their submachine guns. Jenkins pushed past and stepped outside into the frigid wind. He jammed his flight cap on his head and marched down the steps. At the bottom, he stepped to one side and came to attention. "Clear the stairs!" he shouted. The soldiers talked in confusion until an officer came forward and barked commands in Chinese. The soldiers split apart, two on each side of the door, came to attention, and ported their arms. "Major William L. Courtland," Jenkins bellowed, "United States Air Force."

On cue, Courtland stepped onto the stairs. "Who is the officer in charge?" he said in a loud voice. "I need to speak to your commanding officer about this unwarranted delay."

The officer on the ground spoke to a second lieutenant who ran to the two waiting cars parked behind the Boeing. One of the cars came forward and stopped at the base of the stairs. A door opened, and a heavyset man wearing the uniform of a PLA air force general got out. He stood for a moment, looking up the stairs as the car pulled away. Then he slowly climbed the steps, never taking his eyes off the open hatch. He walked inside, and the four soldiers standing at attention rushed in after him.

The second car drove up and stopped in front of Jenkins.

He froze at the sight of the beautiful apparition that emerged from the backseat. It was the woman from Lu Zoulin's office. She watched as two soldiers pointed their submachine guns at Jenkins while a burly sergeant clubbed him to the ground with the butt of his automatic pistol.

"He needs a doctor," Master Sergeant Larry Burke said.

Bender leaned over the bunk where Otis Jenkins was lying. He was still unconscious, but the vicious scalp wound had stopped bleeding. "I screwed up," Bender said. He stood up. At least the other three men were OK, and like him, they had only been roughed up when the soldiers stormed the C-137. Luckily, Burke had been able to grab a first aid kit off the airplane before they were dragged to the cell where the soldiers had thrown them. It was a long, L-shaped room, filthy from previous occupants and bitterly cold. Bender told them to cover Jenkins with dirty straw pallets from the other bunks. "Keep him as warm as possible," he told Burke.

"General, I'm freezing to death." This from the copilot, Rod Davis. It was one more item in his long list of complaints.

"We're all cold," Bender replied, telling him the obvious. He walked to the heavy steel door in the far end of the long arm of the room. "Everyone stay with Jenkins and keep out of sight," he said. "Let them focus on me." He beat on the door with his fist. "Guard! We got a problem in here." There was no answer, and he kept pounding on the door.

"You're going to make them mad," Davis moaned.

Stop whining, Bender thought.

"I can hear someone coming," Courtland called from around the corner.

Bender stopped beating on the door and massaged his hand. Now he could hear footsteps in the corridor. The lock rattled and the door clanged open. The woman was standing there with a large group of guards at her back. *The dragon lady returns,* Bender thought. He stood back and she entered. Again, he was struck by the beauty and grace of the woman that contrasted so violently with their surroundings. "Sergeant Jenkins is seriously injured and needs medical attention," he said.

The woman waved a hand, dismissing his plea for help. "You are here under false pretenses," she said in perfect English.

She and Wang are reading from the same script, Bender thought. "Madam, we're here as special representatives from our president and traveling under diplomatic status. I demand our immediate release."

"You have no diplomatic status and can demand nothing," she snapped. "You were sent here by the Turner woman as a delaying tactic, and she never intended to negotiate in good faith."

"If I understood Mr. Wang correctly," Bender said, "you were expecting the president to give you Okinawa in exchange for peace."

"That was our understanding," she said. "Otherwise, you would have never been allowed to come to China."

"Then I am glad that misunderstanding is cleared up," he said. "That is certainly a worthwhile result in itself. Now, I must demand our immediate release."

"The People's Republic of China does not release spies," she told him.

"We're not spies and you know it."

"Do I?" she replied. "We have evidence to the contrary." She spoke to a guard in Chinese, and he held up the copilot's video camera. "We found this among Captain Davis's possessions. Perhaps you've seen it?" The guard jammed the video camera in Bender's face and pressed the play button. Bender could not hear the audio but he saw the action through the eyepiece. Davis had managed to pan the long line of MiG-19 fighters at the end of the runway before Bender had told him to stop recording. "Your voice can be heard discussing the number of fighters," she said. "This is the work of spies."

"We're not spies," Bender repeated. A coppery, bitter taste flooded his mouth, and he felt helpless. What did he have to negotiate with? "Holding us hostage is counterproductive."

"Is it?" she answered. She spoke to the guards in Chinese. Six guards rushed into the cell, and one pinned

Bender against the wall, holding him there with a long wooden truncheon against his throat. The other five disappeared around the corner, and he heard dull thuds that sounded like flour sacks being dropped on a floor.

"Nooo!" Davis screamed. The guard holding Bender pressed harder, cutting off his breath. Two guards dragged the limp copilot from around the corner. "General," Davis pleaded. "Help!" The guard pressed harder against Bender's neck, and his vision started to blur. Bender relaxed, and the guard eased the pressure. The two guards holding Davis forced him to a kneeling position and straightened his arms out behind his back. They forced the American's head down, and the sickly smell of fresh human excrement assaulted Bender.

The woman uttered a harsh guttural command, and a sergeant stepped in from the hall. He drew an automatic from his holster and chambered a round. It played out with an unbelievable swiftness. The sergeant took four quick steps up to Davis, jammed the muzzle of the pistol against the base of his skull, and fired. The single shot rang out in the cell as the guards released their grip on Davis's arms.

"Must I repeat myself?" the woman asked. "You are spies and will be treated as such." She bowed her head gracefully at Bender and left him in silence. The door banged shut, and only the sound of boots marching down the corridor marred the perfect silence. Bender sank to his knees, not able to take his eyes off the copilot's lifeless body. A violent shudder wracked his body. But it was not from the cold.

26

Paris, France

The phone call came at exactly eight o'clock Thursday morning, February 14. Mazie Hazelton's first reaction was to not take it because it was from a clerk at the Chinese embassy. She bridled at the diplomatic slap in the face but took the call. Forty minutes later, she was at the chateau where the talks with the Chinese were held. But this time, she was met by the military attaché who was above her in the diplomatic pecking order. The handoff from the toady to the attaché could mean only one thing: The Chinese were sending a message to the president and she was the courier.

Hazelton tried to be diplomatic, but the attaché was speaking for a new leader in Beijing and not concerned with the normal protocols. He ended his long harangue with "Your president must understand that we are very serious in this matter."

She replied in kind. "And the quid pro quo?"

"Okinawa, of course."

"Unacceptable," she told him.

"Then we will execute them as spies," the attaché said. He dropped an electronic copy of a photo on the table in front of her. Transmission had degraded the photo, but the body of Captain Rodney Davis lying on a cell floor in a pool of brains and blood was clearly visible. "Justice is swift in China."

Washington, D.C.

Madeline Turner's elbows were resting on her desk in the Oval Office. Her hands were pressed together in front of her face, her chin resting on her thumbs, looking over her fingertips. Her eyes were cold and unblinking as she listened to Secretary of State Barnett Francis. "We received this message from Mrs. Hazelton in Paris." He handed out copies of Mazie's message. "She met, in secret, with the Chinese military attaché less than an hour ago." He waited nervously while they read. "Mrs. Hazelton confirms that a power struggle is going on in Beijing, and the military faction is winning."

"So Lu Zoulin is about to be historically revised," Shaw said.

"He's probably suffered the same fate as Captain Davis," the DCI said.

"How dare they execute Captain Davis," Turner said. It wasn't meant to be a question.

"The Chinese are aware of what's going on here," the DCI said. "In their view, you are preoccupied with your own survival, their selective release has gone unanswered, and it's only a matter of time until we abandon the Japanese. Wang Mocun is apparently the new premier and demonstrating his mastery by pushing the United States around and rubbing your face in the dirt. It's an object lesson for his political opponents."

"And the Japanese," Shaw added.

"Mrs. Hazelton," Francis said, "also claims that Wang has a personal vendetta with General Bender."

The president's words were hard and clipped. "If Mr. Wang thinks he can use hostages to blackmail me into selling out Okinawa, he is sadly mistaken. General Charles, I want another selective release, the same target. This time use a submarine-launched Tomahawk missile. I want it done immediately and with as small a warhead as possible."

"Madam President," Francis said, "you realize that a selective release at this time will, most probably, result in

General Bender's execution." Turner's face paled, but she did not answer.

"Yes, ma'am," Charles said, "we can do that. But there are problems." She fixed him with a hard stare over her fingertips and arched an eyebrow. Charles pressed ahead. "First, the Chinese have most of their submarines at sea. When our submarine launches a Tomahawk, it will give its position away and will be at risk of attack." He gulped. "Second, the Tomahawk's warhead has never been tested and only has higher yields. But we have a high degree of confidence that it will detonate."

"How large of yields are we talking about?" she asked.

"It's selectable for either 100 or 500 kilotons. That's equivalent to 500,000 tons of TNT, half a megaton."

She visibly cringed at the thought of an explosion that large. "You only have a 'high degree of confidence that it will detonate'?" she repeated. "You mean, you don't know?"

"Because we have discontinued underground nuclear testing, we can only test the high explosive that triggers the detonation and run computer simulations. It did perform as designed."

Turner was relentless. "Now you're telling me that this bomb, which was not tested, will detonate. What went wrong with the bomb we did drop?"

"The weapons designers disagree," Charles said. "Some claim it's a problem in the physics package or the age of the warhead itself, while others say it's a mechanical problem or in the electronics. Without underground testing, we can never be certain."

"A resumption of underground testing is out of the question," Turner said.

Shaw shook his head. "It sounds like we're caught smack-dab in a pissin' contest and gotta choose which side has the smartest physicist. Now, how are we gonna do that?" No one had the answer to what was a very serious question.

"I want to use a weapon," Turner said, "with the lowest possible yield. But you're telling me that no one can guarantee a detonation. So what do I do?"

Charles looked embarrassed. "The probability of detonation is a factor in target planning. We raise the chances of success by allocating multiple weapons to a single target." He knew he hadn't answered her question. "We can increase the probability of detonation by thoroughly checking the weapon out first."

"My physicist is smarter than your physicist," Shaw muttered sotto voce.

Charles's face turned beet red. "We have some high-powered experts at the Sandia Labs in New Mexico and the Lawrence Livermore Labs in California," he said. "It would take too much time for them to check out a Tomahawk, load it on a submarine, and position the sub for a launch. But we can fly the team to Okinawa, where we still have three B-61s. Once there, they can test the bombs and select the best one. The target is less than fifteen minutes flying time from Okinawa."

Turner thought for a moment. "Do it. I want a selective release executed within twelve hours."

"We can't do it that fast," Charles said. "We need at least forty-eight hours."

"You've got twenty-four," she replied. "If you can't do it by"—she looked at her watch—"seven o'clock tomorrow morning, I will hold you and every officer, every bureaucrat, everyone involved, fully accountable. You will all be on the streets looking for a job, and the next ground zero will be the Pentagon."

Charles believed her. "Please excuse me, ma'am. I've got work to do."

Shaw watched the general bolt from the Oval Office. "The clock is wound tight and tickin'." He turned to look at Turner. Her hands were still together in front of her face, not like a steeple but poised like an ax.

"Barnett," the president said, "keep beating the diplomatic bushes. Also, call Mrs. Hazelton in Paris and have her deliver a message to the Chinese attaché. Tell them that I want General Bender and his crew released immediately or there will be very grave consequences. I want her back here by this evening."

"She is not to wait for a reply?" Francis asked.

"General Bender's release is the only acceptable reply."

She stood and paced the floor. "Patrick, Mrs. Bender needs to know what has happened to her husband."

"I'll tell her," Shaw said.

"No," Turner replied. "I'll do it. Set up an appointment for later this afternoon. Hopefully, we'll have good news by then. Also, brief key members of Congress on what's happening and continue the hourly briefings for the press." She sat down. "Patrick, we have another problem."

"What's that, Mizz President?"

"We need another way to send a message to the Chinese."

"Like a reporter with an inside to the White House?"

"As long as he has a big audience."

"I can take care of that."

Shahe Air Base, China

Jenkins was conscious and sitting up. "Them miserable suckas," he moaned, holding his head.

Bender sat on the bunk beside him. "I screwed up," he said.

"We had to try something," Jenkins allowed. "Does anybody in the real world know what happened to us?"

Bender looked at his watch: nine o'clock Thursday night, eight Thursday morning in Washington, D.C. Twenty-seven hours had passed since their scheduled take-off. "Someone should be asking questions by now," he said.

The steward, Larry Burke, had his ear against the wall in the far corner. "I hear footsteps," he told them, "coming this way." The pilot, Bill Courtland, stood and headed for the door.

"I'll do it," Bender said. Courtland stood back, relieved that the general was still taking the lead, butting heads with their captors. Bender walked around the corner of the room and stood by the body of the copilot. The door swung open, and two guards stepped into the room. The woman he thought of as the dragon lady stood in the doorway and looked at him. He followed her eyes as she lowered her gaze to the body. "How much longer?"

Bender asked. Her face was a mask, unreadable and unmoving in the dim glow of the one light bulb. *Come on, answer,* he thought. He was using the one bargaining chip he had left.

"How much longer before what?" she finally replied.

"Before you realize you're making a bad mistake."

"Are we?" she asked.

Now it was his turn to be silent. Timing was everything because her next command would set the guards on him. He watched for the telltale contraction of facial muscles. He spoke just as her lips opened. "Most assuredly," he said. "Unfortunately, Mr. Wang does not understand President Turner. That could lead to a terrible tragedy. So unnecessary." From the look in her eyes, he was certain she was listening.

"Chairman Wang understands all that is important," she said.

"He doesn't know what President Turner will do next," Bender said.

"And you do?"

"Most assuredly," he repeated. "Perhaps you should tell him that I know." They stared at each other a few seconds. It seemed like hours. She spoke to the guards, and they picked up Davis's body as she turned to leave. "We need blankets and food," he said to her back. The door banged shut, and the Americans were alone.

"What are you doing?" Courtland asked.

"Negotiating."

"Someone's coming," Burke cautioned from his listening perch by the back wall. The door lock rattled, and the door burst open. A guard shoved the muzzle of his submachine gun in, and for a split second, Bender was certain they were dead. Another guard threw in a bundle of blankets while a third placed a basket on the floor. They backed out and closed the door.

Courtland passed out the blankets while Burke checked the basket. Inside were four plastic bowls, four spoons, and a covered pot. "Negotiations are in progress," Bender muttered. *She's lying,* he thought. *Wang isn't the chairman, not yet.*

Lawrence Livermore Labs
Livermore, California

Tobias J. Malthus was sitting at the shot director's console in the control room of the Nova Laser Facility. Toby Malthus was a bearded teddy bear of a man in his late fifties, six feet tall with soft brown eyes and the disposition to match. Women wanted to cuddle him and thought of him as a muffin. Secretly, Malthus often wished they would add "stud" to the "muffin," but he couldn't change what he was, a gentle human being who played with nuclear fusion, the stuff that powers our sun and the distant stars. On this particular early Thursday morning, he was about to create a tiny star of his own that would live for a billionth of a second.

Malthus gave the word to start the three-minute countdown to another shot, their term for an experiment. Because computers handled all the necessary tasks, little was said.

In the basement of the Nova Laser Facility, the 10,000 capacitors released a large burst of electrical energy into the ten laser beamlines in the main bay. Each of the beamlines was approximately thirty inches in diameter, about the length of a football field, and resembled a Rube Goldberg collection of sewer pipes connected with coffinlike transformer boxes. The beamlines were stacked in banks of five, and an unwary visitor might think he or she was in a plumbing warehouse suffering from an overdose of steroids. Ten trillion watts of energy went down each laser beamline and was focused into a target chamber that might have once been a deep-sea diving bell. Suspended in the target chamber was a fuel pellet the size of a grain of salt. For most humans, what happened next equated to magic. The laser beams compressed the pellet to a density twenty times greater than lead, reduced its size by a factor of thirty, and caused a nuclear reaction.

In quiet moments on long walks, Toby Malthus ran the mathematical probabilities of a shot releasing the full potential of the energy in the small pellets they bombarded with lasers. There was no danger of a mushroom cloud rising over Livermore, everyone agreed on that. But they were trying to fuse two forms of hydrogen to generate heat. That also created radiation. What if they were too successful and the Nova Laser Facility got an unexpected dose of radiation? Then his dreams of being a studmuffin would have to go on permanent hold while the physicists returned to their computers and drawing boards. But even then, he would be that much closer to giving the world the gift of a clean, safe, and unlimited source of energy in the form of heat. It amused him that the hope of the future might be found in the same weapons laboratories that designed thermonuclear weapons. He was a very contented man.

The director of Lawrence Livermore buzzed for entrance into the control room. He was a friendly man, superintelligent, given to expensive suits, and an astute scientist who could explain nuclear physics to kindergarten children and, therefore, politicians. "Toby," he called, "you free to talk?"

"Uh-oh," Malthus replied. He knew how the director worked.

"Weren't you involved with the W-40 warhead?"

"I was young then," Malthus told him. "That was way before your time." As a young physicist, Malthus had predicted that the type W-40 thermonuclear warhead would, under the right circumstances, not detonate or only achieve a low-order detonation. It had been an esoteric argument based on Malthus's calculations pitted against those of another physicist. The argument had raged hot until it was settled in a tunnel deep underneath the Nevada desert. "It was one of the last underground tests before the ban," Malthus said. "I was wrong."

"You heard about the Chinese?"

"Who hasn't," Malthus replied. In the world of nuclear physics, a nuclear explosion was a main event roughly equivalent to the second coming.

"We responded," the director said.

"I didn't hear about that."

"We dropped a B-61."

Malthus's mind raced with implications. The B-61 used the W-40 warhead.

"It turns out," the director said, confirming Malthus's

suspicions, "that you were right. You're leaving for Okinawa."

"When?"

"Twenty minutes ago. Don't bother to pack. A helicopter's waiting."

Washington, D.C.

Ben stood behind at the rear of the news studio evaluating the intern on the center camera. She was a tall and lithe tomboy with dreams of a career in TV news. She reminded him of a young Liz Gordon, fresh from Seattle twelve years ago. Liz came onto the set and sat down opposite Paul Ferguson, the network's aging superstar. They exchanged small talk and Ben smiled at Paul's pose: all friendliness, teeth, and smiles. *And this is the woman who Paul pronounced dead two days ago,* he thought. *Things do change.*

At exactly twelve o'clock, the director gave Ferguson the cue that they were live. "Good afternoon, America. We are in the fourth day since China detonated a nuclear weapon over the East China Sea and brought the world to the brink of nuclear war. While other nations wait and look to the United States for leadership, our president has not responded. Here with me for an update is Elizabeth Gordon." He turned to face her. "Liz, you were at the White House from the very first. Do you have an explanation for this apparent paralysis we are seeing."

"At this point," Liz replied, "I wouldn't call it paralysis. It is fair to say that the only person not panicking and demanding a knee-jerk reaction is the president. While it has been slow to emerge, we are now seeing a deliberate strategy of—"

Paul interrupted her. "But she has done nothing other than issue appeals for peace."

"That is the public, visible part of her strategy," Liz answered. "But there has been a flurry of diplomatic and military activity behind the scenes." She ticked off what had been accomplished. "But there is more. For example, the national security adviser, General Robert Bender, is conducting secret talks with the Chinese.''

She's got an inside! Ben thought, chalking one up for Liz. Her revelation would cause a big wave in the day's news. ''But the fact remains,'' Paul persisted, ''she has given in to nuclear blackmail.''

''Sources high in the White House,'' Liz said, ''tell me the president is still exploring every possible avenue for peace. These are uncharted waters and she is going slowly.''

''At this point, it is fair to ask,'' Paul said, deliberately mimicking her, ''will the president act?''

''Paul, in talking with my sources, I sensed a building momentum in the administration. You'll have an answer to your question in a very short time, probably less than twenty-four hours.''

Ben laughed to himself. *You got him again!* he thought. *And if you're right—move over Paul Ferguson, there's a new kid on the block!*

27 —

Shahe Air Base, China

"**I** hear footsteps," Larry Burke whispered. The sergeant was lying on his bunk in the early-morning dark, his ear against the wall. "Coming this way." Bender rolled over and sat on the edge of his bunk, his blanket draped over his shoulders. He put on his shoes and stood up, adjusting his clothes and knotting his tie. The door banged open and the lone light bulb flicked on. The woman was standing in the doorway flanked by two guards.

Unconsciously, Bender checked his watch: 2:15 Friday. It's still Thursday in the States, he thought. Nancy is probably just returning from lunch. The woman spoke in Mandarin, and two guards grabbed him, pinning his arms, while a third slapped handcuffs on his wrists. He stared at her passively. "Where are we going?" he asked. She spoke to the guards, and they shoved him into the hallway, slamming the door. "They need more blankets and drinking water," he told her.

The woman gave a command in Mandarin, and a guard swung his truncheon, laying it across the back of Bender's shoulders. He staggered but did not fall. "You will only speak to answer questions," the woman told him. The guards half pushed, half dragged him to a waiting van and shoved him into the back. The woman climbed into a waiting limousine that led the two-car procession to Beijing. Bender struggled to a sitting position and looked

416

out a window, surprised that the base was so busy at such an early hour. A guard pushed him back to the floor and barked a command that he did not understand. "And up yours, too," he answered in what he hoped was a servile tone. The guard picked up a thick rubber hose and hit him across the shoulders. It hurt much more than he expected.

"I speak English," the guard said. Bender nodded, not answering this time. They rode in silence until the van reached the same nondescript government building in central Beijing. A guard grabbed him by the arm and jerked him out of the van, ripping his coat sleeve at the shoulder seam. Bender almost said, "Made in Hong Kong," but thought better of it when he saw the rubber hose still in the guard's hand. They hustled him inside and up the stairs. The guards were breathing heavily by the second floor. He increased the pace and made the guards hurry to keep up. The one with the hose was gasping for breath by the time they reached their floor. The woman was waiting in the hall and glared at the panting guards. *I won't get away with that one again,* he decided.

"Chairman Wang wishes to speak to you," she said.

"Does that require an answer?" he asked. She spoke in Mandarin, and the guard swung his hose. But he was still suffering from the run up the stairs, and the blow had lost its punch. Bender faked it and gasped for air as he fell to the floor. He rolled in what he hoped was fair imitation of someone in pain. A guard kicked him in the side, and he came to his knees. *They know what the real thing looks like,* he decided.

She confirmed his guess. "No more games, General." The guards pulled him to his feet and pushed him into a room. It was an austere office with a single table and two chairs. A single filing cabinet stood against the bare walls. The woman sat down in one of the chairs, and they waited. She crossed her legs and lit a cigarette. "What are you thinking?" she asked.

"Why would such a beautiful woman smoke," he lied.

"I don't believe you."

"I told you the truth."

She nodded at the guard, and he laid the rubber hose across Bender's back. But he had regained his strength, and this time drove Bender to his knees. "I didn't ask a question," she told him. They played the game for an hour as they waited. She would speak to him, and he would only answer when she asked a direct question. Once, he hesitated too long before answering and was rewarded with another blow across the back. "Whatever is taking the chairman so long?" she asked.

"I have no idea," he replied.

She spoke to the guard, and he swung the hose. "That was a rhetorical question not intended for you." She tilted her head to one side and nodded at him. He closed his eyes and nodded back as if saying "I understand." And he did. She was softening him up and conditioning him for the meeting with Wang. "What are you thinking now?" she asked.

"I'm being mugged by a beautiful butterfly who likes to hurt people." He braced himself for the blow that never came.

"I believe you," she said.

The door opened, and Wang walked into the room. He was wearing a classic Mao Tse-tung suit and his hair was cut in the same manner as the famous Mao. He sat down and crossed his legs. "A chair for the general," he said.

Magically, a third chair appeared, and Bender sat down, surprised how relieved he felt. An alarm went off inside his head. *I'm caught in a good cop-bad cop routine,* he thought.

"The games are over," Wang said. "I am told you have information of value."

"Not if your goon keeps beating me with that hose," Bender answered. He braced himself for the blow. Again, it didn't come.

"Don't waste my time," Wang said. "What is it you have to say?"

"I know what President Turner is going to do next."

"It doesn't matter what she does next," Wang replied.

Then why are you here? Bender thought. "I assure you that what you are interpreting as weakness and the inability to act is wrong."

"You are full of assurances," the woman said.

"But they are valid," he replied. It was time to start

the bidding. "I'm sorry that what I have to say has no value for you. I had hoped that—"

She interrupted him. "You wish to cut a deal?"

"Your command of the English language is excellent," he said.

"There are no deals to be made," Wang said. "It is beneath me to haggle."

But you are here, Bender reminded himself. He half expected the guard to go back to work with the hose. But Wang just sat and stared at him, his face impassive. Then Bender saw the corner of Wang's eye twitch. *You're running out of time,* he thought. "My concern is for my crew," he said.

"And not yourself?" the woman answered. "How altruistic."

"What are your concerns?" Wang asked.

It's still good cop-bad cop, Bender decided. "That my men should be reunited with their families at the earliest possible moment."

"Why should I release spies?" Wang asked.

"Because they are not spies," Bender replied.

"And you are," the woman said. It was not a question.

Bender took the mental equivalent of a deep breath. "That is for you to decide in your own time." The deal was on the table.

"I see," Wang said. "The crew goes free and you remain with us. In exchange, you tell us what your president will do next. Perhaps, we can reach an understanding. If what you tell us proves to be true, then we will release your crew. But not until then."

It was all Bender was going to get. "I trust you to keep your promise," he said. "Unless you return to the status quo, President Turner will respond, in kind, to your actions."

Wang laughed. "She won't. Your president is a foolish woman. She is afraid of real power, real war, and real nuclear weapons. But she is not alone, your countrymen tremble in fear."

"You are misjudging her," Bender replied. "You shouldn't believe what you read in the newspapers or what your ambassador tells you."

Wang laughed again. "And when will she do this?"

"In the very near future."

"Where?" Wang demanded. Bender didn't answer.

"Do you believe him?" the woman asked in Mandarin. Wang answered in the same language. "No."

"Are you going to tell Lu Zoulin?"

"There is no need," Wang replied. "He would only argue for caution, and the generals are demanding we proceed as planned. Besides, it is too late to cancel the operation."

The woman smiled. "Shall I have them shot?"

"Not yet," Wang answered. "They may still be of some use."

"But if Bender is right and the American witch does as he says, it will be, ah, most embarrassing when the generals discover we were warned."

"Then immediately execute them, and the generals will never learn of it."

"General Bender," the woman said in English, "this has been a waste of time."

"You need a lesson in etiquette," Wang said. He spoke to the guards in Mandarin. They dragged Bender to his feet and jammed a canvas bag over his head. One grabbed it and jerked, led him back to the van, and pushed him inside. He hit his knee on the edge of the van's door frame and pain shot up his leg and into his groin. The driver slammed the van in gear and pulled away, throwing him around. His hurt knee smashed into the wheelwell and he almost lost control of his bladder as pain ripped into his body.

The woman watched the van until it disappeared. No sign of emotion or worry marred her smooth face as she stepped into the waiting limousine. There was no doubt in her mind that Bender had been telling the truth and that Wang should have heeded his warning. That was a problem.

Bender tried to get his bearings as they drove through the city, but he could only tell it was still dark. He counted the passing seconds, and when he estimated an hour had passed, the van slammed to a halt. He was hustled out of the van, and he felt a hand grab the top of the canvas bag.

The rough fabric tore at his skin as it was pulled off. He blinked in the bright light. He was standing outside his cell with four guards. Each had a rubber hose or truncheon shoved under his belt. One unlocked the door and pushed him inside. The guards followed, swinging their hoses and truncheons. A heavy rubber hose slammed into his mouth, and he tasted blood. He fell to the floor and curled into a fetal position. The guards beat on him until their arms were tired.

Finally, they stopped and removed his handcuffs. A swift kick into his side, and they were gone. Burke was over him in a flash as Courtland grabbed the first aid kit. Jenkins hobbled over from his bunk, still suffering dizziness from his own beating. "They really did a number on you," the flight engineer said.

"What the hell is going on?" Courtland asked.

Bender managed to sit up and spat out two teeth. "Negotiations," he mumbled.

Washington, D.C.

Mazie Hazelton walked into Bender's corner office in the West Wing just after six o'clock in the evening. She was exhausted from the hurried flight back from Paris and discouraged by the lack of success. She dropped her briefcase in a chair as Norma helped her off with her coat. "The president wants to see you immediately," the secretary said. "She's in the Oval Office." She reached out and stopped Hazelton with a gentle touch. "What's happened to General Bender? We're hearing terrible rumors."

"I'm not sure," Hazelton answered. "I imagine that's why the president wants to see me." She glanced in a mirror and decided to hell with the way she looked. She hurried down the hall and met Shaw as he came out of the Oval Office.

"Mrs. Bender's with Maddy," he said. "Go right on in."

She knocked twice and opened the door. Nancy Bender was sitting on a couch with the president. Maura was perched on the edge of the opposite couch and came to her feet. "You look tired," Maura said. "Can I get you a cup of tea or coffee?"

"Coffee please," Hazelton said. "Black." She sat in the corner of Maura's couch.

"I've told Mrs. Bender about Robert," Turner said. "Unfortunately, you were the last to hear anything."

"When will the Chinese let them go?" Nancy asked.

"I honestly don't know," Hazelton replied, taking the cup Maura offered her.

"It's unheard of," Maura said, "what they're doing. I just can't believe they'll—" Turner's look stopped her in midsentence.

"He's been in dangerous spots before," Nancy said. "He's a survivor."

"We're doing everything we can to get them out," Turner said. She paused, taking the measure of Nancy Bender. Was she a woman who had to be gently handled and shielded from the truth? Her instincts told her to be honest. "But so far we haven't met with much success."

The corners of Nancy's lips flickered. Was it a smile? "I imagine the Chinese are finding him a bit of a handful."

"How so?" Maura asked, amazed that a hostage could cause his captors problems.

"He's probably negotiating to get his people released," Nancy told them.

"What can he negotiate with?" Mazie asked.

"With whatever he's got," Nancy replied. "You don't know him. He'll get his people out."

"I don't want to mislead you," Turner said. "Please don't get your hopes up."

Nancy turned to face her. "Robert knows you can't give in to this type of blackmail, that you may have to sacrifice—" She couldn't finish the sentence. "But he can accept that if his crew is safe."

"Is their safety that important to him?" Maura asked.

"Oh, yes," Nancy answered. She had to talk, to tell them about her husband. "They're his people, his responsibility. He says it goes with the territory." She looked at Turner. The president understood. "Sometimes he forgets that he is not a rock, safe from the emotions that tear other people apart. When he's hurt or disappointed, he pulls into his cave. He won't say a thing and refuses to let other people help him.'' She blushed. ''Robert would die of shame if he heard me say that.''

Hazelton wanted to reassure Nancy that her husband would be safe. But that would have been misleading. She leaned forward, offering what consolation she could. ''Mrs. Bender, there's something you should know. He needs you.''

''I know,'' Nancy answered. ''But he's so damn—'' Her voice trailed off.

''Close mouthed,'' Turner said, finishing the thought for her. ''You're fortunate. I never know what he's thinking.'' She looked at her watch. ''You'll have to excuse me, I need to meet with my advisors. Mother, will you please see that Mrs. Bender gets home?''

''Thank you, Mrs. President,'' Nancy said as they stood up. ''I can manage on my own.''

''We'll let you know the moment we learn anything,'' Turner promised.

Maura led Nancy out and turned her over to a Marine sergeant who escorted her to her car. ''Drive carefully, ma'am,'' the sergeant said, closing the car door.

Nancy sat in the car and leaned her head against the steering wheel. ''Oh, Robert,'' she whispered.

The Situation Room rapidly filled as the president's security advisors filed in. Hazelton joined the crowd and stood behind Bender's seat next to the DCI. The number of people and the tension in the room left no doubt that this was a full-fledged council of war. General Charles was standing at the far end with the JCS hovering at his back. Barnett Francis and the head of the State Department's Far East Desk were opposite her. The key players from the Intelligence community clustered around the DCI. Shaw stepped through the door. ''Ladies and gentlemen, the President.'' He stepped aside, and Turner walked in.

She sat down. ''Please be seated.''

The DCI held Hazelton's chair as she sat down, a touch of old-world courtesy, and remained standing. The room was absolutely silent. ''Madam President,'' the DCI began as the TV screen opposite Turner scrolled to an area map centered on Okinawa. "Chinese paratroopers have been inserted on the atoll where they detonated their nuclear device. The airdrop began approximately one hour ago and so far, we estimate they have air-dropped approximately 500 men on the atoll. The airdrops are still in progress as heavy equipment and artillery arrive."

"When did we learn about this?" Turner asked.

The DCI checked the time/date stamp on the message. "Four minutes ago."

"Where is General Bender?" she demanded.

The head of the National Reconnaissance Office answered. "Satellite imagery taken two hours ago show his plane is still at Shahe Air Base. Shahe is near Beijing."

"I know where Shahe is," Turner snapped. "When did the Chinese start this airdrop operation?"

"As best we can tell," the DCI replied, "the aircraft launched from mainland China less than two hours ago."

Turner studied the TV screen. "I assume this is their answer to my demand that General Bender and his crew be released."

"Madam President," Secretary Francis said, "this is consistent with their strategy from the very first."

"Salami tactics," Shaw muttered from his end of the room.

Turner ignored him. "General Charles, what is the status on Okinawa?"

"The island is at maximum alert. The team from the States should arrive in five hours. They need some time to inspect the weapons, but we can meet your deadline."

Turner pointed her pen at the secretary of state. "Barnett, continue with your diplomatic offensive. Pull out all the stops. Someone, somewhere, must be able to reason with those idiots in Beijing." The pen moved to the DCI. "Find General Bender." The pen moved and pointed to Charles. "You have exactly twelve hours to execute that selective release. Make it happen."

"Ma'am," Charles said, "we can have an ICBM on target in forty minutes."

"Too big," she said. "I want to move down the scale, not up. And besides, what is the reliability of that weapon?

How many missiles will it take?'' An embarrassed silence met her questions.

"Mizz President," Shaw said, "press conference in five minutes."

She stood up. "You know what I want done. Stay on top of this, and we will reconvene at five o'clock tomorrow morning. Sooner if we need to." She paused, considering her next words. But she said nothing and walked briskly out the door.

Madeline Turner's kitchen cabinet was waiting for her in the family dining room on the second floor when she finished the press conference. Dinner with her friends was exactly what she needed to break her hectic schedule. They clustered around one end of the table and sat down to eat. "Lord, child," Noreen Coker said, "that was a 'come-to-Jesus' press conference if I ever saw one."

Richard Parrish laughed. "Isn't that the bell you used when you were a state senator?"

"When I was a freshman," she replied, "I was the only woman in the senate and none of those old curmudgeons would listen to me. I rang it to get their attention. It seemed like a good idea to stop those reporters from asking the same questions over and over."

Maura smiled. "It worked. You didn't have to ring in once in the last few minutes. You reminded me of a schoolmarm with a bunch of unruly children. I think you made some of them very angry."

"It did speed things along," Coker said.

They deliberately steered clear of China as they ate and talked to give Turner a break and restore her strength. They all felt the pressure she was under and wished they could ease her burden. But the best they could offer was support and a few moments of quiet companionship. When the dinner was over and coffee served, Turner turned to business.

"I was very angry that not one reporter asked about Sam," she said.

"I visited the vice president this afternoon," Parrish said. "He's in good spirits after the amputation. The doctors say he's doing fine and they didn't have to take as much of his left arm as they originally thought. They're still a little worried about lung infection. But it is yielding.''

"What's Leland up to?" Turner asked.

Noreen Coker's chair groaned as she heaved her bulk to a more comfortable position. "That snake?" She humphed. "Laying low in the grass for now. His most recent internal tracking polls are shaky.''

"So are ours," Turner replied. "Do you have any idea what his are showing?"

Coker shook her head. "He may be sensing a new trend. I don't know.''

Parrish set his coffee cup down. "What are you going to do with Shaw?"

"I can't do anything until this is over," Turner answered.

"Give him to me," Coker said. "He'll be squealing soprano for the rest of his life after I'm done with him.''

Turner was alone in her private study when Maura and Sarah joined her. Sarah was in her pajamas and ready for bed. She cuddled against her mother for a few moments. Brian burst through the door and skidded to a stop in front of them. "On the TV," he gasped. "There's a story about General Bender. Liz Gordon said he was being held hostage by the Chinese.''

"It's true," Turner said. "He's being held with the crew that flew him into China.''

"Why?" Brian asked.

"The Chinese say they're spies," Turner told him. "I sent him on a secret mission to talk to them. But I wouldn't give them what they wanted, so they took him hostage.''

Sarah cried. "That's not fair.''

"Many things in life are not fair," Turner said. "But I'm doing everything I can to get them out." They talked for a few moments before Maura took them to bed.

Maura returned a few minutes later and sat beside her daughter. "Are you OK?" she asked.

Turner shook her head. "I'm so worried, Mother. I've

made so many mistakes. I don't want to fight a war, I don't want to use a nuclear bomb."

"Then don't," Maura said.

"I don't have a choice."

"You always have a choice, Maddy."

Madeline Turner shook her head. Maura didn't understand. "No, Mother. The president doesn't have a choice."

Washington, D.C.

Jessica was waiting for Shaw when he arrived at his Watergate condominium. He was tired and wanted nothing more than a tall glass of bourbon and a leisurely soak in his Jacuzzi. "The senator wants to see you," she said.

"Not tonight, Jess. I'm bushed. I've got to be back in a few hours and it's been a hell'uva day." *If only she knew,* he thought. The White House was controlled chaos.

"Now," she ordered, handing him his topcoat. "I'll drive."

"I can't believe this," he muttered as he followed her to the elevator. Jessica was true to her basic instincts and drove like a maniac, thrilling Shaw in ways he hadn't experienced since he was a teenager. They reached the farmhouse in record-breaking time. No one was waiting for them, and the house was dark. He followed her inside, not liking her easy familiarity with the house. *She's just another power groupie,* he told himself. *Use her like all the others.*

Leland was alone and waiting in the den. He waved Shaw to a chair and looked at Jessica. She left the room. "I'm worried about you, son."

Shaw heard the patronizing tone in Leland's voice and felt his skin prickle. He tried to settle into the chair, but no matter which way he squirmed, he couldn't get comfortable and kept slipping forward. It was an old trick Shaw had perfected in his earlier days to handle reporters and lobbyists. Now Leland was doing it to him. Shaw stood up and leaned against the mantle, his foot on the hearth. It was time to go on the offensive. "I've been having some doubts of my own."

"I've always believed in rewarding my friends and burying my enemies," Leland replied. "But I can't figure out which group you fall in. You assured me you were in control in the White House and Turner was isolated. You failed to deliver on both counts and some of our mutual friends have raised serious questions about your loyalty."

Loyalty! Shaw thought. *What would Leland and the group know about that word?* "I take it, our 'friends' are losing their nerve," he said. All traces of his southern accent were gone, and his voice was flat and hard.

"Not losing their nerve," Leland replied. "They feel you have caused them to, ah, take a premature course of action by your rash promises."

"I delivered Jackie Winters," Shaw replied.

"Did you? A friend tells me the FBI is certain the, ah, undergarment found in her desk was planted and they're following up on it. That's a trail that will undoubtedly lead to you and ultimately to here. That was a stupid thing you did." Leland held up his hand to silence Shaw. "Now let me tell you what *you* are going to do. You're going to tell the world how our president is being screwed silly by her national security advisor, a married man, in the White House."

Shaw tried to conjure up an image of Bender engaging in sex. Even for his fertile mind, it was beyond him. But Maddy was there, alone, demanding his attention. It wasn't a politician he was sacrificing on the altar of power but the young and idealistic woman he had taken under his wing years before, the grieving widow, the caring mother with her children, Brian and Sarah. *Brian and Sarah,* he thought. *What will they think of their mother when I do this? Kids! Since when did they vote?* He forced a laugh he didn't feel. "Maddy and Bender! No way, no how."

Leland ignored his outburst. "According to our polls, that will drive the last nail into her coffin."

Shaw came even more alert. He knew all about internal tracking polls, and the White House had its own number crunchers who constantly sampled the public's mood swings. According to their latest polls, Maddy's approval rating was low but holding steady.

"Perhaps," Leland said, "a word in the shell-like ear of Liz Gordon?"

The first touches of panic brushed Shaw. Did Leland know about their relationship? What else did he know? Shaw clicked through the implications. Slowly, he calmed and held his panic at bay. He had to keep Leland looking in the right direction. "For openers, Bender hasn't got a prick. Think what you want, but there's nothing between them."

"Son," Leland said, "we're very serious about this. If Turner survives, I'll personally cut you up for shark bait and feed you to the media. You'll be dead in this town." The threat was very real, and Leland had the power to make it happen.

Shaw's panic was back, much stronger this time. He fought the urge to find a bathroom. "Senator, you and me have butted heads before. We both wound up with headaches."

"I'm not alone in this," Leland said, his voice matter-of-fact. "A lot of good folks are going to be very upset. They can hurt you in ways I can't even imagine. If I were you, I wouldn't make them mad." He paused, ratcheting up the tension before extending the olive branch. "On the other hand, if you help us render that bitch and get her out of the White House—" He smiled and did not finish the offer.

Shaw stiffened, and the urge to urinate went away. Relief shot through him, not because of the senator's offer, but because of what he heard behind the words. It was a subtle nuance, a change of tone, the echo of fear. Leland was on the defensive. Why? Had Leland's polls caught an early trend that his experts had missed? Was Maddy Turner gaining in the public's esteem? He needed to check it out. He muttered a few words and beat a hasty retreat, leaving Leland alone in front of the fire. *Don't threaten old Patrick,* Shaw thought. *Not while I've still got another time at bat.*

A side door opened, and four people filed in. The last was Gwen Anderson, the secretary of health and human services who Shaw had crushed with revelations about her bouts of depression. "Did you get the bastard's attention?" she asked.

"You'll get your pound of flesh," Leland said. "But he's being obstinate and says there is nothing going on between Turner and Bender."

"He may not be willing to give her up on this," Secretary of Defense Elkins said. "They go back a long time."

"My God," Anderson said, "we're talking about Patrick Shaw. Everything's for sale."

Shaw slipped into the passenger's seat of the waiting Jaguar. Jessica's feet danced on the pedals, and her legs flashed in the glow from the instruments. The car leaped forward and accelerated down the narrow lane. "Is everything OK?" she asked.

"Ab-so-loot-lee," Shaw blustered. Whatever he told her would be back to Leland within minutes after she left him. "We had a meeting of the minds. Toot-sweet." She smiled at his twisted French. *What a mess*, he thought. *What a terrible, fuckin' mess.*

She pulled up at a stoplight and reached across to touch his cheek. "You look tired." Her words were soft, full of concern.

"It's been a hell of a Valentine's Day, Jess."

Okinawa, Japan

Bob Ryan stood on the parking ramp with Pete Townly as the KC-10 tanker taxied into the chalks. Ryan shifted his weight from foot to foot as the boarding stairs were pushed into position. The door swung open, and a bearded bear of a man stepped into the hot and humid noonday sun. He shambled down the stairs, followed by seven men and one woman. Townly stepped forward. "Dr. Malthus?" he asked. The beard bobbed up and down in answer, and Townly made the introductions. "Major Ryan and I are your escorts," he explained. "We're going directly to the command post where General Martini is waiting for you."

Martini was waiting at the entrance of the command post, and Townly made the introductions. "We're set up in the Intelligence vault." Martini said. He led the civilians, Townly, and Ryan into the vault. "We've received a valid emergency action message for a selective release with an execute time of no later time than 2100 local," Martini told them. "Eight hours from now."

Malthus's beard dropped to his chest. "You don't want much. OK, let's go to work. First, we need every scrap of information you've got. While we're crunching the numbers, those misfits from Brand X"—he pointed to four engineers from Sandia National Laboratories—"will validate a weapon and check out the circuitry." He looked around the vault. "Can we work in here?"

"It's all yours," Martini said. "If you need anything, tell Pete here. He's got the security clearances to get you anything you need. Doc Ryan is the head of our Personnel Reliability Program. He can escort you anywhere on base."

Malthus grinned at Ryan. "You a shrink?"

"Flight surgeon," Ryan replied, instantly liking the big scientist.

"Always good having someone watching for the gonzos," Malthus said. He flipped open his briefcase and pulled out a laptop computer. The others did the same and linked them together. Ryan stared at the computers in disbelief. Malthus laughed. "Did you think we still used slide rules?"

"Major Ryan," Martini said, "please take the gentlemen from Sandia to the fuel cells building."

The turnstile at the end of the first vertical tank storage system clanked as the long line of drop tanks moved around the track. "Some dry cleaning store," one of the civilians quipped as the tanks swayed and jerked. The operator stopped the track, and the mechanical loading arm gently extracted a tank. Two sergeants lowered it onto a dolly and pushed the tank into a corner of the main hangar bay where a huge curtain had been rigged for privacy. The dolly and the four engineers from Sandia disappeared behind the curtain. Ryan waited as the machine-gunlike sound of air wrenches split the air. Soon, a disassembled drop tank was shoved out.

"You ever seen a weapon up close?" one of the civilians asked. Ryan shook his head and followed him behind the curtain. He stopped, frozen in his tracks. The men were bent over a sleek silver dart, and if Ryan hadn't known what it was, he would have said it was beautiful. "It had better be eleven feet, nine and one-half inches long," the civilian said, "and weigh exactly 716.3 pounds."

"And if it doesn't?" Ryan asked.

"Then we got bigger problems than we thought," the engineer answered.

Ryan stood back as the men started the first of their

tests, a simple weighing of the weapon. He was surprised by their speed and was shocked by their cavalier attitude. The main hangar doors cranked back, and he heard the unmistakable bellow of Master Sergeant Ralph Contreraz as another F-15E Strike Eagle was tugged into the maintenance bay. Like the bomb, the F-15 gleamed with care. "It's fresh off the wash rack," Contreraz told him.

"Why?" Ryan asked.

"Why not?" came the answer.

Shahe Air Base, China

"Someone's coming," Burke said. He moved away from his spot by the back wall of the cell. "What d'you think?"

Bender looked at his watch. It was two in the afternoon. "Dinnertime," he answered. His mouth still hurt, and it was difficult to talk.

The door opened, and a guard carried in the same basket and pot as before. The woman stood in the doorway and watched as Burke ladled out the thin gruel of rice and vegetables. "Who's the dragon lady gonna beat the shit out of this time?" Burke muttered.

"Eat," Bender said.

She waited until they were finished and a guard had taken the basket away. "We are not barbarians," she said. Bender eyed the guards and said nothing. He would wait for a direct question. "You may speak," she told him.

"My mouth hurts," he said.

No sign of emotion crossed her face as her fingers touched his bruised face. "You were presumptuous," she said, pulling her fingers away. "But I found your concern for your men most touching. Why should we let them go?"

"Because Mr. Wang—"

"Chairman Wang," she corrected.

"Is he?" Bender replied. Her facial muscles tensed. He had made a telling point. Now he had to recover before the hoses came out. "Because Chairman Wang promised he would."

For the first time, she smiled. It was beautiful but did not match her words. "Why should he honor a promise made to a spy?"

It was his turn to smile. "Because I told him the truth. Sooner or later, Chairman Wang will have to negotiate with President Turner. By releasing my crew, they are proof that he keeps his word." Had he made a point with her? He couldn't tell.

"You are asking too much for too little," she replied. "Chairman Wang desires more details. You only said she would respond in kind. That is not enough. If she is going to drop a nuclear weapon, we need to know when and where."

"I don't know."

She gave a little sigh. "If I fail, I will lose much face with the chairman. I could start shooting your men one at a time until you tell me."

"I'd lie first."

She spoke in Mandarin, and two guards grabbed Courtland. They straightened his arms out behind his back and twisted as they forced him to a kneeling position. She spoke again, and the same burly sergeant charged into the cell, his gun drawn.

"The island of Kumejima," Bender said. "It's the closest Japanese territory you've occupied and most of the civilians have left." The sergeant froze, and they all looked at the woman. Did she believe him?

She barked a command, and the sergeant backed off, his automatic lowered. "When?" This was in English.

"It should have happened by now."

"Why should I believe you?"

"That's why I had a deadline to get out of China," he answered.

Again, the passive look without any sign of emotion. "Chairman Wang is right. Your president won't act and will only talk."

"You're misjudging her," he said.

"Are we?" She turned to leave. She stopped and turned. "If you have lied to me, I will personally shoot you. In the mouth." She smiled. "But then, perhaps Chairman Wang will have it done first." She spoke quietly in

Mandarin and left. The guards withdrew behind her and slammed the heavy door. The Americans waited in silence as the lock rattled. Burke ran back to his position around the corner and pressed his ear against the wall.

"She's leaving," he said. "I can tell her walk."

Courtland stood up and rubbed his arms. "Damn. I thought I was dead. What's going on?"

"I'm negotiating for your release," Bender told him.

"It sounds like you're collaborating," Jenkins said from his bunk.

"Is it 'collaboration' when you tell them the obvious?" Bender asked.

"General," Courtland said, "that woman will shoot you if you lied to her."

Okinawa, Japan

Toby Malthus kicked his chair back and stood up. He paced the length of the big vault. "Well, Ev, what do you think?" The one woman on the team typed a command into her computer and waited. Like him, she was a brilliant physicist. But she kept it hidden behind a pleasant and cheery personality. People often made the mistake of only seeing an overweight and hardworking single mother of two teenage girls. Malthus knew better.

"Everything checks so far," Ev told him. "What are the Sandia toads saying?" The rivalry between the Sandia and Livermore Labs was an old one but more friendly than vicious.

"So far, the circuitry on the weapon they're dismantling tests perfect. They're almost finished and should be here any minute with the final results."

"Maybe we just had a lemon," Ev ventured.

"Possible. It would help if we could find the bomb. Townly tells me an SR-71 overflew the atoll and they couldn't find any trace of the weapon or the parachute. Because it was a parachute-retarded airburst over a small atoll, the wind may have blown it over the ocean when it didn't detonate."

"And it landed in the water," Ev added. "Lovely. An

armed nuclear weapon set for a ten-megaton yield just laying there.''

"If that's the case," Malthus said, "we'll find it— eventually.''

"Eventually ain't soon enough," Ev said. She considered another possibility. "If there was only a low-order detonation or only the high explosive went off, we should be able to measure an increase in airborne radiation and plot the fallout.''

Malthus double-checked his notes. "According to the atmospheric samples taken by a reconnaissance aircraft before and after the release, there was no increase in radiation.''

Ev looked at him sadly. "It's in the primary, isn't it?'' The B-61 was a two-stage bomb. The *primary* was the fission assembly, or atomic bomb, that set off the *secondary,* the thermonuclear part of the warhead. "So what do we tell the general?'' she asked.

"I need to talk to the Sandia troops first," he answered. They waited until the four civilians walked in, still escorted by Ryan.

"The weapons check perfectly," their leader said. "As best we can tell, they're all good to go.''

Malthus rifled through his notes and reread the crew's debriefing. "The weapon system officer reported that the arm light took approximately ten seconds to change to green when he rotated the wafer switch. Check out the arming circuits on the aircraft.'' He picked up the phone and called Martini as the Sandia engineers left.

The general was waiting for the call and walked quickly to the vault. Malthus explained where they were. "Damn,'' Martini grumbled. "We don't know any more than we did two days ago.''

"General," Malthus said, "I've got a suggestion. We know the circuitry and batteries are good on the last bomb we checked. Upload it and get ready to launch. While you're doing that—''

Ev interrupted him. "Toby, don't do it. We haven't got the right equipment.''

The physicist smiled at her. "I've done it before.''

Martini was an impatient man and not given to collegial discussions. "Do what?" he grumbled.

"We've got a bomb disassembled," Malthus replied. "If you give me the go ahead, I'll cut into the primary. If it's OK, then you drop the bomb that's already loaded." He described the process of cutting into the core and what he was looking for. He concluded with "It will take about three to four hours." Everyone in the room looked at their watches. They had exactly four hours and forty-eight minutes to go.

"What do you need?" Martini asked.

"A big pit, a couple tons of gravel, a steel barrel, and lots of concrete," Malthus said. "Ev knows the details and what has to be done."

Martini's fingers drummed the table. "We got a concrete pit in an old maintenance hangar you can use."

"General," Ryan said, "can you do that? I mean, dismantle a bomb."

"Why not?" Martini said. "I signed for the damn things." He paused for a moment. "Do it."

Ryan paced back and forth outside the old maintenance hangar. His agitation was growing with each step, and he was convinced that Martini had cracked under the stress and had become delusional, turning into a Dr. Strangelove. He wondered if PACAF or the Pentagon knew what he was doing? Probably not. He walked over to the frumpy-looking woman. "Excuse me, exactly why do you need a concrete pit to work in? And why did you cover it with gravel?"

Ev gave him a kindly look and tried to explain. They were disassembling the "physics package" and cutting into the basketball-sized core of the primary so they could examine the very heart of the weapon; specifically, the neutron-emitting initiator at the center and the plutonium surrounding it. But the core was covered with a dark waxy high-explosive material far more powerful than TNT, and there was a chance it might accidentally explode. If that happened, the plutonium, which was highly radioactive, would be dispersed into the air. "The gravel will rise a few feet and settle down, containing the explosion and the radiation," she said.

"But what about the people in the pit?" Ryan asked.

"No one could survive the blast," Ev replied. "But Dr. Malthus knows what he's doing so there's not much chance of that happening. When he cuts into the plutonium, there's going to be a lot of radioactive dust, which will be contained in the pit. We have to run a lot of tests, but it's all pretty straightforward."

"But the radiation," Ryan protested.

"That's why we have to work fast. With a little luck, no one should receive over one or two rems. We can live with that."

"What do you do with the bits and pieces after you're finished?"

"Burn the explosives, grind up the subassemblies, and put what's left of the core into a special container we brought with us and ship it to Pantex in Texas for storage."

"But what if that container leaks? What do you do then?"

Ev was a patient woman. "If we detect any leakage, we encase the container, in concrete, in a barrel. If it's still leaking, we place the barrel in the pit. There's a great deal of radioactive dust down there and the test equipment is contaminated. So we're going to bury the whole thing in concrete when we're finished. No problem."

No problem! Ryan thought. An image of mad scientists flashed through his mind. He saw Master Sergeant Contreraz walk out of the hangar and climb into a waiting van. Ryan excused himself and flagged the van down. "Can I hook a lift to my car?" Contreraz told him to climb in, and they motored slowly across the ramp. "Do they have everything they need inside the hangar?" Ryan asked.

"Oh, yeah," Contreraz answered. "The general is treating them like 500-pound gorillas." They pulled up to Ryan's car and stopped. "They get whatever they want."

"Are any of your people helping Dr. Malthus?"

"He's down there all alone," Contreraz said.

Ryan's head snapped up. Suddenly, he had a vision of

himself as the courageous individual who stopped the madness and Martini's headlong rush to nuclear war. "Thanks for the lift, Sarg." He jumped into his car and sped toward the Security Police shack. He had to find Daguerre, the Security Police captain.

Washington, D.C.

Shaw reached out and hit the alarm before it went off. The green numbers on the clock flickered to 0400. He lay still, not moving. Jessica's hands moved over his back, massaging his muscles. "Did you get any sleep?" she asked.

"No," he answered. He swung his legs out of bed and sat up. "I've got to go. Early meeting." She watched him as he hurriedly shaved and dressed.

"What do you want me to tell the senator?" she asked. He gave a little snort. "Anything you want, darlin'."

"Let me help," she offered.

"There's nothing you can do." Again, he snorted. "Old Patrick screwed the pooch big time on this one." He laughed. "Maddy surprised all of us."

"What are you going to do now?"

That's a good question, he thought. *What am I going to do now?* Suddenly, it came to him. "I'll be gawd-damned," he said. "If old Patrick ratted once, he can rerat right back. Darlin', you can tell Mr. Senator John Leland that I'm not giving Maddy up." Jessica bounced out of bed and threw her arms around him. He stroked her bare back and felt the tears on her cheeks. "Now what brought all this on?"

"Leland will kill you," she said.

"In this town, darlin', you can kill people, but you can't kill them dead. Besides, Old Patrick has a trick or two left in the old hip pocket." He hurried to the elevator, feeling more alive than he had in weeks. His limousine was waiting for him in the garage, and he settled into the backseat for the short ride to the White House. He gazed out the window, trying to anticipate what the day would bring. But he kept thinking about Jessica. *Well, I'll be damned,* he thought, realizing he had an erection.

Shaw was waiting in the hall when Madeline Turner came out of her bedroom. "Good morning, Patrick," she said. "You're looking tired. Didn't you get any sleep last night?"

"As a matter of fact, Madam President, I didn't sleep a wink." They walked quickly down the corridor.

"Patrick, are you all right? You sound different."

"I'm fine, Madam President. Ab-so-loot-lee fine."

She arched an eyebrow and looked at him. "What happened to the 'Mizz'?" she asked.

"Don't know. I guess it sounded a bit presumptuous." They walked in silence to the Situation Room. The stairs and hallways were packed with aides and staffers, poised to be of instant service to their masters inside. They pressed back, clearing a passage for the president. A Marine guard pulled the door open, and Shaw entered first. "Ladies and gentlemen," he announced, "the President."

Turner entered and sat down. "Good morning. I see that you all slept well."

The DCI waited while a little chuckle worked its way around the room. "Madam President," he began, "at last count, the Chinese have landed 986 troops on the atoll and reinforced them with antiaircraft artillery batteries and surface-to-air missiles. A reliable source has located General Bender and his crew. They are being held in a cell"—a TV monitor displayed an aerial view of Shahe Air Base—"in this complex." His laser pointer circled a set of buildings near the center of the base. "Their aircraft has been moved undercover." The pointer circled what looked like a small hill.

"Barnett, have you made any progress on the diplomatic front?"

"None worth mentioning," the secretary of state answered. "We're encountering a singular reluctance on the part of the Chinese to talk. Perhaps they are waiting for new instructions from Beijing."

"I'm done waiting," she answered. "General Charles?"

"No word from Okinawa. But they have not declined the emergency action message."

"What does that mean in English?" she asked.

"They intend to execute the mission no later than 0700 our time, this morning. If something happens, like the runway gets bombed or they haven't got the aircraft—"

"Or a bomb that works," Shaw said.

Charles ignored the interruption. "—then the commander can decline the mission."

"I see," she said. "If they cannot do it or"—she fixed Charles with her pen—"we experience another dud, I want a submarine-launched Tomahawk on target immediately. If that one also fails to detonate, do it again." She stood up to leave.

"Madam President," the DCI said, "the Chinese will probably execute General Bender and the crew in retaliation."

Madeline Turner paled, but her voice was hard and unflinching. "That would be a very serious mistake on their part. Whether they release General Bender or not, the Chinese will have exactly twenty-four hours after our sel rel to convince me *not* to take further steps. Specifically, I will order the Navy to sink any Chinese warship found in the East China Sea. I hope our Navy is up to it."

"Yes, ma'am," the chief of Naval Operations answered.

"Are there any questions about my intentions?" she asked. There were none, and she left with Shaw still in tow.

"She seems to like twenty-four-hour deadlines," Charles said to no one in particular.

"She's taking it one day at a time," Hazelton replied.

29

Okinawa, Japan

Captain Terrence Daguerre leaned cross his desk in the Security Police shack. "Is this a formal complaint?" he asked.

Ryan bit his lip, afraid to take the final step and commit to a course of action. "As the head of the Personnel Reliability Program for this wing," he said, still trying to hedge, "I am bringing to you a valid concern."

"We've talked about this before," Daguerre replied. "Since your so-called concern involves the wing commander, I'm not about to do squat-all unless you file a formal complaint and produce hard evidence."

"I'm filing—" Ryan's voice cracked when he spoke. "I'm filing a formal complaint. General Martini is destroying government property and deliberately violating two-man control procedures required for the handling of nuclear weapons."

Daguerre shook his head. "Exactly what is he destroying?"

"Nuclear weapons."

"Son of a bitch!" Daguerre said, jumping to his feet. "You got proof?" Ryan nodded dumbly, relieved the captain was finally acting. Daguerre jammed his blue beret on and headed for the door. "Show me." He stopped and waited for the doctor. "But you had better be right."

* * *

442

It was sunset when Malthus climbed out of the pit dragging a steel case the size of a wastebasket. He crawled into the makeshift plastic tent set up over the ladder, and the decontamination team sprang into action. In short order, he was out of his lead-lined apron, heavy gloves, respirator, and clothes. He kicked them into the pit and crawled out of the tent, still dragging the steel case. He dressed while Ev checked his dosimeter. She chanced a sideways glance at the naked physicist, taking a not so professional interest in his body. "Not bad," she said. "Ah, I mean there's less than two rems on your dosimeter." She ran a Geiger counter over the steel case that held the plutonium from the bomb's core. "It's a little hot; we better put it in the container."

While two of the Sandia engineers placed the steel case inside a larger insulated steel container, a team of civil engineers started pumping concrete into the pit. "It's pretty hot down there," Malthus said. "But the concrete should do the trick."

"Did you find anything?" she asked.

"Nothing," he said. "I cut and tested three samples and everything tested perfect."

"We're burying over $200,000 of test equipment in that hole and learned nothing?" she complained. "What are you going to tell Martini?"

"I need to think about it."

Martini paced the Intel vault like a caged tiger. "So what you're telling me is that we're still at square one."

"Not entirely," Malthus said. "There's one other thing: the time delay in the arming sequence Captain Byers mentioned."

"The arming circuits tested good," one of the Sandia engineers replied.

"Let's arm it on the ground," Malthus said. "If the green light cycles on like it should, go with the mission."

"I know," Martini said, "that the bomb still needs to sense delivery parameters to detonate. But you ever heard of Murphy's Law? It seems to be in effect around here. There is no way that I'm going to let one of my aircraft take off with an armed nuclear weapon.'' He glared at them. "Not on my base."

"Arming is a two-way street," Ev said. "The crew de-arms the bomb after we check it. If, at any time, the bomb doesn't arm as programmed, abort the mission."

"With all the checks we've done, we've got a higher probability of detonation than any other weapon system in the stockpile," Malthus added.

Martini's face turned to stone as he worked the problem. His entire career had been focused on the mission. It was the touchstone of his existence, the reason for everything he did. Now his mission was to drop a single nuclear weapon on an enemy who had threatened his base and killed people he liked and admired. But did they have the weapon to do it? He checked the master clock on the wall. He had run out of time. "Do it. I'll give the final go-no go decision then."

The two captains stood in front of Martini. The pilot, Chet Woods, did the talking. "We want a second chance," he said. "Let us fly the mission."

"Give me one good reason," Martini demanded.

The WSO, Ray Byers, answered him. "General, it fig-ures that if we're going a second time, you've checked the bomb and the systems out. The only thing that we know that went wrong the last time was the delay on the arming light. I'm betting that was the problem, and we're the guys who will know if it's happening again."

Martini's fingers beat their relentless tattoo on the desk. "Good thinking," he said. "You've got it."

"Over there," Ryan said, pointing out Master Sergeant Ralph Contreraz. "He saw it all." Daguerre stopped his staff car by Contreraz's van and motioned for the sergeant to get out.

"Sergeant Contreraz," Ryan said, "I want you to tell Captain Daguerre exactly what you saw in that hangar."

Contreraz gave them the respectful NCO look that he saved for such occasions. He had developed it over the years in dealing with officers he didn't like or considered incompetent. Ryan met both criteria but he only detested the security cop. "Yes, sir. But I've got to ask first if the captain's got a need to know?"

"Sergeant," Daguerre answered, "the major has filed a formal complaint under the Personnel Reliability Program. I am required by regulation to investigate."

Contreraz decided it wasn't worth arguing about and recounted what he had seen inside the hangar. "Dr. Malthus was in the pit alone, but the pit was under constant surveillance. So what's the problem?"

Daguerre rubbed his forehead. "Very unusual. This is a hard one."

"What's so hard about it?" Ryan snapped. "We've got a commander who is breaking down under stress. He's aberrating, and we have to do something about it."

"I'll have to take this to my boss," Daguerre said. "If he buys it, he'll take it to the vice commander who will have to notify PACAF."

"We haven't got time!" Ryan shouted.

"This is pure bullshit," Contreraz grumbled. The two officers stared at him. "You're wasting my time." He climbed back into his van.

"Why is it bullshit?" Daguerre asked.

"I don't pretend to know all that's going on around here. Hell, I don't need to know. The old man trusts me to do my job as best I can. I haven't got the time or the energy to worry about him and the high rollers in the command post doing theirs."

"You trust Martini?" Ryan asked.

"Damn right. I was his crew chief on the Thunderbirds. Every day, every time he flew, I saw the trust he had in the team. I mean every pilot, every crew chief, everyone. That's why the Thunderbirds were so damn good." He slammed the van into gear. "That's why this base, this wing, is so damn good."

"I can't walk away from this," Ryan said.

"Then try talking to the general, Major. He'll listen." Contreraz let out the clutch and drove away.

"The sergeant's got a point," Daguerre said. "Go talk to him or drop this."

"But he's—"

"Try listening," Daguerre said, interrupting him. "Either talk to the general or drop it. Otherwise, I'll arrest you for inciting a mutiny. Did I use any words you don't understand?''

Ryan shook his head.

The right engine of the Strike Eagle shrieked to life, filling the fuel cells building with sound. The small crowd gathered around the jet stepped back. Toby Malthus plugged his headset into the ground communications cord and spoke to the crew as they went through the before-taxi checks. Finally, it was time to do it. Byers dialed in the PAL code. ''The bomb is unlocked and I've got an orange light,'' he said. ''Nuclear consent switch.''

A slight pause. ''On,'' Woods replied.

Byers took a deep breath and rotated the arming wafer switch to AIR. The light blinked green. ''There was no delay in the bomb arming,'' he told Malthus.

''De-arm it and stand by,'' Malthus said. He ran to a wall phone to call the Battle Cab on a secure line. ''It worked!'' he shouted into the mouth piece.

Martini punched the off button and dangled the phone by its cord. He looked at the colonels clustered in the Battle Cab. ''Malthus says the weapon is good to go.''

''We can make the time over target,'' the Ops Group commander said.

Martini dropped his chin. *What if we fail a second time?* he thought. *It doesn't matter, we have to try. This is what it always comes down to: We have to try.*

He closed his eyes for a moment. He could hear the men breathing in the cab. His eyes opened. ''Go.'' The order went out, and Martini stared at the big status boards on the wall. But he wasn't seeing them. He was with the crew. Then, ''Get Dr. Malthus in here, I need to speak to him.''

The Strike Eagle lifted off runway 5 right and headed straight ahead, to the northeast, away from their target. The island of Okinawa flashed by underneath, and in less than two minutes, they had crossed the island and were over the Pacific. But they were still on a heading away from their target. The pilot flipped off the jet's anticollision beacon and nav lights before wrenching the big fighter onto a southerly course. He dropped to 100 feet above the water, rounded the southern tip of Okinawa, and headed directly for the atoll. Ahead of them, the dark outlines of the Kerma-Retto island chain loomed out of the sea. They were using the islands for terrain masking.

The TEWS, the F-15's tactical electronic warfare system, came alive. A hostile search radar was sweeping the skies in front of them. "They haven't got a paint," Ray Byers said. "The islands are still masking us."

"Not for long," Chet Woods replied from the front seat. He dropped the jet a little lower and flew around the first of the islands. The chirping from the TEWS grew stronger. "Arm it up," he ordered. They ran through the checklist, arming the B-61.

"The green light came on as advertised," Byers told him.

"Shit hot!" Woods barked. They rounded the last island in the chain and headed for the atoll, ninety miles away.

The TEWS chirped at them, filling their headsets with a warning that a hostile radar had found them. Byers checked the symbols on the radar warning display. "It's a search radar," he said, his words fast and clipped. "Coming from the atoll." The defensive part of the TEWS came alive. The system made no attempt to jam the radar but sent out false signals to confuse the enemy's radar as they made the long, high-speed dash across the open water onto the target. "Eight minutes to go." Woods nudged the throttles up, and the airspeed touched 660 knots. They were going .98 Mach 100 feet above the calm ocean surface. At that speed, every second ate up 1,100 feet of the remaining distance.

The TEWS display flashed, and the symbol for a radar-aimed antiaircraft artillery battery appeared. "That ain't gonna save their butts," Byers muttered. But the AAA would be a brief threat when they tossed the bomb and made their escape. A new symbol appeared on the TEWS. "Fuck me!" Byers roared. "They got a monopulse radar on the island. I don't believe this. It's a Gadfly. Where the hell did they get that?" The Gadfly, or SA-11, was a deadly Russian-built surface-to-air missile. It had a range of 21 miles and could engage an aircraft down to fifty feet off the deck. Woods squeaked the F-15 down to fifty feet. "Can you get it any lower?" Byers asked. "Five minutes out."

Byers called up the FLIR, forward-looking infrared, on his far right display scope. The FLIR was a passive system and did not announce their presence by emitting electronic signals like the radar. But at their low altitude, its range was extremely limited. "We're gonna have to use the radar," Byers said. "Four minutes out." Forty-four miles to go.

"Make it quick," Woods grunted. Sweat was pouring down his face, stinging his eyes. Ahead of them the first line of AAA tracers streaked into the sky. "We ain't there, assholes," Woods muttered. The TEWS had worked as designed and had meaconed the hostile radar. When they were inside thirty miles, a curtain of tracers lit the sky. "But they know we're coming," the pilot said.

Byers raised his head to look and quickly looked back down at his displays. He wished he hadn't seen it. He hit the EMIS button and the radar came to life. Byers's fingers played the buttons on his right hand controller like a piccolo and he drove the radar crosshairs over the atoll. He locked it up and stabbed at the EMIS button, returning the radar to standby. The radar had been active less than seven seconds, but it had sent a wealth of information to the F-15's computers. The weapons delivery system could do its job now without the radar. The attack display in the pilot's HUD came on.

Ahead of them, the Gadfly's guidance and tracking radar keyed on the F-15's radar signal and four transporter-erector launchers, each with four missiles, slewed to the northeast.

Four bright rocket plumes—Gadflies—lighted the night as the missiles launched and converged on the F-15. Woods lifted the Strike Eagle to 100 feet and turned twenty degrees to the right. When he was certain the Gadflies had turned with him, he slammed the F-15 down to the deck and turned ninety degrees back to the left. The first two missiles tried to turn with him but overshot.

Woods reversed his turn back to the right, pulling over 6 *g*'s. The third missile tried to turn but broached sideways, tumbling into the sea. The fourth missile flashed overhead and exploded. The expanding rod core in the missile's warhead flayed the night with shrapnel, cutting into the top of the F-15.

Byers felt a stinging in the back of his neck. He knew he was hurt but not how bad. "You with me, babes?" he asked the pilot.

A pained "Yeah" answered him. "I lost the HUD."

"Manual release," Byers said. "Pull on my count." He talked the pilot through the attack as they flew into the hell in front of them. "Come left five degrees, five more, steady, steady, steady, *pull!*" Woods pulled smoothly back on the stick into a sixty-degree climb. Byers watched the altimeter increase. "Ready, ready, ready, *pickle!*" Woods hit the pickle button, and the B-61 separated cleanly from the centerline and arced high into the sky. Woods's left hand jabbed at the weapons jettison button just in case it hadn't released. "Bomb gone!" Byers yelled. Woods rolled the jet and dove. Byers twisted around in his seat and checked their six o'clock position.

The night was blanked by streams of tracers rising from the atoll and sweeping the sky. A finger of fire reached out to touch them. But only one fifty-seven-millimeter shell hit their left vertical stabilizer. "Fuck!" Woods shouted as he retarded the throttles and fought for control. The jet twisted twice and stabilized. They were still flying. Two rocket plumes streaked out of the curtain of tracers etching the sky above the atoll. "Break left!" Byers shouted. "Two SAMS on us!"

The staff car pulled off Perimeter Road and stopped. Martini got out and walked to the guardrail on top of Habu Hill and looked over his base. It was enveloped in darkness, but he could still see vehicles moving in the moonlight. A gentle breeze off the East China Sea washed over him, and he savored the fresh tang of salt air. Toby Malthus joined him, and the two men stood quietly, each lost in his own thoughts.

"Is it going to detonate?" Martini finally asked.

"It should," Malthus answered.

Martini was incredulous. "You mean you're not sure?"

"No" came the simple reply. "You can never be sure in this business." A long silence.

"Why do you do this?" Martini finally asked.

Malthus considered his answer. "When I was in high school, a teacher I respected said nuclear physics was the hardest subject there was. I guess it was the challenge."

"But you stayed with it, so there must have been more to it."

A little smile played across Malthus's face. "Sometimes, when the answers are simple and clear, it's like touching the face of God." He laughed. "It doesn't happen very often. But when it does, it makes it all worthwhile."

"You're not talking about designing nuclear weapons, are you?"

"No. Not at all. What we're doing now is because of what we learned."

A bright, incandescent, man-made sun lit the southwest horizon. They both turned as the fireball began to rise into the sky. Even in the dark and at their distance, they could see the fireball mushroom into a canopy cloud of bright spectral blue as the superheated air cooled in the upper atmosphere. They watched in awe as it faded into the night.

"Oh, my God," Martini whispered.

"There is no joy in this," Malthus said.

Washington, D.C.

Madeline Turner was alone in the Situation Room. Every chair was occupied, and Shaw was standing against the wall behind her, but she was alone. INCOMING MESSAGE blinked at her from one of the TV monitors. She waited. The DCI stood and read the message aloud as it scrolled onto the screen. "Kadena Air Force Base, Okinawa. 1005 Greenwich Mean Time, 15 February. Nuclear detonation observed over target coordinates at 1000 GMT. The time, location, size of yield, consistent with parameters of sel rel mission." He paused and was met with silence. Then he read the last paragraph. "All contact lost with mission aircraft, aircrew assumed lost. Search-and-rescue mission underway." He sat down.

"Casualties?" Turner asked.

Her question was met with silence. Mazie Hazelton lowered her head and spoke, her voice clear and distinct. "The pilot of the delivery aircraft was Captain Chet Woods and his backseater was Captain Raymond Byers, Jr. Our last estimate held 986 Chinese troops on the atoll. We can assume they all perished."

Nothing in the tone of Turner's reply revealed what she was feeling. "And Captain Rodney Davis. And Technical Sergeant Otis Jenkins. And Master Sergeant Larry Burke. And Major William Courtland." She paused. "And Lieutenant General Robert Bender." She stood up. "I only knew one of them."

They all stood as the president walked from the room, still alone.

Shahe Air Base, China

"Someone's coming," Larry Burke whispered. He was in his usual position beside the wall. "It's her." He looked at Bender, fear in his eyes.

Bender walked to the door, straightening his tie and tucking his shirt in. He pulled at his coat, straightening it as the lock rattled. The door swung open. She was standing there, wearing an army officer's uniform devoid of rank. Eight guards stood in the hall behind her, their submachine guns at the ready. Bender froze as she stared at him. "We had a deal," he said, trying to keep his voice steady.

For what seemed an eternity, she did not respond. "You lied to me," she finally said.

"Only when you asked me the details that compromised my country. But I was truthful when I said President Turner would respond in kind."

Again the silence. Then, "Your crew is free to go."

He watched them as the men filed out. It was enough.

Now, the only question left was when. But that was for him alone to discover. He stared at the wall above the woman's head. *Oh, Nancy,* he thought, *I'm so frightened.*

"General Bender?" her voice was there, the same, without emotion. "General Bender?" He looked at her. She was holding a white envelope. "Chairman Lu requested that you deliver this letter to your President." She smiled. "Perhaps you will also mention that we keep our word."

"Most assuredly."

Epilogue —

Okinawa, Japan

"Go right on in, Major." Ryan tried to read the secretary's expression. No luck. He squared his shoulders and pushed through the door into Martini's office.

"Major Ryan reporting as ordered," he said, snapping a crisp salute.

Martini waved a salute back and pointed to a chair. He waited until the doctor sat down. "This came in from the Security Police," Martini said, handing him a one page report.

Ryan gulped hard and read. It detailed his accusations about Martini to the Security Police and was signed by one Captain Terrence Daguerre. "Sir, I want to speak to a lawyer."

Martini stared at him for a moment, his look unreadable. "You'll know when you need a lawyer. Do you remember when I told you to keep an eye on me?" Ryan nodded in answer. "I was mostly concerned with fatigue but the moment you had doubts, you should have come to me immediately and raised your concerns. Failing that, you should have gone to the vice commander. He's the IG's local representative and it's his job to hear complaints."

"Sir," Ryan bleated in self-defense, "you wouldn't have listened to me and what vice commander is going to let a junior officer criticize his commander?"

"You're right about the first part," Martini conceded.

453

"I was pressed for time right then. But he'd have listened or I'd have fired his ass. As it was, you almost got in the way of the mission at a very critical time."

"Sir, I want to speak to a lawyer."

Martini fixed the doctor with a hard look. He had no intentions of pressing charges but was more than willing to let the young major dangle on the hook. The longer the better. "Fine. But first, you're going to do some listening. Ryan, you are an excellent doctor with the potential to make a difference. A big difference. But you can't seem to get past being a self-centered, egotistical prima donna without someone giving you a swift kick in the butt." He held up a hand, stopping anything Ryan might say. "You can separate from the Air Force in about six months. It might be a good idea if you looked someplace else for gainful employment. This isn't the place for you."

Ryan couldn't help himself. "Why?"

"Because you're not in the same league with Chet Woods and Ray Byers." Martini shook his head at the confused look on Ryan's face. "Surely, you remember them. The crew that dropped the bomb?" Ryan remembered. "The Air Force is not about making money, major, or getting your name in lights. We're concerned with accomplishment. We do it by placing service, sacrifice, and obligation over the individual. Woods and Byers understood that. Pete Townly understands that. Sergeant Contreraz understands that. You don't. Now you can go talk to a lawyer."

Ryan saluted and spun around to leave. He almost made the door. "Ryan," Martini said, "everyone benefits this earth. Some do it by living, others only by dying and freeing up space. You've still got time to make a choice."

Washington, D.C.

Ben smiled at Liz Gordon when she walked onto the news set. She glanced at the cameraman, returned his smile, and quickly turned to speak to the director. Ben had seen it before. Liz had moved beyond him, and they would never work together again. He listened as Liz and the director discussed how much leg she should show. "They're not your best asset," he said to himself. Finally it was decided to place a small writing desk beside Liz's chair so she could swivel around to face the camera while she talked. When it was time for a commercial break, she could turn to the desk, giving the camera a profile shot. *Very good,* Ben admitted to himself.

The lights came on, the director cued her, and Liz turned to face the cameras alone, on center stage and in prime time. "Six months ago this evening," she began, "the nation watched in stunned silence as President Turner held her first press conference after the death of President Roberts. At that time, I asked, Who is Madeline O'Keith Turner? We simply didn't know, and within weeks, an untried Madeline Turner faced her first major crisis."

Ben half listened as Liz recounted Turner's first six months in office, cutting to sound and photo bites for emphasis and punctuation. The new intern he had seen before slipped onto the studio and stood beside him. Liz's words came at him in fragments. "Sidestepped the sellout of Taiwan only to be confronted by an aggressive and expansionist China . . . a China driven by an internal power struggle . . . she engaged in a relentless search for peace . . . responded to nuclear blackmail by a singular, decisive show of force and discredited the Chinese generals bent on aggression . . . in the chaos, Lu Zoulin, the moderate premier, regained control and begged for peace."

Ben studied the intern. She didn't seem so tomboyish as before and was dressed as a reporter. *Maybe she needs a videographer,* he thought. The idea appealed to him. He focused on Liz. She had captured the cameras and the audience. "Finally, Madeline Turner has imposed her own style of leadership on the White House. The flamboyant Patrick Shaw has been reassigned as the White House director of communications and Richard Parrish, the former secretary of the treasury and an old friend, is now her chief of staff."

The demotion of Shaw was, indeed, news. Ben almost laughed aloud. *Turner's on to the bastard,* he thought. The image of Shaw shuffled into purgatory in the basement of the White House appealed to him. No longer was Shaw the puppet master pulling strings. Maybe the news desk would assign him and the intern to interview Shaw. He made a mental note to check into it.

A camera zoomed in on Liz's face. "Who is Madeline O'Keith Turner? The answer is simple: She is the president of the United States."

Bethesda, Maryland

Shaw's limousine was caught in heavy traffic a mile short of the Naval Medical Center. Jessica reached out and held his hand. "Are you worried?" she asked.

"Just a regular physical," he replied as the limo accelerated, finally free of the traffic. "Haven't had time for one in years. About time." He grinned at her. "Nothin' wrong with the old machinery."

She returned his grin. "I know. I think it was the stress."

"That's the nice thing about being director of White House Communications," he allowed. "No stress." He brooded for a moment. *And no influence or power either,* he told himself. "I don't know how Maddy fingered me. I thought I had covered my tracks better."

"At least you're still in the White House," she replied.

"But totally off the power curve." He gave a rueful laugh. "When you're caught out all alone, buck naked, like Cinderella after midnight, you got to take what you can get. Sic gloria transit. But old Patrick will be back. Sooner than you might think."

"Do you have a magic wand to make it happen?"

He didn't answer her. Shaw had gotten inside the secret internal tracking polls that were Leland's lifeline to the public's mood. Everything the senator did, whether it was crafting strategy or decision making, was based on what his polls were telling him. It had been amazingly simple to slant the results just enough to feed Leland bad information. Shaw had simply bribed the genius who ran the computers that crunched the numbers, and sooner or later, he would turn it to his advantage. "You're not going to tell me, are you?'' Jessica murmured. ''What would it take to convince you otherwise?''

The limousine pulled up to the entrance of the hospital, and he got out. ''Darlin', these days it wouldn't take much.''

Washington, D.C.

Noreen Coker was the first of Turner's kitchen cabinet to arrive in Richard Parrish's corner office in the West Wing. The black congresswoman dropped her bulk in a chair. ''I cannot imagine Shaw risking all this,'' she said. The vice president walked in with Maura. The empty left sleeve of his coat was tucked into the side pocket, and he looked pale and drawn. Coker sprang to her feet, amazing them with her speed and grace. ''Child, you sit right down.'' Sam Kennett did as she commanded. They waited while he caught his breath.

''We're all here,'' Parrish said. He led them down the hall to the Oval Office, matching Kennett's slow pace. He knocked twice on the door, unable to suppress a smile, and ushered them in. Coker laughed at the shocked look on Maura and Kennett's face when they saw Gwen Anderson, the secretary of health and human services, sitting on a couch next to Turner's rocking chair.

''I'll be damned,'' Kennett said. ''I thought you went over to Leland.''

''I did,'' Anderson said.

''I asked her to,'' Turner told them. ''Jackie was her contact, and they passed information back and forth.''

Kennett nodded, thinking about Turner's personal assistant who had committed suicide. ''Very clever, getting someone on the inside like that.''

''It paid dividends,'' Anderson said, ''when Elkins and Shaw showed up.''

''Speaking of miserable bastards,'' Coker said, ''where is Shaw?''

''Recovering from surgery,'' Turner replied, ''prostate cancer. It was serious, and they had to remove his prostate gland. The doctors say they got all the cancer, but he'll probably be impotent."

Coker let out a whoop. "Banished to the bowels of the White House in a nothing job, and now he can't get it up? Oh, Lord, there is justice out there."

"I'll never understand why you're keeping him," Maura said. Coker and Kennett agreed with her.

"I believe Gwen knows," Turner replied.

"In the final crunch," Anderson said, "Shaw couldn't give you up. Besides, what he's doing to Leland is priceless."

"Which is?" Coker asked.

Anderson laughed. "Don't ask me how, but I think he's cooking Leland's internal tracking polls. And you know how closely the good senator guards them. The results of his polls are slightly out of kilter with what the public is really thinking. Leland is ending up on the wrong side of key issues, and he hasn't got a clue why. I just wish I knew how Shaw is doing it."

"Well, Gwen," Turner said, "as long as you're still on the senator's good side—"

"I'll keep an eye on him," Anderson replied. "But I need a new point of contact. I'll be dead in the water if I'm seen here for anything other than cabinet meetings."

"Jackie will be hard to replace," Turner said.

"Did anyone ever find that Polaroid I gave her?" Anderson asked. "It was a photo of the farmhouse where those bastards meet."

No one could remember seeing it. "It doesn't matter as long as Shaw doesn't have it," Kennett answered. "Sooner or later, he'd piece it all together. I can just hear him." He put on a decent imitation of Shaw's southern drawl: "Gawddammit, Mizz President, you just can't go trustin' anyone around here these days."

Maura gazed contentedly at her daughter. *You beat the bastards,* she thought. *Savor it, Maddy. Enjoy the victory.* Then she saw the slight squint and amusement sparkle in her daughter's eyes as a half smile played across her mouth. Madeline O'Keith Turner was enjoying her triumph. She had weathered her first six months in office and emerged from the crisis stronger, more sure of herself, ready to face the battles looming on the horizon. But for the moment, the sweet taste of success was hers.

Langley Air Force Base, Virginia

Martini moved through the crowd in the Officers' Club. The reception was packed with dignitaries who had attended the Thunderbirds' first show of the season. Begrudgingly, he gave the team high marks for their performance flying the new F-22 Raptor. But he was still convinced his team had been much better in the old F-16. He worked his way past the Thunderbirds who were still in their flight suits and surrounded by a large crowd of admirers. He recognized the president's son, Brian Turner, who was following the left wingman's hands as he demonstrated a high-g maneuver.

"There goes a future fighter pilot," a voice behind him said. Martini turned to see a tall, gray-headed, four-star general.

"General Bender," Martini said. They shook hands, meeting for the first time. "Congratulations on your fourth star and your new command." Bender had assumed command of ACC, Air Combat Command, two days before. "I imagine this is more to your liking than the White House."

"I wouldn't wish that on anyone," Bender said.

"I've heard a rumor that she's looking for a new aide."

"It's true," Bender said.

"The poor son of a bitch," Martini muttered.

"I recommended you for the job," Bender said.

Martini's face turned livid, and he sputtered. "She doesn't even know me!"

"She needs to," Bender said, turning and leaving the speechless brigadier in his wake. He looked for Nancy and found her with Brian.

"Robert, we really must go. Brian has to get back to Washington, and we're invited to dinner with General Charles." Bender agreed, and they made their way toward the exit. But a procession of four waiters and two Thunderbird pilots pushing a serving cart with a large cake blocked them. "We really must go," she repeated.

Bender's face was granite hard as he stared at the cake and the pilots gathering around it. "It's time to do something about that," he muttered.

"Robert," Nancy whispered, "don't. Let it be." But Bender ignored her and walked toward the Thunderbirds who split apart, making way for him.

"What's wrong?" Brian asked. "Is he mad?"

Nancy put a hand on his shoulder. "It's a Thunderbird tradition that the right wingman cuts the cake with a karate chop. He thinks it's childish and always said he'd stop it if he could. They know he hates it." She felt she had to explain. "Sometimes," she searched for the right words, "he can be so, so rigid and prudish."

Bender spoke to the right wingman who was poised to do the honors. The young captain's face showed his disappointment as he moved aside. "Ladies and gentlemen," Bender said, "to the Thunderbirds and the new season." His hand flashed down in a karate chop, cutting the cake. He looked at the startled captain, his face a blank mask. "That's how it's done, Captain."

Nancy joined him and blinked away her tears. "Robert, you just might make it."

The Wit and Wisdom of
Patrick Flannery Shaw

- Politics is like showbiz: Give 'em what they want and they'll come out every time.
- The White House is like a tight pair of pants: Not enough ballroom.
- Keep 'em laughing. But if you're smart, you'll keep 'em looking in the wrong direction.
- When someone screws up in politics, someone loses their balls or as the case may be, their titties, but not necessarily the someone who screwed up.
- Money is the mother's milk of politics (attributed to Jesse Unruh).
- Everyone has their own wagon of manure they like to spread around. Don't stand behind the wagon and never upset it. You may have to clean it up.
- Most elected politicians are professionals. It's the amateurs who scare me. They want to do the right thing.
- I'd rather be a hooker than own a politician. A hooker gets to spit it out afterward.
- Quid pro quos bite you in the ass every time.
- In politics, you can kill someone, but you can't kill 'em dead.
- Loyalty is the currency that you exchange for power.
- Most politicians are like overripe melons: Thump 'em a little and they crack wide open.

- Never trust a politician who can't be bought. They don't know what they're worth.
- Besides losing an election, the worst thing that can happen is to be found in bed with a dead girl or a live boy.
- The best kind of congressman is so crooked that if he ate a nail, he'd shit a screw.
- Never play hardball unless you got another time at bat.
- Political capital is like fuel in the gas tank. The more you use, the sooner you stop.
- Never pass up a men's room to take a precautionary piss. You never know when you'll get another chance.
- Know when to get out of Dodge.
- Always know how to get out of Dodge.
- Congressmen are like dogs: Some learn quicker than others.
- It's best to start in politics when you're young, dumb, and full of cum because two out of three ain't bad.
- The whole truth speaks for itself. Stick to the half-truths where you can do the talking.
- When you're losing, leak.
- When taking a poll, always get the best results money can buy.
- And now abideth in power with information, money, and access. But of these three, the greatest is access to the president.

Glossary

ACC—Air Combat Command. The operational arm of the U.S. Air Force that trains, equips, and maintains combat-ready aircraft within the continental United States.

AMRAAM—the advanced, medium-range air-to-air missile. It has a range of approximately 30 miles and a launch-and-leave capability. Very cosmic and bad news for bandits.

Angels—altitude expressed in thousands of feet. "Angels ten" means 10,000 feet.

AOA—angle of attack. The angle between the wing's chord line and the relative wind.

AWACS—airborne warning and command system. Provides surveillance, command, control, and communications to commanders. Based on the E-3 Sentry aircraft, a much-modified Boeing 707 airframe with a 30-foot diameter radar dome on top.

Bandit—an aircraft identified as being hostile.

BDU—battle dress uniform. The latest name given to the uniform worn in battle.

Bogie—an unidentified aircraft.

BOQ—bachelor officer's quarters.

CAS—control augmentation system. Senses pitch, roll, and yaw rates; vertical and lateral acceleration; angle of attack; and *g* forces; and provides the proper input into the control surfaces of an aircraft when a pilot commands a maneuver.

CAP—combat air patrol.

CINC—commander in chief.

CINC PAC—the admiral in command of Pacific Unified Defense Command.

CNO—chief of naval operations. The admiral on the Joint Chiefs of Staff in command of naval operations.

DCI—director of Central Intelligence. An individual appointed by the president and approved by the Senate who is in charge of all U.S. intelligence agencies and functions.

DEFCON—Defense Condition. A series of alert stages preparing for war. DEFCON ONE being the highest just prior to the outbreak of hostilities.

DIA—Defense Intelligence Agency. The Department of Defense's intelligence branch.

EMIS limit—emission limit. A circuit that shuts down electronic emissions coming from an aircraft that might be detected by an enemy.

EOR check—end of runway check. A final inspection of a fighter aircraft performed just prior to takeoff. Sometimes called the *last chance* or *quick check*.

Flanker—NATO code name for the Su-27, a Soviet clone of the F-15. The Su-33 is a carrier-borne version of the Flanker.

Fox one—a code meaning a radar-guided air-to-air missile has been fired.

Fox two—a code meaning an infrared-guided air-to-air missile has been fired.

Fox three—a code meaning a fighter's machine gun or cannon has been fired.

Fulcrum—NATO code name for the MiG-29. Looks like an F-15 but smaller, roughly the size of an F-16.

GCI—ground-controlled intercept. A ground-based radar providing control to fighter aircraft.

HUD—head-up display. A device that projects vital flight information in front of the pilot so he or she does not have to look inside the cockpit to check the instruments.

IG—inspector general. A military organization that investigates complaints and conducts inspections.

IP—instructor pilot.

J-8—a Chinese twin-engine variant of the MiG-21 with a top speed of approximately 1.4 Mach and a combat range of 500 miles.

JCS—joint chiefs of staff.

Jink—the constant and random changes in heading and altitude by a fighter aircraft to avoid flying straight and level. The goal is to defeat enemy tracking and is vital to survival in an hostile environment.

KS-1—a PRC surface-to-air missile with a range of approximately 25 miles.

Little creek—the code name given to the SR-71 area on Kadena Air Base, Okinawa.

MCC—mission crew commander. The officer in charge of the working troops in the back of the AWACS. The MCC is responsible for mission accomplishment and must never lose situational awareness.

MEACON—a form of electronic countermeasures where one black box spoofs another by sending out misleading electronic signals. All very cosmic.

MIG-29—see *fulcrum*

MOPP—mission operative protection posture. The protective suit and equipment worn to counter chemical warfare. It is very hot and cumbersome to wear.

MRE—meal ready to eat. The replacement for the venerable C-ration. Some are reported to be quite good.

MUNS—munitions storage squadron or area.

NCOIC—noncommissioned officer in charge. The sergeant who runs things.

NEO—nonessential personnel evacuation operation. The name of the operation to evacuate families and nonessential personnel from bases in the forward area prior to the outbreak of fighting.

NIO—national intelligence officer for warning. The bureaucrat in the CIA who is responsible for forecasting impending crisis or sneak attacks on the United States.

NMCC—National Military Command Center. The Pentagon's "War Room."

NRO—National Reconnaissance Office. The supersecret agency responsible for spy satellites.

NSC—National Security Council. Consists of the president and his/her top foreign-policy advisors.

OMB—Office of Management and the Budget. The agency in the office of the White House that creates the national budget for submission to Congress.

OSI—Office of Special Investigations. The U.S. Air Force's plainclothes criminal and counterintelligence investigators.

PACAF—Pacific Air Forces. The fighting arm of the U.S. Air Force that conducts air operations in the Pacific.

PAL—Permissive Action Link. The security system that prevents nuclear weapons from being armed by unauthorized personnel like terrorists.

PDB—President's Daily Brief. The slick product of a committee in the CIA that summarizes the best intelligence the agency has to offer the president. It has a very limited distribution.

PLA—People's Liberation Army. The collective name given to all the armed services of the People's Republic of China.

Popeye—the AGM-142 "Have Nap" medium-range, standoff missile acquired from Israel. The 3,000-pound, precision-guided missile has a 750-pound warhead and a 50-mile range.

PRC—People's Republic of China.

PRP—personnel reliability program. The program that monitors the mental stability of personnel working around nuclear weapons.

ROE—rules of engagement. Normally, a collection of very good rules designed to keep fighter jocks alive in combat. They get complicated when politicians get involved.

SAM—any surface-to-air missile.

SIB—Safety Investigation Board. A U.S. Air Force team that investigates aircraft accidents and issues a mishap report. Their goal is to find out what happened and prevent it from happening again. A SIB does not administer punishment.

Silk Worm—a PRC antiship missile. Notoriously inaccurate and short ranged. The version depicted in this book does not exist—yet.

Sidewinder—the name for the air-to-air, infrared-guided AIM-9 missile. Latest versions are very cosmic.

SU-27—see *flanker*.

Tallyho—a code meaning "target visually sighted."

VTSS—vertical tank storage system. A rack that resembles a dry-cleaning storage track that holds clothes. But this one is on steroids and holds drop tanks for fighter aircraft.

WATCHCON—a "watch notice" issued by the DIA's National Military Intelligence Center in the Pentagon to American forces. A III is the lowest possible level.

Wizzo—the nickname given to weapon system officers. The second crewmember of a fighter aircraft. By nature, a very trusting soul.

WSO—See *wizzo*.

Acknowledgments

F ew writers work in a vacuum, and I owe a debt of gratitude to three friends who gave so unsparingly of their time and support to make this book happen. Mel Marvel, Lt. Col. USAF (Ret.), set the wheels in motion with two simple questions that begged for answers. Robert Beckel, Lt. Gen. USAF (Ret.), introduced me to the Thunderbirds, set a challenge I could not ignore, opened doors of all kinds, and made me deeply envious of those who served under his command. I only wish I had had the chance. William P. Wood guided me through the arcane world of national politics with humor and indulgence. Without his expertise, I would have lost my way countless times.

On Okinawa, Colonel James "Jammer" Jackson, his pilots at the Forty-Fourth Fighter Squadron, Chief Master Sergeant John Clancy, Twelfth Fighter Squadron Maintenance, and the men and women of the Eighteenth Wing, Kadena Air Base, retaught me an old lesson: The machines and technology may change, but people still make the difference. And Habu Hill is really there.

Two nuclear physicists, Dr. Ron Lehman and Dr. Bill Dunlop, at Lawrence Livermore National Laboratory, Livermore, California, opened up the exciting world of inertial confinement fusion and nuclear weapons design. I hope I came close.

To all of you, I can only say thanks.

Finally, without the patience, understanding, and boundless love of my wife, Sheila, I would have never written a single word.

Enter the World of Richard Herman

After serving in the United States Air Force for twenty-one years, Richard Herman has a story to tell.

On the face of it, Herman's novels are techno-thrillers and he writes about the aircraft he loves. But there is much more. His stories are really about the men and women who would fight in defense of their country—and Herman knows them well. His characters chronicle the way of leadership and the obligation for service that was formed in the distant past. Yet they are all too human, replete with frustrations and frailties, the wants and weaknesses we experience every day. They struggle and fail and triumph. And they die.

Herman writes about things his characters would never admit to openly: duty, honor, trust, and the best reward of all, homecoming. They are as true to life as your next door neighbor and, occasionally, they mirror the best in this strange tribe of people called Americans.

But, like his characters, Herman would never admit it.

AGAINST ALL ENEMIES

At the end of the millennium, the United States of America is a country on the edge. As tempers ignite over racial differences, the court-martial of a traitor fuels the madness sweeping the country. It is a firestorm only Jonathan Meredith, a ruthless and charismatic manipulator of crowds, can exploit for his own ends.

At the heart of the battle is Hank Sutherland, a principled prosecutor determined that justice be done. It is Sutherland who must unravel the conspiracy that is threatening the very fabric of American life and, in the end, he must stand alone Against All Enemies.

5:50 P.M., Thursday, March 4, The White House, Washington

Three men clustered around the TV in the President's private office in the residence. The sound was turned low and the voice of the reporter at the scene was only a murmur. The grisly image on the screen said more than any words could describe. The president hit the remote control and turned off the sound. The silence was complete as the men continued to stare at the screen. "Do they have a casualty count yet?" the president finally asked.

Kyle Broderick, the chief of staff, picked up the phone and asked the same question. He didn't like the answer. Broderick was a young man, hard and street savvy, who delighted in using the power that went with being the President's chief of staff. "I want a hard number in the

471

next five minutes or you're history.'' He punched off the connection and turned to the President. ''Sorry, sir. Everyone seems asleep at the wheel.'' Almost immediately, the phone rang. Broderick picked it up and listened. He hung up without saying a word. ''The initial count is over two hundred and rising fast,'' he told the President.

''You'll have to go there,'' the Vice President said to the President. He was a handsome man who had his eye on the presidency in five years. But first, they had to survive the upcoming election. He looked at his watch. ''Time your arrival for early in the morning while it's still dark. Make it look like you've been up all night. We'll work the networks at this end and have you lead the morning news.''

The President nodded in agreement. Again, they stared at the TV. The silence was broken by the distinctive beat of a helicopter's rotor as the aircraft settled to earth on the South Lawn. ''That must be Nelson,'' the President said. A few minutes later, the door opened and a stocky man with thinning brown hair was ushered in. Nelson Durant was fifty-four, and his rumpled clothes gave no clue about who, or what, he was. He was average looking in the extreme and could disappear into a crowd with ease. His image shouted ''wimp'' but his blue eyes carried a far different message. ''Thanks for coming so quickly,'' the President said. The Vice President moved over so Nelson Durant could sit next to the President.

''Have you seen the TV coverage on the bombing?'' Broderick asked.

The answer was obvious and Nelson Durant ignored the question. Besides, Broderick wasn't worth his time. ''What can I do for you, Mr. President?'' Durant asked.

''We need quick answers on this one,'' the President replied. ''Can you help?''

Durant ran a hand through his thinning hair. For those who knew him, it was a warning gesture that he was wasting his time and had better things to do. ''If you're referring to the Project, we're still a month away from startup and then we're looking at another year before coming on-line.''

The President looked disappointed. The Project was a

highly advanced intelligence-gathering computer system that one of Durant's many companies was developing for the National Security Agency. If the Project lived up to Durant's promises, it could find and track any foreign or terrorist threat targeting the United States.

"But I'll have my people check into it," Durant said. The President looked pleased. Durant's worldwide business contacts gave him an intelligence database that rivaled the CIA's. A discreet knock stopped him from saying more. Broderick opened the door and Stephan Serick, the national security advisor, stomped in.

"You need to see this," Serick said, holding up a videocassette. Stephan Serick's childhood Latvian accent was still strong, and the basset hound jowls, heavy limp, and twisted cane were famous trademarks of the man who had served under two presidents of different political parties. "Communications took it off a satellite feed." He collapsed into a chair while Broderick fed the cassette into the TV. "A tourist filmed it. Damned videos."

At first, the scene was a repeat of what they had seen before; the huge crater in Market Street, the mangled cars and the gaping hole that once was the façade of the San Francisco Shopping Emporium. Serick shuddered. "They even got BART." BART was the Bay Area Rapid Transit subway that ran under Market Street. Then the scene on the TV changed as the tourist ran through the debris following a fireman. The camera jolted to a stop and focused on a man emerging from a cloud of dust and debris, his clothes smoking. He was carrying an unconscious girl in his arms.

"That's Meredith," Serick muttered. They watched as Meredith handed the woman to the fireman, his face racked with anguish.

"Just like Oklahoma City," Durant said in a low voice. On the screen, Meredith collapsed to his knees, panting hard. A blanket was thrown over his shoulders.

A voice from off screen said, "My God, the man's a real hero."

Meredith looked up, his lean, handsome face ravaged. He pointed to four firemen wearing respirators descending into the smoke billowing from the underground BART station. "There's your real heroes." He struggled to his feet. "I had to do something. . . . I was there." The tape ended.

"Son of a bitch!" Broderick roared. Then more calmly, "Would you care to guess when this will hit the air?"

"About the time the President lands in San Francisco," the Vice President replied. Meredith was going to preempt the President's arrival on the morning news.

Broderick looked at Durant. "Can you stop it?"

"I don't see how," Durant replied.

"Well," Broderick said, "Meredith is your boy."

Durant's face turned to granite. Kyle Broderick, arguably the second most powerful man in the United States government, had overstepped his bounds. Durant's next words were spoken quietly. "Nothing could be further from the truth." Durant was seething at the suggestion he would have anything to do with Meredith. He stood up to leave.

"Ah, Kyle," the President said, frowning at his chief of staff, "why don't you check with the communications section for foreign reaction?" Broderick nodded and hurriedly left the room. Durant sat back down. "Sometimes I think that boy is suicidal," the President said soothingly. "But seriously, we are concerned about Meredith and there have been rumors. . . ." He deliberately let his words trail off.

Durant looked at the Vice President and Serick. "I need to speak to the President in private."

The two men stood and Serick led the way out, his limp more pronounced. The President's personal assistant took the opportunity to stick her head through the open door. "Mr. President, the British Ambassador and Secretary of State are waiting in the Oval Office." She looked at her watch, a sign they were far behind schedule.

"Ask the ambassador if she'd like another cup of tea," the President said. He waved a hand and his personal assistant closed the door. "What's bothering you, Nelson? If it's Kyle, he's gone."

Durant shook his head. Kyle Broderick had only given words to what the President was thinking. Chasing the chief of staff out of the room had been enough to set things right. He looked at his hands. "I'm not in contact with Meredith. We have no common interests." The President was stunned. It was a tacit admission that Jonathan Meredith was beyond Durant's influence. "And Meredith is running for President," Durant added.

"You're not telling me anything I don't already know," the President replied.

"Jim, Meredith fancies himself an American Caesar, and he's about to cross the Rubicon." Durant's analogy to Caesar taking the fateful step and ordering his army to cross the Rubicon in his quest to become Rome's emperor hit home. Nelson Durant stared at his President. "All of Rome couldn't stop Caesar. Can you?"

1:00 A.M., Friday, March 5, San Francisco

"It was Oklahoma City all over again," Marcy said. She was sitting beside Sutherland in the hospital's waiting room, which had been turned into a makeshift emergency ward. The room was filled with walking wounded from the explosion. "The doctor said you've got a bad concussion," she told him. "They want to hold you awhile for observation."

Sutherland reached for her hand, needing human contact. She responded, her hands clasping his. "The other people on the roof?" he asked.

She shook her head, and he could feel her tremble. "We were the only ones. Hank, you saved me. I was going over the side, you grabbed me . . ." She lost her voice.

"The waitress?"

"She's going to be okay." Then, stronger, "Thanks to you. I could've never gotten her off the roof or gone down that stairwell by myself. If you hadn't been there . . ."

The enormity of it all came crashing down on him. "Oh, shit," he moaned as a new emotion swept over him, driving him into deep despair. "The hostess, she jumped me to the head of the line, if she had sat us at any other table . . ." That was all he could say as guilt claimed him, demanding a penance for being alive.

"It was just one of those things," Marcy said, understanding what he was going through. "It was just coincidence."

Sutherland lay his head back. *Just coincidence,* he thought. *We're alive and they're all dead because of coincidence.* He tried not to think about it and focused on the TV in the corner.

"The FBI is now certain," the commentator said, "that this was a calculated act of terrorism gone wrong. The bomb exploded prematurely while being moved down Market Street. So far, the death toll has reached four hundred twenty-two and is expected to go higher. We're awaiting the arrival of the President, who is due to land at any moment."

"Screw the President," Marcy grumbled.

As if on cue, the commentator held his hand to his ear to be sure he heard right. "The video coverage we are about to show was taken by a tourist moments after the explosion." The screen flickered and the back of a fireman appeared as he ran toward the collapsing building. The camera came to stop and Meredith appeared running out of the building with an unconscious girl in his arms. Sutherland pulled himself into a half-sitting position. The movement made his head hurt. "That's the waitress," he said. "Holy shit, it's Meredith!"

Marcy waved a hand at him, commanding him to be quiet as the scene played out. Meredith's face filled the screen as he uttered, "I had to do something. . . . I was there." The scene cut back to live coverage. Meredith was being interviewed by Liz Gordon, CNC-TV's premier reporter. In the background, floodlights lit the façade of the Shopping Emporium. Sutherland had to concentrate as his mind reeled.

Meredith was forty-six, handsome, six feet tall, with dark hair that was lightly streaked with gray. His lean body was taut and conditioned, the result of countless hours of exercise. But it was his voice, full of warmth and honesty, that captured the moment and came through the glass. "We could have prevented this," Meredith said. His face filled the screen. "We need to go after these cowards and stop them dead in their tracks. We've been too concerned with *their* constitutional rights. Where are the rights of the victims? We need to send a message to our leaders, our judges, that this must stop. Give the FBI, our police, the power they need to root out this evil before they kill again.''

"He's right," Marcy whispered. Then, louder, "So right." Sutherland turned away from the screen and studied Marcy, taking the measure of her reaction. She stood up. "My editor wants a follow-up. I've got to go."

Sutherland sat up but almost passed out. "Marcy, take some time to get over this."

She stood and touched his hand. "Do we ever have enough time?" She bent over and kissed his cheek. "See you around."

He watched her walk away. "See you around," he repeated as the guilt came crashing back.

THE WARBIRDS

In The Warbirds, *Richard Herman's first edge-of-your-seat Air Force thriller, all Colonel Anthony "Muddy" Waters ever wanted was to command a tactical fighter wing. When the call comes, he will discover what true leadership and sacrifice means in the face of real danger, real bullets, and real death. But first, the call must come.*

The crew chief marshaling the F-4 into its parking spot on the ramp at Luke AFB crossed his wrists above his head, signaling for Waters to stop, then made a slashing motion across his throat, the sign to cut engines.

Waters' hands went over the switches, shutting the big fighter down. He unstrapped and threw his helmet and then the small canvas bag carrying his flight publications to the crew chief, who motioned toward the edge of the ramp, pointing out the waiting staff car. Waters scrambled down the boarding ladder and quickly walked around the Phantom during a post-flight inspection, before heading for the car. The wing commander, Boots McClure, crawled out from behind the wheel and stood by the car, a slight smile on his face.

"Congratulations, Muddy. You've got yourself a wing—the 45th at Stonewood. The word came down about thirty minutes ago." McClure grabbed Waters' right hand and pumped it.

Waters just stood there, unable to speak.

A command . . .

A wing . . .

The fulfillment of his dream. The years of hard work, loneliness and frustration suddenly evaporated . . . A wide smile came across his face. A warmth that he had only experienced at the birth of his daughter captured him. It was a high few men ever realized.

"It's going to be different from anything you imagined," McClure said softly, doubting that Waters could catch his meaning. "Why don't you tell your bride and get her away from the O' Club pool." McClure laughed and pushed Waters towards the car. "She's driving some of my young jocks bonkers . . ."

Later, Anthony was ragging Sara a bit about Boots Mc-Clure's randy comments, and acting—well, partially acting—a little teed-off. She picked it up fast, and fed him a few more anxiety moments before playing it straight.

"I met Mrs. McClure the other day at a luncheon and liked her," she said. "She doesn't wear her husband's rank like some of the other wives do. God, what a sad crowd they can be. You'd think in this day and age they'd get out and do *something* besides eat lunch and sit around the pool and gossip, gossip, gossip. For some reason, I think the lieutenant colonels' wives are the worst—do you suppose it's because they're bucking with their spouses for the big eagle and letting off *his* frustrations? Oh, never mind—now what about the big news? Where are we off to in the wild blue yonder and so forth?"

"No way, lady. You got to pay for your intelligence. Ante up . . ."

And she did, and afterward, his head against her bare breasts, as she checked carefully for more signs of gray— "I love a mature man, stop worrying"—he told her it was England, and she told him that that was too easy, that she had paid too much for such available info.

"You've just begun," he said, and proceeded to make love in a way he never thought he could again, the inhibitions from the tragedy of the past finally giving up the ghost.

FORCE OF EAGLES

The legacy of Muddy Waters is safe with Jack Locke, a superb and dedicated fighter pilot. In Force of Eagles, *282 men and one woman from Muddy's 45th Tactical Fighter Wing are POWs in a terrifying hostage situation in Iran. In mounting their rescue, Jack proves he is that rarest of individuals, a true combat leader, when he defends a lone C-130 against a sky full of hostile aircraft, including U.S. built F-4s, an aircraft he loves.*

The two F-4s had a late tallyho on Jack and barely had time to split, one going high and to the left, the other diving to the right. Jack chose the high man and went for a head-on pass. He selected guns, snap-rolled to the right, squeezed the trigger for a long burst of cannon fire and brought the F-4 aboard, passing almost canopy to canopy. He saw smoke puff from behind the F-4 as he turned his attention to the other bandit. "Watch him," he told Byers, "don't lose sight."

Byers turned to look at the rapidly disappearing F-4

behind them just as Jack wrenched the fighter after the other jet. The sergeant's head snapped to the left and his helmet banged off the canopy, but he did keep his eyes on the first Iranian . . .

The second Iranian, for his part, was concentrating on the C-130, trying to get behind the slow-moving cargo plane. Actually Kowalski's low altitude and slow speed were causing problems for the Iranian pilot . . .

Jack selected a Sidewinder and sweetened the shot, taking his time to get well inside the launch parameters of the missile. The reassuring growl of a lock-on grew louder and louder. He pressed the pickle button and watched the missile streak home. The rear of the Iranian jet flared into a long plume of flame as the plane spun into the ground.

"My guy ran away," Byers told him. "What happened?"

"We got one," Jack said as he flew past Kowalski. "You did good, Byers. Rule number one is always check six. You did that. That guy died because he forgot rule number two."

"What's that?"

"Never forget rule number one—"

"Bandits," Kowalski called over the UHF, "ten o'clock high."

A welcome voice came over the radio. "Snake and Jake on the way." Snake Houserman and his wingman were now off the refueling tanker and headed into Iran.

"Hurry, Snake," Jack answered. "Multi-bogies on us." He checked his armament-control set. Two AIM-9 missiles and 450 rounds of 20mm showing on the rounds-counter were left. In a hurry, Jack missed that he still had one Maverick left hanging under the right wing and creating drag. He turned toward the four Floggers that had their noses on him . . .

FIREBREAK

First Lieutenant Matt Pontowski is a wild playboy, a pilot whose career in the Air Force owes more to his grandfather's position as President than to his own undoubted, but unreliable, talents. As Matt parties and drives his commander, Jack Locke, crazy, Iraq's leader, infuriated by the loss of the Gulf War, directs an arsenal of devastating chemical weapons against Israel. But the Israelis are prepared to respond with nuclear warfare. It's a desperate gamble when Matt's wing of F-15E Strike Eagles is sent to the Gulf. In the heat of battle, Matt Pontowski will be forged from a reckless boy into a determined and dangerous man.

Matt concentrated on his attack run. "Skid," he called his wingman, "take the lead, we'll lase. Ripple two." Matt had told his wingman to lead the attack and pickle both his bombs on the first pass. Matt would take spacing and follow on the opposite arm of the *B'nai* attack and do the lasing. "Then get the hell out of Dodge," he ordered.

"Roger, copy all," Skid answered.

"Sounds good," Martin's voice said.

My God! Matt thought. How can he keep what he's doing sorted out and still pay attention to what's going on down here?

The two fighters started their run in. The TEWS scope was a mass of symbols and the audio was deafening him with chirps and wails. He turned the audio off and would rely on Furry to do his job. Now he could clearly see the compound housing the nerve gas plant and storage bunkers on the Nav FLIR. Furry worked the Target FLIR and told him, "Target identified." It amazed Matt how familiar the target complex looked.

Sweat poured off him as he concentrated on the run. A string of tracers from a ZSU-23-4 arched across the sky in front of him. He heard himself breathing hard. "Piece of cake," Furry said, his voice rapid and high-pitched. More tracers crisscrossed in front of him and he saw the bright flash of two Gadflies launching. Now Matt "paddled" off the autopilot and hand-flew the jet as they swung in on their side of the pincers.

Then: "Bombs gone." It was Skid coolly announcing that he had gotten his bombs off onto their target, the main production plant. Matt had lost sight of him when they split up for the attack and it was reassuring to hear from him.

A Gadfly exploded, lighting the sky. In the bright flash, Matt could see Skid escaping underneath the fireball and more tracers reaching toward him. The second Gadfly exploded, but this time, there was no trace of his wingman.

"Lasing," Furry shouted. Matt was concentrating on the Nav FLIR, using it to fly around the target. It was a good run and all systems were working perfectly. A Gadfly streaked by less than a hundred feet above the canopy. For some reason, its proximity fuse didn't work and the missile went ballistic.

The plant erupted in an explosion as the first bomb hit within inches of where Furry had laid the laser. The bombs were fuse-delayed and the first one penetrated to the first basement before it exploded. The second bomb flew right through the explosion and burrowed through to the third basement, burying itself in four feet of concrete before it exploded. The labs and test chamber where the nerve gas had been developed disappeared in a fiery blast. But the scientists who had given Iraq the deadly weapon had been paid off long before and were safe in their homes in Europe and China. Only two technicians were on duty. A series of secondary explosions turned the plant into an inferno and flames belched and mushroomed over three hundred feet into the air.

Furry shouted, "GO!" as a wall of tracers mushroomed

in front of the F-15. Matt broke hard left, still below a hundred feet. He flew around a radio tower and headed for safety as Viper 07 and 08 hit the first of the storage bunkers.

Then it was all behind them and Matt became aware of the chatter over the radios. He had effectively tuned it out. Still, he had been conscious of what was going on around him throughout the attack. It was called situational awareness. He reengaged the autopilot and coupled it to the TFR. He checked his fuel and ran a cockpit check, making sure they had not taken little damage. Then it hit him, the simulator rides the Gruesome Twosome had put them through had been worse.

CALL TO DUTY

Matthew Zachary Pontowski has the loneliest job in the world: the presidency of the United States. As a young man, he answered the Call to Duty *and flew Mosquito fighter bombers with the Royal Air Force in the air war against Nazi Germany. Now he must order young men to risk their lives against a different enemy in Burma's golden triangle, where drugs are the common denominator. But the past will not let him go and he is the link between two missions separated by fifty years and two continents.*

"The press conference has been set up for two o'clock this afternoon," Leo Cox told Pontowski. The two men were sitting in the Oval Office going over the day's revised schedule with the press secretary.

"We expect most of the questions will be about the kidnapping," Henry Gilman, the press secretary said.

"Any feel of the mood of the press corps?" Cox asked.

"Still digging for angles," Gilman said. "Right now they are neutral and waiting to see what develops."

"Good," Pontowski said. "Leo, have the Vice President cover the luncheon with the delegates from the American Bankers Association for me. I'll have lunch with Tosh and join you both in the Oval Office for a final review before the press conference. Have all the players there." The two men rose and left the room.

Outside, Press Secretary Gilman said, "He always talks to Tosh before a press conference."

"She's still his best adviser," Cox told him.

Pontowski walked upstairs to his wife's bedroom. He knocked gently at her door and waited until the nurse answered. It was one of the small things he did to keep his wife's morale up; she always wanted him to find her looking her best. The way the nurse smiled at him as she held the door open signaled that Tosh Pontowski was having a good day. A smile spread across his face when he saw her sitting at the small table near the windows. He walked across the room and joined her.

Tosh Pontowski smiled at him. "The wolf is losing today," she said. As always, her lilting accent captivated him and touched the love he held for her, a love made stronger by her courage in coming to terms with and fighting the disease that ravaged her—systemic lupus erythematosus (lupus—the wolf). The disease was well named for the way it came and went unexpectedly, suddenly leaping out to rip and tear at human flesh and then sneaking away, only to return without warning to attack another part of the body. At first, it had only been a mild skin rash and Tosh had not been overly worried by the flare-ups that continued for a number of years. But then lupus had attacked her joints, and then had returned as kidney paralysis. But that had disappeared and then the wolf had returned again, this time attacking her heart.

He reached across the table and took her hand, hoping that she was in remission again. But his inner alarm warned him otherwise. How much longer? he wondered. He knew he could go on without her but life would lose most of its luster.

As usual, Tosh Pontowski refused to give in to her

disease. "Press conference today?" He nodded a yes. "L'affaire Courtland no doubt."

"Can't hide much from you, can we?" Pontowski observed. Charles, his valet, entered with a tray holding his lunch.

"Courtland will turn this against you," she said, watching him eat. "He knows he must discredit you if he is to defeat the candidate you endorse in the next presidential election."

"I know," he answered. "No matter what we do, he'll claim it isn't enough. He'll work the sympathy angle for all it's worth."

"Then you must defuse it," she counseled. "Recall your own escape."

"But I was never in captivity."

"No, but you were wounded, frightened, and pursued. It was a near thing. Build on that."

Matthew Zachary Pontowski leaned back in his chair and recalled when he had indeed been a terrified, desperately wounded fugitive.